ROOMS OF RUIN

BLOOD OF THE ISIR
BOOK TWO

ERIK HENRY VICK

Ratatoskr Publishing

New York

Ratatoskr Publishing
2080 Nine Mile Point Road, Unit 106
Penfield, NY 14526

Publisher's Note: This is a work of fiction. Names, characters, places, and incidents are a product of the author's imagination. Locales and public names are sometimes used for atmospheric purposes. Any resemblance to actual people, living or dead, or to businesses, companies, events, institutions, or locales is completely coincidental.

Rooms of Ruin/ Erik Henry Vick. -- 1st ed.
ISBN 978-0-9990795-3-9

In memory of Henry "Hank" M. Vick, teller of hilarious tales, man of a thousand voices, grandfather extraordinaire.

All is silent in the halls of the dead. All is forgotten in the stone halls of the dead, Behold the stairways which stand in darkness; behold the rooms of ruin. These are the halls of the dead where the spiders spin and the great circuits fall quiet, one by one.

—Stephen King

I hope you enjoy *Rooms of Ruin*. If so, please consider joining my Readers Group—details can be found at the end of the last chapter.

ONE

Then I was fertilized and grew wise;
From a word to a word I was led to a word,
From a work to a work I was led to a work.
—Vafþrúðnismál. (The Poetic Edda)

She sat on her sunbaked, impromptu throne like the queen she was, pale golden locks stirring in the hot wind blowing from the depths of Kleymtlant's deserts. Her gray eyes sought his, and when their gazes met, Luka Oolfhyethidn's stomach twittered. When she smiled, he thought he might melt.

"What news, my Champion?" Hel asked.

"My Queen, the rebels left Trankastrantir on horseback, but they rode east, not south."

One of her eyebrows quirked. "By sea then?"

Luka nodded once. "They may avoid our trap despite their complete ignorance of its existence."

"Oh come, Luka," she said. "Do you think me so easy to thwart?" She cocked her head to the side, a small smile playing on her lips. "Your part of the plan is in readiness?"

"Of course, my Queen. I spoke with him. He knows his role."

"Superb. I heard from one of Vowli's *oolfa* this morning. His part of the plan is in place, ready, and waiting."

"And can we trust our agent?"

Her gaze hardened. "Am I so easily fooled?"

"No, my Queen. I meant to wonder at the strength of Vowli's conditioning methods."

She arched her eyebrow. "Beyond reproach. But come, enough of this petty jealousy, Luka. We must drive them back to the course we prefer."

"Yes, my Queen. Shall I—"

"I will handle that part."

"Yes, my Queen."

"We have a challenge before us. One to which we must rise."

He arched his eyebrow and scratched his chin. "Tell me, my Queen."

"We have a game of *hnefatafl* to play, and you and I stand against many."

"And which side are we?"

She smiled a lazy, crooked smile. "The attackers, of course."

He grinned and inclined his head. "I understand, my Queen. We erect barricades to keep them from straying from the path we choose."

"Indeed, my Champion. Indeed." She waved her hand toward a pen of human and subhuman thralls the army had gathered from the sparse civilizations of Kleymtlant. "In the meantime, are you hungry? You are much more mischievous on a full stomach."

Luka let his eyes wander about the pen, and his mouth began to water. "I could eat, my Queen."

She nodded. "Then choose our prey." She stood and let the cool, loose robe fall at her feet. "*Byarnteer*," she murmured and began to stretch and morph.

An intense pleasure, mingled with lust, swept through Luka. The last time they had hunted together had been on Mithgarthr. He pointed out a thrall. "That one," he said to one of the pen's guards. He glanced up at Hel's new bear-like form and smiled. "*Oolfur*." Luka took a deep breath and began his own change into a beast out of nightmare.

TWO

The hot sun pounded against the dock and the deck of the ship next to it, but to me, the heat was a godsend. I'd used the last of my "miracle drug," my methotrexate, months before, and despite the pain-masking cloak Meuhlnir had commissioned for me on our trip to Nitavetlir, and Sif's best efforts, my joints hurt, and the heat helped. "I wish you had stayed at Veethar and Frikka's estate," I said for the fourth or fifth time.

"Hank Jensen, bring that up again, and you're going to limp the rest of the way to Pilrust," said Jane. "And not because of your illness."

"Tell him, Jane," said Yowrnsaxa. "He's as stubborn as my husband."

"Oh, god, not that!" said Meuhlnir with mock horror. "Surely, no man aspires to emulate the Isir that spawned an entire mythos. Not to mention a film franchise!"

Sif turned a baleful glare at Meuhlnir. "Hank, I wish you'd never told him of these things called movers."

"Movies, Auntie Sniffles," said Sig.

"Yes, movies. Wasn't his head big enough?"

Meuhlnir grumbled something under his breath and turned away to gaze out at Stein Tuhn Haf, the great ocean that bordered Suelhaym Eekier to the east.

I took Jane's hand, suppressing a sigh. "I don't want either of you getting hurt." Life on Osgarthr had been pleasant and bucolic since we'd rescued Jane and Sig from Luka and Hel. It was a grand place, full of interesting people, but being trapped there rankled, and since my family's rescue resulted in the closure of the *preer*, we had to go to the *Herperty af Roostum*—to the so-called Rooms of Ruin—and get the *preer* functioning again. *If* we could.

The *Herperty af Roostum* were located far to the north, on the northern continent known as Kleymtlant. We needed to go to a place named Pilrust—a long disused citadel of the *Geumlu*. The journey would be a long one, fraught with dangers we couldn't predict—and that's if the Dark Queen and her minions left us alone.

"And still he carries on," said Yowrnsaxa in an exasperated tone, but with a glint of humor in her eye. "Why can't men ever see when they're beaten?"

"Might as well ask the sun to set in the east," said Jane.

Meuhlnir glanced over his shoulder. "That one wasn't that bad, Jane. You're getting the hang of it."

"Awesome. I'm happy I graduated to 'not that bad,'" said Jane in a droll tone.

"Don't listen to him, dear," said Frikka. "That one has always been slow to admit defeat."

The ship looked like a logical evolution of a Viking longship from Mithgarthr—long and narrow, but with three masts, multiple decks, and a hold for the horses. The captain and crew had taken our coin without comment, despite the looks they'd given each other when Meuhlnir had told them the party's ultimate destination.

"Defeat? Me? I haven't even begun."

"You've finished. Everyone knows this but you," grumbled Sif.

"Woman, one day your mouth will get you into trouble that your pitiful shield—"

"Oh, here it comes," said Mothi. "Good, I haven't seen my father thoroughly thrashed in a flyting for months. Go on, Father." Beside him, Sig snickered.

"I can see I will get no rest on this trip," said Meuhlnir.

"Keep flapping those lips, *dear one*, and you'll be whining and whinging about the amount of rest you get," said Yowrnsaxa.

Meuhlnir looked first at Yowrnsaxa, and then at Sif. With a long-suffering sigh, he closed his mouth and boarded the ship. "We're losing the tide!" he called.

"Now he thinks he's the captain," murmured Mothi. "The man has a difficult time navigating out of his own bedroom in the morning."

"I heard that," said Meuhlnir. "You're not so old I can't ground you."

Mothi rolled his eyes but turned his head, so his expression was only visible to Sig. "Yes, Father," he said.

"And don't think I don't know you're over there rolling your eyes, showing off for your young cousin."

The stevedores finished loading the last of the party's luggage and the provisions for the voyage, and the captain paid them in Meuhlnir's silver coins. "Let's get going," he said. "Before we lose the tide."

Althyof scowled as he stepped off the gangplank and onto the deck. He walked as if the deck beneath him might break with each step.

"The ship is sound, sir," said the captain, coming up the gangplank behind him.

"Sound? *Sound?* It's made of *wood.*"

The captain shook his head and strode back to the bridge of the ship. Meuhlnir turned and walked toward the captain.

"Oh, for Isi's sake, Meuhlnir. Leave the man be so we can get underway!" snapped Yowrnsaxa.

"I think I'll stand with the captain for the beginning of our voyage."

Sif tapped her foot and crossed her arms. "I think you'll stay out of the man's way before I clout—"

"Father, come stand next to Sig and me. Tell us a story to pass the time," said Mothi.

Meuhlnir glowered at his wives but came to stand in the bow next to Sig. "You see, Sig? Mothi's got the right of it. It's better to stay single than to—"

"Single, you say?" chuckled Sif. "We can arrange that."

"You never learn, do you, old man?" asked Frikka, trying to hide a grin.

"One day, I will beat them—"

"At flyting? It's not likely," said Veethar.

"*Now* you speak? You don't say a word all the way from Trankastrantir to the coast, you don't say a word while we arrange for transport, not a word over a meal, nothing while the roustabouts load our luggage, and the words you choose to break your verbal fast are those?"

Veethar looked Meuhlnir in the eye. "Everyone knows this, Meuhlnir. Everyone."

Meuhlnir harrumphed. "Well, I hadn't finished. Perhaps I meant to say, 'with a stick' or 'at dice' or 'in wrestling.' Did you consider any of those, O God of Silence?"

"None of those, either," said Veethar quietly. "Everyone knows this." Veethar glanced at Frikka as she came to stand by his side. She smiled at him and put her arm through his.

Meuhlnir shook his head. "Is no one on my side?"

"Might as well ask grass to grow downward into the dirt," I said.

Meuhlnir's cheeks quivered, and he tried to keep the smile off his lips, but he couldn't. He glanced at Frikka. "You see? That is true mastery of the craft, and here I am admitting Hank has become a master."

"Anything to turn attention away from how badly your wives trounced you," said Veethar with the slight stretching of his lips that served him as a broad smile.

"You only say that because you think Yowrnsaxa will give you extra helpings from the cook pot."

"And he's right," said Yowrnsaxa.

"Are Skowvithr and Yowtgayrr on board?" asked Jane with a hint of impatience.

"They are below. They don't enjoy traveling over water," I said. "Sif made them a draught so they will sleep."

"If only I'd made one for my husband," Sif said behind her hand.

"Why is it everyone in my family thinks I'm deaf?" grumbled Meuhlnir.

The ship lurched away from the dock as they laughed, thralls on the deck closest to the water pulling on the oars to get them through the breakwater. The spray from the waves crashing against the bow was frigid, but once they cleared the breakwater and turned north, the spray lessened to a mist.

"How long will it take to get to Suelhaym?" asked Sig.

"Don't start that, Siggy," said Jane. "We'll get there when we get there."

"I just wanted to know if there's time for Cousin Mouthy to teach me to use one of his axes."

"No," said Yowrnsaxa. "Because the second he starts, I will break his legs, and he'll have to heal up before you can continue."

"Aw, come on, Auntie Yarns! Mom gets to learn to use a shield and axe! Why don't I get to learn to fight?"

Meuhlnir glanced at me. "With your father's permission, young Sig, I will teach you to *vefa strenki*."

"Only his father's permission?" asked Sif with an arched eyebrow.

"Er...that is, I meant that..."

"It's okay," said Jane, laughing.

"Fine by us, Meuhlnir. Thank you." I scratched my chin, trying to keep from smiling. "But no lightning. Not for a long while."

Meuhlnir drew his head back as if I had spit at him. "Of course not! I do know a thing or two about teaching a youngster to *vefa*."

"Sure, sure," I said. "But you *do* enjoy lightning."

Meuhlnir grinned. "That is true." He took Sig off to the side and began instructing the boy in hushed tones.

"And what about you, Jane? Are you ready for another lesson?" asked Frikka.

"Yes!" Jane stood and dug out her wooden practice axe. The three Isir women smiled at each other and got out their own training weapons.

"Guess that leaves us chickens," I said.

Veethar grunted.

"I'm surprised you consented to go by ship, Veethar. You opposed it when we discussed the route."

Veethar waved his hand over the rail as if that was answer enough.

"No forests?"

"No horses, either," said Mothi with a grin.

"At least we're bringing the horses with us," I said.

Veethar shook his head. "And yet, instead of riding them, we stand on this glorified raft and hope we don't encounter rough weather." He walked away from Mothi and me and went over to stand next to Althyof, who stood next to the mast, twitching at every groan the ship made.

The women set up a large square, three paces by three paces, using a length of rope to mark the boundaries. I watched Jane limbering up, rolling her shoulders, taking practice swipes with her wooden axe.

"She's a fine woman, if you don't mind my saying," said Mothi.

"Why would I mind? She is."

With a cry, Frikka leapt into the square, putting her weight behind an overhand blow. Jane stepped forward, forcing the leap to end awkwardly, and swept her shield up to meet Frikka's practice sword.

Frikka smiled. "That was good."

"Thanks," Jane said, returning the smile. "I was—" She yelped and backpedaled as Frikka came at her, first barging Jane with her shield, then swinging the practice sword in a vicious flat arc.

"You're not here to talk, girl!" growled Frikka. "Talk when the fight's ended."

Jane blushed, but set her feet and leaned into her shield, taking Frikka's blows on its face. Frikka slammed blow after blow on the shield, and Jane winced. Sensing a quick victory, Frikka closed the distance and raised her sword. Jane thrust under the bottom rim of her shield, poking Frikka in the stomach with the head of her axe.

Frikka doubled over, laughing. "Oh, Sif, my sister. You taught her that trick?"

When Jane straightened, Frikka favored her with a half-mocking bow and stepped out of the square, rubbing her stomach. Sif nodded and strapped on her shield. "Let's see if you can use that trick on me."

Jane smiled and beckoned Sif with her shield.

"She fights well," said Mothi. "Learns quick."

"When she sets her mind to something, no one can stop her."

"Strong woman. Admirable."

I glanced at him, narrowing my eyes. "I'm not going to have to break your legs, am I?"

A broad smile split Mothi's face. "Why? I'm not going to teach Sig how to use one of my axes." Mothi rested his hand on my shoulder, and I winced. "Bad today?"

I looked away. "No. It's okay."

"That awful, is it? The cloak doesn't help?"

"Oh, the cloak helps. Without the cloak, I'd be in bed somewhere."

"This poison you used to take, this…"

"Methotrexate."

Mothi shook his head. "The *Gamla Toonkumowl* has words easier to remember."

"If you say so," I said and laughed.

"Mother Sif was working on something to replace the meth…the poison."

"Methotrexate. Yes, she is, but so far she hasn't come up with a replacement that is potent enough to make a difference."

"She'll find it," Mothi said with confidence. "She's like your Jane—when she sets her mind to something, it's best to just get out of her way."

"I heard that!" Sif called without breaking the rhythm of blows she was trading with Jane.

Mothi rolled his eyes. "This family…"

I chuckled. "Indeed." I nudged Mothi with my elbow. "Without being too obvious, look at Althyof."

Mothi glanced at the Tverkr, who had graduated to crouching next to the mast, looking up into the rigging as if he expected something to fall on his head. "Poor guy. Too bad ships can't be constructed using granite."

"Meuhlnir! I expect battle pay for this voyage!" yelled Althyof.

"Is it so?" asked Meuhlnir without turning away from Sig.

A loud buzzing sound vibrated through the ship, starting in the stern and sweeping forward toward the bow at an alarming rate. The noise ceased, leaving my feet tingling. Everyone froze for a moment. "What the hell was that?"

"Not sure," Mothi said. "I've never heard anything like it."

Meuhlnir ushered Sig away from the gunnels. He handed Sig off to Jane and turned to Veethar. He opened his mouth, but a loud, pulsating throb made speech impossible. The vibrations it sent through my body nauseated me—it was similar to the deep throb of double bass drums at a heavy metal concert, but far more intense.

Mothi pulled me away from the bow, concern etched on his face. "I don't like this, Hank."

The captain of the boat was shouting orders at the crew, his face pallid, expression grim. He ordered the oars pulled in and shipped, and their holes plugged.

"What is it?" bellowed Meuhlnir.

"What we wanted least to meet," said Veethar. "A dragon."

The captain snapped orders, and the crew leapt to answer his demands. They set the sails and the rigging for speed. "Wind, Yarl!" he called.

Meuhlnir raised an eyebrow at Veethar, who made a mocking half-bow. "*Vintur plowsa*," he said, raising his arms wide. The wind doubled, then trebled, until it howled through the rigging, snapping at the sails, stretching the ropes that held them. The big ship leapt forward in the water and accelerated hard.

"More, if you can, Yarl," called the captain. He kept glancing off the stern at something in the water.

"How much can your ship take?"

17 ✪ ERIK HENRY VICK

"More than this!" snapped the captain without turning from the stern.

"*Sterkari vintur, sterkari*," chanted Veethar.

"Oh, by the *Plauinn*," snapped Althyof. "Can you Isir only think in one dimension?" The Tverkr knelt next to the mast and withdrew one of his twin daggers. He chanted under his breath, but without enough volume to be heard over the thrumming coming from the sea beneath us. With sharp, quick gestures, he carved runes in the planking that made up the deck we stood on, and then did the same to the mast. Without breaking the rhythm of his song, he moved to each of the other masts and carved runes into them. When he stood, he glared at Veethar. "Now, make the damn wind *blow*, Isir."

Veethar shrugged and drew a deep breath. "*Andardowhtur kuthadna!*" he boomed, his voice echoing like thunder. The wind surged, blowing like the leading edge of a hurricane.

The ropes sang with tension when the wind caught the sails, and the ship lurched forward as if shot from a cannon. The masts creaked and groaned, but they held.

"Can we outrun it?" asked Meuhlnir.

"Hope that we do," said the captain. He turned and stared off the stern.

My gaze went to Meuhlnir's, and we hurried toward the stern of the ship. "How do we fight a sea dragon?" I asked.

Meuhlnir shook his head. "I've not had the occasion to do it."

"But still, you must have an idea."

He glanced my way but didn't meet my eyes. "Let's get a look at the thing before we decide whether to fight it or not."

The pulsating throb changed pitch, becoming a booming click that rattled through the ship, making anything not secured jump and dance. "What the hell is that?" I asked, not expecting an answer.

"The dragon's roar," said Meuhlnir.

We reached the stern as the beast broke the surface of the water. Where the white dragon I'd fought had been streamlined for flight, massive chest and shoulder muscles built for controlling its huge wings, the sea dragon was long and thin, similar to a snake, or a Chinese dragon. It had no arms or legs, and though it had wing-like appendages, they looked more useful in the water than the air. Iridescent scales covered its body, and the reflected sunlight glinted and shimmered with a thousand different colors at once. Mouth stretched wide, the dragon emitted another series of clicks at such a volume I thought my head might explode. I felt hot, skin super-heated by the sound waves.

"Still want to fight it?" asked Meuhlnir.

"Not in a million years," I whispered.

The dragon was twice the length of the ship, with fins and sails designed for speed in the water. It couldn't fly *per se,* but it could glide through the air for a short span. It used the time to shift its gaze back and forth amongst the people on deck as if marking them. When the dragon's gaze lingered on Althyof, it hissed, and its eyes glowed a fiery orange.

"Your reputation precedes you, *Runeskowld*," said Meuhlnir.

Althyof made a disparaging sound. "I've bound stronger dragons than this."

The dragon's eyes narrowed, and it hissed again before ducking its head and plunging into the water.

"Can dragons understand us?"

"Of course, they can," snapped Althyof. "How else would my bindings work?"

"The runes I saw on Friner's belt—"

"Maintain the binding in my absence, but the binding must come first."

"Can you...can you—"

"Not from atop this floating disaster! I can't concentrate in this claptrap."

"You cut the runes into the deck and masts."

"A ship has no will."

Meuhlnir grunted.

"Captain, what's the draft on this vessel?" I asked.

He turned to me with a scornful expression. "The last place you want to flee from a sea dragon is in the shallows, you fool!"

Meuhlnir cleared his throat. "You forget yourself." He said it in a hard-edged tone and didn't even glance at the man, but the captain blanched, and his eyes widened a little.

The captain bowed to Meuhlnir. "I meant no disrespect to you, Yarl," he said.

Meuhlnir chuckled and hooked his thumb at me. "He's the last of us you want angry with you. Disrespect *him* at your peril."

The captain turned back to me, confusion written on his face. "But...but he's...he's not even..." The man's eyes roamed my body, lingering on Kunknir and Krati and the strange belt that had been made for me by Prokkr, the Tverkr Master Smith.

It dawned on me that he was looking for melee weapons, and I couldn't help myself. I laughed. Holding my hands out, palms toward the captain, I shook my head. "It's okay, Captain. You don't owe me—"

"It most certainly is *not* okay, and he certainly *does* owe you respect, Aylootr." Mothi stepped onto the bridge and glared at the man. "Have you not heard?" he asked, his tone dripping disdain. "You are in the presence of Aylootr, slayer of dragons, slayer of *oolfa*, pursuer of the Black Bitch herself."

The captain's eyes bounced between Kunknir and Krati again, getting wider and wider. "And these?" he asked.

Mothi clucked his tongue. "You've been at sea too long, Karl." He stepped to my side, face set, muscles across his shoulders bunching. "Do you know me?"

The captain nodded. "You are Mothi Strongheart."

Mothi's nod was curt. "I respect this man," he said, lifting his hand toward my shoulder. "If I, Mothi Strongheart, respect him, what should you do?"

"Mothi," I said, using the quiet voice I used to calm drunks back in New York. "There is no—" His hand came down on my shoulder and squeezed.

"Respect, Captain. It is granted to you because of your position on this ship. It can be given to your first mate, instead."

The captain bowed to me, a deep bow from the waist. "I apologize, Yarl Aylootr."

"Good, now we can be friends again. Answer his question!" Mothi's voice cracked like a whip, and the captain jumped.

"The draft of this vessel is shallow for its size and displacement. It was built for speed, long and narrow, with a flat bottom. We can sail tight to the shore, but as I said before, that's the last place we want to be with a sea dragon close."

"Why?" asked Meuhlnir without turning.

"They spring off the bottom, leaping high in the air. From the air, the damn things spit poison on ships beneath them. The poison is like...like...well, I don't know what to compare it to. It eats into the skin and burns while it does so."

"Acid," I said.

"Poison," said the captain with a shake of his head. "Once touched, a man dies. Of that, there is no doubt."

"Okay, so shallow is out, but that's fine. What I'm interested in is the shape of the keel and the bottom of the ship."

Mothi grinned and struck the captain on the shoulder with the back of his hand. To look at Mothi, it was just two friends horsing around, but to look at the captain, Mothi's blow hadn't been a playful one. "You see? Next time, answer without all the fracas."

"Why, Hank? What difference does the bottom of the ship make?" asked Sif.

"Friction...to be fast, a ship needs a shallow draft. Isn't that correct, Captain?" The captain nodded, rubbing his shoulder. "The heavier the ship, the deeper it sits in the water, and that means friction with the water increases. We need this ship to ride higher—out of the water if we can achieve it."

"Out of the water?" asked Althyof. "What ship sails out of the water?"

"One enchanted by Master Enchanter Althyof," I said.

"You over-estimate my skills."

"And one with the help of a *vefari*," I said, turning to Meuhlnir.

He glanced at Althyof. "Well, Tverkr? Shall we try?"

Althyof tucked his head to his chest, but even over the wind, the snapping of the ropes, and the sound of the sea pounding against the hull, we could hear him muttering. When he looked up, his eyes glinted. "If this fails, it *will not* be because of my enchanting, Isir."

Meuhlnir nodded.

Althyof began chanting again, and walked to and fro on the deck, squatting now and again to carve a rune or two into the planks. The more he carved, the faster the ship went.

Meuhlnir grunted. "I'm not sure what will work, if anything."

"All we can do is try," I said. The clicking sound boomed through the ship again, sounding as if it originated beneath the keel. "No time like the present."

Meuhlnir nodded and said, "*Veka midna.*" The timbers that made up the ship groaned, and the ship rode a minuscule amount higher in the water.

"No, no!" snapped Althyof. "I've already made the wood light!"

The water astern began to churn and roil.

"Do something else, Father," said Mothi. "Now."

Meuhlnir shot a glare at him. "*Taka plug*!"

The ship began to skim and skip across the water, like a flat stone thrown side-arm. Behind us, the water erupted in a column of frothy white water, and sunlight glinted from iridescent scales at its center.

"It attacks!" yelled Frikka.

Kunknir and Krati came out of their holsters in my palms without my decision to grab for them. They would be useless once the beast returned to the water, but when it was in the air…

Jane stepped up beside me, her shield on her arm and a sharp axe in her other hand. She wore a winged helmet and a mail shirt that was a little too big for her. Even so, she was beautiful.

"More speed," said the captain, his voice almost inaudible in the din.

"Not yet," I said, cop-voice coming to the fore.

When the water cascaded down the length of the dragon and the beast's entire body was in the air, I fired. Kunknir roared and bucked, slinging hot brass across the bridge. Krati crashed in counterpoint, and more hot brass flew. The rounds flew true, the .40 caliber rounds from Krati glancing off the iridescent scales, and the .45 caliber rounds from Kunknir slicing through them as if they were *papier mâché*.

The dragon made a sound like a baby rabbit in the jaws of a cat. Its eyes sought mine, but I remembered how the white dragon had mesmerized me that day on the plain and avoided its gaze. Kunknir fired dry, locking the slide back. Still firing Krati, I released the magazine from the .45 into the pouch Prokkr had designed for that purpose, the weight and momentum of it triggering the clever device that propped another magazine away from the belt. I slammed the pistol onto the fresh magazine and released the slide, chambering a round.

The dragon hissed, and then the booming clicking noise hit me full force. It was loud, as loud as anything I'd ever heard, and it hurt—not only the sound but the physical impact of the sound waves as they slapped against my body. I shifted Krati to fire at the dragon's eyes and brought up Kunknir.

The dragon shrieked as the hot lead from Krati ricocheted from the scales around its eyes. At that moment, the ship skipped off the last wave and skimmed a foot or two above the water. Without the friction of the water slowing it down, the ship accelerated away from the dragon at an increasing pace. The dragon hissed like a teapot about to burst, and, in an acrobatic feat, folded itself in half to dive back into the water. It dove deep until I could no longer see the sun glinting off its scales.

"Has it gone?" asked the captain.

"No idea. It's too deep—invisible." As soon as I'd finished, the deafening clicking hit us again, vibrating the entire ship with its intensity. "I guess that answers that question."

"Dad!" yelled Sig.

I glanced at the mast where Veethar stood, arms still raised, concentrating on keeping the wind blowing, but Sig was not there. "Sig?"

"*Oh my God!*" cried Jane. "Sig! *Get away from there!*"

I followed her gaze to where our son stood—*stood*—on the gunnel. He was pointing at something straight below us. "Sig, get down from there!"

Jane was sprinting toward our son, maternal instincts in overdrive—or maybe she had a bit of what Frikka had. I followed her, putting fresh magazines into both pistols as I shuffled that direction.

The clicking was louder, making the entire deck jump and heave. As I reached the halfway point to where Sig stood on the rail, and as Jane stretched her arms out to grab him, the dragon slammed into the bottom of the ship between the bow and midships. The ship rolled to starboard as if it would capsize in midair, and the dragon executed another of its acrobatic folds and dove into the water again, its tail slamming into the port side. Jane screamed and leapt toward the port rail, fighting the momentum of the heaving deck plus gravity itself.

Her boots skidded against the wood planks, but she had no traction, and she began to slide back toward starboard. She uttered an unladylike curse and a set of black raven's wings sprouted from her shoulders, emerging from the clever slits worked in her mail shirt for that purpose. Her wings beat once, twice, and she was away from the deck and rising toward the port rail where we'd last seen our son.

I slid toward the starboard gunnel, feet scrabbling against the rough wooden planks, as unable as Jane had been to defy gravity and reach the port side.

Meuhlnir stomped his heavy boot against the deck. "*Stuthva!*" he shouted, and the air crackled with power. The ship shuddered and stopped tipping to starboard. "*Pletya oot!*" The ship righted itself with a wobble toward port.

"Jane!" I shouted. I forgot my aching joints and ran toward the port rail. Beneath us, the dragon splashed and clicked. "Meuhlnir! Jane and Sig went over!" His heavy footfalls sounded behind me as Mothi raced past me. Mothi skidded to a halt at the rail, peering over the side.

"There," he shouted, pointing behind us and port.

I turned and ran to the stern. Jane hovered six feet above the waves, holding Sig, who was soaked to the bone. She struggled to gain altitude and to lift our fourteen-year-old son out of the sea at the same time.

The water beneath them churned and boiled. "Jane! The dragon!" I waved Kunknir over my head, willing her to hear me, to notice me. Sig glanced at me, then down at the churning water below him. He looked up into his mother's face and pulled her hands off his arms. "No!" I shouted and stumbled into the rail.

Jane shrieked as he fell and tucked her wings to dive after him. She shouted, her words lost in the wind and the incessant, infernal clicking.

The distance was a problem, and every second we moved away from them. "Turn the ship!" I yelled.

"Are you crazy?" shouted the captain. "It's better that two should die so the rest of us can escape! I'll not—" His words became an agonized wail, and he slid to the deck.

Althyof stood behind him, eyes blazing, the captain's blood dripping from one of his polymorphic daggers. He was singing in that strange language he used during battle. "Better that one than two, fool." He motioned at the great wheel on the bridge. "Someone drive this accursed floating trap!"

The first mate jumped to the wheel and spun it, but nothing happened. The rudder was out of the water, flapping free in the air.

"*Snoothu vith*!" yelled Veethar and the wind that had been blowing from behind us changed to blow from the bow in an instant. For a moment, the ship shuddered as the sails flapped, but then the wind began to turn the ship.

Jane hovered mere feet above the roiling white water. Sig had surfaced behind her.

"Jane!" I called. "He's behind you!"

The ship was floundering around, spinning her out of my line of sight. I followed the rail as it spun, screaming at the top of my voice and waving my pistols above my head, but it was no use. She couldn't hear me over the booming clicks coming from the dragon, and she didn't notice the change in the wind. Sig started swimming toward her, and something inside me snapped. I swung my leg up and over the rail, meaning to get down there and *help*.

Mothi grabbed me from behind, using his immense strength to lift me off the rail and away. "No, Aylootr!"

It enraged me, and I turned on him. Kunknir and Krati were in my palms, and the urge to do battle sang in my veins. I shouldered past him, or tried to, but he looped an arm, thick with muscles, around me and spun me back.

"No!" he said. "You can't help from the water! Aylootr! Hear sense!"

Yowtgayrr stumbled out of the stairwell that led to the sleeping deck. His eyes were glassy, and his bluish-ivory hair stood on end, but he held both of his blades naked and ready for battle. "What?" he demanded, gaze going first to Althyof and then finding Meuhlnir.

"Sea dragon," Meuhlnir said as if it were nothing more exciting than a brisk wind. "Jane and Sig are overboard. The boy in the water, Jane flying on raven's wings."

Yowtgayrr's eyes sought mine, noting the stand-off with Mothi. He reversed his grip on his blades and stabbed them into the wood. He pointed at me and glared. "You, Hank Jensen, do *not* leave this deck." I opened my mouth to argue, but with staggering steps, Yowtgayrr ran toward the rail closest to Sig. He leapt from the rail and dove into the water.

"By the balls of all the *Plauinn*," Althyof yelled. "No one else leave this damn boat!"

Mothi stared into my face. "Hank? Will you stop fighting me?"

I nodded and, when he released me, stepped past him. Yowtgayrr had covered half the distance to my son, his arms lifting and burying themselves in the waves at a rapid pace.

"What have I done to earn such loyalty?" I muttered.

"Well, for one thing, you do a good job of teasing Father," said Mothi. His eyes never left Sig, but his hand found my shoulder and patted it. "Get those noise-makers ready. The beast comes."

My eyes snapped to the seething white water, then to Jane, who hovered a few feet above it. Without giving myself time to think, I lifted Krati and put a round in front of her. She wore the ring Althyof had enchanted—she could heal herself if the bullet went awry. The same ring that let her fly on those beautiful sable wings.

The round splashed into the water in front of her, and her gaze snapped up and to me. I waved her away from the moiling water, and Mothi pointed at Sig. She got the message and veered away, just as the dragon broke the surface of the water.

Yowtgayrr reached my son and hooked an arm around the boy's chest. Sig struggled as Yowtgayrr started to pull him away, back toward the ship.

"No, Sig! Go with him!" I yelled.

The dragon hissed at the ship, then saw Jane. It lunged at her, mouth open wide. Jane juked to the left and darted back, wings working hard. The beast snapped at her again, and again Jane dodged away, flitting this way and that like a hummingbird on methamphetamines. The sea dragon emitted a long series of loud clicks, and Jane weltered in the shock wave that followed. When it saw her wallowing, moving like a drunk butterfly, it hissed and arched its neck while tilting its head to the side, preparing to strike at her and snap its jaws around her body.

Kunknir and Krati roared and boomed, and lead flew toward the dragon's head and neck. The bullets might have hit Jane, but I didn't know what else to do.

I kept firing until Kunknir's slide locked back, and as I ejected the magazine and fed in a fresh one, the bullets from the gun rived through the dragon's scales covering its jaws and the side of its neck. The dragon heaved its head away, ducking behind the bulk of its own neck. Jane cried out, and I cringed, wondering if one of the rounds from Krati had hit her.

The dragon emitted a string of pops and whumps in rapid succession, the clangor stunning Jane further, and she dipped close to the perilous waves. When it turned, the dragon hissed at me, its eyes gyrating like a Hollywood special effect. Yowtgayrr and Sig drew its attention, and it blasted them with a long volley of loud clicks that agitated the surrounding water, making the surface of the sea carom and dance with its intensity. The dragon lunged at them, mouth dripping a foul-looking arylide yellow, viscous fluid into the waves below it.

"Yowtgayrr! Poison!" I screamed it so loud that my voice cracked.

The Alf redoubled his efforts, using his free arm to scoop at the water. Sig had stopped fighting him and instead, kicked his feet and paddled in the water as if he were doing an upside-down butterfly stroke. Even with both of their efforts, they stood no chance of outpacing the behemoth beast.

Jane shook her head and beat her raven-black wings hard to gain altitude. She glanced around in time to catch the dragon preparing to strike, towering over Yowtgayrr and our son, jaws dripping acid. "No!" she screamed, and as she did, a bright carmine aura flashed around her and, a heartbeat later, around the sea dragon.

The clicking from the dragon ceased, and it spasmed and convulsed, its head flopping this way and that as its body performed a strange dance in the water. The beast's entire body stiffened and fell to the side with a tremendous splash, reminding me of a tree felled into a lake.

After the booming clamor of the dragon's clicking and hissing, the sound of the roaring wind seemed trivial, a welcome respite. Jane listed sideways, head lolling.

"What did she do?" murmured Mothi.

"Althyof," I said.

"What?"

"The ring gives her the power to kill by a force of will alone. She said she'd never use it."

"Her son had never stared into the jaws of an angry sea dragon when she said that."

"No doubt," I said.

Jane rolled her head to stare at the long, iridescent body of the beast, seeming to see nothing else—not Sig, not Yowtgayrr, not the ship. I thought she wallowed in remorse, that she was busy cursing herself for killing the beast, but it wasn't that. Or at least not all of it was. Her magnificent black wings stopped beating the air and disappeared as her eyelids sank closed. She tilted to the side and fell into the sea as if dead.

"Get us down!" I shouted and ran toward the rail.

"You stay here!" Mothi yelled at me. With a running leap, he jumped to the gunnel and dove into the sea.

"*Setyast til syowvar*!" Meuhlnir commanded, and the ship sank to the surface of the water.

"*Vinturidn er rowlegur*," said Veethar, and the sails slackened as the wind died away.

I twisted out of my belt and swept the cloak off my shoulders for the first time since I'd run out of my methotrexate. Caustic pain descended from my shoulders to my hips, ripping a harsh gasp out of me. I stripped off my armor, and let it fall to the deck. Tunnel vision swept in from nowhere and I staggered as the ship lurched through the waves.

"No," said Meuhlnir in a calm voice. He wrapped the cloak around my shoulders and relief sang through me. "Mothi's already there. He has her, Hank."

I forced my eyes open and saw he was right. Mothi had his arm across her shoulder and was pulling her toward the boat with long, efficient strokes of his other arm. Yowtgayrr had Sig and was angling toward Mothi in case he needed help. I sagged against Meuhlnir, fighting the urge to vomit.

"Sif!" Meuhlnir called.

Veethar snapped his fingers at the first mate. "Get them all on board."

The first mate glanced at Althyof, and the Tverkr gestured at the rail with impatience. "Don't look to me every moment! Do your job!"

The first mate—now the new captain—yelled orders at his thrall crew and they hustled to get our four companions back on board. The ship maneuvered close, and the crew threw netting over the side to act as an impromptu ladder. Yowtgayrr set Sig to climbing the net and then took one of Jane's arms so he and Mothi could bring her up the net.

My attention shifted back and forth between Jane and Sig. Jane's head lolled from side to side with the movement of the waves. Her eyes were half-open but empty. "Jane!" I called. She gave a start and turned her head toward me, but she didn't seem to recognize me.

Sif gave me a cursory look. "I'll deal with you later," she promised. "You made your own pain, you can live with it while I treat your wife."

I nodded, eyes only for Jane.

Sig cleared the rail and ran over to me. "Daddy! What's wrong with her?"

"I don't know, Son."

"Don't worry, Sig. Auntie Sniffles is here." She put her arm around Sig's shoulders. "But don't you think for a second I didn't see the silly thing you did and won't have words with you about it later."

Mothi and Yowtgayrr reached the gunnel and handed Jane over the rail to Meuhlnir and Sif. They set her on the deck, and Sif examined her.

"What is it? Did the dragon—"

"No," said Sif. She closed her eyes, lips moving. Jane's body convulsed, and she regurgitated sea water all over the deck. Sif nodded and put her ear to Jane's chest, expression tight, worried. Then, she smiled. "All is well. She's in a kind of sleep. Whatever she did, it drained her body to dangerous levels. I cleared the water from her lungs, and she is breathing on her own."

A sigh of relief gusted out of me. "When will she—"

"Telling the future is Frikka's department, not mine," said Sif. She glanced up at me, and her eyes softened. "But don't worry, she *will* wake. For now, we make her comfortable." She stood and began issuing orders to the thralls to bring up blankets and the rocks they used below deck for heating the cabins.

"Dad!" murmured Sig, and I tore my gaze away from Jane and put my arm around my son. "Is she going to be okay?"

"Yes, Son," I said. "Auntie Sniffles is better than an emergency room any day of the week."

"Did you see what Mom did to it? The dragon, I mean? It fell over dead!"

I flinched and put my arm around his shoulders. "Mommy will feel bad about that, I think, so maybe we shouldn't make too much of it when she wakes up."

Sig glanced around me at his mother and looked up at me. "Why? I don't understand."

"It's no small thing to kill another living being, let alone one that might be intelligent. It affects almost everyone, but in different ways."

"But, it was a dragon, and it was trying to kill me!" His whisper was fierce.

"Which is why your mother acted as she did. Her choice was between her beliefs and your life."

He nodded after a moment of thought. "Oh."

"Let's tread carefully for a while, make things easy for her."

"Yeah, Dad. I can get with that program."

"Good. Now you'd better get out of those wet clothes before you turn into a Sigsicle."

"It's not that cold, Dad. I want to talk to Mommy when she wakes up. To thank her."

"Get yourself changed, Sig, then we'll see."

I turned back to Yowtgayrr and Mothi. "Thank you, both of you. I don't know what I've done to deserve friends like the two of you."

Mothi grinned at me, but Yowtgayrr shook his head. "Don't be silly, Hank. The boy is a fine addition to the party, and it was my honor to help your family. As for thanking me, that is unnecessary. Recall my mission, recall my beliefs."

I nodded but didn't let go of his forearm. "Yes, that's all well and good, but recall *my* beliefs and accept my gratitude."

Yowtgayrr shrugged and smiled. "Fine. You're welcome, Hank." He squeezed my forearm for a moment, then broke away. "It's very cold in this wind. I'll go below and get warm."

"Do that," I said.

Mothi clapped Yowtgayrr on the shoulder and together the two men went below to get dried off and warm. The new captain was shouting more orders to the thrall crew, getting them underway again, but he wasn't turning the ship back to their original course.

"Captain!" shouted Meuhlnir. "Our destination lies to the stern."

The man shook his head and pointed back toward the port we'd sailed from. "You'll have a refund minus expenses and a funeral, but I'll not risk the ship."

Meuhlnir turned to look at me and raised his eyebrow.

"Why is it at risk? The sea dragon's dead."

The captain nodded but didn't spin the great wheel. "That one is dead, yes. But sea dragons hunt in pods."

"Pods?" asked Meuhlnir.

"Groups," I said. "I wouldn't think they'd act that way. Aren't they territorial?"

"To non-dragons, yes," said the captain. "And to dragons outside their pod, but the dead sea dragon called his mates."

"How do you know?"

"The other sound it made, not the clicking," said the captain. "We're in a race now, whether we like it or not. We need speed, now, or you will have to fight other dragons."

"*Andardowhtur kuthadna*!" commanded Veethar, and the hurricane-like winds filled the sails again.

THREE

I carried Jane down the gangplank and onto the docks. Her head lolled with each step, and she hung as limp as a rag doll in my arms. Sig trotted next to me, concern-filled eyes on Jane's slack face, laden down with his pack and his mother's.

Meuhlnir arranged rooms for us in the tavern next to the docks, and I took Jane straight up the narrow stairs and lay her on the bed. Sif followed on my heels. I stepped back, worried that she hadn't even twitched during the entire process of disembarking the ship.

Sif put her hand on my shoulder. "All is well, Hank. She sleeps and will awaken when her body is ready for her to do so."

I nodded, not taking my eyes off Jane's face.

"All is well," repeated Sif. "There's nothing more to do. She will be fine." She looked me over, assessing my condition, gaze darting from my face to my stance, to the hunch of my back. I'd grown used to such looks in the years of my illness, first from Jane, and, since we'd been in Osgarthr, from Sif *and* Jane. Sif reached into her ever-present bag and pulled out the small container of foul smelling ointment she dosed me with when my Personal Monster™ got the better of me. She raised her eyebrows.

"Not yet," I said. I still hadn't gotten over what Jane called the Calculus of When—the feeling that I needed to conserve things that worked to reduce my pain and discomfort, only using them when I absolutely had to. I didn't think Sif's cream would fade away as the drugs from Mithgarthr had, but the lizard part of my brain didn't care what I thought.

Sif's gaze drifted to Jane's unconscious face. Sif's face settled in an expression I recognized from previous conversations. "You're no good to her if you're laid up next to her, Hank."

"Oh, all right," I muttered. Stress, my ever-present enemy since the Dark Queen's curse wrecked my life, had taken its toll during the battle with the sea dragon and the flight back to the safety of the harbor. My worry about Jane only acted as cement to the always present stiffness in my joints. My back hurt as if I'd been in a car wreck, and my knees didn't want to bend.

Sif closed the door and said, "You know what to do."

I stripped off my outer layers and my shirt and pants. "How come you never run out of that smelly stuff?" I asked.

Sif put her bag on the foot of the bed and pushed me toward the room's only chair. I winced as I sank into it, weary and sore. Sif shrugged. "You need it, don't you?"

"Yes." I sighed as she worked the cream into my shoulders and neck. The ointment worked by overloading the neural pathways that conducted pain and irritation. It burned like menthol sports cream, but more so.

"I'm still working on the substitute for your poison, though I have made little progress. But I still object to the process on principle."

"Yes, I know you do, but I don't know anything else that works as well as the methotrexate."

She grunted and smeared the noxious-smelling cream into my knees. "I've been thinking about that. This poison, this methotrexate, it doesn't seem that its poisonous qualities are what affect your curse."

"No?"

"No. I think it's another effect. It reduces inflammation, and that improves your condition."

"If you say so," I said. Sif hadn't gone to medical school, but I'd put her up against anyone who had, any day of any week. She understood things about our bodies because she could *see* them—she saw what made them go astray and had the herb lore to set them straight again.

"I do. Maybe I don't need to duplicate this foul poison. It could burn your lungs, you know."

"I do," I said. Methotrexate was a chemotherapy drug, and in large doses, it caused horrible side effects. "But I don't take enough of it for that to happen."

"Oh, is that so?" The sarcasm dripped from her voice.

"According to Western medicine."

"And you know what it's doing to your kidneys? Your liver?"

"No," I said. "When I was back home, I had to do monthly blood tests to watch all that, but here…"

"Here, you must rely on me. Your kidneys are recovering nicely since you ran out of the stuff."

"Perhaps, but you've seen how much worse I've gotten."

Sif grunted. "I suggest we try an experiment."

"Oh?"

"Yes. I suggest you stop thinking and let me do my work. I suggest you leave it to me for two months. You do what I tell you, you take the preparations I make you—no matter how bad they taste—and we see how you do. Do you agree?"

"Will you continue to work on the methotrexate-substitute while the experiment runs?"

She stooped to work on my knees and treated me to an awkward shrug. "Of course. It will be our backup plan."

"Then there's no downside."

"Good. I hope to get you doing better *without* risking your health."

"Now that's a novel concept."

"Yes, well, I can't speak to the practices of the healers in your *klith*, but here, we try not to poison our patients."

"What is this great idea you've been working on?"

She clicked her tongue. "This *great idea,* as you call it, is a chemical made in certain glands of pigs, a blend of herbs, minerals, vitamins, and a little *vefnathur* to bind it all together."

"And what does it do?"

"Curtails the urge your body has acquired to inflame its own tissues at every turn." She pulled me out of the chair and turned me, so she could work the cream into the small of my back.

"So, it's an anti-inflammatory? And the chemical sounds similar to a glucocorticoid. Prednisone."

"I have no idea about that gobbledygook you just spouted, but, yes, it's a *potent* anti-inflammatory— like your poison, but without the poison."

"I've tried crazier things," I said.

Sif swatted my backside. "You needn't try it if you think you know best."

"No, no," I said. "I'm happy to rely on your knowledge."

"You'd better be since as far as I can tell, my 'smelly ointment' does more than that cloak for your mobility." She put the lid back on her little jar of miracles. "I'll see if I can buy the chemical extract here in town. If not, I can buy a supply in Suelhaym. I need to shop there, at any rate, to buy Dragon's Kiss so I can formulate something to replace the dwindling supply of your pain pills."

"Either way, the anti-inflammatory will be a relief. I should have brought more methotrexate, but I never thought I was going on an extended stay to another planet. To be honest, I believed I would either die in that cave or be back home by dinner." I shrugged and flashed a rueful smile at her.

"It's no matter. We can make efficient substitutes." She grinned at me. "Or better. Now, let's get you downstairs before my husband makes a mess of things. I'll stay with Jane."

I pulled my clothes back on and said, "But he's so good at that."

"And you've known him such a short time!" Laughing, she shoved me toward the stairs and closed the door to my room behind me.

We gathered around a big table in the port-side tavern's private dining room. A fire burned in the large stone fireplace, and dirty sunlight streamed in through the grimy windows on either side. The Alfar looked groggy, especially Skowvithr, who'd awakened a few minutes earlier.

"And how is Jane?" asked Frikka.

"According to Sif, she's recovering. She needs rest, that's all," I said.

"Good. But returning to our conversation, I say we should go overland," said Althyof. "I'd rather walk than get on that flimsy craft—or one like it—ever again."

"Time, however, is not on our side," said Meuhlnir. "If not for the sea dragon, we'd be over halfway to Suelhaym by now."

"My point," said Althyof. "What is a collection of sticks compared to the might of a sea dragon? Nothing but kindling."

Meuhlnir puffed out his cheeks and let the air whistle between his teeth. "Yes, but—"

"No buts, Isir. What I said is the truth and nothing else."

Meuhlnir glanced my way, his posture stiff, lips pinched together to form a fierce frown. "What do you have to say, Hank? By ship or by land?"

"Why did it attack?" I asked.

Veethar nodded at me, face set in grim lines. "That is the question."

Meuhlnir rubbed the back of his neck as if he'd slept on it wrong. "Is it? Does it matter?"

"Of course, it matters," said Yowtgayrr.

"If *she* sent it to harry us, it's one thing," I said. "If it's a random attack, an innocent attack if you will, we can assess the risk of returning to the sea, but if the Dark Queen sent the beast at us, the risk is one hundred percent."

Mothi leaned forward, resting his elbows on the table, drawing a frown from Yowrnsaxa. "If she sent the beast, won't she send something else if we travel by land?"

"Maybe," said Frikka, pulling her lip. "But maybe not."

"Why not?" asked Meuhlnir. "If her point is to harry us, why not harry us on land?"

"She may want to *delay* us," said Veethar.

"Yes, and it could be that going overland is slow enough she'll leave us alone," said Frikka.

"You've *seen* this?" asked Meuhlnir.

"Look, we still don't know if she even sent the beast," I said when Frikka looked down at the table without speaking.

"That's the beauty," said Mothi. "Whether she sent it or not, we are delayed, and we delay ourselves further sitting here arguing the point. She has as much time as we allow her to set up a trap in Suelhaym."

"But would she?" asked Meuhlnir. "Would she risk her sister's wrath?"

"As much as I love her, Freya has never been one to stand up to her sister," scoffed Yowrnsaxa. "Do you not recall our last trip to Muspetlshaymr?"

Meuhlnir's face darkened. "Do not think I forget."

"Then you know Freya may not like what her sister does, but she will allow it."

"Even now?" asked Veethar. "Even after the war?"

Frikka tapped the table. "I think not."

"You think not, or you *know* not?" asked Meuhlnir. When she didn't answer, Meuhlnir leaned back in his chair, tugging his beard. "Just once, it would be nice to have a straight answer," he muttered.

"This is pointless," said Mothi. "We can't know if she sent the sea dragon or not...or if she's trying to delay us to set a trap in Suelhaym."

"We *could* find out," muttered Meuhlnir.

"Stop your sulking," said Yowrnsaxa, but she smiled to take the sting out of the words.

"Okay," I said. "Let's look at it another way. Is there any chance another captain will agree to take us to Suelhaym now that the story has no doubt spread across the dock?"

Althyof scoffed. "Not likely. I wouldn't."

"Yes, but you wouldn't be a ship captain, either."

"No."

"What's the real difference in travel time?"

"Had we left from our estates, we would now be a day away from Suelhaym," murmured Veethar.

"But, we didn't. We came here and spent a day getting a ship and another day loading and killing sea dragons. So, from *here*, how long by horse, and how long by ship?" I asked.

Mothi scratched behind his ear. "Getting another ship—*if* we can, given the pod of sea dragons in the area—loading our luggage and getting underway, those could each take a day or more. The voyage itself would take two or three days, depending on the weather."

"And the sea dragons," said Yowtgayrr.

Mothi nodded.

"Veethar? By horse?"

Veethar looked down at his lap. "We are marginally closer here, and we can follow the coast road. Three, or perhaps four days of hard riding."

"Even with young Sig, here?" asked Yowrnsaxa.

"Yes, I think so. Young Sig is becoming quite a horseman." Veethar's lips twitched at my son, and Sig smiled his widest smile.

"Then the easiest route is by land," I said.

"I wish we'd—" started Meuhlnir.

"We didn't," said Veethar.

I inclined my head. "Done is done and wishing won't change it. The time we spent on the sea route is gone, we have to move on."

"I'll go see about getting the horses cared for until Jane wakes." Meuhlnir stood and darted a quick look at Yowrnsaxa. "Are we adequately provisioned for traveling by land?"

Yowrnsaxa's gaze swept around the room, and she stood. "I think we could survive, but I'll purchase a few more things."

"I'll go with you," said Frikka.

"Good," said Meuhlnir with a glance in my direction. "The rest of you should try to rest. We all have rooms upstairs, and we can't leave until Jane recovers in any case." Meuhlnir grimaced as he rose and tromped toward the door.

"I'll come with you," I said.

"Make sure the horses don't outwit him," said Mothi with a grin.

Meuhlnir grunted and pushed out through the door.

I pushed away from the table and went after him. By the time I got over to the stables, Meuhlnir was already finished and standing outside, waiting for me.

He stopped and shook his head. "I'm not happy about the sea dragons."

"Neither am I, but we survived."

"That's not what I meant." Meuhlnir gestured with his chin, and I turned to look at the mouth of the harbor. A stone breakwater bordered the harbor, and in its opening to the sea, the water moiled, stirred by the cavorting of sea dragons. Geysers of water splashed the rocks on either side, and beyond the disturbance, large wakes creased the water. I whistled.

"Indeed," he said. "But the dragon's pod heard its call."

"Do they normally act this way?"

"You mean, 'do they pursue a ship for leagues and then guard the mouth of the harbor the ship took shelter in?'"

"Yeah, that."

"I'm not an expert on sea dragons, but I rather doubt it."

I nodded my agreement. "Should we do something about this? The port can't function with these monsters swimming around."

Meuhlnir rocked his head from side to side. "The real question is: *Can* we do something about this? I don't know the answer to that question."

"What will happen if we leave without clearing the danger away from the port?"

"I would assume that, *if* the Black Bitch sent these creatures, when we leave town, they will lose interest, or maybe even follow us up the coast if we travel close enough to the water."

"And if they weren't sent by her?"

"They will forget why they are there in a short time and swim away."

I scratched my chin, looking at the waves made by the pod of water dragons. "Are they... I might have misunderstood, but Friner was...well, *smart*."

Meuhlnir arched his eyebrows.

"Are these sea dragons smart? Can they reason?"

"I'm not sure anyone knows how smart they are. To my knowledge, no sea dragon has ever been bound—despite what the Tverkr said. And yet the one your wife killed acted like it understood our intentions whether it understood the language or not."

A stable boy came over and tugged on Meuhlnir's sleeve. "All done," he said. Meuhlnir ruffled the boy's hair and slipped him a piece of silver.

"Come on, *Tyeldnir*, our work here is done."

"Oh, no, not another one."

"Oh, yes," said Meuhlnir. "I heard the stable boys refer to you thus."

"And it means what? Loud person? Noisemaker?"

"No," he said between guffaws. "It means 'wand bearer.'" He pointed to Kunknir and Krati in turn.

"They're not wands." Even to myself, I sounded silly.

"No, they are not. But to these boys, they are."

"Why do I get the feeling that by nightfall everyone will be calling me Tyeldnir?"

Meuhlnir affected innocence. "Why, I have no idea, *Yarl Aylootr*."

"Does no one ever forget anything in this place?"

Meuhlnir laughed again. "No. Haven't my wives taught you anything?"

FOUR

Being a one-eyed man, wearing a dark cloak and a floppy hat had its advantages—the inhabitants of the port town all knew who I was. The karls and thralls of the port town stayed out of my way when they could, and when they couldn't, they bent over backward to help when I asked for it.

By the time Jane came around, and Sif pronounced her fit enough to travel, a day and a half had passed, and our party was scattered to the four winds. Even with the help of two scullery maids and three boys, it took an hour and a half to get everyone rounded up and ready to travel.

None of us had seen Althyof, who had disappeared in search of "supplies," and it took forty-five minutes to find Althyof—and two of the three boys, plus myself—plus another forty-five minutes to make him sober enough to stay on a horse. I thought Meuhlnir would come out of his skin as we looked for the Tverkr. I've not heard such profanity since the last time Jane almost hit a car on I-590 back home. He hid his impatience about as well as a hyperactive four-year-old, and by the time we got Althyof straightened out, I feared for Meuhlnir's life at the hands of his wives.

We'd ridden north on the field-stone paved coastal road from the port town at a slow pace, both in deference to Jane's recovery and to Althyof's woozy head. After a few hours, Sif had insisted we stop for the day and allow Jane to rest. The sea dragons followed us along the coast, cavorting in the waves, and hissing at us every now and again.

"Guess that answers that question," grumbled Meuhlnir.

"My question is this…"

"Yes…Tyeldnir?"

"Funny," I said. "If sea dragons have never been bound, how does the Dark Queen control them?"

Althyof grunted. "*Control* them? She doesn't control them. She *points* them in a direction and tells them to go have fun."

"But—"

"She gives them a target and, afterward, lets them do what they want. It's much *simpler* than what I do. She doesn't bind their wills at all; she gives them suggestions that are almost what they wanted to do in the first place. It's a subtle change, like telling a child that they want to eat cake instead of pie."

"Or cake and pie, instead of cake alone," said Sig.

"Shaddap, you," I growled at him, and he smiled.

"But, didn't they have to travel to us? Didn't they give up on hunting things they could eat to chase us down the coast this afternoon?"

"Of course, they did."

"So…"

"Think it through. She convinced *one* sea dragon, and probably one that was already in the area, to attack the ship. We did battle; it sent out a call to its pod for help. It said, in effect, these people are hurting me, come avenge me. The pod came, and the Dark Queen only had to convince them to stick around until we left and shadow us up the coast."

"And this is their pie? Following us all day when they know they can't get to us?"

"Revenge is their pie. She tells them that if they follow us, eventually there will be an opportunity to take vengeance."

"And they are dumb enough to believe that they will sprout legs if they swim far enough north?" asked Jane in a groggy voice.

"They aren't dumb at all," said Althyof. "They—"

"They *are* dumb," insisted Jane. She shuffled out of camp.

"But she doesn't understand—"

"Later," I said and followed Jane into the darkness. She heard me coming and stopped so I could catch up without killing myself in the underbrush.

"You don't have to follow me. To…to coddle me!" she hissed when I was close enough.

"I'm not coddling you, Jane. I know what it's like—"

"You know what it's like to be shot at *by your husband*?" she snapped.

"Did I… Did I hit you? When I was shooting at the dragon?"

"Well, I hope you weren't shooting at me. Not *that* time, at least. And no, you didn't hit me, but I *felt* the bullet go past my side. Do you know what that feels like, Hank?"

"You know I do, Jane. And you know I didn't shoot *at* you. I shot *in front* of you because I couldn't get your attention any other way, and Sig was behind you. Yowtgayrr already had him—"

"Don't you think I know that?"

"I'm only saying I didn't mean to hit you, *ever*, but I had to distract that damn sea snake, or it would have gotten you or Sig, and ring or no ring, I don't think you would survive a dragon's bite."

She stood there, fuming but not talking, close to tears. It wasn't about the shooting. She knew how proficient I was with my pistols, and that Kunknir had been enchanted for accuracy. It was about killing the dragon—about *Jane* killing the dragon.

"Hon, I know you didn't want to kill it. You never wanted to kill anything, but the choice was—"

"Between Sig and the stupid sea dragon," she said with tears in her voice.

"Yes," I said and waited.

"Oh, Hank, I don't want to kill things with…by… I didn't even think about it! But I did it…I just did it! I…I…I—"

"Had to, to save the life of your son. Jane, you had no choice, and it would be no different if a man attacked Sig, and you had a pistol. You'd have shot him—*protected* Siggy—only to feel bad about it like you are now." She took a step closer and burst into tears, so I held her while she cried.

"I don't like it," she said after a while.

"Don't like what, Jane?"

"I don't like being…"

"An action hero? Too late, Supergirl." That earned a chuckle. "You know I love you, no matter what you do."

"Even if I make you eat burnt kale?"

"Well, let's not get all crazy here. I mean, *burnt kale*?"

"You'll eat it and like it, Mister!" She was still crying a little, but she chuckled deep in her throat.

"Better now?" I whispered.

"Not better but *getting* better."

"Good, because all this coddling you was starting to cramp my style."

"If you weren't already broken, I'd hit you right now."

"Why do you think I'd risk talking to you like that? You know if you punch me you'll have to take care of me all the more."

"Who says I'm taking care of you now? I only need you healthy until we get back home, and *then*

I'll collect the life insurance and move to Tahiti." She stepped back, wiping her eyes.

"Toledo, maybe."

"Toledo, Spain."

"They wouldn't take you. Your accent is horrible."

"If you have finished making a fool out of yourself, Hank, let's go back and see what's in the cook pot. Besides, my legs are shaking, and my head feels like Althyof's face looks."

I draped my arm over her shoulder, and she snuggled against me. "What do you suppose the miraculous Yowrnsaxa has in store for us tonight?"

"It doesn't smell anything like kale."

"Thank God!"

We walked back into camp, and the Isir all did their thing of pretending nothing had happened. A moment later, Yowtgayrr and Skowvithr also came into camp, one on each side of us. Jane glanced up at me, and a blush crept up her neck. I gave her a squeeze and mouthed the word "Elves", and she grinned. Of Althyof, there was no sign.

We sat on the logs Mothi had dragged close to the fire. He and Sig were locked in a conversation that involved a lot of hand gestures and funny faces. "He's a big kid," whispered Jane.

"Not around Svartalfar," I said, remembering the damage he'd done to his own hands while shoving them down the throat of a Svartalf that had attacked Veethar's compound.

"What?"

"Never mind," I said. "Mothi likes Sig, and will entertain him, but when push comes to shove, he's no child."

"Are you hungry, Jane?" asked Yowrnsaxa from across the fire. The Isir woman was bent over the pot, inhaling the scent, and stirring its contents with a long-handled wooden spoon. She peeked at Jane, and her eyes darted away again.

"Starved, and whatever is in that pot smells like heaven."

Veethar grunted his agreement.

"Eat double tonight, dear," said Sif without looking at her. "I will be watching."

Frikka came and sat on the other side of Jane. She didn't look at her, but she took Jane's hand and gave it a squeeze. "You know of the troubles the Black Queen has caused here."

"Yes," murmured Jane.

"Did you know we fought a war to get free of her?"

Jane nodded. Around the campfire, silence descended as everyone turned to listen, even Mothi and Sig.

"During that war, we fought our friends, our families," said Frikka in a quiet, restrained voice. "We did...many things."

"Frikka, it's okay. I'm—"

"She caused so much pain—even in the getting rid of her. I made my first kill in that war, but I should have killed sooner than I did."

Yowrnsaxa passed out bowls of steaming roasted vegetables in a thick beef broth. She paused next to

Frikka and put a hand on her shoulder, squeezed, and then turned back to her task.

"Before the war, we all thought we were hardened *skyuldur vidnukonur*—shield maidens. The men believed their duties as *vuthuhr trohtninkar*—the Queen's Guard—prepared them, but, nothing can prepare one for war…"

FIVE

Nothing can prepare one for war, thought Frikka as she surveyed the bloodied and mutilated bodies lying on the muddy, bloody ground of the courtyard, moaning in pain or unconscious. Some bore terrific bite wounds, and some had gaping, parallel wounds made by the claws of a beast of prey—one of the *oolfa*, the elite shape-changing warriors that now fought with the Dark Queen.

The thought of the tall, lanky bestial forms their enemies took during battle made Frikka's stomach churn. There was only one way an Isir could harness such power—breaking the *Ayn Loug*—the ancient law of the Isir against consuming human flesh to increase one's power.

She was sick of the war. Sick of seeing her people hurt at the hands of former friends who seemed to revel in the pain they wrought. Suel had become so...*bloodthirsty* since that day in Muspetlshaymr.

What was worse, neither set of leaders seemed interested in bringing the fighting to an end. Meuhlnir wouldn't consider any plan that led to the deaths of Suel, Luka, or Vowli, no matter how evil their deeds. For her own part, Suel always pulled out her troops when they would overrun the rebels. It was as if the war were a mere lark for the queen, and she wished to sustain the fighting for as long as possible.

How far she's fallen. Frikka shook her head. Her auguries hadn't shown her an end to this miserable war—only more strife, more death, more pain. Endless insanity.

"Frikka!" shouted Veethar from the other side of the square of carnage. "Are you hurt?"

She shook her head, unable to muster a smile for her lover. "No, Veethar. I'm fine." She turned her gaze back to the bodies of the thralls, karls, and lesser yarls that lay helter-skelter around the hall, bleeding, crying, dying. "This is…"

"Senseless," said Veethar, striding over to stand next to her. "But, do not despair, my beauty. It is about to end."

She flashed a quick smile his way. "You're sweet, Veethar."

"No, I mean it. Suel wants a palaver."

Frikka raised her hands at the throng of casualties surrounding them, and let her hands fall. It seemed easier than speaking, easier than raising an argument—as if arguing with Veethar was a worthwhile pursuit to begin with, he only grunted and looked away if she disagreed with him. *God of Silence, indeed.*

"She's tired."

Frikka nodded. Her auguries had shown nothing of the sort, but again, Veethar wasn't the one she had to convince. She turned on her heel, and, grabbing Veethar's arm and pulling him along, went to find Meuhlnir.

As usual, he lounged in the great hall, sitting at the head table as if surrounded by feasting men and women. It irritated her, but she couldn't say why. "Here you sit," she said by way of a greeting. "Do you ever leave this hall?"

Meuhlnir inclined his head and stroked his beard, tearing his eyes away from the fire long enough to glance at her and nod to Veethar. "Might as well ask if Nithukkr leaves his mountain of stone."

Frikka scoffed and shook her head. "Our men...all of us...we need a *leader*, Meuhlnir. We need a general who stands—"

Meuhlnir held up his hand. "Please, Frikka, no more of this."

"But, Meuhlnir, don't you see—"

Veethar put his hand on her arm and when she glanced at him, shook his head once. She fought to suppress a sigh and lost.

"I know what you will say, Frikka. You've said it all before, and, for what it's worth, you are right. I *should* be out there…" He waved his hand at the door behind her. "I should be walking amongst the wounded, or helping Sif organize our forces. There are many things I *should* be doing, but since…ever since the day that…" His voice wound down like a wind-up toy at the end of its spring. He shook his head, eyes drifting to the fire once more.

He didn't need to say more, she understood. She nodded in sympathy.

"There's news," said Veethar.

Meuhlnir's gaze crawled away from the fire, across the floor, onto Veethar's boot, and up the side of his body, lingering near his face, but not quite reaching it. "News? Another battle?"

Veethar nudged Frikka.

"He said Suel wants a palaver."

Meuhlnir's gaze snapped to her own. "Palaver?"

"It's what he said." She hooked her thumb at Veethar, and Meuhlnir's gaze swam toward Veethar again.

"Details?" he asked.

Veethar shrugged. "The messenger came…a thrall on a beautiful horse…said Suel is tired of the war…wanted to know where we could meet, face-to-face."

Meuhlnir swept to his feet, melancholy gone like mist on a bright morning. "Where is this thrall?"

Without a word, Veethar turned and strode out the door. Frikka shook her head and followed him, leaving Meuhlnir to follow or not.

The messenger's youth shocked her. He was nothing but a boy atop a magnificent roan. His eyes darted everywhere, trying to see everything at once. His fear was palpable, and as she and Meuhlnir stepped out into the sun, the color ran from his face as if someone had unplugged a drain. Frikka smiled at him.

"Boy!" snapped Meuhlnir. "Give me your message."

The boy's gaze slithered to Veethar's face, to Frikka, and back to Meuhlnir. "Yes, lord," he said. "The Queen Suel summons you to a palaver, to discuss the end of this war. She commands you to name the place and time, and she will consider your request."

Behind her, Meuhlnir tensed, and the air seemed to crackle with tension—or maybe it was static electricity. Frikka shook her head and stepped forward.

"Boy," she said, almost a whisper.

The boy's gaze snapped to her own.

"Tell Her Majesty the Queen that we will make ourselves available to her at her pleasure. Our only request is that we meet outside Suelhaym, for obvious reasons."

The boy nodded once, swallowing hard. His hand holding the reins twitched, almost as if to question whether he could leave.

"Fair enough, Meuhlnir?" she asked, not taking her eyes off the boy.

As if it were an answer, Meuhlnir grunted and turned back into the building.

Frikka smiled up at the thrall. "Go on, boy. Back to the queen."

The boy nodded once and swept the magnificent horse in a half-circle before giving him the spurs. The horse raced through the gates, leaving a swirl of dust in his wake.

"Could be a relative of yours, Veethar," she said, hiding a grin.

Veethar grunted and put his hand on her shoulder.

The queen's response came in less than an hour. She'd chosen a traveler's inn, near to, but outside, the city of Suelhaym.

Meuhlnir gathered the yarls in the great hall for a Thing—a democratic convocation—to decide what to do. He stood in silence while they gathered, and when the last woman arrived, he cleared his throat and stepped up on a stool. "I will go to the palaver alone," he announced.

"No, you won't!" snapped Yowrnsaxa.

"I lead this rebellion, and I—"

"Oh, you lead us, do you?" asked Sif. She stood shoulder to shoulder with Yowrnsaxa, her face as fierce as her friend's.

"It makes sense not to risk—"

"No," said Veethar, a note of finality in his voice.

Meuhlnir turned to him. "Come now, Veethar. You know as well as I that—"

"How many fighting pairs should we take?" asked Yowrnsaxa, turning to the assembly.

"A *trachkar's* worth?"

"Now, wait just a moment," said Meuhlnir, but no one paid him any mind.

"50?" asked Sif. "Suel will bring more. Maybe some of those beasts, too."

"Why not take her at her word?" The question came from the back of the room, and Frikka couldn't pick out the speaker. That the rebellion contained spies was a given, but she'd never considered there might be a traitor among the yarls. The room was silent for a moment.

"Who spoke?" asked Meuhlnir.

No one answered, but the room erupted with the rustling of armor as men and women craned their necks to see.

"I'd say we need at least a hundred yarls—and make most of them *vefari*. Also, at least two hundred karls, and a full contingent of thrall support troops," said Frikka into the silence.

"Six hundred? To a palaver?" asked Meuhlnir. "That seems—"

"Justified," finished Yowrnsaxa. "We'll keep them back. They will reveal themselves only in the event of trouble. Now, get off that stool and come stand with me."

Meuhlnir glanced around the room, a long-suffering expression on his face, and the room erupted into laughter, the suspicions of the previous moment forgotten—or at least ignored.

With the familiar smile he'd worn almost constantly in better times, Meuhlnir shrugged and stepped off the stool. He walked over to Yowrnsaxa and kissed her cheek.

"You're not as stupid as you look," said Sif with a wide grin.

"Keep sweet talking me, and I'll marry you, too," said Meuhlnir.

Veethar laughed. It was a loud, braying laugh he reserved for those he knew best. Sif looked at him and winked.

"Those two would be the death of you," Veethar choked out between guffaws. "You could never keep up."

"When you are always out front, you never need to 'keep up,'" said Meuhlnir, and the room erupted in laughter again. "What?" he asked. "What?"

Sif patted his arm and turned to the Thing. "Six hundred. Anyone object?" Meuhlnir opened his mouth. "Good! Let's get going." Sif swept out of the room, a small smile on her face.

The troop readied gear and mounted horses, standing in the field outside the fortress gates. Meuhlnir, Sif, and Yowrnsaxa were the last to arrive, and when they did, Sif rode to the front of the assembled troops. "*Klyowthstirkidn*," she said, and when she spoke next, her voice carried to all those assembled, though she didn't raise her voice to shout. "We go to speak with the queen. Hopefully, all is as it appears, but it may not be. This may be a trap, and there is no way to know, except to go."

Voices rustled in the ranks of thralls standing in the back.

"Now, there is no cause to fear. We are taking a large number of fighters. You are the stick we carry in our hands as a warning, like a man carrying valuables through the dark night might carry a club to warn away harriers. You will stay back until we call for you—until we need you."

Sif turned her horse and walked him to the road. "Be aware," she called over her shoulder. "Be vigilant." She spurred her horse into a gallop, and the troop followed, Meuhlnir with a bemused expression on his face.

They rode for half a day and reached the valley that held the inn by midafternoon and sat on a bluff looking down at the inn. It was nice enough, as inns went, and the valley gave every appearance of normality. Sif turned to Frikka, and said, "Well, what do you think?"

"What do I *think*?"

Sif frowned and pinched the bridge of her nose. "You know what I mean."

Frikka smiled, but she didn't feel like smiling. She felt as she always felt when someone pressed her for an augury—uncomfortable and a little sick to her stomach. "I haven't seen this," she muttered.

"Well, then, we are on our own," said Sif. "Who goes?"

Meuhlnir looked at Veethar, Frikka, Yowrnsaxa, and turned his gaze back to Sif. "I've already said I prefer to go alone, but—" He held up a hand to forestall Yowrnsaxa's objections. "But, I bow to my wife's wishes. I say we five go."

Sif nodded. "How do we call the troop if we need them?"

Meuhlnir grinned, but his expression was cold, hard. "If they see lightning, they should come on the run."

Sif conveyed orders to the leaders of the reserve forces and led the party of five down into the valley. What had looked like normalcy from the bluff, now looked like an utter lack of life—no one worked the fields, no travelers walked the roads, nothing. They approached the inn with only the sound of their footsteps breaking the silence. Sif pulled up in front of the inn, eyeing it with suspicion. "Where is everyone?" she hissed.

The door banged open, and thralls dressed for war poured out of the inn.

"It's a trap," snapped Sif. "Run!"

They wheeled their horses, but *oolfa* stood behind them, drooling bloody pus, fur bristling. Thralls kept pouring from the inn, surrounding the party.

"Finally," said Suel in silky tones. "What's that adage? Cut the head off the snake?" An *oolfur* growled and snapped its teeth, eyes blazing at Meuhlnir. "I know, dear one," Suel said. "You can have him as soon as I'm done."

Suel spoke from hiding, but Frikka closed her eyes and *saw* where she stood. *Cut the head off the snake?* She could end it; she could end the terror, the misery, *the war*. All she had to do was say one word in the *Gamla Toonkumowl*. Just one small word.

Frikka stared at the spot in the woods where Queen Suel hid. *Say it! Say* "tayia!" she raged at herself. She wanted to say it, she wanted the queen dead, and that one word, that one command in the *Gamla Toonkumowl* would end the queen's life as surely as a dagger between the ribs. She opened her dry mouth, and drew breath, focusing her mind on Suel, on her essence.

"Yes," hissed Meuhlnir. "Come, *my brother*, we have much to...*talk* about." The *oolfur* snarled and took a step.

"No!" said Suel. "Not yet."

Say it! Frikka screamed in her mind. *Do it! She deserves no quarter, no mercy!* Her lungs were full, the word was on her tongue, ready for breath to give it life, and still, she hesitated.

"I wanted to thank you," said Suel. "To thank you for coming, for giving yourselves to me. Did you think I would entertain a palaver with a bunch of traitorous fools?"

Why can't you say it? This wasn't Suel—not the Suel she'd grown up with, not the pleasant, fair-minded queen she'd respected. This woman was an abomination, a mistake. *She deserves nothing but death for what she's done*! Still, the breath remained trapped in her lungs.

"Sif, my childhood playmate, my *friend*!" Suel spat the words into the air as though they were venom aimed at Sif's eyes. "I never expected you would betray me."

"*You* betrayed *me*, Suel, along with the memory of your father."

"Ha! Another fool. Your barbs have no point, *Trohtninkar Tama*." Suel stomped her foot. "Even the sound of your former title makes me angry."

End this! End it now! Frikka closed her eyes, blotting out the scene, the war, the queen. One word. One little word.

"Enough of this! *Ehlteenk*!" screamed Meuhlnir and lightning arced from the sky to the sound of crashing thunder.

Even through her closed eyelids, Frikka saw the brilliant blue bolt descend into the knot of thralls surrounding them. An *oolfur* snarled, another howled. Horses whinnied and jostled around her. Weapons rang as they were unsheathed. *DO IT!* she screamed in her mind.

"Kill them all!" snarled Suel.

Do it now! Say the word! Say it! But she couldn't bring herself to utter the word that would drain the life from her one-time friend and queen. She couldn't kill in cold blood.

"Frikka!" shouted Veethar.

Her eyes snapped open and pandemonium erupted around her. Thralls pressed forward with spears and shields, and the *oolfa* snarled and snapped behind them, working themselves up to charge. Meuhlnir stood in his stirrups, pointing his hammer at one of the *oolfur*—his brother, Luka, no doubt. Sif and Yowrnsaxa had their shields on their arms already, and their weapons in their other hands. Veethar sat on his horse at her side, his expression serene, but his eyes contained a little wildness, a little fear, a little excitement. As she watched, his lips moved, but whatever he said was too low for her to hear. His eyes changed from pale blue to blazing yellow, and he pointed at the forest.

Green growth exploded through the underbrush, trees sprouting and shooting skyward. The underbrush thickened, vines reaching and grasping at the queen's forces hiding in the woods. Shrieks came from the deep woods, and Veethar's face wrinkled in an ugly smile.

Frikka looked for Suel, but she was no longer hiding in the bushes—she'd stepped out into plain view. *If Veethar can do his part...* She raised her hand and pointed at Suel. She opened her mouth to speak the word, to kill her friend.

Suel's eyes snapped to hers and blazed like twin suns. "No!" shouted Suel. "*Thun!*"

Frikka let the word loose, breathing life to it, caressing it with her tongue, a silly half-grin on her face. Nothing happened. No sound issued from her throat, no word of power fell from her tongue. *Thun...silence.*

She stared at Suel, fury burning in her heart, while lightning bolts danced around her. Horses screamed and lashed out with metal-clad hooves. Beside her, Veethar whispered to himself, pointing here and there, smiling as nature took vengeance on their attackers.

Suel still stared at Frikka, anger and hatred burning in her eyes. She lifted her hand and pointed at Frikka. "*Kvul!*"

Frikka's nervous system lit up like she'd touched the sun. Agony ripped through her body in wave after wave of burning, tearing, breaking, smashing agony. She screamed, and her muscles convulsed all at once, throwing her to the ground at the horses' feet.

"No!" shouted Veethar. He leapt from his horse, drawing his sword and standing over her as she writhed in the dirt.

A sound like the pounding surf rang in her ears, and she thought it was her own pulse. She tried to open her eyes, to see what was happening around her, to avoid being trampled by the horses at least, but the effort was too much amidst all the misery that had become her entire existence.

"Sif!" shouted Veethar.

"Frikka! Yowrnsaxa, get these horses away!" yelled Sif.

Frikka wanted to tell Sif to focus on the battle, to stop worrying about her, but then another billow of torment crashed over her, and the world outside her misery disappeared.

SIX

"**I** didn't want her to worry about me. I wanted her to focus on the battle. I tried to tell her that, but another flood of anguish overcame me, and everything went black for a while."

"But what she didn't know, couldn't know, was that the Dark Queen's forces were already in flight. Between Meuhlnir's wanton use of lightning, and Veethar's nature-magic, the enemy turned and ran," said Sif.

"Not to mention the six hundred fighters pounding down from the hills," said Meuhlnir.

"Yes, there was that, too."

"The battle?" I asked.

Meuhlnir shrugged, pursing his lips. "Not much of a battle, to be honest. The *oolfa* took one look at the forest going crazy at their backs and ran for it. The Black Queen was never a stupid woman, and she had a gift for sensing the tide of battle turning. I didn't see how she got away."

"She took the form of a bear and charged down the road, maiming her own troops if they got in her way," said Yowrnsaxa in a bland tone.

I glanced at Jane, who was staring at the flames licking the cook pot. Her lips pursed and relaxed, pursed and relaxed, but the rest of her face bore no expression. "Penny, Supergirl," I whispered.

She started, then flashed a quick smile at me. "That was quite a story, Frikka. Thanks for telling me."

Frikka stared into the fire. "Who knows? Maybe I could not have killed her had I tried." Frikka glanced at Jane and patted her hand. "I should have killed her when I first saw her. Her forces would have fallen apart as each ambitious leader claimed the throne. You see?"

"Yes," said Jane.

"I might have saved so many lives. I could have saved *your family* from this ordeal."

"Yes," said Jane. "Though as hard as it was in the beginning, things…"

Frikka chuckled. "Not everything has been bad? You say this even *after* meeting Meuhlnir?"

"I heard that," said the lightning god.

"I intended you to."

Jane smiled. "Yes, good things have come out of our ordeal," she said, looking at Mothi and Sig joking and play-fighting at the edge of the fire's light. She took my hand and squeezed. "And this idiot here finally has a doctor who seems to know what she's doing."

Sif smiled and bowed her head once.

"But even so," said Frikka.

"Yes," said Jane for the third time. She looked at Frikka, and something seemed to pass between them. "There's no point feeling guilty, is there?"

"None," said Frikka. "The Sisters wove your fate eons ago. You can only do your best."

Jane smiled and squeezed my hand. "I tell this lunkhead that all the time, but he's got this thing about making everything perfect."

Frikka glanced at me. "Men," she said with a smile, and the other women repeated the word in the same tone.

Meuhlnir glanced at me across the fire and shook his head. "There will be no living with them, you know. *You* kill the next dragon, please."

I laughed and shook my head. "Let's avoid the next dragon and call it a win."

"Hmmm," said Sif. "You see, dear? Not all men are idiots."

"Who knew?" asked Frikka, her eyes on Veethar's pale blue ones across the fire.

"I did," said Jane. She punched me in the arm. "Because my friend married one of the non-idiots. I bet *he* never shot at *her*!"

"A guy makes one mistake…" I said, doing my best mournful voice.

"Exactly!" said Meuhlnir. "One mistake, and—"

"Shut it," said Sif without looking at him. She tried not to, but she couldn't help smiling.

"Might as well ask sand to turn back into rock, as ask a woman to let things lie," Meuhlnir muttered.

"Heard that," said Yowrnsaxa. "What are you eating for dinner, dear?"

Meuhlnir shook his head. "I should know better than to say anything."

"You really should, by this point," said Veethar. "Everyone knows this."

"Knows what?" said Althyof, walking back into the camp.

"It's nothing," said Meuhlnir.

"Tverkar jokes? Again?"

Meuhlnir held up his hands, palms out.

Althyof glared at everyone sitting around the fire. "I hope no one laughed…"

"Really, Althyof, there were no—" Jane began.

"Got you," he said and roared laughter at the night sky. When he'd laughed himself out, Althyof slumped onto one of the logs circling the fire. "Okay, so guess what I just did."

"Um, I think you tried to pull a joke, but I'm not entirely sure," said Meuhlnir in a droll tone.

"Not that," said Althyof, with a wave. "While I was away."

"We don't discuss such things in mixed company," said Veethar, his face grim.

"What? No, I…that is, I—"

"Got you," said Veethar, and, this time, everyone laughed.

Yowrnsaxa doled out portions of another delicious, if improbable, trail stew, which was better than the fare I'd eaten in many fancy restaurants back in Mithgarthr.

"There's something I don't understand," I said, looking at Althyof.

"Yes?"

"Why did Jane pass out? The ring—"

"Ah, that. The ring allows her certain abilities, but at a price, as with anything."

"A price?" I asked, my voice grave.

"Oh, nothing to be concerned about. For the enchantment to work as it does, it needed to be bound to something. Given the nature of the work, I bound the power of the enchantment to her will—to her spirit, or whatever you Isir call it."

"Fettle," said Sif.

"Wait a minute—"

"No, hold on," Althyof said, pointing at me with his spoon. "There is no permanent damage done. Her spirit will replenish itself over time, as anyone's does. There is no danger."

"Well, she passed out and almost drowned," muttered Yowtgayrr.

"Well, yes, but—"

"So, there are limits to what she can do. If killing something will knock her out for a day and a half, what about—"

"The time, the *impact* of the deed depends on the power of the creature. How much of its own will it raises in its own defense."

Jane nodded. "The more powerful the...will, the more it takes out of me."

"Yes," said the Tverkr around a mouthful of stew. "Meuhlnir, here, you—"

"No. No jokes," said Jane.

Althyof bowed his head. "Ah, yes. No jokes," he said.

"What about the confusion? The healing? The wings?"

He waved his spoon. "No, only the offensive abilities. Well, yes to the confusion. It will drain you, but not to the extent of killing your opponent."

"And does the cost scale?" Jane demanded.

"I don't follow."

"If killing one sea dragon knocked me out for a day and a half, would killing ten million ants do the same?"

"I'm not sure that's a good—"

"*Fine.* If I confuse one man and it takes one unit of energy from my...from my spirit, would confusing ten men take ten units?"

Althyof nodded. "I would think so, yes, but it's complicated by the fact that not all men are equal. Some are weak, some strong." He shrugged. "You will feel the drain. With the dragon, it was—"

"Too quick," she said.

"Yes. Too quick. In the future, you will have to assess the creature you wish to kill, to judge the impact to your will."

Jane nodded and looked out into the darkness surrounding the camp. We went on eating, talking about lighter things, and after everyone finished stuffing themselves, between the full bellies and the roaring fire, eyelids drooped, and conversations petered out. While Jane helped Yowrnsaxa clean up, I rolled into the large bedroll Jane and I shared, groaning under my breath as my creaky joints settled on the hard ground. I had meant to wait for Jane, to warm her side of the bedroll, and to hold her until she fell asleep, but the events of the day snuck up on me, and I slept.

When I woke, the fire had burned down to coals, and it was still dark—still the middle of the night dark. My knees, ankles, and feet burned with a persistent, low-level pain. Jane lay beside me, her breathing deep and relaxed. I lay there, trying to escape the pain by sinking into the warm embrace of sleep, but deep down, I knew it was a lost battle. Once the pain reached the level where it could wake me, it would keep me awake for as long as it wanted, and there was not much I could do about that. I could take a pain med, but since I was one of the lucky few for whom narcotic pain meds prevented sleep and made me groggy at the same time, that would only guarantee I wouldn't sleep for the rest of the night. It was a win-win for my Personal Monster™. It made no sense, but then again, where was it written that things must make sense?

There was a part of me that had grown to hate night. I kept it from Jane—she had enough to worry about—but the act of getting ready for bed, the settling into bed, the silence, the darkness, all of it contributed to my insomnia. There's an unfortunate side effect of chronic pain—in the absence of other sensory input, pain gets louder—more intense—and much harder to ignore.

I thought about taking a pain med anyway…maybe I'd fall asleep before the damn thing set my brain to "wake." There was a part of me that recognized the fallacy inherent in that thought, but another part of me didn't care. It's not like I'd fall asleep if I *didn't* take the pill. The pain would be there, waving its arms and shouting for the rest of the night. The only hope was a distraction that wouldn't, in and of itself, keep me awake, but had enough *oomph* to lower the volume of the pain.

Yeah, right.

I rolled up on my side, facing Jane. At times like this, I missed being back home, where books were as close as my phone, and I'd be able to read away the hours until dawn. I had my phone, of course, I'd buried it away in my pack, but with no way to recharge the thing, the battery had gone flat.

Hell, if we were back home, I could get up and go search for the end of the Internet. Or maybe watch YouTube videos of idiots doing stupid, yet interesting things. Or I could play a game—my hands felt fine for a change. I flipped to my other side and stared into the darkness while my legs sang their litany of pain and discomfort in my ear.

Reciting the things I couldn't do wasn't helping anything. Why did my mind run to things that amped up my stress instead of repressing it? It never failed—when I felt my worst, I worried about all the things I was missing out on, all the things I could no longer do. It was stupid, but I seemed powerless in the face of that brand of self-torture.

I wondered what Luka was doing at that moment. He'd taken damage in our fight in Piltsfetl, not only from my pistols but from Urlikr's swords. Even Jane had gotten in a few licks. I didn't imagine any of the wounds still existed or had even slowed him down that much, but still…

And the Dark Queen…Elizabeth Tutor on our *klith*…Hel on Osgarthr…She-who-waits…the Black Bitch…Queen Suel of Suelhaym… She had a new kingdom in Fankelsi—the land Meuhlnir had exiled her to at the end of their war—didn't she have to *run things* there? Or did Vowli act as her regent? How come she had so much time to make our lives miserable? And why did she care? Because she hadn't liked my attitude when Jax and I interviewed her back home? It's not as if *she* had been pleasant. The whole interview would have gone another way without *her* attitude. But hell, as long as I was wishing wishes, if she and Luka hadn't come to my turf and started eating people, I'd still be back home, living the life I loved. I'd still be healthy.

I flopped onto my back and sighed.

"What's the matter? Can I get you a pill?" asked Jane in a sleep-blurred voice.

"Sorry I woke you," I whispered.

"Want a pill? A hot-pack?"

She wasn't awake. There were no microwaves, no hot-packs on Osgarthr. "No, no. Go back to sleep, Supergirl. I'm fine."

"Sure, sure. Nothing wrong with you."

I smiled in the darkness—even half-asleep she still had the ability to bust me for being a "big, dumb Norwegian." It was one of her gifts, I suppose. Her breathing deepened and evened out. I held still long enough to be sure she was asleep before lifting the edge of the blankets and rolling out from under them.

The air was frigid, shocking as I shuffled over to the glowing coals of last night's fire. I stirred them with a stick and fed them fresh kindling. In a few moments, I had a small fire going again, and I huddled in its warm glow. The eastern horizon was still dark, not even a hint of color. Salt and sea came to me on the breeze, and the scents seemed pure, clean. Sea air back home had much the same effect on me, but here, where the seas *were* clean and fresh, the effect was stronger. Waves pounded on the thin shingle of beach across the road from the campsite.

As I watched the dark, misty shoreline, my eye caught on a stygian patch of shadow. *Is my mind playing tricks or did that black hunk of night move?* I wondered. I stared at the black patch and waited. As a cop back in New York, I'd learned that my eyes were sometimes smarter than my brain—at least my conscious brain. Maybe it was some lizard part of me, buried deep, that was still worried about the tiger in the night, or the part of my mind that wasn't distracted by actual thought, but when my eye snagged something in the night, there was usually something to it.

Of course, I pretended *not* to watch, looking off to the side, watching from the corner of my eye. Years of being a cop had also taught me that when people are up to no good and know you are watching, they have the patience of the saints.

I pretended to be interested in the fire, in the night sky, in the sole of my boot, and through it all, the patch of blackness remained still. I half-believed my lizard brain had made a mistake this time and had almost stopped paying attention when it finally moved again.

Whatever it was, it moved without making a sound—no chink of armor, no rustling of cloth or leather. Its steps made no sound either, as it backed away, moving south from the camp along the dark swath of beach.

I stood and stretched, still not looking at the thing. As I let my hands fall to my sides, I realized my pistols and gun belt were over near the bedroll, in a heap under a cloth. Three steps brought me to them, and I grabbed the belt without pausing, moving into the darkness on the other side of the fire with as much stealth as a big, dumb, disabled Norwegian can.

"Do you need a pill?" I heard Jane ask in a bleary voice.

"Go back to sleep," I whispered.

I walked through the darkness, parallel to the road, eyes straining to adapt to the lack of light. It was still over there, still moving, still not making a sound. Whatever it was, it didn't seem to be aware that I had left the camp, let alone that I was shadowing it from across the road.

The thing stopped—all I could see of it was a patch of black darker than its surroundings—and turned as if it were looking out to sea. Shaped like a woman, or a slender man, it stood, straight-backed and stiff-legged. I crossed the road in the hunched-over trot that was the best I could do given my condition, and still, the thing didn't turn. It didn't move, as if it were a statue of onyx rather than an animate being.

My palms rested on the butts of my pistols, landing there as if by their own accord, and as I closed the distance to the thing, I slid Kunknir and Krati out of their holsters.

"You don't need your wands, Tyeldnir." The voice lacked the characteristics I associated with live people. It was without warmth, without emotion of any kind.

"I'll be the judge of that. Let me see your hands."

The shadowy figure raised its arms out to its sides, and a spooky sound escaped it. "I am no threat to you, Hank Jensen. To the contrary."

"How do you know my name? Let me guess: the Black Bitch sends her regards."

A shudder wracked the thing, seeming to send ripples through its shadow stretching across the ground. "No. I do not serve *her*. I serve…Roonateer. Or I serve myself. I serve the three Sisters, the Weavers of Fate."

"The Nornir?"

"The very ones."

I sidled around the thing, wanting to see its face, but I might as well have stayed where I was. The thing had no features, no face. It stood but seemed no more solid than the surrounding air. "Who...what are you?"

"I am of the Tisir. I am *filkya*."

"*Filkya*. I know that word. Are you telling me you are a ghost? A spirit? Entwined in my fate?"

The Tisir laughed, and it sounded more than a little like a bus grinding its gears. "I am *filkya*," it—*she*—repeated. "I am Tisir."

"Is that a name?"

Again, she laughed. "The name of my kind, yes. I am called Kuhntul. It means 'wand wielder,' the same as you, Tyeldnir."

"Don't call me that. My name is Hank."

Kuhntul cocked her head to the side but said nothing.

"Why are you here? Why do you come sneaking up on our camp in the middle of the night?"

"I am here to warn you, Hank, son of Yens."

"Warn me? About what?"

"A betrayer," Kuhntul hissed. "A traitor."

"What, in our party? I don't believe it."

"Believe what you want, my duty is dispatched in this." Kuhntul turned and drifted to the south, skimming above the sand without touching it.

"Wait just a minute," I said. "You can't say something like that and walk away into the night."

"No?" Kuhntul didn't slow, but she wasn't moving much faster than a walk.

"If you are a *filkya*—my *filkya*—fate binds you to me, right? That means—"

"I never said I was *your filkya*."

"You implied it."

"Did I?"

I didn't know why, but I had the distinct impression that Kuhntul was laughing at me. "It doesn't matter. I don't believe anyone in our party is a traitor."

"That is your business, Tyeldnir."

"Meuhlnir's family is beyond suspicion, they've proven their willingness to die for my family. Likewise, the Alfar. Veethar wouldn't betray anyone to whom he's given his word. He's not made that way."

"Is he not?"

The feeling she was laughing at me was so thick it seemed hard to breathe. "And Frikka? There's no way...she has no motive. None at all. Neither does Althyof, as much as he plays his Tverkr role, he's an honorable man."

"Is he?"

"Yes, he is," I snapped. "Then who? Jane? Even if I saw her betray me, I wouldn't believe it of her. Sig? My own son? Don't be ridiculous."

"And yet, the skein of fate says you will be betrayed by a member of your party."

I scoffed. "And this skein is never wrong?"

Kuhntul shrugged and laughed. "It is not."

"Why are you really here? Who sent you?"

"I've told you why I am here, and I came of my own accord. I have no...what did you call it...no *motive* for dishonesty."

"If you are one of the Black Queen's pets, you've motive aplenty."

"I am no creature of the Dragon of Fankelsi. I'd sooner yield my soul to the mists than serve one such as she."

I believed her—about not working for the Dark Queen, at least. Nothing she said caused any pings in my Cop-radar.

"Be on your guard, Tyeldnir. Don't be caught unaware." With that, Kuhntul dissipated like smoke on a windy day, leaving me alone on the black shingle of beach. I slipped Kunknir and Krati back into their holsters and blew out a breath. I *had* wished for something to distract me from my aching legs. As I walked back to camp, I didn't feel them at all.

SEVEN

When the sun finally broke across the eastern horizon, I'd thought myself in circles at least fifty-seven times, and still, I couldn't say if anyone in the party could be suspect—let alone *should be* one. Who could I suspect? No one, that's who.

"Morning, you idiot," said Jane.

"I love you, too."

"Did you sit up all night?"

"Not all night."

"You are a big, dumb Norwegian. Do you know that? Stubborn. Head-strong."

"Handsome. Pretty, even."

"Pfft! Why didn't you wake me? I'd have gotten you a pill, or a hot rock or something."

"The pill would've kept me awake anyway. And I can get my own pills, woman."

"Yeah, sure, as if you can be trusted with your own meds. I should pop you right in the lip."

"I'd love a kiss, thanks."

She pretended to glare at me the whole time she walked from the bedroll to where I sat and bent down and kissed me. "You will be a mess all day, Henry."

"Ew," I said. "Dragon breath."

"He's better at this than you are, husband," said Sif from the bedroll she, Meuhlnir, and Yowrnsaxa shared.

"Much," said Yowrnsaxa.

"Ha! He only has one wife, it's hardly a fair comparison."

"No, he's better," said Veethar. "Everyone sees this."

"Silent god, my ass," grumbled Meuhlnir.

"I wish all the Isir would be silent," grumbled Althyof. "How am I to get enough rest to put up with you throughout the day?"

"If only we could get enough rest to make traveling with you easier," said Meuhlnir.

Althyof stood and stretched, a small smile playing on his lips. "Sleep all you like, Isir. It's not like we need anything from *you*."

"Might as well ask if the sky needs the sun," said Meuhlnir, but I thought he was hiding a smile. "You know, I was foolish when we bargained. You should be the one paying us."

"Whatever for?" asked Althyof. "People follow me around for days, hoping to catch a touch of my magic. Hoping to learn how to be witty, to be brave."

"Hope is such a cruel mistress," said Sif, not bothering to hide a smile.

"Ah, my lady, you cut me." Althyof pretended to stagger, clutching his chest. "Remove your barb."

Sig sat up in his bedroll, rubbing his eyes. "You guys know I'm fourteen, right?"

"What of it?" asked Althyof.

"Fourteen-year-olds need to sleep in late in the mornings. It's a biological necessity."

"Speaking of biological necessities," said Althyof as he walked away from camp.

"I thought he'd never leave," said Frikka.

"I heard that!"

"As I intended!" yelled Frikka.

Mothi groaned and rolled out of his bedroll. "This inn has such thin walls. I heard everything everyone said."

Jane tweaked my ear. "Don't think I've forgotten how badly you were losing our argument."

"As if," I said, pulling her down for another kiss.

"I win sometimes," she said.

"When I let you."

"Do you see, Meuhlnir?" asked Sif. "He's better at it. It's plain to see."

Meuhlnir blew a raspberry and stood, stretching his back. "Maybe you are just better at flyting than

Jane is. You have several centuries of experience more than she does."

"So, I'm old?" asked Sif, in a light, jovial tone that made Meuhlnir turn and stare at her. "A crone? You'd prefer someone younger, perhaps?"

"No, no. Not at all. I—"

"Does he truly never learn?" asked Veethar. "I find this incredible."

We went about our morning ablutions and ate a cold breakfast. As we were packing, Sif walked over, pretending nonchalance while her critical healer's eye roamed my body, lingering on the spots that hurt me the most. I didn't know how she could do it, but it was like she could see pain. Given the *vefari* that surrounded me, maybe she *could* see my pain.

"It hurts," she said without preamble.

"I'm okay," I said. Jane grunted and shook her head.

"Okay, are you?" said Sif while arching her eyebrows.

"Yeah. It is what it is."

"And since no one gifted at healing travels with the party, I guess you'll have to suffer through stoically. Right?"

"It's the Calculus of When," said Jane. "And a big dose of Norwegian."

"Of what?" asked Skowvithr.

"His internal calculations of how bad he has to hurt before he will do something sensible, like let Sif help him." Jane straightened so she could add her disapproving glare to Sif's.

Sif looked at me, her expression hardening into a stern, forbidding frown. "You will not do this Calculus of When anymore, Hank Jensen. Not when I can help."

I kept fiddling with the straps that held my pack behind my saddle. Even Slaypnir turned his big head to look at me, and it seemed he was glaring at me, too. What could I say? They were right, and I knew it. There was no doubt, but even so, there was something in my head that made me want to conserve things that worked, to only use them when I felt "bad enough."

"I *will* have Jane hold you down, Hank," said Sif.

"And I will help," said Yowtgayrr.

"I know," I whispered, fighting emotion. "I know."

"So let her help," said Jane, exasperation at war with her empathy. She glanced at Sif. "It's the Norwegian genes that make him this way."

Sif chuckled. "It is the *Isir* genes, or maybe only the genes of Meuhlnir's family. Mothi is no better."

"Leave me out of this, Mother," called Mothi from across the camp.

Sif laid her hand on my shoulder. "Let me help, Hank."

I didn't know why I put them all through this time and time again. I had to learn the lesson—learn to take the help that was available—and, after enough time had passed, I'd have to learn the same lesson again.

"Legs," I muttered. "Knees, ankles, and feet."

Sif kicked a log near the now cold fire. "Sit."

I sat and kicked off my boots, peeled my socks, and removed my pants. Somehow, the last few months had robbed me of being ashamed to sit around outdoors in my underwear.

Sif rummaged in her bag and came out with her stinking pot of balm. She rubbed her hands together to build up some warmth and smeared great gobs of the malodorous stuff from the balls of my feet to mid-thigh. A stinging burning sensation followed her hands, and the pain began to abate.

"Is it only the balm?" I murmured.

"The balm works as I told you, overloading the pain pathways with the burning sensation."

"But…what about your other gifts?"

"As a *vefari*?"

"Yes. Are you *vefa strenki* as you apply the balm?"

"Do you think I am?" she asked, keeping her head down as if she was focused on smearing the balm across my knees.

Since I'd been tricked into traveling to the *klith* of Osgarthr, my pain had never been beyond the limits of Sif's balm. Yes, I had the cape Meuhlnir had commissioned for me that reduced the pain I felt to a certain threshold, but I learned what that threshold was when I'd lost my left eye during the battle with the demons and the white dragon. "I think you are," I said.

"Very astute of you, Hank," she said.

"What…"

"What am I doing? I *vefa strenki* to increase the effect of the balm, exciting certain parts of your body—the channels that convey sensation to your brain—and doing the opposite to others."

"Nerves."

"If you say so."

It made sense: excite the irritation pathway, suppress the pain pathway. Since the irritation pathway was starting at a higher level of excitation, the nerves fired more readily. Since the pain pathway was suppressed, it took more stimulus to fire the neurons. "Well, thanks."

Sif shrugged and looked me in the eye. "It's what I do, Hank. Try to remember it this time."

I chuckled. "Does Mothi?"

"Cousin!" he yelled from where he was wrestling one-handed with Sig, his tone one of mock exasperation.

"Might as well ask if stone remembers that the wind can cut through it, given time," said Meuhlnir.

"That was…painful," said Jane.

Meuhlnir smiled a wide, tooth-filled smile. "As was that!"

"So many puns," I said. "Too little time. Let's get a move on before I'm forced to vomit."

We mounted and walked the horses up to the stone-paved road. In the sea to the east, sea dragons cavorted, hissing and clicking at us as if inviting us to come for a swim. "How close can they come to the shore?" I asked.

"Right up on the sand," said Althyof. "But they can't stay for long, or their skin will dry out and crack."

"If I were to go to the beach, could they attack me?"

"Oh, yes," said Althyof.

"Do they see well at night?"

"Better than in the daylight." With that, the Tverkr spurred his mount and cantered to the head of our column.

I'd been on the shore hours ago, putting myself in danger without knowing it, but they hadn't attacked. *Why? The Tisir?* I walked Slaypnir over to Sinir. Meuhlnir glanced at me as we approached and raised an eyebrow.

"What is a Tisir?"

"Where did you hear that word?" he asked.

I glanced at the others. Only Yowtgayrr looked our way, the others seemed lost in thought, or involved in their own conversations, except Veethar and Skowvithr, who rode together in absolute silence. "From someone—*something*—that claimed to be one."

Meuhlnir glanced at me. "Yes?"

"Yes. Last night."

"Tell me of it." He appeared nonchalant, uncaring, but his eyes burned with intensity, and he leaned toward me in his saddle.

"I woke in the early morning and couldn't get back to sleep. I got up and built up the fire, and sat there, watching the flames. Out of the corner of my eye, I saw something shift down there on the beach. I waited, wanting to be sure I hadn't imagined it."

Yowtgayrr clucked at his horse and rode up on the other side of Meuhlnir. "Did it come into camp?"

"No. When it moved again, it took off to the south. I left camp, paralleling the road, and—"

"You should have woken me," said Yowtgayrr.

"Time for that later," murmured Meuhlnir. He twirled his fingers at me.

"I followed it from across the road, and after a little while it stopped and stood with its back toward me, gazing out to sea. I snuck up on it and confronted it."

"Describe it," said Yowtgayrr.

"She was black. Like a shade—like a shadowy demon. She said she was a Tisir, sent by the Nornir to deliver a message. She also said she was *filkya* but wouldn't name who she was bound to."

"Did it give you a name?" asked Veethar. He'd drawn up on my other side without me noticing.

"Yes. Um…Guhnter?"

"Kuhntul?

"Yeah, that's it." Veethar's eyes left mine, and I tracked his gaze to Meuhlnir. "What?"

"What was her message?" demanded Meuhlnir.

"It's nothing. Nonsense. Who is this Kuhntul?"

"Tell us what she said, Hank," said Yowtgayrr.

"Fine. She said there was a traitor in the party." As one, the Isir and Alfar turned their gazes forward, coming to rest on Althyof's back. "No," I said. "Althyof wouldn't betray us."

"The Tverkar differ from us," said Meuhlnir.

"That may be, but that Tverkr is no less honorable than any of us."

"Still, he bears watching," murmured Yowtgayrr, his hand coming to rest on the hilt of his narrow-bladed longsword.

"Look, I don't believe the message. None of us are betrayers, traitors. Not Althyof, not any of you."

"Of course not," murmured Meuhlnir, his eyes never leaving Althyof's back. "He has quite a way with dragons, though, doesn't he?"

"Tell me about Kuhntul," I said and sighed.

Meuhlnir cleared his throat. "It's Veethar's area of expertise."

I glanced to my side. Veethar's eyes were on his saddle horn. He waved his hand at Meuhlnir.

"Oh, very well," said Meuhlnir. "A Tisir is a spirit-being, something foreign to all the races known, including the demons. Their origins are unknown—none of them will speak of it. Their role in the history of Osgarthr is…complicated."

"Complicated? How?"

"They are neither good nor evil—"

"Or they are both, like all living things," interjected Yowtgayrr.

Meuhlnir nodded. "Sometimes they act as a guardian, a benevolent spirit, but other times they act as antagonists."

"And Kuhntul?" I asked. "To which group does she belong?"

Meuhlnir cleared his throat and looked at the back of Althyof's head. "We believe that when we perceive the color of their body, it's an omen of how the Tisir is disposed toward us—either toward us personally, or toward our quest."

"And black means what?"

"Seeing a black Tisir is an omen of ill-tiding," said Yowtgayrr in his quiet, understated way.

"Then she was lying?"

Meuhlnir shook his head. "That is not clear, and it's not necessarily true that Kuhntul is an enemy. In the war, she fought against the Black Bitch."

"She seemed adamant she did not serve the Dark Queen," I said.

"Whatever their intent, the Tisir serve only themselves," said Veethar.

"Well, Kuhntul claimed to be serving the Nornir in this."

Veethar shrugged.

"And she may be," said Yowtgayrr. "But only because serving the Nornir in this serves Kuhntul's own purposes."

"Then she can't be trusted, right? What she said...we should ignore it."

Meuhlnir shrugged and stroked his beard. "At our peril."

"Would a Tisir keep one of our glittery friends at bay?"

"If the sea dragon were smart," said Veethar.

"You were on the beach? Alone?" asked Skowvithr.

I hunched my shoulders. "Yeah. That's where Kuhntul was. I didn't know the sea dragons could come up there."

"And why wouldn't they?"

"Well, they are *sea* dragons, right? No legs, no wings." We rode on in silence for a while, lulled by the ring of the horses shod hooves on the stone. "What I can't figure," I said at last, "is *why* Kuhntul would come at all. Why would the Nornir care what happens to this party? To me?"

"Maybe they like you," said Meuhlnir with a shrug and a forced smile.

"Someone has to, after all," said Veethar. He spurred Ploetughoefi forward to ride next to his wife. After a while, I rode over to Jane.

"That was quite a meeting of the minds," she said.

"Yeah," I said. "How's Sig handling all this?"

"Are you kidding? He loves it." She gestured to where Sig rode Lyettfeti next to Mothi on Skaytprimir. "Just look at him eating up Mothi's attention."

Mothi waved his arms around like a madman, deep in the telling of some heroic tale, no doubt. "How lucky I've been," I murmured, recalling all the hazards, all the dangerous beings I'd encountered since coming to Osgarthr, and yet the first four beings I met were Meuhlnir, Sif, Yowrnsaxa, and Mothi.

"Yes," said Jane. "It's not so bad here."

I looked at her askance. "No?"

"No."

"You don't miss being home?"

"Well, sure I do, but there are far worse places to be trapped." Her face clouded over, and I knew she was replaying events from her captivity at the hands of Luka and Hel.

"I know it was bad, but we got you out of there."

She smiled at me and winked. "Yeah, because you needed someone to cook and clean."

"No way! I'm not so shallow as all that. Besides, Yowrnsaxa is a better cook. I needed someone for laundry."

Her lips parted, and her tongue darted out. "I'll wash your laundry, all right. And you just wait until we stop for lunch and I tell Yowrnsaxa you were mean to me."

"She likes me better," I said.

"I do not!" called Yowrnsaxa from behind us.

EIGHT

That day we rode hard, passing an inn just before noon. The inns were spaced to be an easy day's ride apart, and I thought we'd be sleeping rough again because of our late start the day before, but by some miracle, we made it to the next inn right after night fell.

I groaned as I swung my leg over Slaypnir's rump and dismounted. Slaypnir turned his head as if to ask what the big deal was, after all, I rode him, not the other way around.

As I turned, Sif caught my eye. She patted her medicine bag, and I nodded. No use arguing about that again. Not yet, anyway.

"Greetings, lords and ladies," said the rotund innkeeper. "I'm happy you've graced my humble establishment. Will you need rooms for the night or supper, perhaps?"

"Seven rooms, if you please," said Meuhlnir, jingling his pouch, which seemed never to run low of silver.

"Very well, Lord," said the innkeeper. "I'll have to put out three karls, but they can sleep in the stables. I—"

"We can't do that," I said to Meuhlnir. "They got here first."

"You disapprove?" Meuhlnir asked with a shrug. "It is the way of things. If we don't take the rooms, this fine gentleman will kick them out anyway for costing him the trade."

The innkeeper made a little half-bow at me. "Yes, Lord. Please stay, the karls will insist, even if I do not."

The rigid caste structure of Osgarthr still seemed so strange to me. That men would believe it their duty to give up their room for me was beyond the pale. I nodded, trying to conceal my discomfort.

"It's settled," said the innkeeper. He glanced down at Kunknir and Krati on my hips. "Yarl Tyeldnir," he added with another half-bow.

"How do these things get started?" I asked, glaring at Mothi.

He held up his hands in protest. "I have no idea, Aylootr."

I shook my head and sighed. "When do you serve supper?" I asked the innkeeper.

"It's being prepared as we speak," he said, but his eyes were glued to Meuhlnir's hands as the Isir shifted pieces of silver from his purse to his palm. The innkeeper snapped his fingers, and a boy about Sig's age stepped out of the small office.

"Yes, Father?" the boy asked.

"Tell the three karls they need to move to the stables."

"Yes, Father," said the boy, and he trotted up the stairs.

"In the meantime, we'll take any room that's private," said Sif, putting her hand on my shoulder.

"Yes, Lady," said the tavern master. "Take your pick of any room past the first three at the top of the stairs."

My gaze drifted to the narrow stairs, and a sigh escaped my lips.

"Do you have a room on the ground floor? Tyeldnir will only want to climb those stairs once."

"Of course. Take my office for as long as you need." He stepped to the side and swept his arm at the door behind him. "There's no bed, but…"

Sif laughed as she steered me into the little room—it wasn't much larger than a coat closet—and pushed me into the hard wooden chair next to the writing desk. She swung the door closed. "Off with your pants," she said in a brusque tone of voice. She applied her mystery balm in silence, lips pursed at the cherry-red color of my ankles and knees. "Will we need to stay over tomorrow?" she asked.

"No, I can—"

"Hank," she said, putting a finger to my lips. "Quit being a man for a moment and tell me what you will need tomorrow."

I twitched my lips. "What will serve me best is getting to that market in Suelhaym, so you can make the gunk you promised me back in town."

"Yes," she said and left the room, and when I'd corrected my state of dishabille, I followed her, in time to witness the exodus of the karls.

It surprised me that they seemed to be in high spirits, joshing Mothi (though deferentially). The playful banter stopped when they saw the pistols on my hips, and they bowed to me.

Bowed to me, for Chrissake.

I stood there trying to decide what to do in response. *Should I say something? Bow back? Tell them to stop?* In the end, I nodded at them, pretending people bowed to me all the time. Jane sniggered, and Mothi's face was cracked by a huge, toothy smile.

"Lords and ladies, your table awaits," said the innkeeper.

"These fine karls will be joining us," I said, and enjoyed the surprised yet delighted uncertainty in *their* faces.

"Why not?" boomed Meuhlnir, with barely suppressed mirth.

We followed the tavern master into the cramped common room. The décor was dark, with wood stained to the extent it was almost black, either on purpose or by smoke from the immense fire pit in the center of the room. Drag marks on the wooden floor showed that the tables were usually set for four and separated by five or six feet. The tables had been shoved together into one long table with benches along both sides. At the head of the table sat an upholstered chair—from the tavern master's apartments by the look of it.

He rested his hand on the padded backrest. "My *best* chair," he said. "I'd be honored, Yarl Tyeldnir, if it suits you."

"I'd be honored if you called me Hank," I said.

"That's kind of you, Aylootr," said Mothi with a mischievous grin.

"You, sir, may call me Mr. Jensen." I painted a severe, stern expression on my face, which only made Mothi's grin wider. I turned back to the tavern master. "The chair looks comfortable, but Meuhlnir or Veethar will sit at the head of the table."

"If they do, I'll be cracking skulls before dinner," growled Sif.

"And they don't call her the Harvester of Blood because she makes idle threats," said Yowrnsaxa in a tone to match.

Frikka put her arm through Veethar's and led him to the end of the table. "Don't tempt fate, husband. You've seen her fight."

Veethar smiled at Sif and bowed his head once in her direction. "Wouldn't dream of it."

"Sit in the damn chair, Hank," said Meuhlnir. "I'm not going up against *both* my wives. Might as well ask the wind to stop the sun in the sky." He moved to the head of the table and sat in the first spot to the right of the chair. He threw a glance down the table at Veethar. "See? I *do* learn."

"Hold me, Sif, I might faint," said Yowrnsaxa with laughter in her eyes.

"Mothi, come steady your mothers before we both lose consciousness."

The three karls stood—somewhat bashfully—in the corner, looking lost. "Don't mind them," I said. "They do this all day and all night. Consider it dinner theater." That earned timid smiles, but they still didn't move, so I sat in the chair at the head of the table and waved my hands to my right and left. "Come sit with us," I invited.

The karls were large men, though not as large as the Isir, but they looked at Sif and didn't move an inch.

"Sif, please tell these fine men that you won't eat their livers with a side of fava beans," I said.

She looked at me for a drawn-out moment, bewildered. "Of course, they should sit," she said, a blush creeping up her neck like a wild rose.

I turned my gaze back to the karls and smiled. "Come on." They ducked their heads and came over. One sat on the other side of Meuhlnir, and the other two sat on my left. I glanced at the innkeeper. "You were about to tell me your name."

The man blushed and ducked his head. "Oh yes, I'd forgotten. I am Tholfr."

"Nice to meet you, Tholfr. And you three?" I asked turning back to the karls.

"My companions are Uhkmuntr and Neerowthr," said the one to my immediate left. "And I am Lottfowpnir, Lord."

I held up my index finger. "None of that, Lottfowpnir. My name is Hank. It's nice to meet you."

"And you, Lo—uh, Hank. If you'll forgive me, that's a strange name."

I chuckled. "It's the diminutive name for Henry. It was my grandfather's name."

"Ah, a name worthy of respect and remembrance," said Neerowthr.

"Yes," I said glaring at Mothi, who stood next to my son. "That is my son, Sigurd, or Sig, as he prefers to be called." The three karls glanced down the table and inclined their heads. Sig blushed and threw the men a little wave, then glanced at Mothi, who tousled his hair and shoved him toward the table.

Tholfr cleared his throat. "He looks of an age with my boy, Retyinarr, if you'll pardon me saying so."

"I thought the same thing," I said.

"Well," said Tholfr, "I'll see to the food."

"With our thanks, Innkeeper," said Meuhlnir. "And bring us mead in large quantities."

Althyof scoffed and sat next to Frikka. "Ale for me, if you please."

The rest of the party sat, and though the assembled tables had seemed too large for our party, shoulders rubbed, and elbows jostled. I was glad for the chair, and not only because of its padding.

"Tell me, what brings you three to be traveling?" asked Meuhlnir with a casualness that must have seemed genuine to the karls, but which made Sif's head come around as if pulled by her braids.

"We travel together," said Uhkmuntr. "Lottfowpnir's father is attached to a mercantile concern in Suelhaym and sent us to straighten out a supplier near Trankastrantir."

"Is that so?" asked Veethar.

"Yes, Lord," said Uhkmuntr. "There is a spinner, and he is—"

"Come, Uhkmuntr! These lords have no interest in the details of our business." Lottfowpnir's elbow connected with his friend's ribs—a gesture meant to be hidden from everyone at the table.

"No," said Frikka in dulcet tones. "We are interested in the trades."

Lottfowpnir looked as if he couldn't tell if Frikka was mocking him or not. "It's nothing, a matter between karls."

"Speak," commanded Veethar.

Lottfowpnir glanced at the faces around the table. It was clear he'd rather be somewhere else, but he had no choice now. "There is a spinner in Trankastrantir, with whom my father trades. In the past, his yarns have been of the highest quality, but lately, they have been stiff, scratchy, and...well, they have an odor, and it does not wash out. We are weavers of fine cloth, sold to only the best clothiers in Suelhaym, and as such, we rely on quality yarn."

"And you go to collect your payments for the bad merchandise, I'll wager. The spinner's name?" asked Frikka.

"Tofri, Lady."

Frikka nodded, her expression solemn. "Did news of the attack on Trankastrantir reach Suelhaym?"

Lottfowpnir looked at the table in front of him.

"Answer," growled Veethar.

"Speak up, Lottfowpnir," I said. "It is rare, in life, to find friends to whom you can speak your whole mind, the whole truth without fear of reprisal. Veethar and Frikka are two such people. Speak your mind."

"Frikka and Veethar," he murmured. He glanced at me and then away, his eyes roaming the walls opposite him. After a moment of silence, Lottfowpnir gazed down the table at Frikka and Veethar. "We heard, but, with respect, that was seven months ago. We made allowances in the beginning. We paid full price for half-price yarn, and we did it without complaint because Tofri has always dealt squarely with us. But this is business, and everyone has troubles to deal with."

Frikka's eyes were distant, empty. "Tofri is known to me." She grasped Veethar's hand. "To *us*. You recognized our names, so you know why."

"Yes, Lady," said the karl.

"And yes, seven months ago Trankastrantir was attacked by a band of Svartalfar and demons. There was also a dragon, a white dragon that Hank and Althyof killed when it attacked our estate."

Uhkmuntr and Neerowthr stared at one another, eyes wide. Lottfowpnir glanced at Mothi, and then at me. "*Aylootr*," he whispered. "Of course."

"What you haven't heard, obviously, is that there was tremendous damage, both to the town proper and to outlying farms. You did not hear about the high loss of life."

"No," said Lottfowpnir, eyes back on the table in front of him.

"You've done business for years, but I'll wager you that Tofri never told you that he lost five of his children that day, and one of his wives."

"No."

"Nor did he tell you that the sheep he relies—relied—on to make your high-quality yarn were destroyed, that his farm was razed."

"No, he didn't."

"Where do you suppose he's getting the wool now?"

"I...I hadn't thought of that, Lady."

"No," said Veethar in a harsh tone. "You had your silver to consider."

Lottfowpnir grimaced.

"I'll tell you where he's getting his wool. He's buying it from Suelhaym, from the market. He's shipping it to Trankastrantir, spinning it, and shipping it back. How expensive must that be?"

Lottfowpnir shook his head. "He didn't tell us any of this."

"Now you know," said Veethar.

"The question becomes: 'What will you do with this knowledge?'" asked Frikka. "Do you proceed and claim your silver?"

Lottfowpnir shook his head. "No. We can't do that."

"You've said this spinner has been a loyal supplier, yes?" asked Yowtgayrr.

Lottfowpnir glanced at him as if he hadn't been aware the Alf was at the table. "You're…"

"An Alf. Yes."

The karl nodded as if he encountered Alfar every day. "Tofri has been a good supplier, an honest tradesman."

"An evil man might lie to you, take advantage of your good nature, but a good man, as you describe him to be, would not."

"Yes," said Lottfowpnir.

"If you have a friend—a true friend, mind—where's the profit in breaking with him? Wouldn't it be better to speak up, to reason things out?"

"Yes," said Lottfowpnir again, and I thought he'd grown a tad sullen.

"Let's leave it there," I said. "Lottfowpnir has a lot to mull over, and no doubt he will have to speak with his father before any decisions can be made."

"Yes, this is true," said Frikka with a nod toward me.

I cleared my throat as Tholfr set mugs and pitchers of mead on the table. With a glance at Althyof, he broke the seal on a clay jar and poured a dark brown liquid into one of the cups. "Your ale, Master Tverkr."

Althyof grunted and took a sip, his eyes lighting up as the liquid splashed across his palette. He swallowed and took another mouthful, smiling all the while.

"I spoke with Meuhlnir, Yowtgayrr, Skowvithr, and Veethar earlier today about meeting a Tisir. Kuhntul was her name."

Sif and Yowrnsaxa exchanged a look of surprise, but Frikka didn't bat an eyelash. Frikka, the seeress who never speaks her prophecies, I thought with irritation. She probably knows what it all means, whether there is a real traitor in the party or not. I glanced at Meuhlnir, and he nodded as if he knew what I was thinking. As much as he complained about the same, maybe he did.

"Who's this Kuhntul?" asked Jane.

"A Tisir—a *filkya*—who is known to us," said Frikka.

"And that's good or bad?"

Frikka shrugged.

"Tell us about her," I suggested, hoping to draw Frikka out a little.

"She fought in the war. She fought against the Dragon Queen."

"Then she's on our side, right?" asked Sig.

Frikka favored him with a stunning smile, and I could almost hear his insides melting. "We mustn't assume that, Sig."

"Why not, Auntie Flicka?"

"Sig!" said Jane. "Show some respect."

"Sorry," he said, but Frikka only laughed.

"In the war, Kuhntul didn't so much fight on our side as fight against the queen's forces," said Yowrnsaxa.

"Isn't that the same thing, Auntie Yarns?"

"No, Siggy-pig," said Mothi.

"I don't get it," Sig said.

"Kuhntul came to Nitavetlir right before the war here broke out," said Althyof around his mug of ale.

"In a way, she tricked the Tverkar into joining the war and siding with the dissidents against the Dark Queen."

"Is that so? I have never heard of this," said Meuhlnir.

"It is. She came during a time of crisis on Nitavetlir. Two kingdoms, Serklant and Yutlant, were...uh, engaged in diplomacy—"

"Exchanging insults, then?" asked Mothi with a grin.

Althyof returned his grin and nodded. "As I was saying, the two nations had been engaged in a discussion about which kingdom's craftsmen were in more demand. King Hetidn of Serklant grew incensed—that one never could have a conversation without taking offense. He decided to settle the matter following the ancient Tverkar traditions—by combat. He led his men on a long march, and somewhere in the middle of the *Mikitl Skowkur*, he—"

"The what?" asked Jane.

"The *Mikitl Skowkur*," said Sif. "It's a huge 'forest' of stalagmites on Nitavetlir."

"Which ones are stalagmites again?"

"Stalagmites are the ones on the ground," said Sig. "Geesh, Mom, do you even Earth Science?"

"You're in so much trouble," said Jane with her best mock glare.

"*As I was saying*," said Althyof. "King Hetidn got separated—he's famous not only for taking offense at every little thing but also for his propensity to get lost in his own bedroom. King Hetidn wandered around, calling for his men. I was the first to find him, of course, by chanting a *lausaveesa*—"

"A what?" asked Sig.

Althyof sighed. "Am I ever to finish this telling?" he muttered into his beard. "A *lausaveesa* is the short chant of a *runeskowld*."

"A magic spell?"

Althyof scoffed. "Nothing so pedestrian, but given your lack of education, young man, it's close enough. To avoid further interruption, there are two other forms I will define now. A *trowba* is a series of stanzas with a refrain, that is sung by a *runeskowld*, often accompanied by a sort of dance. A *triblinkr* is shorter and has no refrain. It is usually chanted rather than sung."

"*Cool*," said Sig. "Will you teach me to do it?"

Althyof gazed at my son with a stern expression for the space of ten heartbeats. "We shall see how you fare with Meuhlnir. I will say that no Isir has ever mastered the art."

"I'll be the first."

"As I said, we shall see." He crossed his arms over his chest. "Now, does anyone else have questions or comments that can't be held until the end of the telling?" He gazed around the table, one eyelid twitching. Despite the twitch, he seemed secretly pleased by Sig's request, but the twitch *was* a nice touch. "Then I will continue the telling.

"I found King Hetidn, by chanting a *lausaveesa*. His mind was blurry, and I could smell the *strenkir af krafti* all over him." Althyof paused for a quick glare around the table as if challenging someone to interrupt. "He said he had met a woman..."

NINE

Althyof chanted a *lausaveesa* as he trotted between the stone trees of the *Mikitl Skowkur*. King Hetidn had gotten himself lost—again—damn the man. He emerged into a clearing of sorts, and across the small clear space, Hetidn leaned against a thick stalagmite. "King Hetidn!" he called.

The king looked around, his gaze passing right over Althyof the first time, and then meandering back. "Is it you, Althyof?"

"It is, Your Majesty. I will lead you back to the others."

"Good, good," said the king, but his gaze kept losing track of Althyof as if the king were drunk.

"Are you well, King Hetidn?"

"Yes, fine," groused the king with a surly expression crossing his face. "Tired is all."

"Well, let's get you back to the others."

"Did you…"

Althyof crossed the open space and came up short five steps away. He sensed the *strenkir af krafti* wrapping around the king, and the king was neither a *runeskowld* nor a *vefari*. "Your Majesty, are you…alone?"

"I am alone, Althyof! Do you see someone else?"

"No, King Hetidn, no one else is apparent. But… Your Majesty, someone has accessed the *strenkir af krafti* with you as their focus."

"Maybe it was that woman. Did you not see her?"

"Woman, Excellency? Only you stand before me."

"Well, she was…" The king's voice trailed away, and his eyes lost focus again.

"Come, Your Majesty. Let's get you away from here. You can tell me about the woman on our trip back to the others."

"Woman?" The king turned vacant eyes on Althyof. "What woman?" He held out his arm, allowing Althyof to lead him.

"I didn't see her, Excellency. You mentioned her a moment ago." Althyof took the king's arm and walked back to the impromptu camp the king's men had set up.

"Oh, yes. She was quite a beauty, Althyof. Beautiful! She gave me something to drink."

"Something to drink, Excellency?"

"No, I'm not thirsty right now." The king stumbled, and his eyelids drooped.

Althyof didn't like the look of his pallor, nor the decline of his faculties. *Poison?* he wondered. "Tell me more of this woman, Your Majesty."

"Ah, yes. Quite beautiful she was. Blonde-haired, blue-eyed, dressed provocatively." The king's tone was wistful with a dollop of lust.

"Blonde? She wasn't a Tverkr woman, Majesty?"

"No, no. An Isir, but pretty." Hetidn grinned at him. "Her dress was *transparent*, Althyof. Imagine it!"

"Yes, Excellency." Althyof was busy imagining things, but none of them was a scantily clad woman.

"She gave me a drink. I was very thirsty," said the king.

"What did she give you to drink, Excellency?"

"Some draught or another. Mead or something weak such as that. It offended me, of course, but thirst is thirst."

"Yes, Your Excellency, quite right. Did she speak to you?"

"I...I think so, Althyof, but I can't remember what she said. It's as if a fog I can't penetrate wraps the words..."

"Yes, Your Majesty." Althyof led the king back to his men at arms and instructed the captain of the guard to set up a tent so the king could take a few hours' rest. He turned on his heel and walked back into the *Mikitl Skowkur* without another word.

Althyof was already composing another *lausaveesa*, this one intended to bring him across the path of the mysterious woman. There were a number of questions he wanted her to answer. He trotted and chanted the *lausaveesa* in a cadence that matched the pace of his footfalls. The *runeskowld* ran for forty minutes before he realized his path was circling back on itself again and again. He stopped short, standing straight, in surprise. Someone was turning his *lausaveesa* back on him. That hadn't happened since he'd earned the rank of master.

He composed his mind and put together a *triblinkr*, something powerful enough to resist being tampered with. When he had it all in his mind, he began to jog, again chanting in time to his pace. This time, the path his chanting led him down was arrow straight, and he emerged into the same clearing in which he'd found the king. The *triblinkr* urged him on, past the clearing, and into the stone trees on the other side. He ran on, past glittering formations of minerals and ores, past a small, mineral-infused lake. His legs kept pumping, and his lips kept chanting. Finally, he came to another clearing, this one larger than the last.

"Welcome, Althyof, Master *Runeskowld*," said a blonde woman sitting in an ornate chair in the center of the clearing. He thought he detected scorn in her use of his title but decided not to take offense. Not yet.

"And you are, Lady Isir?" He called her that, but it felt wrong on his lips, even as he said it.

"For one, I am no Isir. I could have stopped you, you know."

She really is beautiful, he thought. *For a non-Tverkar*. "Could have stopped me doing what?"

She laughed. "Your little *triblinkr*. I could have looped it back on itself with as much ease as I did your *lausaveesa*."

Althyof took it as bravado. "Then why didn't you?" he snapped.

"You intrigued me. Only rarely does someone of your abilities seek me out."

"What did you do to King Hetidn?" he demanded, stepping forward.

"No, *Runeskowld*," she said, and he froze in place. "I prefer you at a distance."

He tried to move forward again, but the muscles of his legs wouldn't obey.

"What happened between Hetidn and me is our own business and no concern of yours."

"I beg to differ," said Althyof. He compartmentalized his mind, using one part to maintain his conversation with the woman, and using the other part to compose a *trowba* meant to break her hold on him, to turn her spell back on herself and to hold *her* frozen against her will.

"I don't care," she said with a small, triumphant grin. "Well, I've seen you, Tverkr, and my curiosity is satisfied. You'll not see me again."

"Your name," said Althyof. "Tell me your name." As he said the words, he began to sing the *trowba* in his mind, imagining the dance that would accompany it, flinging runes into the world. After a moment, his feet moved to the steps of the dance and whirled across the clearing.

The woman's eyes widened as he moved, and she shrank away from his whirling dance. As she leaned away from him, Althyof sang his *trowba* aloud, increasing his volume with each stanza. By the time he came to the refrain, he was shouting the words in her face.

A stricken expression twitched on her face, and she appeared frozen as he had been moments before. He ended his *trowba* and grinned at her. Her lips twitched, and she was shaking with fear. "And now, woman, you know the depths of my mastery."

The woman burst out laughing. What he had taken for fear was an act—camouflage. She reached forward, moving easily, and pushed him away. She stood, grinning at his flabbergasted expression. "Goodbye, *Master Runeskowld*. You should return to your friends, they are waiting for you," she said and disappeared.

Althyof decided it was time to take offense, after all. "Who *are* you," he muttered. He turned and walked back to the camp.

When he arrived, the king was pacing back and forth, and the impromptu campsite had been struck. "Althyof!" exclaimed the king. "It's about time you returned! We almost left without you. Where have you been?"

Althyof put on the expression he used when he wanted to appear mysterious. "A *runeskowld's* business is his own, Excellency."

"*Runeskowlds* in my employ *have* no business of their own. It would be best if you remembered that in the future."

Althyof said nothing and resisted the urge to bow his head. Hetidn had ruled the kingdom for thirty short years, and Althyof remembered his father with fondness. Hetidn would never match his father as king. The Tverkr was just not suited for the job.

King Hetidn gazed at him coldly for a moment before turning to his men-at-arms. "Let's go, men. We need to be in Yutlant before night arrives." He glanced over his shoulder. "Althyof! A *trowba* for speed, endurance, and a direct path to Hokni's summer palace." He snapped his fingers as if he were calling his dogs.

Althyof decided it was high time to take offense, but he didn't let it show. He set off at a quick pace, one sure to tax the indolent king, singing a rote *trowba* of travel rather than composing something tailored to the situation. *Treat me like hired help, and hired help is what you will get.*

They ran for hours, twisting through the stone trees of the *Mikitl Skowkur* like lithe wild animals. When Althyof stopped singing, they were near the summer palace of the king of Yutlant, Hokni by name. King Hetidn stood behind, hands on his waist, gasping for breath. "The summer palace, Excellency, as *instructed.*" Hetidn nodded but didn't have enough wind to make some pompous declaration or other, and Althyof had to suppress a smile.

The king's fighting men stood behind him, most in much better shape than the king, but the number of men who were gasping for breath appalled Althyof. It didn't bode well for the battle to come.

"Well, Your Majesty? Should we set up camp?"

The king shook his head. "No," he wheezed. "No camp. We strike in the night."

Althyof stiffened. "What?" In his surprise, he forgot to use the honorific, but if the king noticed, he let it pass.

"No camp. We strike as soon as the men have rested."

"But, Your Majesty, the conventions of war—"

"Damn the conventions of war," snapped the king. "It's Hokni's wedding night. There will be no better time than this night."

Althyof's gaze slipped to the commander of the king's troops. The man looked back stony-faced, but Althyof thought there was a flicker of discomfort in his eyes. *Worse comes to worst*, he thought. *First, it's a sneak attack after the day is done, and then it's a sneak attack on a wedding party*. Althyof pursed his lips, trying to think of an argument to dissuade the king from this rash act.

The king glanced at his face and shook his head. "It's decided," he snapped. "And I'll hear no arguments against it, Althyof."

"Is this the work of the woman in the forest, Excellency?"

"What woman?" the king snapped.

"The beautiful blonde woman who bewitched you."

"I remember no woman," Hetidn said, but Althyof thought he caught a glimmer of recognition in his gaze.

"Your Excellency," began Althyof, "if you permit me time to examine you, I'm sure I can compose a *trowba* to rid you of this spell." His voice rang with confidence, but even as he said them, he recalled the results of the last *trowba* he'd sung against the blonde woman.

"No," snapped the king. "We attack in half an hour." The king spun on his heel and walked away.

Althyof glanced at the faces within hearing distance. They all wore the same expression: resignation. Shaking his head, Althyof walked away from the small army of men.

It's not honorable, he thought. *But it's also not honorable to betray one's king, even if the king is an insufferable fool.* He shook his head. If he obeyed Hetidn, it would be to perform a dishonorable act. But wouldn't the dishonor rest on Hetidn's shoulders? Then again, if Hetidn was dishonorable, so was Serklant as a nation, and as a citizen of Serklant, the dishonor was his to share.

Althyof strode into the darkness, his mind awhirl, his stomach churning. There had to be an answer, had to be a solution, a way out. The answer came into his mind as if someone had whispered it in his ear, and his pace picked up. He sang a *trowba* of stealth and ran toward Hokni's palace.

Technically, what he had in mind was a betrayal of his king, his countrymen, but outside the technicality, it was the perfect solution. He would eliminate the pall of dishonor from the attack.

Althyof snuck onto the palace grounds, and into a vacant room, where he let the *trowba* draw to an end and composed himself. He beat the dust of travel from his clothes as best he could. He would still look out of place—who attended a wedding in rough traveling clothes? At least he wouldn't look as if he'd walked in from the road itself.

Althyof followed the sounds of merriment to the large hall where the wedding party was in full swing. He slipped into the room unnoticed and stood in the shadows, looking around. Hokni was easy to pick out: a tall Tverkr wearing gold-spun robes and a stone crown on his head, whose gaze was one of lust and impatience. The small woman next to him was beautiful—a dainty Tverkr woman with amazing vermillion eyes.

Like he had every business being there, Althyof walked toward King Hokni. The king saw him approach, and a look of concern flittered across his features. He made a hand gesture at someone behind and to the side of Althyof, but it was too late to change direction or to stop—to do so would be to scream he was a danger to the king.

Althyof didn't see the blonde woman in the shadows behind the table until it was too late. In fact, he heard her whispering to the king before he saw her. Hands fell on his shoulders and upper arms with grips of iron.

"Your Majesty, King Hokni," he said. "I am Althyof, the enchanter and *runeskowld*."

The king nodded. "So I am told," he said in a mild voice.

"The woman behind you, Sire, has led King Hetidn to be outside your walls this very night. She has brought him here, whispering poison in his ears until he is ready to attack tonight. During your wedding party."

"Yes," said King Hokni. He didn't seem surprised, or even concerned.

"Sire! I've known King Hetidn for many years, and I served his father before him. It is not a dishonorable family. Serklant is not a dishonorable nation!"

"Be that as it may, Hetidn is outside, planning to attack," said the king.

"Yes, but *bewitched*, Your Majesty. Bewitched by the blonde woman behind you."

"Do you hear that, Messenger? You've bewitched Hetidn. Have you bewitched me, as well?"

"Of course, Excellency," said the blonde, her tone one of jest, but her expression serious.

"I thought so!" joked King Hokni. "Tell me, Messenger, to what end?"

"To bring Serklant and Yutlant to war." Again, the woman made it sound like a joke, but her eyes told another story.

"She means what she's saying, King Hokni," said Althyof. "She isn't joking as she makes it sound."

"Oh, of course," said Hokni with a broad smile. "Why, Messenger of Suel, do you wish our two countries to come to war?"

"Queen Suel's reasons are beyond the likes of you." Hokni laughed, but the Messenger of Suel didn't. The king didn't seem to notice, but his bride's eyes widened, and she brought a small, perfect hand to her lips.

Queen Suel? Of Osgarthr? What would she gain from this? Althyof squinted at the Messenger and began to compose a *lausaveesa* that would reveal her identity.

The blonde woman winked at Althyof and disappeared. He heard the war cries signaling the start of the attack outside. Hokni looked up at him and grinned. "Seems you will need a new employer soon," he said and laughed.

TEN

"**A**nd Hokni's new bride looked at him as if he were insane. She got up and left the wedding feast, but Hokni didn't even notice. Kuhntul *had* bewitched him, of course. She'd controlled both kings perfectly, playing one against the other."

"Of course, the woman was no envoy of the Dark Queen," said Meuhlnir, stroking his beard.

"No, but none of us knew that at the time. It appeared to be a play, a stratagem designed to make an invasion easier."

"How so?" asked Neerowthr.

"By eliminating two strong nations, thus creating a power vacuum into which the Dark Queen could have stepped," said Frikka.

"Exactly right," said Althyof. "But Tverkar don't think that way. Instead of creating a power vacuum, it galvanized the Tverkar, unified us—for once. We prepared for an attack on Nitavetlir, all nations working together in a common cause."

"And when no attack came?" asked Veethar.

Althyof shrugged. "When no attack came, we decided to go on the offensive, to punish the Dark Queen for her interference. Meuhlnir's entreaty served as a good excuse."

"Hmph. And here I thought my oratory skills had carried the day."

Althyof chuckled. "Not likely. It was a convocation of Tverkar you addressed. You didn't insult anyone; how could we trust you? All that blather about common goals, common enemies."

"Well, it *was* true," Meuhlnir said.

"To you, yes. To the Tverkar?" Althyof spread his arms and shook his head. "There was no profit in your proposal."

"Where was the profit in taking revenge?" asked Sif.

"Sometimes, my Lady Sif, vengeance is profit enough. Eh, Veethar?"

Veethar gazed at Althyof with a placid expression and said nothing.

Althyof shrugged. "We didn't find out it was Kuhntul acting on her own until the battle of

Raytyanes. As you no doubt know, Kuhntul created a bit of a stir."

"How so?" I asked.

Althyof glanced at me, a crooked grin on his face. "She and Skuhgul—another of the Tisir—ripped through the Dark Queen's karls like a *sterk task*, slaying them with a passion. Yarl Howkon stood and died with his karls. Despite his use of the *strenkir af krafti*, he couldn't save his men, or even himself. Kuhntul and Skuhgul were too powerful, too furious."

"And the Tverkar saw it and knew they'd been tricked?" asked Jane.

Althyof waggled his head back and forth. "In a way…We were there, undermining the keep walls. We heard Kuhntul and Skuhgul arrive—who could miss that frenetic bruit—and we rushed out of our tunnels, believing at first a cave-in was imminent. We saw them, sweeping through the men on the walls, white streaks that left blood and body parts in their wake. We didn't recognize what they were at the time; we thought it might have been the work of a powerful *vefari*. When the din ceased, the gates of the fortress were thrown open, and two women stood inside, making gestures of welcome. One of them was the blonde woman from the tale I told. Kuhntul."

"And? What about your vengeance?" asked Mothi.

Althyof scoffed. "We'd just seen the two of them decimate an entire fortress of men—*vefari*, yarls, karls, thralls—indiscriminately. We may be a grumpy bunch, but we aren't a *stupid* grumpy bunch."

"Did anyone confront her?" I asked.

"I did," said Althyof. "I demanded her name, and this time she told me. I demanded she explain herself, and she laughed at me. Skuhgul came to stand by her side, glowering and humming a spooky little tune. I thought it prudent to leave."

I glanced at Meuhlnir, then shifted my gaze to Veethar. "The Tisir helped you in the war?"

Meuhlnir glanced at Veethar and said, "Yes."

At the same moment, Veethar said, "No." The two Isir locked eyes for a moment.

"Which is it?" I asked, but neither man would elaborate on his original answer.

Frikka took a drink of her mead. When she swallowed, she said, "Kuhntul and Skuhgul wore white during that battle. Are you aware that they appear as white or black depending on their intentions?"

I nodded.

"Well, in other battles, they or others of their kind appeared dressed in black."

"And so we arrive back to 'I don't know' as the answer *du jour*?"

"The what?" asked Meuhlnir.

"It means 'of the day.'"

"Oh… As I said before, the role of the Tisir on Osgarthr is complicated."

"These Tisir are fickle," said Jane.

"They may be," said Frikka. "But even so, ignore them at your peril."

"But how can you trust what they say? How can you ever be sure if they want to help you or hurt you?" asked Jane.

Frikka shrugged and took another sip of mead.

"Well, using the color guideline that seems to be the only constant in the subject, Kuhntul's appearance, in this case, is malevolent."

"Yes, but to whom?" asked Veethar.

"I'm the one she came to."

"Sure, but perhaps by manipulating you, she is acting *against* someone else," said Althyof. "There's no telling what any given Tisir is up to. They are a cantankerous lot."

"Coming from a Tverkr, that says a lot," said Mothi.

Althyof squinted at him and laughed. "I like you, lad."

Mothi grinned. "I'm a likeable fellow."

"Even if you do smell like dirty socks," said Sig in a stage whisper.

"I'm not the one who doesn't enjoy bathing."

"Well, Cousin Mouthy, thanks for telling my mom."

"Your mom had already discerned your lack of bathingness. I do have a nose." Jane cocked her eyebrow at him. "I'm getting a prophecy. You will be bathing tonight."

"Too bad you don't follow Auntie Flicka's example and keep your prophecies to yourself."

"Boy," I growled.

"*Kidding*, Dad. Geesh."

I smiled and winked at him. "Me too."

"Dadgumit! Foiled by Cop-voice. Again!"

Tholfr and his son banged in from the kitchen, each carrying three times as much food as our party could eat in two sittings. I didn't complain, though, the scent of it made my mouth water.

After we finished supper, Jane and I went up to our room. I felt the way I did most nights after my Personal Monster™ had kept me awake throughout the previous night: groggy and fuzzy-headed. There was a fire blazing in the room's little stone fireplace, and the room was sweltering. It felt good for a moment, but I had to open the window and let some of the brisk air in.

"What are your thoughts about all that?" I asked, trying for casual, but hitting the mark for awkward instead.

"About those three men who have to sleep in the stables because of this weird caste thing they've got going on here? I don't like it."

"Neither do I, but that's not what I meant."

"About this Kuhntul woman? She sounds like someone we don't need to invite over to dinner."

"Ten-four on that."

"What was it she told you?"

"She said there was a betrayer in the party. A traitor."

"Naw," said Jane. "They could have betrayed us during the battle at Piltsfetl."

"I know, that was my thought as well. Some of the others immediately pointed at Althyof."

"Why?"

"Tverkar have a mercenary reputation."

Jane shrugged and slipped into the bed. "Ah!" she exclaimed. "Bed! Warm and cozy."

I shook my head. "You're insane. It's sweltering in here."

"Well, I'm cold, so there. Plus, I don't care if you're hot, get your ass in bed and get to sleep. If you pull another all-nighter, I'll have to beat you, and then your fancy new friends will know what a wimp you are."

I climbed into bed and shoved the covers off.

Jane shrugged even further under the covers. "More for me!"

"Hog them all you want, dear," I murmured and fell asleep.

EL'EVEN

Mud mired us, Veethar and I, buried under a thousand tons of rock and swathed in darkness. A terrible beast lived in the darkness with us—I could hear it breathe and sniff, looking for us.

I couldn't see an inch in front of my face, but I knew Veethar was in front of me, trying to lead me out of the blackness and into the light once more. He whispered incessantly, which rang false, but he kept it up as we trudged on and on.

The beast followed us, its steps just a fraction of a heartbeat off-time from ours. It was big, from the sound of it, and it was angry.

"Veethar, we have to get out of here," I hissed. "There's something in the darkness with us."

Veethar turned as if in a dream and looked at me. His eyes were empty, dull, but his lips moved constantly, a susurration of sibilants sang in my straining ears.

"Would you stop that? I'm trying to listen for the beast."

He nodded but didn't stop.

A great, shaggy arm swept out of the darkness behind Veethar. I tried to speak, tried to shout a warning, but the words stuck in my throat. At the end of the shaggy arm gleamed four long, silver blades that whistled through the fear-thick air.

As I watched, the arm swept into Veethar's exposed back, the blades slicing through him as if his body were made of tissue paper. His head separated from his neck, falling sideways in the great arm's wake, lips in constant motion, empty, dead eyes glued to my own.

The beast was coming for me next. It clanked and banged toward me in the darkness, crying out and grunting.

TWELVE

I awoke breathing hard, ears straining for the clanking, banging advance of the thing from my nightmare. Outside, practice blades crashed against shields, and a woman grunted. I peeled my eyes open and winced at the sunlight streaming in through the open window. The position of the sun meant it was late morning—around 10 or 11 if my guess was right. The thick comforter draped over me, weighing me down. I flung it off and swung my legs to the floor, groaning at how stiff I was.

My head felt as if I'd spent the previous night doing a week's drinking and my mouth tasted like a monkey's asshole. I stuffed my legs into my pants and dragged a shirt on, wincing at the myriad of aches and pains.

Someone had decided I needed rest, and it rankled. *Why ask me if you're going to do what you want, regardless of my answer?* I shook my head, trying to rid myself of the irritation at the women who had my best interests at heart. Even so, being disabled didn't mean I was a child. *I can still make decisions about my own body, thank you very much.* That wasn't a fair thought, but I felt like shit and was grumpy to boot.

I blinked hard a few times, trying to clear the bleariness from my eyes, but it was obviously going to be *one of those days* in which my vision was blurry, my body was stiff, and my demeanor was bear-like. I wished it was as easy as that old Toys-R-Us commercial (*Turn that frown upside down!*), but it wasn't that easy. It seemed as if changing my mood had been that easy before the advent of my Personal Monster™, but maybe that was just green-grass syndrome.

I glanced out the window, a bit amused by the grunting, the battle cries, the whump of wooden weapons on shields, the cheering. *Wait, cheering?* I lurched to my feet, shuffled my way over to the window, and squinted out.

In the empty space between the inn proper and the small grazing pasture kept for the horses of the inn's guests, a fighting square had been laid out. In it, Jane stood, crouching behind her shield. Yowtgayrr stood opposite my wife, his narrow longsword and dagger held at the ready, sunlight skittering along the naked steel. As I watched, Jane leapt forward, feinting with her shield at Yowtgayrr's head and slashing at his throat with her wooden axe. At the last moment, Yowtgayrr dodged to the side and swatted her across the rump with the flat of his longsword. Jane yelped and whirled to face him, eyes blazing, but the Alf was already gone, circling as she moved.

Jane struck with her axe, swinging blind, and it clattered across Yowtgayrr's shoulder. Mothi, Sig, and the three Isir women cheered. Yowtgayrr staggered back, almost tripping himself.

The memory of Yowtgayrr fighting three Svartalfar during the attack on Veethar's estate swam into my mind. He'd been so graceful, so *capable*, that he'd made his three opponents look like children fighting a master swordsman, but in the square below, he appeared slow and clumsy.

I turned from the window and laced up my boots, sitting in the chair next to the door. I thumped downstairs, pressing both palms into the walls in opposite directions. There was no handrail, of course—Osgarthr had no Americans with Disabilities Act. There wasn't room for a handrail anyway. My knees and ankles screamed at me the whole flight of stairs.

Tholfr sat in his tiny office, almost dozing. When he heard me at the bottom of the steps, he sprang up and came out to greet me. "Was the room satisfactory, Yarl Tyeldnir?"

"Hank," I said in a gruff, grouchy voice. "And yes."

"Ah, yes…Hank," he said with obvious discomfort. "Would you care to eat?"

"God, no. But I'd take a cup of clear, cool water."

"It would be my pleasure." He turned to go to the kitchen.

"I'll be outside," I said, gesturing to the side of the inn where the impromptu lesson was going on.

"Yes, Yarl Ty…Yarl Hank. I'll bring it to you."

"Thanks," I called after him. I turned and tromped outside, squinting against the bright sun. The air was crisp and smelled of the sea. *Wonder if those sea dragons are still at it.*

I glanced seaward, but the inn was nestled in a copse of trees, so though I could catch glimpses of the brilliant emerald water, I couldn't see any dragons. I rounded the corner of the inn in time to see Jane barge into Yowtgayrr with her shield, sending him sprawling into the dirt. Her audience cheered.

Sig saw me coming and ran to greet me. "Dad! Mom's kicking Yowtgayrr's butt!"

"Is she now?" I said. I glanced at Yowtgayrr and met his bland gaze.

"No, she isn't," said Jane. "Yowtgayrr is a very capable opponent, and he's also a good enough teacher not to make me feel like a stumbling old cow."

Yowtgayrr's expression glimmered toward a smile for a moment, then Jane barged into him with her shield again, and his gaze snapped back to the fight.

I walked over to stand next to Mothi. "How's she really doing?" I asked under my breath.

"Against an Alf *sverth hoospownti*—swordmaster? She'd be dead in fifteen seconds or less. But against a karl? She could hold her own."

"What about against an Isir *uhxl mathur*?" I asked with a smile.

Mothi shrugged and grinned. "Sixteen seconds, but about a second later you'd put a bunch of holes in me." His expression grew serious. "As your *skyuldur vidnukona*? I might run."

Jane and Yowtgayrr circled each other, eyes locked, footsteps almost in unison. "Last exchange," Jane said, her color high in her cheeks. "Don't hold back."

"My lady, there's no point in—"

"I want to understand where I really stand."

Yowtgayrr's eyes flicked toward me, and I shrugged. He nodded to Jane. "When you are ready."

Jane sprang at him, shield arcing toward his throat, axe chopping down toward his bicep on his sword arm. Yowtgayrr spun to the side, his longsword flicking out twice, and Jane cried out in surprise, watching her shield and axe go spinning into the dirt outside the square, landing before she did.

She stood there a moment, staring at Yowtgayrr. "I'm *definitely* not kicking Yowtgayrr's butt, Siggy."

"I guess not," he said, sounding concerned.

Yowtgayrr made a small bow in her direction. "It has been my pleasure to spar with you, Lady Jane. You did well."

"Well? After what you just did?"

The Alf shrugged. "I've been practicing my art for centuries. You've been practicing for months. You did well, and I say this as a qualified judge of your progress."

"If you say so," she said, looking at her shield, her axe, then her unmarked hands and forearms.

"I do say so," said Yowtgayrr.

"As do I," said Sif.

"Will I ever be able to move like that?" Jane murmured.

"Sif, would you do me the honor?" asked Yowtgayrr.

"My pleasure." Sif strapped her shield on and hefted her axe—her real axe, not a practice weapon. "Try not to die," she said with a smile.

Yowtgayrr smiled back and dropped into a crouch as Jane stepped out of the square. When Jane was clear, Sif screamed and sprinted at Yowtgayrr, shield up, axe whirling at her side. Yowtgayrr feinted to the right and danced away to the left, his sword and dagger blurring out, once, twice, and a third time, each blow caught on Sif's shield. They exchanged blows at lightning speed, metal rasping against metal, feet blurring, feinting, stomping. It was like some elaborate dance.

I thought I saw blows that could have landed, but if they had, death would have followed, and at the last possible moment, the blows were checked or turned away. They fought back and forth, back and forth, dancing across every square inch of the fighting square. It was almost impossible to follow, and the whole thing had the flavor of unreality that I associated with vintage kung-fu movies.

Abruptly, both combatants stepped back and bowed to one another. Neither seemed to even be breathing hard. Jane shot a look at Sif. "Guess you've been holding back, too," she laughed.

Sif smiled. "Had that been a real fight, Yowtgayrr would have killed me numerous times. He is a *sverth hoospownti* of the highest order."

Yowtgayrr bowed his head. "Thank you, Sif, but you might have killed me multiple times as well."

Sif laughed and shook her head. "No, you'd have decapitated me in that first exchange, as you well know."

Yowtgayrr shrugged and sheathed his weapons.

Sif turned to Jane. "Do you see?"

"Yeah," said Jane. "I see I need more practice."

"Yarl Hank, here's your water," called Tholfr, coming around the side of the inn. "Are you sure I can't bring you some food?"

"You can," said Jane. "He'll be eating bread and cheese this morning."

Tholfr looked at Jane and opened his mouth but closed it and nodded before looking at me and nodding. "Bread and cheese, Yarl?"

I shook my head and laughed. "You heard her. She has an axe now; I'm not going to argue." Tholfr smiled uncertainly and turned back to the inn. "Where are the others?" I asked Mothi.

"Veethar and my father are talking to the karls, inviting them to travel with us back to Suelhaym. Althyof is off doing Tverkar things, probably practicing his scowl in a mirror. Skowvithr is walking in the woods."

"Are we ready to travel?"

Mothi shook his head slowly, and his eyes darted to his mother. "I thought we'd take the day in rest," he said.

"No, we should move on. Sig, would you go round up the others?"

"I wanted to watch Mom fight some more."

Jane locked eyes with me, judging my pliability, assessing my physical state. "No more fighting today, Siggy. We've got to get back on the road."

"Aw, man…" said my son, the orator.

Sif pointed at me. "You go eat. I'll get my bag. If we're getting back on those horses today, you're getting a dose of the ointment."

"And you will go on a full belly," said Jane coming to stand shoulder to shoulder with Sif. "Or I'll spank you."

"Couldn't resist it, could you?" I laughed.

"Nope." Jane cracked a grin.

We filed into the inn, the others heading upstairs to pack, while I slouched into the plush chair in the dining room.

It didn't take long to get the party ready to move. The karls had accepted the invitation to travel with us, and as Sif and I came out of Tholfr's tiny office, everyone was mounted and waiting out front.

As we exited the inn, Meuhlnir leaned down and said, "You know this is foolish, right, Hank?"

"How so?"

"These inns are built so that they are a day's ride apart. If we leave at noon, we either have to camp for the remainder of the trip or have another half day of travel. You might as well rest—"

"No. I don't need a day of laying around." My voice sounded petulant, even to me.

Jane shook her head and rolled her eyes up.

"But—"

"And to be honest, I'd rather not stay at another inn and run the chance of forcing more karls to sleep in the stables."

"But that was only right," said Uhkmuntr.

"It was our pleasure and our duty," said Neerowthr. "You are yarls."

I shook my head. "We're all men, same as you."

"Speak for yourself," said Jane. "But I can't say I was very comfortable putting you out, either."

The karls glanced at one another. "It could not be otherwise," said Lottfowpnir. "You are yarls, and we, karls."

"We are no better than you," I said.

"Hank," said Meuhlnir in a soft, but firm voice. "Don't argue with them. They are not upset, why should you be?"

"Maybe because it's not right to treat people differently because of who their ancestors are?"

Meuhlnir shook his head. "That's where you are wrong, Hank. It's how our society works. Your mistake—which you repeat often, I might add—is in the arrogant assumption that what your society considered right and correct should apply to other societies, other cultures. Your values are your values, and you are free to keep them, as long as you allow us the same freedom."

I glanced at Jane, and she looked up and left while lifting her eyebrows. "I'm not here to tell you what to believe," I said softly. "That *would be* the height of arrogance. It seems unfair, given my upbringing. That's all."

"The Isir culture has existed for eons—longer than any I am aware of on Mithgarthr, I might add—and it was *designed* to include this caste system that you rail against. There has never been an uprising against the caste system."

"But you fought a war—" began Sig.

"*Not* against the caste structure," said Meuhlnir. "We went to war against a government that had become unjust. Nothing more."

"But you keep *slaves*," said Sig. "How can you think that's right?"

"Thralls are not slaves as you understand the word. No one *owns* them. They are free men. Destiny attaches them to a specific yarl house for whom they work. Many thralls live their whole lives without even seeing a yarl. They are not bought and sold; they are not kept from marrying, from having a family."

"No," I said, "but they are not free to seek employment elsewhere, correct?"

Meuhlnir sighed and glanced up at the sun. "It is our way, Hank, and no one is complaining but you three. In any case, the day is not getting any closer to morning, so I suggest we head out. I also suggest you three consider my words." With that, he tapped

Sinir's flanks and trotted back out to the road, and everyone followed.

Yowtgayrr rode to my left, looking ahead, but glancing at me from time to time. "Thank you," I said.

"For what?"

"For working with Jane. And for not killing her by mistake."

Yowtgayrr smiled warmly. "Oh, it was my pleasure. And I would no more allow harm to come to her than I would you. Your son, either."

"That's why I said thank you."

We rode in silence for a while, and as the road came out of the woods, I glanced at the sea. The dragons were still there but were considerably farther offshore. "Still with us," I mumbled.

"Yes," said Yowtgayrr. "Like lice, they are."

"Tell me something, Yowtgayrr."

"If I know it."

"You told me about the *Plauinn*, and how the Tverkar, the Alfar, and Svartalfar races came to be."

"Yes," he said. "The First War. What of it?"

"Well, you told me that everyone descends from the *Plauinn*."

He nodded and made the go-ahead gesture with his free hand.

"What I don't get is this. The three races have a few distinguishing characteristics that make them seem related. Humans—the people of Mithgarthr—and the Isir also have similar characteristics, but the two sets of peoples, those that fit the Alfar mold, and those that fit with the Isir, don't seem to be related genetically."

"Genetically?"

"Ah. A word from my *klith*. You referred to them as bits of the *Plauinn*."

"Oh, yes. The bits govern how a race might look but is not limited to outward appearances."

I nodded and shrugged. "Okay, but what about the demons? The fire demons from Muspetlshaymr, for instance. They seem to have fire *inside* them from the way Meuhlnir describes them. And the demon whose blood took my eye...I mean, it had acid for blood. How can they be related to us? Even remotely?"

Yowtgayrr threw back his head and laughed. "Now you finally understand how we feel about the Svartalfar!" He clapped me on the shoulder.

"Sure," I said, but without conviction.

"I'm not saying the *Plauinn* looked like Alfar, though some believe that. We are the closest representatives to the *Plauinn*...uh, genically."

"Genetically," I said. "So, even though they have mutated—changed at the genetic level—very far from the *Plauinn*, the Alfar believe everyone is still related?"

"Yes," said Yowtgayrr. "Some are *more closely* related, that's all. And, keep in mind that the First War fractured the very universe itself. There are *strathur* in which the physical laws are different, *strathur* in which we would die if we were to travel there. The people in those places are vastly different from us, but they are still related to the *Plauinn*."

"I have a hard time seeing how that can be possible."

Yowtgayrr shrugged. "How could it not be so? The *Plauinn* were the First People."

"Okay, leaving that aside, but assuming it to be true, you've heard about Isi and his genetic manipulation of the Isir—specifically how he defined the castes?"

Yowtgayrr nodded.

"Are the Alfar... Don't you—"

"The Alfar don't judge, Hank. Neither should you." His voice was friendly but firm.

"You've been practicing not judging for eons," I said mimicking his tone in the fighting square. "I've only been practicing a few minutes."

Yowtgayrr grinned. "But remember, we are all just men, Hank, and no man can be perfect. Do you remember Freyr's reaction to you?"

"How could I forget?"

"Judgmental, wasn't he?"

That scored a hit. "Is that how I sound to Meuhlnir and the others? As Freyr sounded?"

Yowtgayrr shrugged. "You've only been practicing a short while compared to Freyr. You haven't yet reached his level of arrogance." He said it with a smile, but the words still stung. "Hank, every man has the right to determine what is right and what is wrong. No one has the right to tell someone else how to think, no matter how much they believe they are right."

I nodded, remembering how some people back home had turned an initiative of acceptance—no, a celebration—of the differences between Earth's races into an excuse to chastise people who believed differently from themselves. It rankled that I was coming across like the PC-police back home. "Accept diversity as long as your views are the same as mine."

Yowtgayrr shrugged. "None of us are perfect."

Althyof trotted his horse up on the other side of mine. "Speak for yourself, Alf."

Yowtgayrr sighed, but he hid a grin behind it.

"And what can I do for you Althyof?" I asked.

"It's what I can do for you, Isir."

"Oh?"

"I could hobble together a *trowba* that would give these horses some pep and a lot more endurance. We could make it to the next inn by nightfall."

"Hmm," I said, glancing at Yowtgayrr. "And what would that do to the horses?"

"Just think of it! A hot meal, a stout ale! A bed! A pillow! A roof to cover this infernal sky!"

"And the horses?"

Althyof shrugged, looking sour. "It would be hard on them, but they are mere animals."

"In that case, I don't think you should do it," I said. "Plus, Veethar would probably have words for you."

"Ha! That one barely has enough words for himself, let alone to share with others," he snapped. The Tverkr scowled and spurred his horse on. He galloped around a bend ahead without looking back.

"He takes rejection well," I muttered.

"For a Tverkr, he does," said Yowtgayrr. "Many Tverkar would have demanded to fight you."

From around the bend ahead, I heard Althyof laugh, a loud booming sound filled with derision and scorn. "Be off!" he shouted.

With a glance at Yowtgayrr, I gave Slaypnir his head and galloped around the bend, the Alf half a step behind.

A band of men stretched across the road, and Althyof sat on his horse. He held one of his daggers in each hand, and the distinctive cadmium red aura flickered around the blades. "You fools! Do you know who I am?"

"Hopefully a rich Tverkr."

Without slowing, I pulled Kunknir out of its holster and took aim. *With the* preer *closed, the only ammunition available is what I carry*, I thought, trying to do a quick mental inventory of how many rounds I had left. I holstered Kunknir and drew Krati. If I was going to run out of ammo, I'd rather Krati be the well that ran dry. I leaned forward in the saddle, extending my arm so Slaypnir could see the pistol. He snorted without missing a step, and I sank back, letting the pistol wander down the line of highwaymen until I found the biggest one. I snapped off two quick shots, sending the rounds whistling by his head, one on either side.

Every eye in the band of outlaws snapped up and found me charging toward them on Slaypnir. They exchanged glances and dropped to their knees.

I brought Slaypnir to a halt next to Althyof. "I was not in danger," he murmured. I shrugged, keeping the pistol moving back and forth along the line of kneeling men.

"What is your purpose here?" I called to them.

"Forgive us, Yarl Tyeldnir!" cried the big man.

"Why? You've accosted my friend, Althyof. Who, I might add, was about to kill you to the last man. Don't you know better than to threaten the man who defeats trolls in single combat? He's a *runeskowld,* you bunch of idiots!"

"We didn't know, Tyeldnir!"

I glanced at Althyof, who, despite rolling his eyes, looked pleased with what I'd said about him. "Now you do," I said. "Why are you here? Who sent you to harry us?"

The big man glanced up at me, craning his neck at an awkward angle. "No one, Yarl. We are poor, and we need to eat."

I sat back in the saddle, tapping Krati against my leg. It was an excuse I was well familiar with from Mithgarthr. It carried about as much weight on Osgarthr as it did there. The rest of the party trotted up behind us, as the big man's eyes darted from one to the next, his complexion getting more and more mealy as he progressed.

"What's this, Aylootr?" asked Mothi.

"It seems these men are poor and need to eat," I said in a mild voice.

"Is that so?" asked Meuhlnir.

"They think to fill their bellies by taking from us?" asked Veethar in an algid voice that might have tempered molten steel. His horse took a step forward, lips twitching.

"Forgive us, lords and ladies," said the big man, his voice shaking.

"Are you aware of what happened to the last band of harriers that bothered us?" asked Meuhlnir.

"No, Lord."

"No, you aren't. Any idea why?"

"No, Lord."

"Because none of them lived to tell the tale." The line of kneeling men glanced at each other, seemingly at a loss for what to say or do next.

"Well, fools?" demanded Mothi, unsheathing his axes. "What are you still doing here?"

They looked up, expressions of shock on their faces. I gestured at the wooded side of the road with Krati. "Run that way. There are sea dragons about today." I pointed at the big man. "Remember your life belongs to me now. Don't make me come and collect."

"Thank you, lords!" said the big man. He got up and sprinted away into the woods, followed by his merry band.

"And give up robbery," I yelled. "Or I will come back for another visit."

"Yes, Yarl Aylootr!" the big man yelled back over his shoulder. "I'll see to it!"

I sighed and glared at Mothi. "I hope you're happy," I said.

"Oh, I am, Aylootr, I am." He grinned at me, and I couldn't help laughing.

THIRTEEN

The sun flirted with the mountains girdling the western horizon as we crested the last rise and glimpsed the city stretching out along the shore for what must have been miles and miles. Suelhaym. "Bigger than I thought," I said.

"You should have seen it before the war," said Sif in a wistful voice.

Muddy red tiles capped the buildings, and smoke from cook fires billowed skyward. An ivy-covered granite wall surrounded the city, and it must have stood forty feet high. Docks stretched far out into the natural bay that was the eastern border of the city.

Ships teemed in the harbor, leaving with the evening tide, their lanterns and navigation markers bobbing about like fireflies in a breeze. There was no sign of the sea dragons that had escorted us down the coast. The muddy red tiles must have once been bright red and shiny, and the wall straight and kept clear of the creeping ivy that climbed it now. "It must have been beautiful from up here."

"Oh, it was," said Frikka. "In time, it will be again."

"I'm hungry," grumbled Althyof. "*And* thirsty. I wonder if anyone here has a proper ale?" He tapped his horse with his heels and cantered down toward Suelhaym's massive North Gate at the foot of the hill.

The gates stood open and seemed to be unattended. As we approached, I understood why: they stood open because they no longer closed. The left gate leaned propped against the granite wall, its massive hinges twisted and broken, the gate on the right still hung by its bottom hinge, but the top hinge had melted after contact with something extremely hot, and the inner tip of the gate had buried itself in the ground.

"This is where she made her last stand," said Veethar in a quiet, almost mournful tone.

"We had to attack our own city," murmured Meuhlnir. "Break our own gates, fight our former neighbors street by street to the palace in which we used to serve."

"Then the real battle began," said Frikka, brushing at her cheeks.

"Yes," said Veethar and walked his horse off the road and into the trees on the inland side.

"Come on," said Mothi. "Let's leave them to their reminiscences."

"Lead on," I said, and we followed Mothi through the gate.

Once we'd ridden a block or two, Mothi said, "I'm glad I was born after the war. So many places are nothing more than reminders of the worst times in their lives."

"Understandable," I said. "It must have been the hardest thing they'd ever done."

"I don't know how Pratyi and Freya can stand to live here."

"Did they fight?" I asked.

"Oh yes, despite how Freya was at the beginning of it all, by the end, by the battle of Suelhaym, she'd enlisted with my father to unseat her sister."

"Why didn't Freya become the queen?" asked Jane. "I've always liked the myths about her."

"They offered the kingdom to her, but she refused. She said she'd lived in her sister's shadow her whole life, and she didn't want to live in the shadow of her sister's fall from grace."

"Do they live inside the walls?"

"Yes," said Lottfowpnir. "Their estate lies down near the northern gate. Other side of the city. It used to be the Dark Queen's palace."

"So much for moving out of her sister's shadow," murmured Jane.

"It's where we are heading," said Mothi with a curt nod.

"We'll take our leave here, Yarls," said Lottfowpnir. "Our path leads toward the harbor. Many thanks for your generosity. Please pass the sentiment on to the others."

"We will," I said. "I hope everything works out with your spinner."

"I'm sure it will," said the karl. "If not now, when Lord Veethar and Lady Frikka return to Trankastrantir." He nodded at Sig and somehow managed a graceful bow to Jane from horseback. To Mothi and me, he raised his hand to his forehead and tugged his hair. "Lords."

"Goodbye, Lottfowpnir," said Mothi. "Uhkmuntr, and Neerowthr, farewell."

The karls mumbled their farewells and the three of them took the next right without a backward glance. "I'll never get used to it," I murmured.

"Yes, you will," said Mothi in a matter-of-fact tone. "Your legend grows daily, and even if you weren't Isir, people would assume you were one and, like it or not, the people would treat you like one."

I nodded.

"Oh, great. Thanks a lot, Mothi, now his head will be as big as a...as an..."

"As my father's?"

"*Exactly*," laughed Jane.

I glanced behind us, sure Meuhlnir would claim to have heard the conversation in a thunderous voice, but the others had not entered the gates yet. "They'll be along soon, I trust?"

"Yes," said Mothi. "Before true night falls." He led us on, nodding to the karls and thralls who dropped what they were doing to come pay their respects to our passage. Mothi sat straight in his saddle, despite the weariness he must have felt. He presented a regal figure—a stern-faced hero, back from the wars.

I could see the northern wall by the time Mothi turned to the east. The broad avenue he led us to had a flower-filled median and smelled of honeysuckle and fresh bread. The businesses and homes along the avenue seemed to be of a richer variety than the gate road.

Ahead of us stood a smaller set of walls made from the same stone as the outer walls, but the gates of the inner walls were in good repair, and the stone was polished, almost like a fancy counter-top back home. As we approached, the gates swung open, revealing an inner courtyard bedecked with garlands of tropical flowers.

A woman whose beauty eclipsed Frikka's (but not Jane's!) stood on the other side of the courtyard. Her hair was blonde and hung to her waist. Her smile beamed radiantly through the gloaming like a lighthouse in a storm. She stuck her tongue out at Mothi, almost skipping over to take the reins of Jane's horse. "Hello, Sister," she said.

Jane glanced at me, a terror-struck expression on her face. She slid to the ground, and before she could say a word, Freya embraced her and kissed her on both cheeks. "I'm so glad you are here," Freya exclaimed. "We have so much to talk about." The blonde woman linked her arm through Jane's and turned to Sig. She beamed a smile at him, and said, "Welcome, Sigster. I hope you're hungry. We don't have the same kind of kitchens as you do on your *klith,* but I had my cook prepare the fingers of chickens for you. Oh, and fried cheese."

Sig darted a look of wonder my way. "Thank you!" he said, turning back to stare at Freya. "Those are my favorites. How did you know?"

Freya winked at him and smiled as would a carny huckster. "Magic." She laughed and turned to meet my gaze with curiosity. She looked so like her sister that for a moment, I could see her snarling at me as she cursed me in the *Gamla Toonkumowl.*

"I am *not* my sister," she whispered.

"Forgive me," I said. "The resemblance is uncanny—took me by surprise is all."

"And she re-earned her nickname—the Black Bitch—in what she's done to you and your family. I understand."

"Are you done ignoring me?" demanded Mothi.

"Did someone say something?" she asked Sig.

"It was only Cousin Mouthy."

"Cousin...*Mouthy?*" Her gaze snapped around to Mothi's, merriment in her eyes. "What an appropriate nickname." She laughed, and it was as if someone had struck a chorus of glass bells. I remembered Meuhlnir telling me Suel had laughed that way before her fall, and it was every bit as beautiful as he had claimed.

"I allow Piggy to call me that, and sometimes Hank, but you? No, I don't think so."

"Like you could stop me, you big lug." She took a few steps, dragging Jane along, until she was close enough to punch Mothi in the shoulder. "Don't think you've gotten so big that I can't spank you."

Mothi grinned and winked at me. "She's all talk, this one. Never does as she promises."

"Flirting with my wife again, youngster?" boomed a man's voice from a darkened doorway. The voice was melodious, like that of a trained opera singer.

"Flyting's more like it," said Freya, "and he has as little chance in one arena as the other."

"She started it," said Mothi, a toothy grin splitting his face. "Anyway, old man, if you can't keep her home, that's your problem."

"Suddenly, I feel like a cow," Freya said. "Be careful, boys, lest you find yourselves outside the gates looking for a place to sleep."

"I don't think Suelhaym could handle Pratyi and me spending a night out on the town."

"Neither could Pratyi," said Freya. "Now, stop being crass, the both of you, before Jane takes offense. She's been working with her shield, I understand."

Pratyi stepped out into the twilight and sauntered toward us. He was tall, as were all the Isir, and broad across the shoulders, and yet he moved with a dancer's grace, not quite the flowing elegance with which Yowtgayrr moved—not like a master martial artist—but as if he listened to a music none of the rest of us could perceive. He squinted past me toward the gates. "Noble Alfar, welcome to our home."

"Thank you, Pratyi. I am Yowtgayrr, and this is Skowvithr."

"Are you here looking for your kinsmen? The five Meuhlnir sent last spring?"

"We are Hank's *tutha verntar*."

I glanced at Yowtgayrr, eyebrows arched. "It means bodyguard."

"Don't gild the lily, Yowtgayrr." Pratyi turned to face me. "It means 'death protectors,' the implication being they will die before you do."

"Oh," I said. "I knew they felt that way."

Pratyi fixed his gaze on me. "Language is more than a tool to hack about oneself with like an axe." Without looking, he swatted Mothi on the shoulder. "It can be a weapon, it can be a balm, it can be a caress, or it can be a club wielded by a clumsy ogre."

"Very poetic imagery, husband," Freya said in a risible long-suffering tone.

"I try," said Pratyi with a smile.

"Are you done with the pedantic sermon?" she asked, her tone sweet and cajoling, but with the promise of hidden barbs.

"I think I am," he said, rolling his eyes at Mothi.

"Let's all go inside. Pratyi talks less when he's inside." Freya flipped her hair and batted her eyelashes at her husband demurely and led us into the main house. "I take it the others are mooning about outside the gates?" she asked over her shoulder.

"Yes," said Mothi. "They'll be along when they are ready."

She sighed. "If they would accept that this is now my fiefdom, instead of living in the past..."

"Wife?" said Pratyi.

Freya glanced at him. "Husband?" she mimicked.

"Shut up."

Freya stuck her tongue out at him but said no more.

"Is anyone hungry? Thirsty?" asked Pratyi. "We've had the cooks busy all day preparing a feast of favorites, both from Osgarthr and from Mithgarthr."

"I told them," said Freya.

"Oh." Pratyi winked at Sig and boomed, "Lead us to the dining hall, woman!"

The hall was much the same as Veethar's and Meuhlnir's before him but on a much grander scale. It was a huge rectangular room, with a row of fire pits running down the center and long picnic-like tables on either side. There was a dais at the end, and on it sat another table, this one grander than the rest, with gilded carvings running down the legs. Elaborate scenes of ships, dragons, and Isir doing various tasks lined the walls and columns—carved into them by master craftsmen.

The last table on our side was set up for eating, and a fire babbled next to it in the fire pit. Dishes of all kinds, some I recognized from Mithgarthr, some from Osgarthr, and some I didn't recognize at all, covered the center of the table.

Freya nodded toward the table. "I thought we could be informal. Does it suit?" She looked at me with quirked eyebrows.

"I guess you've never seen Mothi and my son attack supper. Informal is a step up."

She laughed and swept her arm at the table. "Sit. Eat. Drink. Ignore my blowhard husband."

Pratyi shook his head and sat next to Mothi. "Tell me, youngster, what mayhem have you wrought since we last spoke?"

Mothi grinned at his plate heaped with roasted and smoked meats. "Have you heard how the mighty Aylootr slew the dragon at Trankastrantir?"

"Oh, no," I said. "But at least you didn't come up with a *new* nickname for me."

"Don't worry," said Pratyi. "The locals already have."

I groaned. "Do I even want to know?"

Pratyi shrugged.

"Tell us," said Mothi, grinning from ear to ear.

"Valkyosanti," said Pratyi. "Chooser of the slain."

I grimaced. "I think I prefer wand-bearer."

Mothi's wide shoulders twitched. "It's not as funny as wand-bearer, I'll give you that."

"Why is there a need to give me a different nickname every other day?" I asked. "Does Mothi have a bunch of these nicknames?"

"No, he's too inconsequential," said Pratyi with a grin. "Meuhlnir, on the other hand…"

"Oh? Tell us," I said with a chuckle.

"My favorite is Rimr," said Freya. "It means 'noise.' I always thought it suited him."

"I heard that!" said Meuhlnir striding into the room, followed by the other Isir.

Sif wore a wide grin. "My favorite is Ednlinkr."

"Oh, no," muttered Meuhlnir.

"What does that mean, Auntie Sniffles?" asked Sig.

"It means 'the big-headed.'" Everyone laughed at that.

"Well, technically, it means 'the one with the big forehead,'" murmured Pratyi.

"Back to pedantry, Husband?" asked Freya with a hint of acid in her voice.

"Did I speak aloud?" he asked Mothi.

"Don't worry, Hank. These nicknames are just something that someone of your and my caliber has to endure. Admiration of the common man and all that."

Veethar snorted and set off another round of laughter.

I was glad to see the others falling back into familiar routines. "Speaking of big heads, did you run across Althyof?"

"Might as well ask if the sun noticed a firefly as it passed," said Meuhlnir.

"Boo," said Pratyi.

Meuhlnir cast a rueful look at Freya. "Can you yell at your husband more? He's getting mouthy again."

"Leave me out of this," said Mothi.

Meuhlnir let out a gusty sigh and turned on his son. "How long are you grounded for again?"

Mothi smiled. "Four hundred years? Five? Who can keep track?"

"We'll make it an even six hundred in that case."

"Fine, fine," said Mothi around a mouthful of smoked venison.

"And leave some food for the rest of the Isir!"

"I have to eat fast, or Piggy-Sig will eat it all."

"As if," said Sig in a voice that dripped scorn.

Again, the room filled with laughter—even the Alfar joined in—and it warmed my heart. I caught

Jane staring around the table too, her gaze bouncing from Frikka to Sif to Yowrnsaxa to Freya and back again. She caught me looking at her and wrinkled her nose at me, and I grinned at her like a love-struck idiot. Her eyes drifted past my shoulder and locked onto something.

I turned and saw nothing of interest at first, but the fire guttered, then blazed as if there were a strong wind. The flames leapt and danced for a moment, before the fire went dark, along with the torches and braziers hanging from the walls of the great hall. The room plunged into darkness.

"*Lyows*!" yelled Freya, and the big room filled with bright white light.

A woman stood in the middle of the fire pit, where the flames had leapt and cavorted moments before, long blonde hair cascading down from her bowed head. I stood, almost overturning the bench, and jerked Kunknir and Krati out of their holsters.

It was the woman I knew as Liz Tutor—the Dark Queen, the Black Bitch...*Hel*.

Her head snapped up, gaze locking on mine, a sneer on her lips. "Pathetic," she whispered.

"Sister! You are not welcome here," hissed Freya.

Hel threw back her head and laughed. "The moment I need your permission to do *anything*, let alone visit my own palace in my own capital city, *teekur*, I hope someone kills me."

Pratyi lurched up from where he still sat, eyes blazing. "Don't you call her that! That is *your* nickname!"

"Ah, another relic heard from. Will you sing us a song, poet?" Hel's eyes tracked down the table, lingering on Sif before moving on and freezing when her gaze rested on Meuhlnir. "*You*," she muttered.

"*Me*," Meuhlnir agreed, mocking her tone. "Look, here's the hammer you gave me." He whipped the hammer forward, underhand, and it whistled across the room and passed through Hel's head.

She laughed and pointed at him. "Still slow, still stupid, I see. I'm not *there*, you great idiot. You can't touch me, and luckily for you, I can't touch you."

Meuhlnir smiled, but it was ugly, cold. "Can't blame me for trying, though, can you?"

Hel rolled her eyes and shook her head. "I can blame you for many things, and I do." Her gaze continued around that side of the table, stopping on Sig. "Oh, look, it's family time! How fun!"

Sig looked at me but kept his lips pressed shut.

"Nothing to say, little son of Hank? Just as well, you aren't very smart."

"Fuck you, you *bitch*!" snapped Jane.

"Ah, another quarter sings forth." Hel's gaze snapped to my wife's. "And how are you, Jane?" Her gaze whipped across Jane's form and settled on the hand on which she wore the platinum ring Althyof had enchanted for her. "Ah! How cute. Tell me, woman, do you love your crippled husband that much that you will die with him? Because that's what that trinket means—when he dies, you die."

"I know," said Jane.

Hel shrugged. "How predictable. And *boring*." Her gaze moved past Jane and seemed to stutter across the Alfar's forms. "Who's with you? Who else have you brought into this, Cripple?"

Yowtgayrr shook his head, putting his finger to his lips.

"Your insanity is showing…uh, what should I call you?" I asked. "Black Bitch seems most appropriate."

Her eyes snapped to mine, and she took a step forward, her feet passing right through the stones lining the edge of the fire pit. "You be *careful*, Cripple. There's more I can do to you, even at this distance."

"Want to bet?" asked Freya in snow-capped tones. "This is now *my house*, sister."

Hel laughed. "Well, in that case, *thank you* for the invitation. It was so nice of you, *Sister*." The Dark Queen walked forward, and Mothi and I lurched backward so she couldn't touch us. She continued as if we didn't exist, her eyes locked to Freya's. Hel didn't stop until she stood in the center of the table, various dishes and pitchers of mead seeming to poke out of her body, her legs invisible beneath the table. "I should have killed you when you didn't support me. You are such a disappointment, little sister. Father would cry to learn what you've become."

"Being called a disappointment by you is the greatest praise I can think of," snapped Freya. "Father would have hated to see what you've become."

"Good thing he's dead then," said Hel with a cruel twist to her lips.

"Well, isn't this fun?" asked Meuhlnir. "Are you just here to charm us with your wit, or do you have something to say?"

Hel glanced at him with mild annoyance. "Never stop being smug, Meuhlnir. It suits you." She whirled to face me and stood stone-still for the space of five breaths. "This all started with *you*!" she spat at me.

"Oh, I don't know—"

"No, this all started with your depravity," jeered Sif. "We should have killed you."

"Aw, Sif, you wound me. Shall we not play dolls together anymore?"

Sif shook her head and turned her back, angry tears shimmering in her eyes. "What happened to you?"

"I grew up. Why haven't you?"

"You never answered me," I interrupted.

"What?" She looked at me with scorn. "Answered you what?"

"So, my opinion is that I should call you the Black Bitch. How's that sound to you?"

Her eyes narrowed to slits, and her nostrils flared. "Be careful," she whispered.

"Here's an idea," I said. "You say whatever you've come to say and then get the fuck out of here, so we can get on with our business—which is getting close enough to you that I can put a bullet between your fucking eyes." Sig gaped at me, open-mouthed.

Hel glared at me, her expression twisted with loathing. "Fine," she snapped. "Vowli says your presence here has caused too much of a distraction. He urged me to come tonight, to...*negotiate* peace, so *we* can get on with our business. We will restore the *preer,* and you and your stupid little family can go back to your paltry lives on Mithgarthr."

I pursed my lips and stroked my goatee, pretending to think about it. "I'll tell you what..." I started but let my voice trail away.

"So? Tell me!" Hel stomped her foot like a five-year-old.

"When you can restore the *people* you killed in Mithgarthr, I'll consider leaving you alone. No, on second thought, reincarnate everyone you've killed, everyone Luka and Vowli killed, and I'll think about only locking you away in a deep hole for the rest of time, rather than spraying your brains on whatever's behind you."

She smiled a slow smile with one side of her mouth. "I told him you would—"

"*Get out of here, you miserable bitch*!" I screamed. "Haven't you figured it out yet? Where is your vaunted intellect? Let me spell it out: We don't give a *shit* what you propose."

She laughed, her gaze sliding around the table. "Good," she crooned. "Good. We will meet in battle—"

"Oh, shut up!" I snapped. "Here's something I've learned since I followed you and the dog-faced boy to Osgarthr. Are you listening?"

"Tell me. What have you—"

"*Kverfa*!" I shouted, and her eyes popped big and round before she disappeared. Behind me, the fire roared back into existence as though trying to make up for lost time.

"Nice pronunciation," said Pratyi in the silence that followed. He walked around the table to stand next to Freya, his arm around her trembling shoulders.

Mothi put a finger in his ear and made a show of wriggling it around, face scrunched up. "Yes, definitely well said, Kuhtlunkr."

I turned to Meuhlnir.

He shrugged. "It means 'one who yells.'"

I rolled my eyes and sat down with a thump, shoving Kunknir and Krati back into their holsters. "Awesome."

"Dad, you *cursed* at her. You told me never to curse at a lady."

"She's no lady," said Yowrnsaxa.

"Well," said Freya with forced levity. "Let's get back to our dinner."

"I seem to have lost my appetite," said Meuhlnir. "*Aftur*," he muttered, and his hammer came spinning back to his hand.

"Me, too," said Sif, her eyes on her lap.

"Let's not let my sister ruin our evening," said Freya with sadness in her eyes.

"I'm sorry, dear one," said Frikka. "It's hard to see her as she has become. So hateful."

"Do you think it's easy for me?" demanded Freya, tears brimming in her eyes. She shook her head and dashed out of the room.

"Now, we could have handled that better," muttered Yowrnsaxa.

Anger twisted Pratyi's face into ugly lines. "Her damn, *damn* sister!" he hissed. "Will she never be free of her?" He stood. "I'll go see to her."

"No, Pratyi," said Sif. "Let us go." The three former *Trohtninkar Tumuhr* stood and, after a moment, so did Jane. The four women followed Freya out of the room.

"It's the same every time that damn woman speaks to her," muttered Pratyi. "The Dark Queen knows what Freya sacrificed for her." Meuhlnir cleared his throat and looked down at his hands. "Oh, we know you don't think she did enough, but she did what she could!"

Meuhlnir met the other man's gaze. "I didn't say anything, Pratyi."

"You didn't have to." Pratyi got up and stormed out into the courtyard.

Meuhlnir sighed and shook his head. "Some wounds never heal," he muttered.

Veethar stood and followed Pratyi outside.

"If you are still hungry, Sig, you better eat up," I said, but my son only shook his head, a forlorn expression on his face.

"Why is she so...so...*hateful?*" he asked.

"Because, Sig, she is broken inside," said Mothi.

"One thing's certain," said Meuhlnir. "She knows we are here."

"Yes," I said. "And she'll no doubt have the exits of the city watched."

"And harass us every step of the way." Mothi shook his head. "That'll make for a fun trip."

FOURTEEN

The next morning, we awoke to the wonderful smell of fried ham and eggs. The rooms Freya and Pratyi had provided our party opened onto the great hall, so as soon as we were decent, Jane and I stepped out, sat down, and dug in.

Veethar and Meuhlnir sat across from us, each intent on a bowl of something that looked like steaming mud. Of our hosts and the others, there was no sign.

"Early birds?" I asked between mouthfuls.

Veethar glanced at me and turned his gaze back to his mud, or whatever it was.

Meuhlnir swallowed and took a drink. "No birds," he said. He pointed at his bowl with his spoon. "It's a mixture of—"

"No, like the expression…you know, the early bird gets the worm?"

Veethar shook his head without looking up. "All birds eat worms," he muttered.

"Oh," grunted Meuhlnir with an amused glance at Veethar. "The women are still sleeping or doing whatever woman-thing they do in the morning."

"I can see why they threaten to beat you all the time," said Jane with a quirky smile.

"They do that because my prettiness leaves them in a state of exultant awe, and they don't want anyone to know."

"Ah," said Jane. "Good to know." She looked around the hall. "Are Mothi and Sig outside?"

Veethar nodded and spooned another glop of the foul-looking stuff from his bowl into his mouth.

"They were leaving as I came out," said Meuhlnir. "Boys will be boys."

"Could… I mean, given last night, could that be dangerous? Sig running around Suelhaym?"

"Mothi is with him," said Meuhlnir with a shrug. "And in any case, I don't think the Black Queen is prepared to act at this moment."

Jane nodded.

"But she knows where we are," I said. "And that's not good."

"No," said Veethar.

"I gave this some thought last night. We will need to evade her watchers as we did before we traveled to Piltsfetl to rescue Jane and Sig."

"Another glamor? Would that work twice?"

Meuhlnir shrugged but looked uncomfortable. "Who can say? But letting her maintain such an advantage is sheer folly."

"Agreed. We don't need more sea dragons following us. I wish I had any idea how we could pull it off."

"It's good I came along, then," boomed Mothi as he came through the door.

"Oh, yes," said Meuhlnir. "We need someone to wash dishes."

"I'll wash you, old man. But, hey, if you don't want to hear the answer to your dilemma, I can go back outside and teach Sig more curse words in the *Gamla Toonkumowl*."

"You better not be teaching him to curse," said Jane.

Mothi shrugged. "All boys curse."

"And all mothers kick the asses of those who teach their boys to curse in the *Gamla Toonkumowl*, big-ass axes or not.

"What's the solution, Mothi?" I asked with a wry grin.

"Lottfowpnir, here," he said, stepping aside and ushering the karl inside the great hall. "If you recall, he and his father deal in textiles, shipping goods to and fro along the coast."

"Of course," muttered Veethar.

"Ah, that may be the first good idea you've thought of before I did, Son," said Meuhlnir.

Mothi scoffed, grinning and rolling his eyes.

"Greetings again, Yarls," said Lottfowpnir. "Mothi has said you want to leave town unseen. I believe I can help with that."

"Before you say any more," I said, holding up my hand. "You should know what you are up against. The Dark Queen, herself, is the one we need to evade. She knows we are in Suelhaym—in this house—and she knows where we're going. She won't look kindly on you or your family if you help us."

Lottfowpnir shrugged. "We are beneath her notice."

"Not if you help us," warned Meuhlnir. "The woman holds many a grudge."

"She's an evil woman," said Lottfowpnir and then he paled as if he just remembered we were all yarls. "If you'll pardon me for saying so. She'll manufacture a grudge if it suits her, so I might as well act as I see fit."

"Well said."

"How do we do it?" I asked.

"I have a caravan leaving today. We can hide most of you in the carts until we are well outside the city. We can put your horses in the traces, and no one will be the wiser."

"I'm not sure those horses will appreciate—"

"I'll handle it," said Veethar. "They will do as I ask."

"Has anyone found Althyof yet?"

"He stumbled in around dawn. Drunk." Meuhlnir hooked his thumb toward a room near the door. "That's his."

"At least we won't have to put on a search," I sighed. "Can you accommodate all twelve of us? Is the caravan large enough?"

"There will be fourteen," said Freya from the doorway to the kitchens. "Pratyi and I are coming along, as well."

Meuhlnir and Veethar glanced at each other but said nothing.

"We *are* coming, Meuhlnir."

"Freya, I never said otherwise."

"Well…good. We're packing now. How soon do we leave?"

Meuhlnir arched an eyebrow at Lottfowpnir. "At your convenience," the karl said.

Meuhlnir nodded. "And how do we get from the palace to your caravan?"

"My father owns a warehouse close by. With Lady Freya's permission, I will send carts to pick up linens and rugs, as if you were sending them out for cleaning. From there—"

"No, that won't do," said Freya.

"It's for show, Lady Freya. You won't—"

"No!" she snapped. "My sister would see through that in half a breath."

Meuhlnir quirked his eyebrow at her. "What *wouldn't* she see?"

"Instruct your caravan to stop here on their way out of town. I will make substantial purchases—

enough that the fourteen of us will fit in the space left by what I buy."

"Uh… Yes, Lady," said Lottfowpnir.

Freya tossed a purse to him, and from the look of it, it was heavy with coin.

"No need to pay, Lady. Have your thralls return the goods to the warehouse as soon as we've left the city." He made as if to toss the purse back, but Freya held up her hand.

"No. Take the silver. We will keep what I purchase. There's no reason for your business to suffer losses over this."

"That's unnecessary, Lady. We—"

"You will accept my payment," she said in a tone that brooked no further arguments.

"Thank you, Lady Freya," said the karl.

"Good. How soon can the caravan be here? I still need to pack a few things, and I will need time to make my selections."

"I can have it here within the hour."

"Do that," she said and turned back toward her quarters.

It took five hours for Freya to pick her goods, and Yowrnsaxa pitched in by buying bolts of light linen that Freya would store for her until we returned from *Kleymtlant*. Sif spent the time buying specialized supplies for her medical bag and mixing a batch of the concoction she promised would work better than my methotrexate. In the end, we had enough room in the carts for comfort. Lottfowpnir's men stacked the remaining bundles of clothes and tapestries to form a small room at the bottom of each cart. Our packs and gear took two carts. We piled in, two to a cart, and the caravanners stacked bolts of woven cloth across the top of the hidden place, then put more bundles of clothing on top.

The cart Jane and I shared lurched into motion, the wooden axles beneath us groaning under the weight. It was bizarre, riding tucked down inside, unable to see our progress with our own eyes, and before long, the heat and the gentle rocking of the cart lulled me to sleep.

I awoke when the cart ground to a stop. I was sweating and parched. By the groggy look on Jane's face, I imagined her head felt as stuffed and achy as my own. My knees and elbows had stiffened due to the cramped circumstances. Above us, bundles and the bolts of cloth were removed, and blessedly sweet, cool air flooded into the small space.

"You survived," said Lottfowpnir.

"Had a nice nap, too," said Jane, climbing out of the cart. I followed her out, trying to keep my groans to myself.

The caravan's carts were parked in a circle, with the horses tied to a line stretched between two trees outside the camp. Thralls were busy building a fire and others unloaded the cook's cart, setting up a folding table and benches that could fold flat.

"Quite an operation," I said, pointing with my chin at the table and chairs.

"Travel is no reason to be uncomfortable," said Lottfowpnir with a grin. He and his men moved to the next cart in line and shuffled the bundles around to allow the cart's secret occupants to get out.

"Did you have any trouble?" I asked.

"Trouble? No. I spotted a large number of *tretyidnfukl* on the outer wall of Suelhaym, but none of them followed us."

"You spotted a large number of what?" asked Jane.

"*Tretyidnfukl*. They are small flying creatures that look a bit like a miniature dragon, but act more like eagles or hawks, hunting small game and rodents."

"Is that unusual, that they should roost on the walls of Suelhaym?"

"Yes, it is," said Pratyi, helping Freya out of the cart behind ours. "They are territorial by nature, and solitary. We may see one flying high overhead, but they almost never come close to the town."

"The Dark Queen?"

Pratyi spat over the outside edge of the cart. "Yes. She can influence creatures—"

"Like sea dragons, yeah, we learned that not long ago."

Pratyi nodded, a grave expression on his face. "It's probably how she knew you had arrived at the palace. No one would think to notice *tretyidnfukl* flying high overhead."

"We should have," grumbled Meuhlnir, climbing out of his own cart. "She used similar tactics during the war."

"Yes," said Freya. "She succeeded that time, too."

Meuhlnir looked away and walked toward the fire.

I followed him and stood next to him, though standing in the heat of a blazing fire was the last thing I wanted. "Do I sense an issue between Freya and Pratyi and the rest of you?" I whispered.

Meuhlnir grunted, wearing an expression as if he'd eaten something sour. "Can't discuss it here," he whispered back. "But think back on Kuhntul's warning."

I looked at him askance. "Betrayer?" I whispered.

His gaze flickered to mine and away. "We'll find time to talk later."

"How do we know that the Dark Queen isn't watching us now?" I asked in normal tones.

"She's limited by the creatures she co-opts. If the *tretyidnfukl* didn't suspect the caravan—didn't follow it—the Dragon Queen has no idea where we are. She's not omnipotent, though she does a good job of appearing so."

I nodded. "So we're okay? Until she spots us again?"

Meuhlnir nodded and stretched his lower back, his vertebrae crackling. "No more hiding in the carts."

"Good," I said. "I'd never have thought I'd look forward to spending a day astride Slaypnir's back, but after today…"

"Yes," said Meuhlnir. "Perspective is everything."

Once everyone had disembarked from their carts, we stood around watching Lottfowpnir's crew setting up a comfortable looking campsite, complete with chairs near the fire and large tents for us to sleep in.

We sat at the table, to a chorus of groans, and the thralls began to lay out the meal. We dug in as if we had done more than lie in the back of a cart all day, and it was good, but nothing compared to Yowrnsaxa's camp cooking.

Lottfowpnir's crew ate in silence—awed by the presence of so many Isir. They ate with none of the banter I'd expected, often staring surreptitiously at one of the Isir women, Jane included. After catching me watching them, Mothi caught my eye and smirked.

"So, Aylootr...any plans for the evening?" he asked. "Breaking the legs of people ogling your wife, maybe?"

"Why, do yours need breaking?" I asked, mimicking his tone. After that exchange, the thralls kept their gazes on their plates.

The sun set while we were eating, leaving us bathed in the gloom of early evening. Lottfowpnir stood. "Guests, would you join me by the fire?"

We moved to the fire and sank into the folding wooden chairs that the thralls had set up earlier. They were something akin to Adirondack chairs, and as such, were comfortable, but I didn't think I'd ever get back out of mine.

It was a warm evening, made even warmer by the blazing fire, but it wasn't uncomfortable. We sat in companionable silence for a while before Lottfowpnir cleared his throat. "Yarl Aylootr, it is common practice in these caravans to pass the evening with stories. Would you tell us a story of Mithgarthr?"

"Didn't we agree you would call me Hank?"

Lottfowpnir glanced at his thralls but nodded. "Yes. Forgive me."

"What kind of story? A myth? Something from my life? What would you like to hear?"

Lottfowpnir shook his head.

"I could tell you a tale of my ancestors. It involves a rich king, a young hero, a demon, and the demon's mother."

"Ug, Dad. Beowulf? Really?"

I shrugged. "Do you have a better idea?"

"Aylootr, tell us about something from your life there," said Mothi.

One of the horses screamed before I could speak, and, in the space of a breath, they were all squealing. Something growled in the darkness beyond the horses. I'd grown up with dogs, and as an adult had raised several Rottweilers and the growl that came out of the darkness sounded big and angry.

Veethar was already moving, ducking under the tongue of the cart near the horses. I struggled up and out of the chair, along with everyone else. Sig started toward the carts, and I pointed at him. "No, sir. Don't you dare." He looked at me, a blush creeping up his cheeks, but he kept his mouth shut.

I strode out of the circle of firelight, awkwardly climbing over the tongue of the cart Veethar had ducked under. There was a scent in the air—something wild, something predatory with a distinct charnel edge.

The cart horses were squealing, tugging against the high line that held them, at the edge of panic. My hand dropped to the butt of Kunknir, and my mind inexorably brought up the ever-diminishing number of rounds I had left for the pistol. Until we opened the *preer* again, those rounds were the last rounds in the universe.

Slaypnir stood tall amongst the panicking cart horses, head up, nostrils flared. He stared at a point in the darkness, blowing hard through his nostrils. He pawed at the ground and swished his tail. Skaytprimir snorted next to him, something I'd never heard him do unless he was running full tilt.

"What is it?" I hissed.

Veethar, standing next to the horses, shook his head. His hand rested on the hilt of his sword, but his lips moved without sound.

"*Au noht*," I said, remembering that first fight against the harriers with Meuhlnir's family. During that fight, Yowrnsaxa had said the words, and like that night, a cold, soft pressure encircled my head, and my eyes began to sting and water. But after I wiped away the water, I could see as if it were daylight.

I looked where Slaypnir was staring. A huge, yellow-eyed canine shape stood in the trees fifty yards away. Its pelt was shaggy and black, and its tail was rigid and straight up in the air. Its eyes tracked to mine, and when our gazes met, the thing snarled deep in its throat.

It *looked* like a wolf, but it was too big to be one. Its shoulder was as high as my waist, and it appeared to be close to three hundred pounds. It was thin-hipped, but wider in the chest, with long, narrow legs. Its ears laid back against its skull, and its lips curled, showing its long fangs.

"It's a wolf," I whispered. At the sound of my voice, the wolf stepped forward, stiff-legged and snarled louder.

"Yes," said Veethar. "And no."

"Bring spears," called Lottfowpnir. "Yarl Aylootr says it's a wolf, and where there's one, there's another." Thralls bustled out of the camp, bearing spears and shields, and the wolf glanced at them but snapped its eyes back to mine. It took another threatening step toward me, growling all the while.

I put my hand on Kunknir, and the wolf's eyes followed my movement. I couldn't afford to go around spending bullets as if they were plentiful. Only about fifty rounds remained for Kunknir and a little more than that for Krati. "We can't let it get at the horses."

"No," said Veethar.

Meuhlnir, Mothi, and Pratyi came to stand nearby, and I didn't see them, but I knew my Alfar *tutha verntar* had to be close by. "How do you fight a wolf?" I asked.

"Your guns won't be effective?" asked Mothi.

"Ammunition is…scarce."

"Lottfowpnir has the right of it in that case," said Meuhlnir. "Spears."

While we spoke, the wolf's eyes danced from one to another, following whoever was speaking. Its growling was a constant undercurrent of our words.

I stepped forward and raised my arms. "Get out of here!" I yelled at maximum volume. The wolf tensed, and its growls turned into snarls, but it didn't back off. "Go on! Get moving!" I shouted, using my Cop-voice and putting as much volume into it as I could. The wolf's tail dropped until it was horizontal and held stiff. On a whim, I snarled back it.

"Yarl Aylootr!" called Lottfowpnir.

I glanced in his direction, and he tossed me a spear. It was six feet long and tipped with a nasty-looking barbed metal blade. I caught it but fumbled it a moment before getting a good grip. I lowered the spear to point at the wolf. "Get gone while you still have a choice!" I yelled.

The snarling wolf took a stiff-legged step to the side.

"That's right! Go on!"

The wolf's snarl deepened, and the beast crouched, like a Rottweiler who was about to jump.

"This isn't—" As soon as I spoke, the wolf hurled itself through the air, straight at my throat, mouth wide.

I didn't know how to use a spear, but instinct took over. I planted the butt of the spear in the ground at my feet, angling the point up to catch the leaping wolf on its tip. The weight of the beast buckled the spear's haft, but not before the wolf impaled itself on the blade. Even so, the weight of the huge wolf slammed into me, sending me reeling to the ground, the wolf on top of me. It was still growling deep in its chest, and it was snapping its teeth, but its movements were weak and getting weaker by the second.

The others rushed forward, kicking the wolf off me. "Are you injured?" asked Mothi.

"Sif, get your bag!" yelled Meuhlnir at the same time.

"No, I'm fine," I said. "Not a scratch."

The wolf lay to the side, its flanks heaving as it tried to breathe. Blood trickled out of its maw and pooled beneath its chest. Even dying, its yellow eyes tracked my every movement.

"This is strange behavior for a wolf," I muttered.

"That's no wolf, Aylootr," said Mothi. "That is a *varkr*. See the size of it?"

"What is a *varkr* if not a wolf?" I murmured.

"It's related to a wolf," said Mothi. "But it's different."

"Think of it as a primal wolf," murmured Veethar. "An ancient species from the start of time."

"A primal wolf? A *dire wolf*?"

Mothi shrugged. "It's a *varkr*."

"Are all *varkr* as aggressive as this one? A wolf should have run away when I yelled at it."

"Why?"

"I'm bigger, louder. Scarier."

Mothi shrugged. "Well, this is a *varkr*, not a wolf. They don't run, they attack."

"Now you tell me."

Mothi grinned and slapped me on the shoulder, and I winced.

Something moved in the underbrush beyond the dying *varkr*. The brush parted, and two *varkr* pups stumbled out and trotted to the adult, sniffing the air as they came.

"Brave little guys, aren't you?" I said. One pup stopped and stared up at me, challenge in the lines of his body. He growled at me a moment and continued to the adult's body. The pups sniffed the dead *varkr* before throwing back their heads and yowling as if they were grieving, and it broke my heart. "Come away from there, pups," I crooned. "Lottfowpnir, may I have the leftover scraps of meat from dinner?" I asked.

The karl squinted at me, his head tilting to the side, and I thought he would refuse me for a moment. He might have, I suppose, except for the ironclad rules of the caste system. In the end, he snapped his fingers, and a thrall darted off, returning a moment later with a plate full of gristle and meat scraps.

I nodded my thanks to Lottfowpnir and bent to the task of winning the pups over. "This may take a while," I said over my shoulder. "And will be easier if there's nothing to distract or startle them." They left me then, walking back into camp, all except Veethar, who stood still as a statue, watching me.

The two pups watched me with the intensity of a lion watching a gazelle. I picked up a strip of meat and tossed it in front of them, far enough from the adult *varkr* that they would have to leave its—*her*— side. "Come on, fellas. It's yummy meat."

"Give them a moment," whispered Veethar. "They are uncertain."

I nodded and waited, letting the aroma of the meat do the seducing. Though they were pups, and young ones by the state of their fur, the young *varkr* stood about a foot at the shoulder already. The larger of the two waddled a short distance from his mother's body, eyes glued to mine the whole time as if he were daring me to move.

When he reached the meat, he stood for a moment, staring at me before the puppy in him took over. He dropped his front shoulders almost to the ground, wagged his tail, and yipped at the piece of meat. After a moment, he pounced on it, grabbing it in his teeth and shaking his head.

The other pup gave their mother one last look and trotted over, looking at me with an expectant expression on its little face. I got another strip of meat and tossed it at the puppy's feet. The pup sat and cocked his head to the side, staring at the piece of meat. His brother swooped in and grabbed the meat and ran a few steps away to eat it.

"Hey there, Greedy, there's plenty to go around," I crooned and tossed another piece of meat to the smaller pup.

"You will need names for these two," whispered Veethar. "Keri means 'the greedy one' in the *Gamla Toonkumowl.*"

"Keri," I said. "I like it. What do you say, little fella? Is Keri a good name for you?" The pup who'd stolen his brother's meat looked at me and quirked his head to the side. His little tail came up and wagged back and forth a time or two. "There it is, then."

"Yes," murmured Veethar.

The other puppy finished its morsel of meat and sat back, staring at me. After a moment, he raised a paw and scratched at the air. "Hungry, are you?" I crooned. I tossed him another bit of meat, and he fell on it like he was starving. I glanced at Veethar, who squatted, his face filled with delight. "Well, Veethar, how do I say 'hungry one?'"

"He's not hungry—he's ravenous. Fretyi means 'the ravenous one.' I'd use that."

"Well, little guy? Is Fretyi your name?" Fretyi yipped twice and bounded over to me, sniffing the air, looking for more meat. I put my hand out and let the *varkr* pup sniff my fingers. He wagged his tail and nuzzled my hand. "Amazing he's willing to be my friend after I killed his mother."

"His memory of her is already fading. They are young, and now that you are providing for them, in their eyes, you are their parent."

"Thanks for not saying I'm their mother. How smart are these *varkr*?" I kept doling out the meat, keeping my two new dependents happy.

"They make excellent companions when captured at a young enough age. After they have developed to a certain point, they will always be wild and unpredictable. These two are young enough."

I glanced at him as that was the most I'd ever heard him say at one time. He smiled and shrugged, and his eyes drifted back to the animals. He moved his lips in silence, and the air had the heavy feel to it I associated with Meuhlnir's *vefnathur strenki*. "These two are young enough. They are binding their spirits to your own, Hank Jensen. See that you are worthy of it."

"I will." I turned back to the pups, trying to entice Keri closer by tossing his chunks of meat closer and closer to my feet. Fretyi had moved to sit next to me, leaning against my leg and taking meat from my other hand.

"Dad?" called Sig from the camp.

Keri crouched, ears back and growled his puppy best. "It's okay, Keri. That's your big brother."

"I'll go," said Veethar, rising to his feet and walking away.

"Now, little dorks, let's get back to making your tummies fat." I tossed more meat toward Keri, getting him a few steps closer each time.

FIFTEEN

I f I'm honest, I'd forgotten what life with a puppy was like…and now I had two. We'd slept with them inside our tent, curled around our feet, and early in the morning while it was still dark, they reminded us that they were there. Jane gave me her patented "I'll kill you for this" smile and tried to take the two puppies out of the tent, but they wouldn't have it. I creaked and groaned my way up off the ground and took the little bastards outside. They were hungry, so I fed them more of the meat scraps from the night before. After they ate, they wanted to pounce around at the shadows of the trees in the moonlight, rather than do their business and let me get back to sleep.

I took them outside the circle of carts, around to the opposite side of the camp from the horses, and found two sticks. We invented a new game: I threw the sticks, and they stared at me a moment before attacking my feet. They frolicked and romped, growling and yipping at the shadows, never straying more than a few feet from me. It seemed to me that they'd already grown an inch.

When the black shadow detached itself from the trees on the other side of the road, Keri and Fretyi came to me and stood, one on either side, tails erect, ears up, and eyes glued to the black shape. Growls rumbled from deep in their chests.

"Are you going to tell the Dragon Queen where we are again?" I asked.

Kuhntul solidified out of the shadows, a beautiful woman dressed in black armor and a black cloak. "Why do you accuse me of this?" she snapped, eyes blazing.

"The last time we met, we got a visit from her not two days later."

Kuhntul snorted. "Two days? If I were in league with the Black Bitch, she'd have found you that very night, back on the beach, and you'd never have seen me. I told you: I do *not* serve her. I serve the Nornir." She cocked her head to the side, and her pale green eyes roved my face. "You have eluded the Dragon Queen. For now, it remains to be seen if you will continue to do so or squander this advantage by acting the fool."

I sighed and bent to rub Keri and Fretyi behind their ears, trying to settle them down. "My pups don't seem to approve of you, Kuhntul."

"Animals," she said as if that explained everything. "Tell me, Tyeldnir. What is your plan? To where do you travel?"

"Why would I tell you? For all I know, you wish me harm."

She cocked her head again and gazed at me for a protracted moment, reminding me of the way the pups cocked their heads when I said a word they liked. "Why would you think that?"

I gestured at her armor, her cloak. "You are wearing black."

She shook her head, a wry smile dancing on her lips. "Do you accept everything your Isir cousins tell you?"

I shrugged and suppressed a sigh. "They know more about this place than I do. Who else should I listen to?"

She tossed her head. "A fair point, but they don't know everything." She ran a hand down her side. "I'm dressed this way because this is a mission of stealth. *At night*. I can hardly expect to go unnoticed if I flip around in white, can I?"

"What is it you want?" Keri and Fretyi couldn't be distracted from Kuhntul. Their eyes stuck to her as if she was a dangerous predator. Maybe she was.

"Why must I want something?"

"Because you're here. Again."

"I come as an advisor—an interested, but unattached advisor. I have nothing to gain, so my advice is clean, unfettered by personal desires." She arched her eyebrow at me. "Can your companions say the same? Any of them?"

"It's true that these Isir have an agenda, but that agenda coincides with my own."

"*Does* it, Tyeldnir?" She shifted her weight forward, and the two pups added a ragged note to their growls. Kuhntul glanced down at them and made a face. "Send these creatures away."

"I don't think they would go, even if I was willing to send them, which I'm not."

"The Tisir are above such low forms of life."

I chuckled. "Was that a pun?"

She looked at me, the skin between her eyebrows wrinkled. "Do you mock me?"

"No. You're floating in midair, and these two are a foot or so high. Above these low forms of life, indeed."

She eyed the *varkr* pups and drifted a few steps farther away. "The time of your betrayal approaches, Tyeldnir."

"I wish you wouldn't call me that," I snapped. "My name is Hank."

"Will you go to the executioner's block arguing about trivialities, or will you listen to my counsel?"

"What I will listen to are facts. No more riddles. If you have something to say, say it plain."

Kuhntul sighed and shrugged. "You demand plainness, here is plainness. You will be betrayed in your quest for control of the *preer*. The person who betrays you will be one of your party and the betrayal will come at a high cost."

"Tell me who the betrayer is."

"I can't—I do not know who it is. The Sisters refuse to disclose that. If someone in your party practices *saytr* or has the *syown*—"

"Wait. I know what *syown* is, but what is *saytr*?"

"The word means 'string magic,' but here it refers to string magic of prophecy."

"You know Frikka and Freya are members of my party. You know they practice prophecy."

She gazed at me, waiting.

"Now that we've established there are members of my party with the *syown* or who practice this *saytr*, what about it?"

"As I was saying, a *saytr* practitioner could cast an augury that could tell you the betrayer's name. Or someone with the *syown* might see it. You could kill the betrayer—"

"No."

"Come, now, Tyeldnir. You have killed men."

"Yes, in battle…when I have had no other choice. But killing in cold blood? An execution? No, that's not me."

She squinted at me for the space of three breaths and shook her head. "Such hollow distinctions, Tyeldnir."

"I won't murder anyone, *saytr* or *syown* notwithstanding."

She sucked in a breath, though I doubted she needed to do anything as pedestrian as breathing, and blew it out her nose. "At the very least, you could expel the person from the party—"

"Is that your goal with all this? To split us up?"

"Tyeldnir, I've already said why I am here. Why can't you—"

"And yet all you advise me to do involves killing a member of the party or sending someone away. That weakens us. Together, we are strong, and we've faced down the worst the Dark Queen has to offer. We—"

Kuhntul laughed, her cackle echoing down the road like the cries of carrion birds. "You've hardly seen the worst the Black Bitch can bring to bear. Haven't you been listening to the stories of your companions?"

Keri spun around and growled at something lost in the darkness behind me. "What is it, boy?"

"Nothing to fear," muttered Kuhntul. "It's your pet Tverkr."

Althyof stepped out onto the road, a dagger in either hand. He was chanting something too low for me to catch, his eyes welded on Kuhntul. I felt the heavy presence of the *strenkir af krafti* singing in the air, wrapping around me and the two pups.

"Oh, please, Althyof," said Kuhntul with a forbearing sigh. "You know your *triblinkr* can't stop me if my desire was to harm him. Why bother with this farce?"

Althyof finished his chant and stepped across the road. "So you keep telling me, woman, and yet my paltry abilities seem to keep working."

"I have no wish to hurt Tyeldnir," she said. "Nor his…*animals*. I guess your mastery of the *strenkir af krafti* will continue to be unchallenged by me. What is it you want here, Althyof?"

"Want? I want nothing, unlike *you*. Hank is an honorable man, who doesn't deserve the rank manipulation of your kind."

Kuhntul shook her head and gazed up at the stars. "What would I gain from such manipulation? Why would I invest such time? Why wouldn't I take whatever it is I wanted? None of you could stop me."

"*Your* mastery of the *strenkir af krafti* remains untested, woman. I beg you to try."

"Enough," I said. "This isn't getting us anywhere."

Kuhntul arched her eyebrow at Althyof. "No."

"Do you have more to say?"

She shook her head. "You've listened to my counsel. Act on it sooner rather than later."

A phrase uttered by an uncountable number of lawyers back home came to mind, and it was perfect. "I'll take it under advisement."

"Somehow I think that means you will ignore my advice."

Althyof chuckled. "You're not as dumb as you look."

She sighed and shook her head. "What must I do, Tyeldnir? What must I do to prove myself?"

"Well, to start, you can stop calling me that."

"And you can go back in time and stop yourself from manipulating the Tverkar into fighting in the war," said Althyof.

She laughed, but no amusement reached her eyes. She snapped her fingers and disappeared without even a pop.

"You two *really* don't get along," I said, feeling the weight of my illness like a mantle of stone.

"No, she's a duplicitous, double-dealing, deceitful, duplicitous—"

"You said that one already."

"Well, she's doubly duplicitous then." He glanced down at my hips. "You shouldn't be roaming around without your weapons, Hank. There are dangers here."

I shrugged. "A *varkr* already attacked me tonight. I figured my dance-card was full."

"I don't get that reference, but trust me, Hank, you are never safe here. Not until the Dragon Queen has been dealt with."

"Yeah, I don't need the reminder."

He pointed at my hips with one of his daggers. "Seems you do."

"Yeah, okay. I'll be more careful." I picked up another pair of sticks and threw them. Keri and Fretyi watched them fly, and as soon as the sticks hit the ground, they pounced on my ankles, one to a leg.

Althyof grinned, watching the pups worry at my feet. "You have the luck of an Alf, Hank." He looked up at me, and his face grew serious. "But that won't be enough to save you." He glanced away, shaking his head. "No, not enough. Tomorrow, ride by my side. I will begin to teach you the ways of the *runeskowld*."

My eyebrows shot up. "You told my son that no Isir had ever learned—"

"No, I said no Isir had ever *mastered* it. You may not either, though by my judgment you are the best of them." He glanced at my expression and laughed. "Relax, Hank. That isn't saying much." He squatted and stroked Fretyi's rump. The pup spun to face him, growling, and snapping. "Oh, he's a fierce one, isn't he?"

"I guess so."

Althyof stood up and glared at me. "Now, if you're done raising such a ruckus that no sane Tverkr could sleep, I'll go back to bed!" He whirled and stomped off, but not before I saw the twinkle of amusement in his eye. Fretyi stood, still as carved stone, and watched him, a low growl rumbling in his chest.

"Don't worry, pup-pup. He's not as cantankerous as he pretends to be. I trust him, and so can you." Althyof paused a moment, the flap to the tent he shared with the Alfar held open, but he didn't glance over. I had the impression that every word I said had carried to his ears. "But he *is* as ugly as a stump." Althyof chuckled and ducked inside, letting the tent flap fall closed behind him.

"You were never in danger, Hank," said Skowvithr's disembodied voice. "I was with you all along. Kuhntul would not brush aside my abilities as she thinks she could the Tverkr's."

"What, are you and Yowtgayrr standing watches now?" I asked the empty air, but there was no answer. Of *course* they were standing watches. I should have guessed they would be after the first meeting with Kuhntul. I picked up a stick and threw at the space the voice had come from. The puppies watched it arc through the air unobstructed, glanced at one another, and then attacked my feet. "Some watchdogs you two are turning out to be. We'll have to work on your situational awareness." Keri looked up at me and yipped before going back to trying to kill me from the ankles up.

The puppies weren't interested in going back to sleep, so I played with them until the sun cracked the horizon and announced the coming day. As if they had alarm clocks, Lottfowpnir's thralls awoke and climbed out of their tents, joking and teasing one another until they saw me and pulled on their professional faces. They set about getting the caravan ready to depart, feeding and caring for the horses, packing up supplies that wouldn't be needed during breakfast, and settling bundles in the carts, since we would ride our own horses that day.

Some were curious about the *varkr* puppies, others feared them. None of them wanted to approach, whether it was because of the wild puppies or because of me, I couldn't tell. They kept their heads down and worked.

Veethar was the first of the party to exit his tent, and he walked straight over and crouched beside me, holding out his hand. He uttered a low whistle, and Fretyi cocked his head and trotted over. Keri was still more cautious around others, but Fretyi seemed to have gotten over his natural wariness—at least of Veethar. The pup sprawled at his feet and rolled over for a belly rub, which Veethar seemed delighted to give. "They are in good health," he said.

"They should be after the amount of meat they wolfed down."

A small grin stretched Veethar's lips. "Wait a month or two."

"Have you had *varkr* before?"

He shook his head.

"Kuhntul dropped by again last night."

Moving slowly, Veethar turned his gaze to mine. He quirked his eyebrow, which, given I was speaking to Veethar, was like someone jumping up and screaming: "*What?*" I shrugged. "Same old thing. She wants me to get Frikka, Freya, or Yowrnsaxa to identify the betrayer. She thinks I should kill him. Or maybe her." I glanced at the tent Freya and Pratyi shared. "Althyof came out to play, though, and scared Kuhntul away."

Veethar nodded, eyes pensive, lips taut.

"What do you think about all this? Meuhlnir implied you were the expert on the Tisir."

Veethar shifted his weight and stared down at Fretyi, scratching the puppy's belly while Fretyi preened and rolled around. He made a non-committal sound.

"Do you think she's out to help us or drive us apart?"

Veethar rolled his shoulders. "You shouldn't worry about Freya."

"No? I got the feeling you and Meuhlnir don't trust her."

Veethar glanced at me, his pale blue eyes almost glowing with the intensity of his feelings. "You misunderstood."

"Okay," I said with a shrug. "I don't know the story, but I'll take your word for it. I have no reason to mistrust anyone in this camp."

Veethar nodded and patted Fretyi's tummy. "Good pup," he crooned. He stood with an economy of movement that I envied and turned away, walking over to the horses.

"Good talk," I muttered.

SIXTEEN

After everyone had performed their morning rituals, and we'd all eaten, the thralls hitched the cart horses to the wagons, and we saddled our mounts. Getting into the saddle was an adventure after the long night with too little sleep, but with Sif's ointment burning away on my skin, it was manageable.

The pups didn't approve of me being up there on Slaypnir, and by his twitching ears, Slaypnir didn't care much for the puppies yipping and whining around his hooves. "Sig, hand Fretyi up to me." I twitched my saddlebags around to the front and flipped one of them open.

"Uh... I don't think he wants me to."

"It's okay, Son, be calm and let him sniff your hand before you pick him up."

Sig followed my instructions, and not only did Fretyi sniff his hand, but he also gave him a lick and wagged his tail. Sig picked up the pup with a grunt. "Heavier than I figured he'd be." He held the pup up to his cheek and giggled like a boy five years younger when Fretyi licked his cheek and nuzzled him.

I took Fretyi when Sig handed him up and slid him butt-first into my saddlebag. "Now, do the same thing with Keri. He's a little more skittish, so don't make any sudden moves."

"Can Keri ride with me?" Sig asked.

"No, not today, Son," I said. "I have to balance the weight of the bottomless pit here." I scrubbed Fretyi behind the ears.

Sig got Keri in his arms after a bit of convincing and held him up to me. I put Keri in the other saddlebag, and Slaypnir turned back to scowl at me. I never knew horses could scowl, but Slaypnir left no doubt about it. I patted his neck to placate him. It was turning into a full-time job keeping all these animals happy.

Althyof walked his horse over. "Remember our discussion," he grumbled.

"I do."

"Hold back a little. What I have to teach is not for everyone."

I nodded, and we sat while the caravan rumbled out onto the stone roadway. Sig wanted to hang back, but I sent him ahead to tell Mothi a joke. After everyone else had left, it was Althyof, myself, and the Alfar.

Althyof scowled at them. "What I have to say to Hank is not for your ears."

Yowtgayrr looked at him and yawned as if bored by the Tverkr's words. "Where Hank goes, we go."

"Ride behind us and smell my farts, in that case. You can watch over him from there," snapped Althyof. He glanced at me and twitched his reins, and I did the same. Yowtgayrr and Skowvithr stayed a respectable distance behind us, but their eyes lingered on me all morning.

"I'm going to teach you the ways of the *runeskowld*. It won't be easy. It may be the hardest thing you've ever done—the most taxing mentally and physically. Are you ready? Will you commit yourself to the task?"

"Yeah," I said.

"Because if you don't or can't, there is every chance you will do yourself, or worse yet, *me*, significant harm. There are good reasons we don't teach this art to other races except in atypical situations."

"Have you ever taught anyone before me?"

"Tverkar, yes. Isir, no."

"But you are confident you can do it?"

"Of course," he snapped. "I'm the master here, Hank."

"No offense meant," I said.

He made a face and grumbled into his beard for a few steps of our mounts. "The Art isn't as simple as muttering words in an ancient tongue and concentrating on what you want to happen. Every Isir can do that, after all."

"Okay."

"Some think it's as easy as singing a tune, dancing a few steps, and what you want to happen, happens. It's not that easy."

"What in the history of time ever is?"

"Before we start the first exercise, ask whatever questions you may have."

I scratched my goatee. "What's the difference between what you do as a *runeskowld* and as an enchanter?"

"The medium. When I'm enchanting, I sing a *trowba,* and I inscribe the runes into the thing I'm enchanting. The runes bind the *trowba* to the item."

"I wondered about that."

Althyof glanced at me. "Well, now you know. Anything else?"

"Why are you called a *runeskowld* instead of something else? It doesn't seem you use runes except when you are enchanting."

"Ah, very preceptive…" He smiled at me. "…for a block of wood. Runes are also used in *trowba, triblinkr,* and *lausaveesa.*"

"But how can that be? You never write anything."

"Runes are not just marks on paper, Hank. I am in my most powerful state when I'm singing a *trowba* and accompanying it with a dance. Have you not noticed this?"

"I have, but I wondered if maybe it was a way to keep the rhythm."

Althyof smiled the way an indulgent parent smiles at a precocious child. "Well, it does help with that, especially in situations where your mind must do multiple things at once—"

"Multitasking," I grunted.

Althyof laughed. "Multitasking. I like that. Yes, the dance helps when you must multitask—singing the *trowba*, *stayba runana*, and fighting a dragon."

"*Stayba* what now?"

"*Stayba runana*—it means 'casting the runes.'"

"Well, that clears it up…"

"Don't be a smartass, Hank. *Stayba runana* is how we refer to using the runes without writing them down. It's the process of focusing on the rune or runes you need in your mind and casting them out into the world where their power can manifest."

"Wait a minute. You sing, dance, fight dragons, and imagine runes floating around you?"

"Yes." Althyof smirked. "Now you see why only Tverkar have mastered the art." He tapped his temple. "One must be gifted with a large mind that can run down multiple paths at once."

"Not to mention stubbornness."

Althyof's shoulders hitched up and down. "True."

"Okay, now I have to ask the obvious question."

Althyof waved his hand as if inviting me into his home.

"This seems like a lot of effort to go through to accomplish what the Isir do by...how did you put it...muttering words in an ancient language and imagining what they want to happen."

Althyof laughed, a great belly-shaking laugh. "And how many dragons have you seen bound by Isir? How many Isir *fly* those bound dragons?"

"A fair point," I said.

"And how many have made you things as powerful as the ring your lovely wife wears? How many Isir offered to bind her to your fate? How many offered to make her an Isir?"

"Wait a second...you made her into an Isir? With the ring's enchantment?"

Althyof rolled his shoulders in a kind of shrug. "As good as. Well? Tell me which of the Isir offered to do the same."

"Well, no one."

"And why?"

"I never thought about it."

"The reason is that *it is beyond* what is possible by *vefnathur strenki*—by *saytr*. I am not boasting, Hank. You have seen me in battle, singing a *trowba*, stepping the dance, and *stayba runana*, all while fighting, planning, defending myself, yes?"

I nodded, remembering the way he'd dispatched the white dragon at Veethar's estate.

"By comparison, what would it take to accomplish the same using the *Gamla Toonkumowl*?"

"I don't know."

"It is like comparing cooking one dish at a time over a single flame versus having separate heat sources for each pot—like the difference between one horse pulling a sledge to clear trees versus a caravan's worth of horses and men working to clear the same snarl of downed trees."

"Serial versus parallel."

"What?"

"Doing things one after another versus doing a bunch of things at the same time."

"Yes. The *trowba* has power, the dance also, and the runes most of all."

"Would it be possible to also *vefa strenki* while singing, dancing, and casting the runes?"

"I've never heard of it being tried, which is not to say it hasn't been. More?"

"No. Honestly, I don't know enough about what you do to know what I need to know."

"Based on that sentence alone, Hank, you should do well." He chuckled. "Okay, on to the basics. The first thing you need to know is that the sung or chanted part, that is the *trowba*, the *triblinkr*, or the *lausaveesa,* must be constructed a certain way. Each starts with the identification of the *runeskowld*. For example, each *lausaveesa* I chant begins with the phrase '*Yek air* Althyof *hoospownti runeskowld*' which identifies me. You would say '*Yek air* Hank *neelithi runeskowld*' which means 'I am Hank novice *runeskowld*.' Try it."

"*Yek air* Hank *neelithi runeskowld*. And yours identifies you as a master *runeskowld*?"

"Good. And you are correct, *hoospownti runeskowld* means master *runeskowld*. And while we sing or chant this line, it is important to cast a particular rune. This rune has various meanings, but in this context, it is a dedication, an introduction of sorts. This is the rune." Althyof chanted a short *lausaveesa* and lifted his hand. He drew in the air, and the rune appeared, glowing the same cadmium red that his daggers did when he fought. The rune looked like a diamond. "This rune is *Ingwaz,* and it simply means 'this is the beginning.' Do you understand?"

"Yes, chant my introduction and cast *Ingwaz.* Doesn't seem too hard."

Althyof scoffed. "Well, I would expect saying your name would be easy. The next phrase varies, depending on which effect you want. You would use *Mannaz* if you wanted an augmenting or supporting *kaltrar*." He drew in the air again, and the figure that emerged looked like two vertical lines connected at the top by a sideways X.

"What's a *kaltrar*?" I asked.

"It means 'spell' or 'incantation.' If you meant to do harm with your *kaltrar*, you would use *Laguz* or perhaps *Hagalaz*. This is *Laguz*," he said, drawing what looked like an arrow pointed upward, except the left-hand part of the tip was missing. "And this is *Hagalaz*." He drew two vertical lines in the air and connected them with a crossbar that slanted downward from left to right. It looked a little like a capital H, but for the slanted crossbar. "If you mean to do something for another, you would use *Gebo,* which means 'gift.'" He drew a capital X in the air. Do you understand?"

"I do," I said. "Are there only three possible runes for the second line?"

"For now," said Althyof with an air of mystery. "The simplest *lausaveesa* are only three lines long." He ticked off points on his finger. "*Ingwaz*, the defining rune—*Mannaz*, *Laguz*, *Hagalaz*, or *Gebo*—followed by a representation of what you want to happen, and finally, the closing rune, which is *Sowilo*, or 'success.'" He drew in the air again, this time drawing an S that looked like a childish lightning bolt.

"There's got to be more to it than that."

"Well, of *course* there is. Those are the runes you cast while incanting. The challenge comes from making each line start with the rune."

"What do you mean?"

"*Ingwaz* is equivalent to the letter I; *Mannaz*, M; *Sowilo*, S." He raised his eyebrows.

"I see. I am Hank novice *runeskowld*. Make me strong. Songs are cool."

Althyof nodded but frowned. "It is not a matter for joking, though, Hank. When you learned to *vefa strenki*, I assume you mispronounced words, or failed to focus your thoughts?"

"Sure," I said.

"And what happened?"

"Nothing. You must have what you want foremost in your mind like you do with the runes, I guess, and if—"

"Never make the mistake of assuming *vefnathur strenki* approaches the complexity of a *kaltrar*. When you incant as a *runeskowld*, if you fail, there is a backlash of energy. It may strike you; it may strike those around you."

"Ah," I said. "That sounds dangerous."

"It is, Hank, and I want to impress this on you. I *never* want you to practice the art when I am not with you. I will tell you when you've earned sufficient skill to chant simple *lausaveesa* on your own, and until I do, pretend you don't know how unless I am by your side."

"Okay," I said, trying to sound steady and brave, but with an icy knot of fear in my belly.

He squinted at me. "I see I've planted a seed of fear. That is good, Hank. Never let complacency grow there instead. Even I could break a *kaltrar* and suffer for it."

I nodded.

"Good. Now, let me teach you your first *lausaveesa*. How would it begin?"

"*Yek air* Hank *neelithi runeskowld.*"

"And which rune?"

I flashed him a crooked smile. "*Ingwaz.*" I drew it in the air, but no fancy cadmium red rune glowed there afterward.

"Good. The *kaltrar* is one of support, so what rune must we use?"

"*Mannaz.*" Again, I drew the rune, and again he nodded.

"If you were fluent, you could create a sentence for yourself, and one day, you will. For today, you will speak what I say."

"Does that mean, you can compose a *kaltrar* on the fly? You could make it up as you go?"

Althyof nodded. "*I* can, yes. *You* cannot. Not until I say." He bathed me with a grave stare.

I nodded.

"Good. The sentence I want you to memorize is: '*Mathur ayns ok yek thyowst*.' Repeat it."

"*Mathur ayns ok yek thyowst*."

"Yes. The next line requires you learn the rune *Eiwhaz*. It looks like this." He drew in the air, making a vertical line. At the top, he made a slanted line that hung off the right side of the line like the overhang of a house. At the bottom of the line, he made a line that slanted upward and to the left. "Do you have it?"

"*Eiwhaz*. Yes, I think so."

"No. You have it, or you do not. There is no 'think so.' Not in this."

"Okay, Yoda," I said with half a smile on my lips. Of course, Althyof didn't know what I was talking about. "Never mind, I understand. I have it."

"The line is: '*Iya tyefthu myer frith*.' Say it."

"*Iya tyefthu myer frith*."

"Draw *Eiwhaz*." I drew it in the air, and he nodded. "The last line comes with what rune?"

I fought the urge to sigh. I understood the danger, but it seemed pedantic to quiz me over and over. "*Sowilo*." I drew it.

He ducked his chin. "Last line. *Sintaplowth thehta puhlvun ok truchkma thath*."

I blew out a breath. "That's a doozy. *Sintaplowth theta puhlvun ok truckma thath*?"

"Almost. *Thehta*." He gestured at me.

"*Thehta*."

He nodded. "And *truchkma*."

"*Truchkma. Sintaplowth thehta puhlvun ok truchkma thath*."

"Yes, you have it now. Hank, this is a weak *kaltrar*, but even so, if it backfires, it will hurt."

I shrugged. "Althyof, if there's anything in this universe I'm used to, it's pain."

He squinted at me a moment and pointed to my saddlebags where Keri and Fretyi dozed, lulled by the conversation and the gentle, rocking pace of Slaypnir's walk. "Oh, I forgot them."

"I know, and you must never forget the danger to those around you. Pass them to one of the Alfar."

I nodded and waved Yowtgayrr forward. He came alongside, and I lifted the saddle bag and passed it to him. Keri squirmed, but his little eyes stayed closed. Yowtgayrr nodded and fell back.

"Tell me the runes, in order," demanded Althyof.

"*Ingwaz, Mannaz, Eiwhaz, Sowilo*."

"Good. To *stayba runana*, you must concentrate on the shape of the rune, draw it in your mind's eye. Don't force it to be any color just let it be whatever it wants to be."

"I'll try."

"Okay, I want you to chant the first line, while you cast *Ingwaz*. Go no farther. I will observe." He reined his horse to the other side of the road and waved at me with no little impatience.

I tried it, and a vague tickling of *something* flowed around me. Slaypnir snorted and flicked his ears back.

"Good," called Althyof. "Try the whole thing."

I took a deep breath and steeled myself against the possibility of pain. I recalled the shape of each rune, in the order they would fall during the incantation. After another deep, steadying breath, I spoke the words, casting the runes with the start of each phrase.

When I finished, nothing happened. I glanced at Althyof, tensing against the pain that might wash back on me. Althyof smiled. "How do you feel?" he asked, stepping his horse across the road to ride by my side again. "Physically, I mean."

That's when it hit me. "I feel fine! I mean, there aren't any of the aches and pains that exist even with the cloak. It's like... Is the curse gone?"

Althyof's smile faded a little. "It isn't gone, not for good. In fact, it will come back far too soon, I expect. I said this is the weakest *kaltrar* I can think of that has any meaning for you."

"But still! Does this mean I can lift the Black Bitch's curse?"

Althyof shook his head. "I'm afraid not. Curses don't work that way, and unfortunately, the Dragon Queen is not limited to mere *vefnathur strenki*. She was never taught, not by any Tverkar anyway, but she can do something that approaches *lausaveesa*. Her power is unschooled, untutored, but it's also indisputable." He shook his head again, avoiding my gaze. "I'm sorry, Hank, but the only way to lift the curse is to convince *her* to lift it."

Disappointment swept through me, but I wasn't surprised. Meuhlnir had told me almost the same thing. And, truth be told, I was...*used to it* was the wrong phrase, maybe *resigned* to it captured the way I felt. I tried for a smile and landed on something more akin to a drunken leer. "Ah well, easy come, easy go."

"The pain is back already?" Althyof asked.

"No, it's an expression. It means nothing easy to do is worth much in the long run."

"Ah." He nodded and looked ahead. "I want you to monitor yourself, Hank. When you first begin to experience the effects of the curse, tell me."

"Will I be able to use the *lausaveesa* again? When the pain comes back?"

"Yes, you *could*. I wouldn't advise it on your first day, nor will I allow it. You must build your skills slowly."

I thought of the years I'd spent building my physical strength—all the hours in the gym, all the slow progression from one weight to a little more weight, from ten reps to twelve. It made sense. "I get it."

"You won't argue? You won't try anyway?" Althyof stared at me with assessing eyes.

"No, I won't. I'm old enough to recognize my own foolhardy impulses."

Althyof smiled crookedly and waggled his eyebrows. "Me, too. Mostly."

"Mostly," I echoed, smiling back at him. "So how do I make the *lausaveesa* stronger? More runes?"

"That's part of the eloquence of the Art. Let me simplify the runes a moment. Let's call *Ingwaz*, I; *Mannaz*, M; and so on. The *lausaveesa* you learned a moment ago takes the form I-M-E-S. To increase the strength of any *lausaveesa*, you can add runes as you suggested, or you can repeat the runes. For example, we could construct a *kaltrar* that took the form I-M-E-E-S, and it would be stronger. Or I-M-M-E-E-S. Understand?"

"Yeah. Can I repeat the same phrase three times, too?"

"No." He smiled a crooked smile. "That was imprecise of me. You *can*, but there are diminishing returns with the phrases. If you repeat the *Eiwhaz* phrase three times, it will be only a small amount stronger. If you use unique phrases, it will be somewhere between two and three times stronger."

"Oh. I guess I need to accelerate my acquisition of the *Gamla Toonkumowl*."

Althyof nodded, but there was a glint in his eye that made it seem what I'd said had amused him. "What?"

"Er? Nothing, nothing." He glanced away.

"What's next? Something to protect myself or my son?"

"No, not yet, Hank. We can't rush this."

"Right. I keep forgetting that. My nature urges me to race ahead, to learn as much as I can, as quickly as I can."

"Laudable, but likely to result in your death when it comes to the Art." Althyof sank his chin into his beard and seemed pensive. "This Kuhntul business…"

"Yes?"

"Why does she come to you? From what I overheard last night, I take it she has some prophetic, yet incomprehensible warning?"

I smiled crookedly. "That's the best description I've heard to date. She warns me that there is a betrayer amongst us."

"A betrayer." Althyof scratched a bushy eyebrow. "Of course, you suspect me."

"No, not at all. I suspect Kuhntul if you want to know the truth."

"But the others, *they* suspect me."

I shrugged. "You'd have to ask them."

"I don't need to ask. Of *course* they suspect me. I'm a Tverkr."

"And so they *should* suspect you? Is that what you're saying?"

"No. But they will. They always suspect Tverkar, despite the betrayals by their own people. They glibly accept Freya into their midst, despite what she did in the war, but me? No, I'm suspect, despite what *I* did in the war. It has always been thus, starting with the Alfar, who assumed we took after the Svartalfar more than their fair-skinned race. The Tverkar have a certain reputation—unearned, I might add—for being mercenary, for selling ourselves to the highest bidder. Even the lofty Meuhlnir considers this a fact."

I remembered the bargaining Althyof had done in Prokkr's workshop and cocked my head to the side. "It seems you encourage this belief," I said, keeping my tone neutral, mild.

"Yes, and why not? Why not act the way people expect? Why not play the role?"

"Because it does nothing but reinforce the beliefs?"

"You're young, Hank. I sometimes forget that you've lived only a few decades." He shook his head. "Beliefs like this…they do not change."

One thing I learned as a cop: when someone comes out with a statement such as that, there's no point going on with the conversation. "What did she do?"

"Eh? Oh, Freya?"

"Yes. Meuhlnir and Veethar are tight-lipped on the subject."

"Yes, I bet they are." He rode for a while, swaying with the gait of his horse, stroking his beard and squinting at those ahead of us. "It was late in the war. Causalities on both sides were…horrible. The rebellious Isir had mustered allies from many a *klith*, many a *stathur*, and the Dark Queen had done the same. As the number of combatants swelled, so did the level of violence. While the Isir were…reluctant…to unleash the full brunt of their powers on their kinsmen and friends, they had no such compunction about blasting Svartalfar or Tverkar."

"I don't imagine the Tverkar felt bad about killing Svartalfar, either."

"Indeed not. We unleashed such power—and by we, I mean all the combatants in the war—that the universe shook with it. It seemed hopeless at first— one side would win a battle by decimating the enemy, then the other side would win the next battle by doing the same. It was almost as if we traded fortresses back and forth, the leadership of both sides seemingly wanting to avoid the leadership of the other. But slowly, the tide turned. The allies the Black Bitch had summoned were inconstant, and when things got to be too much for them, they slunk off into the darkness and disappeared home. Soon the rebels outnumbered the loyalists at every battle, and we stopped trading victories. Meuhlnir came up with a plan…"

SEVENTEEN

"**I** have a plan!" Meuhlnir, shouting so that everyone in the large hall in the fortress at Raytyanes could hear him, climbed up on a table. "I have a plan to end the war!"

"Oh, ho! Meuhlnir has *another* plan to end the war," heckled a Tverkr with mossy-green hair standing a few dozen steps from Althyof.

"I deserve that," said Meuhlnir. "It's true my last plan to end the war was a disaster. I admit—"

"And the three before that!" shouted the Tverkr. The knot of Tverkar he stood with laughed, and blood suffused Meuhlnir's cheeks.

"Let the Isir speak!" shouted Althyof, glaring at the heckler. "Let him speak so we can get out of this damn room. Hear his plan so we can get to the ale!" The Tverkar in the hall laughed and cheered, and Meuhlnir's blush deepened. Althyof felt a twinge at that, but if he didn't couch his words in a nest of scorn, the Tverkar would ignore him and continue interrupting, and the damn meeting would take forever. For his own part, curiosity burned foremost in Althyof's mind.

"Well, I don't want to keep you from your ale, so let me get through this quickly. If any want to stay after I'm done and discuss tactics, I welcome it." He glanced around the room, his gaze resting on Alfar and Isir for a moment, but never on a Tverkr, Althyof noticed.

"Get on with it," snapped Althyof to the cheers of his fellows.

"We have discovered where Suel is." Meuhlnir smiled at his woman, the one they called Yowrnsaxa, and she blushed prettily. "Suel lies camped near the pass through the Dragon Spine Mountains and has but a small force with her. She's committed the majority of her forces to the west, lying in ambush in the pass itself. Thanks to Veethar's skills with flora and fauna of the Great Wood of Suel, she believes we have marched toward the pass and are preparing to attack Suelhaym itself. She—"

"What would make her believe tripe such as that?" shouted someone in the back of the hall.

"Veethar created a false trail—one big enough to account for our entire force. The trail begins outside the gates of this fortress and treks northeast toward the pass. Sufficient?" Meuhlnir's tone sounded harried, annoyed. When no one else spoke, he gave a curt nod. "Suel believes she is safe, with the largest part of her army between her and us. Instead, she is horribly exposed. If we act with haste, we can flank her small force and capture the queen before she can alert her main army."

"What's to keep her sitting there, waiting for us?"

Meuhlnir's smile was grim, yet fierce. "I've offered her something she wants."

"And what could that be?" asked Althyof.

Meuhlnir's gaze found his own. "Me."

Althyof shook his head.

"Well, of course, not the real me. I put a glamor on a thrall volunteer and sent him north into the wood. He's an experienced woodsman, and Veethar has enchanted his boots to make the path I spoke of a moment ago. He's already halfway to the pass."

"How can you know where he is?" asked an Alf.

"I have marked him so that Yowrnsaxa can keep track of him via the *syown*."

"Reckless," snapped Althyof. "If she can see him, so can Suel! She will see the deceit!"

"If she knew what to look for, maybe," said Meuhlnir, a ghost of a smile on his lips.

"No. Suel's more than a *vefari*, Meuhlnir. What she does is—"

"Oh, come now. You say that as if being a *vefari* is some small task. As if there are other ways of accessing power that eclipse what a *vefari* can do. We all know you Tverkar have a vested interest in perpetuating such a myth, but we all access the same *strenkir af krafti*. What I can do, an Alf can do. What an Alf can do, *you* can do. Everyone knows this."

Althyof shook his head and caught the eye of a pale Alf standing across the room. He put out his hand, palm up, and shoved the air toward Meuhlnir. *Tell him*, the gesture said. The Alf shook his head and closed his eyes. "If I can find this thrall, will you believe me then?"

Meuhlnir laughed, shaking his head. "That would be cheating, no? I already gave you the key to finding him." He put his hand on the small of Yowrnsaxa's back and smiled down at her.

"Fool," Althyof muttered.

"Now, if I can continue?" Meuhlnir scanned the room and nodded to himself. "Suel will not be able to resist the lure of ambushing me. She will think me unaware of the mass of troops hidden in the pass. She will think I'm easy prey."

"Get on with it!" yelled another Tverkr near Althyof.

"Yes. Veethar and I have been working in secret to amass a set of *preer*, adjusting their endpoints and situating them to facilitate transporting the entire army in short order. We will attack tomorrow at dawn."

"Do you not think Suel can sense the *preer* being moved?" asked Althyof.

"Could you, Tverkr? Even with your 'superior' skills?" Meuhlnir dismissed his argument with a wave of his hand. "Any other objections to the plan?"

"What do we do when we have her?" asked an Alf.

"What do you mean?"

"Do we kill her?" asked Althyof. "She's earned it."

Meuhlnir blanched and blinked. "No. No, we can't kill her. She must be...*contained* somehow. Shown the error of her ways...rehabilitated."

"Lunacy," muttered Althyof. "What makes you think you can—"

"The matter is closed," snapped Meuhlnir. "She will not be killed. Her punishment is for the Isir to decide." He cleared his throat. "That is the essence of the plan. Go drink your ale, Tverkar." As he climbed down from the table, Frikka approached him and spoke, her expression and gestures animated. She gestured at Althyof and spoke with passion, but Meuhlnir waved her away.

Althyof tried to catch Frikka as she strode away, anger burning in her wake, but her lovely legs were too long, and he wouldn't degrade himself by running after a woman. He intended to have a word with her before they trapped Queen Suel. Maybe, between the two of them, they could arrange for an accident to befall the blighted queen. When he lost sight of Frikka as she turned the corner into the wing the Isir had taken over for themselves, he sighed and turned away. After all, there was ale to be drunk and songs to be sung among his own kind.

The next morning, annoyance, and a booted foot, forced Althyof into consciousness. His head pounded like a giant drum, and each sound like a mallet striking that drum. He groaned and forced his eyes open. An Alf stood above him. "What?" demanded Althyof.

"The battle?" The Alf quirked an eyebrow, somehow making the expression appear both amused and condescending.

"It's still dark!"

"Yes, very astute of you. Recall that we are to attack *at* dawn, not noon."

Althyof grimaced and swirled his tongue around the cesspit that had replaced his mouth while he slept. "Something wrong with that ale," he mumbled.

"Indeed," said the Alf. "The problem with the ale is that you drank too much of it."

"Bah," grunted Althyof. "You are now speaking nonsense."

The Alf sighed. "Will you stay awake this time?"

"This time? This is the first time you've awakened me."

"No, it isn't." The Alf narrowed his eyes and scowled. "This is the *third* time we've had this conversation. I'd prefer to get on with my preparations, so this time, I will wait until you are on your feet."

Althyof smirked. "When I need an Alf babysitter, I'll be sure to call on you. Now, leave me alone, or I'll show you how I bested Fowrpauti in single combat."

"Ha! A great *runeskowld* performed that task, not some drunken wretch."

Althyof squeezed his lips together, squinting up at the pale-skinned Alf. "Your name, Alf?"

"I am Fyuhlnir, Tverkr."

Althyof nodded, committing the name to memory. "Good, good. I'll find you, Fyuhlnir, after the battle. We can discuss your errors and assumptions at that time."

"As you will. What is your name, so I can be sure to find *you* if your courage doesn't have the same legs to it as your bravado?"

Althyof smiled a nasty smile. "I am Althyof. You know…Binder of Friner…Slayer of Fowrpauti. Oh, and *master runeskowld.*" He didn't think the Alf could be any paler, but his pasty face blenched even more. Althyof winked at him. "Heard of me, eh? Well, after today, you'll know my capabilities from experience—*first-hand* experience. Now, run away."

To his credit, the Alf nodded. "Until this afternoon." Neither of them knew it, but the Nornir had already clipped Fyuhlnir's thread.

Althyof looked around for his cup from the night before but couldn't find it. He shrugged and grabbed the nearest cup that still had liquid in it and tipped it back. The dreg of ale at the bottom of the cup tasted sour and warm, but it was wet, and it helped wash the cesspit taste off his tongue. Whatever that foolish

Alf thought, Althyof was no novice when it came to drink *or* battle.

The army assembled in the vast square outside the main keep. Isir stood in neat groups, *skyuldur vidnukona* standing next to their companions, looking pretty as if out for a picnic rather than a battle. Alfar stood in precise squares of one hundred, each equipped with a longsword and a dagger. Althyof looked at the rag-tag group of Tverkar, standing or slouching in small knots of men, in various states of undress, and smiled. Only the Tverkar knew how to hold a war. *Who needs all this pomp? All this* discipline *and* order*? Our enemies end up just as dead.*

Meuhlnir bustled out of the keep, flanked by Yowrnsaxa on one side and Veethar and Frikka on the other. He glanced at the Tverkar contingent, and a scowl skittered across his face. Althyof spat on the cobbles at his feet. Self-importance rarely amounted to much in his opinion.

"Men and women!" Meuhlnir yelled. "We go to do battle with the queen. We go to put a stop to this depravity that has come to grip our fair homeland by the throat. Today, this ends!" He beamed a smile at the amassed army, his gaze lingering on a tall Isir, then moving on.

Meuhlnir moved through the troops, patting shoulders, shaking hands, murmuring encouragements—as if any of that was worth a tinker's damn. Althyof sidled closer, interested in the Isir man standing apart.

"Pratyi," said Meuhlnir. "Where is your fair companion?"

Pratyi's face darkened, and he looked away. "Gone."

"Gone? What do you mean? Gone where?" asked Meuhlnir.

"As if you don't know," mumbled Pratyi.

Meuhlnir's face colored. "And you *let* her?"

Pratyi flashed a look of exasperation at the Isir leader. "No, I didn't *let* her go. I didn't encourage her to go. I *forbade* her to go."

Meuhlnir spread his arms wide. "So, where is she?"

"You know where she is!" snapped Pratyi. "She lulled me to sleep and slipped out during the night."

"This puts the entire plan in jeopardy, Pratyi! Why didn't you tell me the moment you realized she'd gone? Why didn't you sound the alarm?"

"Stop wasting time, Meuhlnir," snapped Pratyi. "Open the *preer*! Let's salvage what we can of this."

Shaking his head, Meuhlnir motioned to Veethar, and they began the work of opening *preer* and anchoring them in the courtyard. It was a matter of minutes before they had them all ready. "Through your assigned *proo*!" Meuhlnir shouted. "Be ready for anything; the plan may be compromised!" Meuhlnir glared at Pratyi and popped through one of the *proo*. His two female companions followed him through, and then everyone was moving, loosening weapons, double checking straps of armor and shields, reaching for the silvery *preer*, and disappearing with a pop.

Althyof passed through with a knot of *runeskowlds*, each dressed in enchanted leather robes, each wielding daggers or maces. He appeared on the other side into the middle of a raging battle and launched into the *trowba* he'd prepared, his daggers glowing cadmium red and growing to three times their normal size. The Tverkr spun into the fray, slicing and hacking at the enemy as he whirled, dodging blows, leaping over kicks. He heard other *trowba* and automatically adjusted his tempo to match, lending additional strength to the *kaltrar* and stretching the range of the effects.

He danced through the enemy lines, untouchable by enemy blades. *Thralls! Poorly armed thralls!* he thought. It was a delaying tactic—it had to be. These thralls were not warriors, they had little training, if any, and their arms and armor were pitiful. Those that didn't have farm implements bore rusty, age-dulled swords and axes. Althyof cut through them like a hot knife through butter, never pausing, never taking a wrong step. In his peripheral vision, he saw other leather-robed figures doing the same thing, guided by the *trowba* and their own dancing.

Runeskowlds didn't fight in organized clumps as did the Isir or the Alfar. Each *runeskowld* stood apart, and other warriors stood between and behind them, following their progress across the battlefield. They were best suited as shock troops and could turn the tide of a battle by confusing the enemy alone.

Althyof paused a moment, then turned his dance to the side, knowing his companions would follow his lead, not because he commanded them, but because it was a wise move. They created a boundary of sorts—circling the *proo* they'd come from about thirty yards out, allowing troops to come through and amass without being attacked.

When the space filled up with Tverkr warriors, Althyof spun toward the enemy again, letting the warriors fill in the spaces between him and his neighboring *runeskowlds*. They slammed into the enemy line like a *sterk task* and shattered it, a number of thralls throwing down their weapons and running away.

Althyof danced farther and farther away from the *proo* he'd travelled through, stretching the circle, deforming it into a lopsided oval, heading for the knot of fighting at the next closest *proo*. The other *runeskowlds* sussed out his plan and let him break away, taking a contingent of Tverkr warriors with him, while they continued to guard the *proo* and let more and more Tverkar come across in safety.

Althyof danced toward the *proo*, which was surrounded by a force much more dangerous than the thralls the Tverkar had faced. Tall humanoids with knobby joints and thick skin, dressed in the skins of strange animals, wielded stone and wood weapons, but with massive strength. Althyof grimaced, altered his *trowba* to account for the massive strength of the trolls, and led his force into the fray.

Trolls were large, strong, and bred and raised to fight, but they weren't all that bright. The Tverkar slammed into their flank, inflicting massive damage before fading away. The intent was to draw a small contingent of trolls away from the larger force, deal with them while the Tverkar had superior numbers, and once the first batch was dead, reel in another small group.

It worked, again and again. Althyof's *trowba* lent the Tverkar strength and endurance and sapped the will of the big, dumb brutes at the same time. Althyof danced around them, feinting, cutting, stabbing, kicking, never missing a beat in his song or dance. Trolls fell before him, and the ground ran blue with their blood.

When the troll ranks were sufficiently weakened, Althyof circled, rounding up his warriors, and together, they punched through the troll lines to come to the aid of whoever was inside the circle. They burst through, and the Alfar defending the *proo* parted to let them in. The Alfar fought with courage and dedication, not to mention great skill at arms, but their techniques didn't fare well against the brutish strength of the trolls.

Dead and injured Alfar littered the ground, their dainty longswords and daggers lay beside them, ignored by the trolls. Without stopping his *trowba*, Althyof set his men to bolster weak parts of the Alfar line and struck out in search of the Alf who was giving the orders.

An Alf knelt on the ground next to another prone figure. The prone Alf's head was crushed on the right side, clear fluid running from his ears and blood filling his eyes. His good eye rolled in its socket, flitting from place to place, from Alf to Alf. It finally came to rest on Althyof.

It was Fyuhlnir, and he was dying.

Althyof knelt on his other side, abandoning his *trowba* for long enough to take the Alf's pain away. "Some men will do almost anything to get out of a friendly fistfight," he said.

Fyuhlnir tried to smile, and it was ghastly. Half of his face had frozen in a terrible rictus, his eyelid on that side gaping, letting blood trickle down his cheek. His lips failed to respond to the command to smile, twitching uselessly. "I saw you with the trolls," he croaked. "My apologies, Althyof, master *runeskowld.*"

"Accepted. Now, what are we to do with you?"

"There's nothing anyone can do." Fyuhlnir shifted his gaze to the Alf on his other side. "I put you in Althyof's command until you rejoin the others. Follow his lead, follow his orders." His eyes rolled toward the sky, and he died.

"I don't give orders," said Althyof. "Follow me, follow my men—they know what to do. I won't interrupt my *trowba* once I start it, so if you have questions, ask them now." The Alf looked at him, his face slack, eyes empty. "Right, then," murmured Althyof. "Alfar, hear me!" he shouted, standing straight. "Fyuhlnir has died at the hands of these damn trolls. Before he did, he entrusted your lives to my care. You've not fought with us before, so I will explain this once. I sing a *trowba*. I do not give orders.

My men know how to fight with me and know what I want from them. What I want from *you* is that you stay with my men, doing what they do, when they do it. Questions?"

There were none, so Althyof glanced at his Tverkar and began his *trowba* again, picking it up in the exact spot where he'd left it. He began his whirling dance, darting through the Alfar line to gut a troll here, slice the throat of another there. Once the Alfar picked up on the nature of the Tverkar method of battle, they adapted to it with grace and improvised to fit Althyof's needs as if born to it.

They killed every troll encircling them, the trolls being too battle-hungry—or too stupid—to fall back when they lost the numerical advantage. The other *runeskowlds* and their warriors came jogging over, and the two forces merged into a larger unit.

Again, the *trowba* of the *runeskowlds* overlapped and combined to create a stronger and farther-reaching effect. Sounds of battle came to them on the wind and Althyof moved in that direction, the rhythm and pacing of his *trowba* increasing to accommodate faster travel.

The group crested a small rise and poured down the other side toward the flats where a battle between Isir raged. Althyof led his sprinting warriors and dancing *runeskowlds* into the fray, never hesitating. They smashed into the flanks of the queen's forces to devastating effect.

The *runeskowlds'* songs reached a crescendo and fell on the Isir enemy like a tidal wave obliterating a beach. Melodies and lyrics mixed and wove together to create a blanket of fear and hopelessness for the Isir—friendly and enemy alike, but that couldn't be helped. The joined forces of the Tverkar and Alfar made short work of the Isir enemy, and Althyof steered the *trowba* into a stanza of recovery.

Meuhlnir and his party were not part of the Isir contingent, which was comprised of thrall infantry with a few karls in support. Althyof wanted to get on with the battle—to fight the queen's forces and crush them before reinforcements from the pass fell on them like wolves. He turned and danced toward the area where Meuhlnir had thought Queen Suel camped.

They ranged across a small woodland, forded a stream, and came to another flat area. Arrayed on the other side was the main force of the queen's troops. Svartalfar hovered around the edges, given a wide berth by the Isir troops. In the center of her lines, the queen had placed a knot of trolls—shock troops. Lined up in the center as they were, Althyof could not pull a few away from the troop as he had done back at the *proo*. That made the center dangerous, but the Svartalfar were no easy foe either, with something approaching *runeskowlds* of their own. Even so, the band of Tverkar and Alfar he led summed to almost the same number as the queen's forces.

He danced boldly into the flat space, singing at the top of his voice, dancing in time, and *stayba runana* with all his concentration, and his force followed without hesitation. The queen's army advanced in unison—a well-drilled cadre of professional warriors—except for the trolls, who pelted forward to meet the charge, bellowing war cries and ignoring the directions of their Isir commanders.

When the trolls were halfway across the field, Althyof began a measured retreat—if for no other reason than to see if the queen's Isir forces would stop their charge and let him deal with the trolls alone. The ugly things slowed, but a current of power swept through them, and they began to contort and cry out in pain.

Maybe the rebel Isir have joined us at last, he thought, then the trolls were on them, and he had no more time for idle thoughts. The trolls smashed into them with a combined guttural warcry that sounded like a monster storm roaring onto land from the sea. They swung huge wooden clubs two-handed in flat, vicious arcs that sent Tverkr and Alf alike flying if they were unlucky enough to be in the way.

The trolls had no grasp of unit tactics and no ability to tap into the *strenkir af krafti*, but the threat they represented was significant nonetheless. A group of trolls the size of the one he faced could defeat a larger number of warriors without much effort— unless the warriors had support. Althyof led the *runeskowlds* into a new song, one that emphasized physical agility and speed instead of raw strength and endurance.

He danced among the trolls, spinning, kicking, slashing with his daggers, screaming his *trowba* at the top of his voice, and his *runeskowlds* did the same. They were deep into the troll group, wreaking havoc, sowing confusion in the trolls at the line.

A club whistled by Althyof's head, just missing taking off the top of his skull. Althyof shouted two discordant phrases and the swinger of the club staggered back, clutching his chest, eyes wide. Althyof sprinted at him and, planting his foot on the troll's knee, leapt up and slashed his throat, foul-smelling blue blood showering all over him as he did so.

The warriors he led gave a cheer and pushed into the knot of trolls, silvery blades flashing in brutal arcs that bisected troll flesh, their blue-splattered blades sweeping on through the rest of their swing, flinging troll blood through the air.

Althyof renewed his *trowba*, adding phrases to inspire panic and unreasonable fear. The trolls reacted, bellowing their terror. Some flung away their wood and stone weapons. Others fell to their knees, exposing their throats for a quick, clean death.

A shrieking cry climbed into the air from outside the battle, and Althyof assumed it was the Isir engaging—trying to lend support to the floundering trolls. He continued fighting, singing, dancing, and casting the runes. He slashed about himself in time to his *trowba*, blue blood flying in his wake.

There was a roaring in his ears as he did this, and at first, he thought it was his own pulse in his ears. But when the sound became louder than the surrounding battle, he started to pay attention. He used his *runeskowld*-trained ears to pick out individual sounds from the roar. They were guttural snarls, beastly growling, and roars.

Althyof fought his way free of the trolls, coming out of the knot of swinging steel and pounding clubs just in time to see the band of *Oolfhyethidn* charge. They attacked as men would, but they were huge—three times the height of a Tverkr—and seemed to be a cross between a man and a wolf. They came on, slamming into the back of the trolls, rending troll flesh in their frenzy to get at the Tverkar and Alfar warriors.

As if they had been waiting for a cue, Isir and Alfar poured out of the woods, swarming around the trolls to get at the flanks of the *Oolfhyethidn*. Thunder boomed, announcing the presence of Meuhlnir, and lightning crashed into the *oolfa*, stunning many of them. Althyof shouted five or six cacophonous phrases over the background of the other *runeskowlds' trowba,* and the *oolfa* clapped their hands to their ears.

With the addition of the rest of the rebel army, they made short work of the small force loyal to the queen, *Oolfhyethidn* or not. The queen and her leadership broke away from the battle, sprinting away to escape.

Althyof wanted to pursue them, wanted it with every fiber of his being, but he was enmeshed in the battle with the troops the queen was abandoning to their fate.

As the fight dragged on, fresh units of the queen's forces charged out of the forest on her side of the field, but never *en masse*. No, they came one unit at a time, forty men here, twenty men there. They did nothing to affect the outcome of the battle, but they kept the rebel forces occupied, tied to the fighting so they couldn't pursue Suel.

EIGHTEEN

" **S**uel sacrificed her forces to keep us occupied, bound to that battlefield. They attacked piecemeal, never *en masse*, never with thought or plan, but they allowed her escape, though it broke her army for any practical purpose."

"How did they know where you would emerge from the *preer*?" I asked.

Althyof jerked his chin toward the people riding in front of us. "*She* told her sister."

"Freya?"

"She claims she didn't mean for the counter-attack to happen, she just didn't want her sister killed. She says the Black Bitch took advantage of her, pulled the locations of the *preer* from her with the *strenkir af krafti*." Althyof leaned to the side and spat on the road. "And so, when we finally broke the gates of Suelhaym and won the city, the fools exiled her instead of pursuing and killing her. They said Freya's action made it clear how most Isir felt about their former monarch."

"How many died in that last battle because of what Freya did?"

Althyof shook his head. "Many, but they would have died one way or another."

"Because the Isir couldn't bear to defeat her if it meant her death."

"Yes." Althyof cleared his throat. "After all that, a man needs an ale. And you need to practice your runes. No *kaltrar*, mind. Practice the runes."

"Have you ever spoken of that day with Skowvithr?" I asked, darting a glance back at the Alf.

"No. Why would I?"

"Fyuhlnir was the son of Freyr."

"And?" There was a trace of impatience in Althyof's voice.

"So is Skowvithr."

Althyof sat back in his saddle, a sour expression on his face. "That is…"

"Yeah. From what Freyr said, I don't think they know what happened to Fyuhlnir, only that he never returned."

Althyof grimaced and shook his head. "I've already told the story once today." He glanced at me and away. "Oh, very well." He reined his horse to a stop and waited for the Alfar to catch him up.

I kept riding, replaying the story Althyof had told me in my head. Of course, it was skewed by Althyof's point of view, but even so…Freya had betrayed them. Granted she'd been trying to save her sister, but even so…

Kuhntul kept warning me about a betrayer in our midst. But Freya? I rode on to the muted sound of Althyof's voice telling Skowvithr how his brother had died.

NINETEEN

When the road hooked toward the small coastal towns north of Suelhaym, we left the relative comfort of Lottfowpnir's caravan. We didn't want to risk getting too close to any town and the possibility of drawing the attention of the Dark Queen's lookouts.

Veethar led us straight west, the Dragon Spine Mountains looming in front of us, getting bigger each day. I spent each morning's ride with Althyof, learning to be a *runeskowld*. Jane spent every evening with the ladies, practicing her shield and axe skills.

Sig was learning to *vefa strenki* under Meuhlnir's watchful eye—and from anyone else who would spare him the time. Keri and Fretyi ate, grew like weeds, slept, and attacked my feet at every opportunity.

We arrived at the foot of the mountains on the evening of the third day. By that time, I was exhausted, but thanks to the noxious brew Sif forced on me every morning, my joints didn't feel that bad—relatively speaking. I was stiff, but I didn't think I was any stiffer than I would have been after riding a horse all day while taking methotrexate. I needed less and less of her smelly ointment, and that was as good a measure of improvement as anything. The curse wasn't gone—I still needed the enchanted cloak to avoid curling into a ball—but it was more manageable.

"You want us to go through that?" Jane asked pointing at the cave.

"Not tonight," said Veethar.

"But tomorrow? Will the horses go through there?"

The cave was tall and wide, but I had no doubt it would narrow somewhere in the basement of the mountains.

Veethar grunted and gave a short nod.

I dismounted and took the pups out of the saddlebags that they were rapidly outgrowing. The second I put Fretyi down, the crazy pup ran in a tight circle, barking and snarling at his hind leg. Crazy. When I put Keri down, he tackled his brother, nipping and yipping, before jumping up and sprinting into the forest with Fretyi hot on his tail.

"Those two," laughed Mothi.

"Those two remind me of you and Sig," said Yowrnsaxa shoving past him with her iron stewpot heaped full of supplies for dinner.

Sig did his best, but he couldn't tackle Mothi the way Keri had tackled Fretyi. Not even the loud puppy-like yips helped. Mothi held his hand out, holding my boy away with a hand on his forehead.

"I'm going to have a look around in there," I said.

"Don't stay too long." Meuhlnir glanced up at the sky, checking the position of the sun.

"It's okay, I'm not scared of the dark," I said with a laugh.

"As long as you know the dark isn't scared of you either."

The floor of the cave was hard-packed clay—at least in the part of the cave visible in the sunlight streaming in through its entrance—while the walls and roof were cold grey stone. The sunlight filtered in thirty feet before darkness took over. It was ten degrees cooler in the darkened part of the cave and stepping forward into that morass of inky black suddenly seemed like the last thing I wanted to do.

"*Au noht*," I whispered, and the now-familiar sting and tightness wrapped my eyes. When the stinging faded, I could see again, despite the lack of light. The cave ran laser-straight into the mountain, but a hundred yards from the entrance, it became a man-made thing, the marks of picks and shovels visible on the walls. I shuddered as the memory of the abattoir-like cave Luka and Hel had used in New York came flooding back. That alone-in-the-dark hinky feeling ran chilled fingers up and down my spine, and if I hadn't known it was impossible, I would have suspected Luka of staring at me from the dark reaches of the cave.

I turned around and walked back toward the entrance, my pace increasing as the freak-out ran a little wild. I could see the gloaming settling on the forest outside and had no desire to be inside the cave when the light died.

A heartbeat before I crossed back over the border between dusk and pitch black, something like a caress fluttered on the back of my neck. It didn't feel like Jane caressing my neck though. It felt…greasy, dirty, wretched. I walked faster and whispered laughter slithered out of the darkness behind me.

Meuhlnir was on his feet, staring at the cave entrance when I came outside. "Everything okay?" he asked.

"Sure," I said, pretending nothing had happened. "But what did you mean when you said the dark wasn't scared of me?"

Veethar grunted from his place at the fire.

"It's not important," said Meuhlnir, but he avoided my gaze.

"What?" I said.

"It's no matter. We'll discuss it tomorrow as we trek through the cave."

"Ha!" grunted Althyof. "There are *lantvihtir* in that cave, aren't there?"

Meuhlnir turned a baleful gaze on the Tverkr.

"What's a lanterntir?" asked Sig.

"*Lantvihtir*," said Althyof. "They are…spirits, I guess you could say, that are tied to a particular place, or a feature of the land."

"*Ghosts*?" asked Sig, sounding a bit uneasy.

"Yes, I suppose," said the Tverkr.

Meuhlnir shook his head, glaring at Althyof. "They are mostly harmless, Sig," he said.

Althyof gave him a sly wink. "Don't worry, Isir. I'll protect you. We Tverkar learned how to deal with the *lantvihtir* a long time ago."

Meuhlnir threw up his hands and stalked out of camp. Sig watched him go, concern bubbling on his face. "Dad…" he said.

"Don't worry about it, Siggy."

"Come help me with tonight's stew, little Piglet," said Yowrnsaxa with a wink. "That way you get to taste it before anyone else." Sig scampered over to her side, grinning, ghost stories already forgotten.

I sat next to Althyof. "So, you disagree about the cave?"

"Oh no," he said. "I'm happy to be going back underground where all sane men should stay. And don't worry about the *lantvihtir*. I can keep them at bay with a *trowba*."

"*Them*?"

"Don't worry," he repeated.

"You're not very good at this."

"At what?" He quirked an eyebrow at me.

"At reassuring people."

He laughed and tipped me a wink. "Is that what I was doing?"

We ate our dinner with the normal amount of joking and teasing we'd all become accustomed to. Keri and Fretyi cleaned up the leftovers and lolled near the fire, logy and full. Their example seemed like a good one, so everyone turned in.

In the morning, I noticed a cold wind blowing through the camp—the kind of wind that usually preceded a bad thunderstorm.

"Storm brewing," I said.

"No," said Veethar, jerking his chin toward the cave. "The wind comes from beneath the mountains."

Althyof hawked and spat. "That wind," he said, jerking his thumb at the cave, "comes from the throats of the *lantvihtir*. They are waiting for us."

"What do we do?"

The Tverkr shrugged. "I will sing a *trowba*, and they will not bother us. The rest of you stay together—as close together as you can. Someone must tend to the horses," he said, looking at Veethar.

Veethar nodded and walked to the high line where we'd tied the horses. He began speaking softly to the animals, touching their necks, patting their withers, and they seemed to pay close attention to his words. Even the two *varkr* pups sat with heads cocked and ears up.

"Do we need weapons?" asked Jane, her eyes fearful and on only Sig.

"Shouldn't," said Althyof. "Stay together. You will know if you start to stray too far from me."

We packed up our goods and equipment, tying what we could to our saddles and the pack horses. Yowtgayrr and Skowvithr came to stand by me when we were ready. "It would serve me best if you protect Sig."

"We are sworn to protect you, Hank. We will protect your family if the need arises."

"Listen, Sig is a kid. It might appear that he's almost an adult, but things are different in Mithgarthr—kids don't grow up as fast. If he gets into trouble, I'll have to do what I can, and that means I'll be at risk. You see? By protecting him instead of me, you will be protecting me." They exchanged a glance, and Skowvithr glided over to stand with Sig. "Jane," I said.

She had her shield strapped to her left arm and what she called her "business axe" in her right. She came and stood to my left, looking pensive. "Should we make Sig come with us?"

"It's up to you. But if you think he's less safe with Mothi, you're mistaken. He killed a Svartalf by shoving his hand down the man's throat."

"Yeah, you've told me that story about fifteen thousand times."

"Don't worry, Supergirl, I'm sure I will mention it again. And *don't worry.*"

She flashed a quick smile at me and went back to fidgeting.

"Bet you never expected to be using an axe and shield when you were back in one of those design meetings at work."

"I could've used the axe in some of those meetings," she said. "'We don't own that piece of the application'...thwack!" She mimicked slamming an axe down and grinned a wicked grin.

Althyof started to sing, his words creeping and crawling across the back of my neck like spiders. He motioned us tighter and nodded. He walked into the cave, with the rest of us close on his heels.

With the sun at our backs, the patch of light extended far deeper into the cave than it had the night before, but even so, a chill wriggled down my spine at going back inside.

We walked through the sunlight, peering ahead. When we reached the man-made part of the cave, Althyof's tune changed, shifting toward some harmonic minor key that made my teeth want to jump right out of my mouth and becoming more strident—even creepier than it had been before. The darkness loomed closer, and along with it, a feeling of malevolence. I couldn't see a thing, but I had the distinct impression that a number of...*things*...were surrounding the party—just outside the area of effect of Althyof's *trowba*.

"*Au noht,*" said Yowrnsaxa.

Jane grunted and tried to rub her eyes with her shield arm. In other circumstances, that would have been fuel for a bit of teasing, but in that cave, I didn't want to tease anyone. "Don't worry," I said. "It will fade." And as soon as I'd said it, it did.

With the ability to see in the dark, I perceived faint, blurry forms at the edge of the *trowba*. Most of their features shivered and jittered, but their faces...their faces cleared if I stared at one long enough. Their expressions displayed rage, repugnance, and revulsion.

Ahead, water gushed out of the wall fifteen feet in the air. It cascaded into a pool that almost covered the entire floor of the cave—only a path about three feet wide skirted the underground pool on the side opposite the waterfall. Sunlight streaming in from the cave's mouth bounced and shimmered on the surface of the pool. As we approached the pool, Althyof stopped walking.

Without pausing his *trowba*, he pointed at Veethar and the horses and pointed across the pool. Veethar nodded and led the horses, single file, along the path. Althyof pointed at Jane, Sig, Skowvithr, Mothi, Yowtgayrr and me, and once again pointed at the path. We followed Veethar, who was about a third of the way around the pool. Althyof followed us, straining his voice for volume, his lyrics harsher and stentorian.

When Veethar reached the other side, he stopped and turned back to watch our progress. Althyof lagged behind us, waving the others to come along. He motioned us on with impatient gestures when he saw we'd slowed to match his pace.

I turned and looked back when we reached the other side of the pool. I kept expecting a tentacled monster, straight out of *The Lord of the Rings* books, to attack us from the pool. The walls of the cave toward the entrance sparkled in the sunlight, the cave's mouth blazing with warm yellow light.

Althyof reached us and waved us on, making room for the others. We walked away from the pool of water, which now looked as black as death. It would be the perfect time for Tolkien's beast to attack us if it existed.

I should have been watching the other direction as it turned out.

With a roar, a huge shadow loomed against the darkness of the deep cave. I spun, hands flying to the butts of my pistols. One of the horses snorted, and another squealed in fear. Keri and Fretyi ran to me and pressed against my legs, whining and looking into the darkness with significant anxiety.

With a clatter, Mothi's axes were out, and then everyone was drawing weapons. Althyof's cadmium red cartoon daggers flared to life, their blades pulsing in time with the *trowba*. The roar sounded again, seeming closer and angrier.

"What the hell is it?" hissed Jane, her voice tight.

Keri growled, sounding twice as big as he was, though he remained at my side, pressed into my leg.

"Dad?" asked Sig, his eyes round.

The roar came a third time, and Slaypnir screamed in response. Keri's growl turned into a snarl, and Fretyi barked like an attack dog on high alert.

"Be ready," said Meuhlnir.

"It's not natural," muttered Veethar.

The *skyuldur vidnukonur* stood beside their men, legs apart, shield-side leg forward, weapon-side leg back, shields up, and Jane shifted her stance to match theirs. "Dad?" asked Sig again, fear quivering in his voice.

"It's okay, Sig," I said. "Stay with Skowvithr, no matter what happens."

His expression twitched, seemingly at war with itself—like he wanted to laugh but was too scared. "'It's okay, but if everyone dies, stay with Skowvithr.' You're a dork, Dad."

Footsteps thumped on the cave's floor, and something snarled in the darkness. It wasn't a friendly sound. Slaypnir screamed again, shaking his head and pawing the ground. I drew Kunknir and Krati, holding them ready, and walked forward to clear my sight lines.

The roar sounded again, at a deafening volume. Whatever it was, it stood fifteen paces away, and it was monstrously big. It opened its mouth and roared, and with the noise came the odor of death and decomposition.

"What the hell is it?" I shouted over the din.

As if it had been waiting for us to speak, the thing charged before my shout echoed into the depths of the cave. It came on all fours, chuffing like a steam engine gathering speed. It galloped toward us, claws or talons of some kind scuffing against the hard-packed clay floor.

It emerged out of the darkness like a demon rising from hell. Its eyes glowed red, and its fangs glistened with a ropy slime that dripped over its decaying gums and splattered on the floor. Where it still had fur, it was wiry, coarse, and dark brown, and where it had fallen out, old, dry sores disgorged maggots by the handful. It was a bear.

A Brobdingnagian, brainsick bear. A *dead* bear.

Kunknir thundered in the tight confines of the cave, followed by Krati. The muzzle flashes of the two pistols made the bear stop his charge and shrink back, but the rounds that slammed into the thing seemed inconsequential to the beast. He rocked forward on all fours and roared at me.

"No use!" shouted Veethar, pushing up beside me. He stood tall and threw his arms out to his sides. "*Tvala*!" he commanded.

The bear shook his head, easily the size of Veethar's torso, staggering for a moment, before shuffling forward, eyes blazing.

"*Kera ayns ok yek seki*!" Veethar shouted. "*Tvala*!"

"*Hooth ow yowrni*!" shouted Mothi as he stepped forward. "*Strikuhr risa*!" As he began to swell up like a time-lapse view of a bodybuilder, he sprinted forward, an axe in each hand.

"Mothi!" yelled Sig. He took a step forward, but Skowvithr planted a hand on his shoulder and held him back.

The bear swung his head toward the growing Isir charging him and roared. Mothi roared back and lifted his axes high.

Meuhlnir's hammer whistled by me, end over end, the runes of his name glowing in my enchanted sight. "*Ehlteenk*!" Meuhlnir shouted.

I squeezed my eyes shut before the thunder sounded, wondering for a second how lightning would deal with us being underground. A heartbeat later, the bolt passed by me, the skin on the right side of my body tingling and burning with its passage. I cracked open my left eye. The lightning streamed in a burning blue, *horizontal* line from behind me into the bear's wide chest. It sizzled and popped for a moment, like fatty meat cooking over an open flame, then faded. A large burn in the shape of a rough circle smoked in the middle of the bear's chest, but other than that, he seemed unaffected.

Meuhlnir's hammer bounced off the dead bear's skull, and as it did, two things happened at once: Meuhlnir shouted, "*aftur,*" to bring the hammer back to him, and Mothi struck the bear with both of his double-bladed axes, chopping deep into the thick flesh of the bear's neck. The bear screamed in rage and lashed out at Mothi, but he was already lunging away. Yowrnsaxa leapt forward, shield held high, running to guard Mothi's flank. The bear glared at her and swiped at her shield with his other arm, and the blow sent Yowrnsaxa reeling back, dazed.

Small arms fire would never turn the tide of this battle, even with the enchantments on the pistols. The bear had no wings to puncture to force a retreat. I holstered my pistols, wishing for another kind of weapon.

Keri and Fretyi pressed into my calves, one on each side, alternating whimpering and snarling, tails tucked, ears back. I wondered if they would stand with me if the bear attacked.

A scene from the movie *The Thirteenth Warrior* splashed through my mind like a blast of cold rain. It was the scene in which the party of Norse warriors discovered that the Ven worshiped bears. Ahmed Ibn Fahdlan, the Arabic thirteenth warrior, asks how to fight a bear, and Buliwyf answers: "With spears."

"How do you say 'spear' in the *Gamla Toonkumowl?*" I called.

"It's hardly the time—"

"*Tell me!*" I cried.

"*Sbyowt,*" said Sif from where she was ministering to Yowrnsaxa.

I replayed all the lessons Meuhlnir and Mothi had given me about *vefnathur strenki. Fix the image of what you want to happen in your mind,* they had said. *Then say the words.*

I imagined a twelve-foot-long metal pole tipped with a long, tapering blade. I imagined the blade glowed the way Althyof's daggers did. I fixed that image in my mind, held my hands out in front of me, and said, "*Sbyowt.*"

The spear condensed out of the air, dream-like, solidifying and gaining weight as it did so. The last thing to appear was the tip, which ended up looking more like a lightsaber out of Star Wars than Althyof's blades.

Mothi was leaping and rolling, striking the bear at every opportunity. Meuhlnir came forward, trying to taunt the bear into ignoring Mothi.

I glanced at Jane. "Stay with Sig," I said.

"Hank, don't you go…"

But it was already too late—I was running forward, the huge spear clutched in my fists. The bear's eyes locked on the glowing tip and he chuffed, almost as if he were asking what the red thing was. "Mothi, get ready!" I shouted.

The bear's eyes shifted to mine, and he roared in my face, the stench of death and corruption overpowering. The bear reared back on his hind legs, towering over me. I raised the tip of the spear, waving it in the bear's face. He snapped at the tip, and when it moved, I dipped the tip of the spear in under the bear's chin, meaning to skewer him in the throat, but the beast was wily and cunning, and as I slid forward to skewer him, the bear slipped to the side, allowing the burning tip of the spear to crease the side of his neck. With horrific speed, the bear lunged forward and swung a mammoth, claw-tipped paw in a wide, flat arc aimed at my head.

"Hank!" Jane screamed.

It was as if that massive paw was coming at me in slow motion, but I, too, was mired in sluggish time. It came closer and closer, and as it did, details of the paw grew clearer: the scars on the fleshy pads, the cracked claw on his middle toe, the tufts of dead hair falling from the loose skin of his ankle.

"Down!" yelled Mothi as he leapt at the bear's exposed back.

The puppies knocked me down, one crashing into my legs and the other slamming into my torso. They hit the floor next to me, and scrambled away, their claws scrabbling on the clay. The spear bounced out of my hands as I hit and immediately disappeared. The bear angled his swing down, trying to catch me anyway, and he almost did. His decaying paw swept by my head, missing me by mere inches.

Mothi slammed into the beast's back, sinking both axes in to the haft. The bear roared and shook as if trying to dislodge a fly. Mothi planted both feet between the beast's shoulders and strained to pull the axes apart, tendons and muscles bunching and quivering. The bear twitched his fur again, but otherwise ignored Mothi's efforts.

The bear loomed over me, malevolence burning in his eyes, foul pus dripping from his open maw. I tried to scrabble away, but the beast was too quick. He roared in my face, splattering me with the viscid pus. I gagged on the stench of it, trying to get away— digging into the clay with my elbows and heels, pushing with all my strength. The bear chuffed in my face as if he were laughing at my weakness.

An immense, black power swept around me and slammed into the bear, and though it staggered a half-step to the side, the relentless thing came on.

"It won't die," wailed Jane in a voice with no strength in it. Behind me, she clattered to her knees, too exhausted by the attempt at killing the dead bear to stand.

"He's already dead. Death magic is meaningless against him," said Veethar, in a calm, level voice.

Yowtgayrr whirled by me, spinning in mid-leap, blades flashing in my enchanted vision. He swept along the side of the bear, still spinning, blades slicing into the bear's side, ripping away chunks of dead flesh. The bear turned his head to the side and bellowed in anger, but Yowtgayrr was already gone, circling behind the beast.

"*Ehlteenk*!" Meuhlnir yelled, and again thunder boomed as lightning streamed into the cave on a flat, horizontal trajectory. This time the bolt slammed into the bear's face, igniting some of his loose fur.

Yowtgayrr sprinted toward the wall beside the bear's other flank, planted his foot high up on the wall, and sprang backward, twisting his body as he flew so that his longsword carved a long, deep furrow across the beast's spine.

The bear spun, nearly crushing me as he did, flinging Mothi off without his axes, which were still embedded in the bear's back. The beast swung at Yowtgayrr, moving faster than a bear that size should have been able to. Yowtgayrr feinted to the side, then rolled forward, leaping to the side at the last moment, sinking both his longsword and his dagger into the beast's shoulder as he passed.

I rocked to the side and crawled, wincing, on my hands and knees out of the bear's range. "How do we kill him?"

"He's already dead—" began Veethar.

"*No shit!* How do we kill him *again?*" yelled Jane as she fought her way to her feet through sheer force of will.

The bear roared at Yowtgayrr, but try as he might, the thing couldn't touch the Alf *sverth hoospownti*. Yowtgayrr danced past the bear, making cuts into the bear's dead flesh at will, but he had limits, he would tire, he would make a mistake eventually, and the bear would be on him.

I glanced around at the others. Althyof stood in the center of us all, singing his *trowba,* dancing in place, his cartoon-daggers growing and shrinking, stretching and thinning. He didn't dare stop, or the *lantvihtir* would be on us. Veethar stood, arms at his sides, watching the bear move, almost as if he were entranced. Sif knelt by Yowrnsaxa's side, wrapping her arm where it oozed blood. Jane stood in front of Sig, looking like she'd gone ten rounds with Muhammad Ali, and Skowvithr stood at her side, hand on her elbow. Meuhlnir was dragging Mothi away from the bear, not having an easy time by the look of it. Freya and Pratyi stood side by side, heads together, talking in each other's ear to be heard over the din. Frikka was…not there.

"Veethar! Where's your wife?" I shouted.

Veethar turned as if in a dream and looked at me. His eyes were empty, dull. He whispered something under his breath, lips in constant motion. "What?" I said.

The dream came back to me, the dream I'd had at Tholfr's inn. I'd forgotten it in the days since—written it off as the reaction of my subconscious mind to the sound of Jane practicing with Yowtgayrr. I couldn't be sure, though, if the dream had *really* happened this way, or if my mind was taking events of the present and treating them like a memory, like *déjà vu*.

Even so, the memory of the shaggy arm whistling through the darkness to decapitate Veethar burned and sang in my forebrain. I lurched to my feet and grabbed Veethar by the shoulders, twisting him around me in a circle, so I was between him and the bear. His eyes settled on mine for a moment and cleared. His gaze flicked over my shoulder, and his eyes jerked wide, wide open.

I spun, and yelled, "*Sbyowt*!" The long spear coalesced in my hands, the lightsaber tip gleaming. The huge undead bear lurched at me, one paw whistling at me with all the bear's considerable weight behind the blow.

I dodged to the side, but I was too slow. I jerked the spear into the path of the blow, hoping the metal shaft would be strong enough to deflect the massive paw.

It was an insane hope, and the shaft shattered like ice struck with a hammer. The force of the blow was immense, and it left my arms numb to the shoulder. I staggered back, and the bear roared, his disgusting spittle splattering in my face.

"Look out!" shouted Veethar from somewhere behind me.

The bear's other front paw was sweeping toward me, already too close for me to dodge. I dropped the bottom of the spear and lashed out at the bear's paw with the glowing, flickering tip of the spear. The bear screamed in angry defiance as tip of the spear sliced and burned its way into the center of that massive paw. The bear jerked his paw away, dragging me toward his body until it dawned on me to let go of the spear.

The zombie bear swung his head and looked at the spear impaling his paw. He tried to grasp the spear with his teeth, but on the wrong end, the glowing tip burning his tongue and mouth. The bear glared at me and roared again. I tried to back away, to get out of the bear's reach.

Quicker than thought, the bear lashed out with the paw still impaled by my spear. I dodged to the left and pain exploded on my right side. The broken shaft of the spear skewered me through the right side of my chest.

"Hank!" shouted Yowtgayrr. The bear lifted his arm, dragging me up into the air, and shook it, rattling the bones out of me. The bear kept jerking his arm this way and that in savage sweeps. I flopped to and fro, no thought left.

"*Ayta sbyowt*!" shouted Sif. The spear sticking out of my side dissolved into mist, and I flew away from the bear, six feet above the ground. Jane and Sig screamed a duet.

In the moment before I slammed into the ground, I saw her—Frikka—kneeling against the far wall of the cave in the shadows there. Her gaze met mine, and she was crying, the tears looking like red gold to my magicked eyes. Kuhntul's words sang in my mind. *I am here to warn you, Hank, son of Jens.* I'd asked her what she was there to warn me about. *A betrayer*, Kuhntul had said. *A traitor.*

I crashed into the hard clay floor, the impact jarring all thoughts and memories from my mind. I bounced once and skidded into the shallows of the black pool of water. I lay there, feeling hot and cold all over, feeling sick, not yet aware of any pain, wrapped in a cocoon of shock and concussion.

Frikka raced to my side—she was far closer than anyone else, as if she knew I'd land where I did. She rolled me onto my back, out of the cold water. "I'm so sorry, Hank," she whispered in my ear. "Veethar was to die, and I—" She broke down into uncontrollable sobs while she pressed her hands to my side.

Where she pressed, it burned as if she held a red-hot iron poker to my skin. She kept whispering about how sorry she was, but I couldn't find the strength or the will to care. Dizziness swept through me like a tsunami, followed by intense nausea, before I started to shiver. A burning pain radiated from my side where Frikka worked, something that felt alive, like snakes crawling under my skin, trailing hot wire.

"Betrayer," I whispered and tried to push Frikka's hands away, but I had no strength.

She reacted as if I'd slapped her, head jerking back, eyes popping wide open, a perfect expression of startlement etched on her face. She bent forward at the waist and wailed silently, her mouth stuck open, red gold tears pouring down her cheeks. Even so, she kept her hands pressed to my side, doing whatever traitorous act she'd been doing before.

My blood burned in my veins as if it were laced with boiling acid, searing the inside of my veins, burning my tissues, but leaving my nerves intact so I could suffer through every little thing.

I *had* to get away from her, had to stop her putting whatever poison she had in my veins. I knew I had to or I would die. I was already too weak to struggle to my feet, to retreat physically—too weak to *make* her stop. The cloak was overloaded, pain was my entire world, and my vision was growing dim.

The cloak! But I couldn't twitch the edges of it forward, not with the gash through my chest and abdomen. I couldn't activate it, couldn't twist my *fettle* and get away from Frikka. *The activation word! What is it?* I racked my mind, trying to remember the word Althyof had taught me.

"Oh, Hank," cried Frikka. "Forgive me. I'm a weak old woman."

Vakt! That was it. "*Vakt*," I muttered and turned into smoke.

The relief from the burning pain washed through me as if I'd died and gone to heaven. I moved away from Frikka, and though her eyes tracked my every movement, she stayed where she was, looking dejected, broken.

I didn't have long—a few seconds—and I wanted to get back to Sif so she could save me from whatever Frikka had done.

I almost made it, passing Jane and Sig who were running to where Frikka knelt. Skowvithr watched me, or the smoke that represented me in that plane, and glanced at Jane and Sig. *Go with them*, I shouted at him in my mind.

My *fettle* untwisted, and I appeared standing, but collapsed flat on my face, not even putting out my arms to cushion the fall, as soon as my weight hit my muscles. Yowrnsaxa saw me appear and cried out. Sif rushed to my side and rolled me over.

"Dammit, man, can't you go a day without my help?" she muttered. Behind her, the bear roared, and something crashed into the wall of the cave.

The pups charged over to me, whining and crying, trying to lick my face and getting in Sif's way. She pushed them away. "Get back and let me work, you can lick him after I've made sure he'll live," she said in a stern voice. "If I can." The puppies sat down and watched her as if they understood her perfectly.

She was muttering, shoving something into my side and it felt like the hot iron Frikka had been using. Jane and Sig ran over and hovered behind Sif. Sig's eyes filled with tears and he turned to Jane, pressing his face against her shoulder. Frikka stood behind them, head down, red gold tears raining on the clay floor in silence.

"She…Frikka…" I whispered.

Veethar strode up to his wife, face writhing with rage. "What did you do?" he hissed.

Frikka sobbed, head hanging.

Jane pushed Sig away, but with a gentleness that belied the rage etched into her face. She turned, slipping her axe out of her belt. In two quick steps, she stood in front of Frikka, the blade of her axe shaking. "*What did you do?*" she screamed.

Frikka glanced at her, and another sob burst from her. She hung her head again, unable or unwilling to say anything in her defense.

"Stand away," snapped Veethar, the ring of command in his voice.

Jane barely glanced at him. She lifted the axe, and Veethar stepped between my wife and his.

"No," he said.

"*You bitch!*" Jane yelled. "*What did you do?*" Her voice was filled with tears—tears of anger, tears of betrayal and frustration, tears of fear for me.

Yowrnsaxa ran to her side, putting her arm around Jane's shoulders. "Come away, dear," she said.

"She…she…"

"We will sort all that out later, dear. Your son needs you more than your anger." Yowrnsaxa's voice was soft and yet hard as nails. She pulled Jane away with a firm, but gentle pressure.

Jane let herself be led away, and Frikka sobbed all the louder. The bear roared as if angry that people were ignoring him. "Will someone kill that goddamn bear?" yelled Jane.

A hard expression settled on Veethar's face as he glanced at Frikka, and her sobbing became uncontrollable as she sank to the ground, the very picture of desolation. He spun on his heel without a word, barely sparing me a glance, his face set in ugly, grim lines. "*Kverfa*!" he called, trying to dispel the force that had reanimated the bear. "*Ayta*!"

The bear roared and sent someone flying to land in the water. Mothi.

"*Snooith aftur til mirkurs tautha*!" shouted Veethar.

"What's he saying?" I croaked, for some inexplicable reason, it seemed like the most important question in the world.

"Return to the darkness of death," muttered Sif, still busy with something at my side that had gone thankfully numb. The bear stopped roaring every other second, for which I was thankful.

"*Kvild, ow kowthu*!"

"Rest, Great One," Sif translated.

"Great One?"

Sif shrugged. The sounds of battle had stopped.

"*Ivirtyeva thehta rityi, sova, kvilt.*"

"Leave this realm, sleep, rest," Sif murmured. Somewhere in the cave an immense weight crashed to the ground.

"Why didn't he do that before?" I asked in a cross voice.

Sif shrugged. "Shush now, Hank."

"But I've got to—"

"You've got to do what I say, now, Hank," she snapped in a voice as hard as iron. She looked at me before shaking her head, wearing a grimace. "I'm putting you under." She turned and dug in her ever-present medical bag. She pulled out a stoppered glass container that held a noisome-looking grey liquid and held it to my lips. "Drink, Hank. Two swallows."

I shook my head. "I need to—"

"Oh, for the love of Isi! *Svepn*," she said, touching my forehead with her finger.

It felt as if she put a glob of snow the size of her fingertip on my forehead. The cold wetness spread, covering my forehead, the top of my head, my whole head. Before it progressed further, I slept.

TWENTY

*T*he pain faded, in fact, all sensation disappeared, leaving me floating in a pool of cold, apathetic numbness. I opened my eyes, and to my shock, I hung in the air above the heads of my family and friends. My body lay on the floor of the cave, Sif bent over me, listening to my chest, looking worried. Yowrnsaxa knelt next to her, pushing a linen cloth into my side. Blood and pus smeared my face, and my eyes were closed.

The bear roared, but he sounded far away, unimportant. I glanced at him, and instead of a *rotting, pestilent corpse, the bear glowed with life: magnificent coat of waxy brown hair; clear, intelligent eyes; healthy skin and claws; full belly.*

"Get out! Why did you disturb us?"

I shook my head and blinked hard to clear the vision, the dream from my eyes.

"Just leave! Leave my cave!"

"Can't do that, now can I? That's me, down there." I pointed at my blood-smeared body.

"You! You stuck me! With that…with that red thing!"

"In my defense, you were trying to kill all of us."

"You invaded my home. That short one sang his dirge that pushed the lantvihtir *out of their home and into mine."*

"We're traveling to the other side of the mountains. When I'm awake, you are dead."

"I'm not dead!" roared the bear.

I forced my eyes away from Sif and looked at the bear. Yowtgayrr danced around him, but he looked misty, fuzzy. As I watched, the bear lurched at him, swiping the air with his paw, and missing.

"If you stop attacking, Yowtgayrr will stop fighting you."

"And these?" The bear gestured toward its back where Mothi's axes protruded from his thick skin. "The one that stuck these here…he's insane."

"You don't know the half of it. Be glad you're not a Svartalfar. What's your name?"

"Name? Why do you want my name?" The bear peered at me with open suspicion.

"So we can have a civilized conversation. My name's Hank."

"Hank?" the bear said, making it sound like a cough. "What sort of name is that?"

"My grandfather's name."

"Oh, a thousand pardons." I never knew a bear could look sheepish, but he pulled it off. "My name is Kuthbyuhrn."

"What sort of name is that?" I asked with a smile.

"It isn't the name of my grandfather," said the bear gravely. "But it is a name of respect. It means 'God bear' in the old tongue."

"Old tongue? The Gamla Toonkumowl?"

"Is there another?" The bear had stopped fighting Yowtgayrr, and the Alf stood to the side with his weapons held ready, eyes darting between Kuthbyuhrn and my bleeding form. "What's that female doing to you?"

"Trying to stop me from dying, I'd guess."

The bear glanced at me and somehow managed to appear concerned and sheepish at the same time. "You stuck me with a magic spear."

"As I said, you were trying to kill us. See the woman there? The one who is crying? That's my wife. The boy is my son. I couldn't let you hurt them."

"No, of course not! This has been a grave misunderstanding. The lantvihtir lied to me. I should know better than to trust them." Kuthbyuhrn glanced behind me. "Uh, I don't want to alarm you, but the female may have decided to kill you."

I turned and looked. Sif held a short-bladed dagger to my right side, halfway between my armpit and the bottom of my rib cage. She leaned forward and slid the blade into my skin, and I screamed...

TWENTY-
ONE

...**A**nd opened my eyes wide. My body
convulsed and arched until only my
heels, palms, and the back of my head
still touched the ground.

"Hold him!" shouted Sif.

Skowvithr grabbed my shoulders and pressed me
to the floor with gentle pressure. Veethar squatted
and grabbed my knees.

Fire burned in my side, and I had an almost irresistible urge to vomit. "What…" I moaned.

"Shush, now," said Yowrnsaxa. "Let Sif do her work."

"Blood has filled the right side of your chest, Hank, and is keeping your lung deflated. If I don't purge the blood, your chances of surviving this are quite low."

Somewhere above my head, the undead bear— *Kuthbyuhrn,* a voice in my mind said—made a strange sound, almost like a horse blowing air through its nostrils, but sounding distressed. Then it clacked its teeth.

"Someone kill that damn thing," spat Mothi.

"No." I took a long, slow breath. "Kuthbyuhrn was lied to."

"What's he talking about?" cried Jane.

"The thing seems content to sit and watch," shouted Yowtgayrr. "He's stopped attacking."

"Yes, I told him you'd stop fighting him if he did."

"He's delirious," said Yowrnsaxa.

I tried to shake my head but only managed to turn my head to the side before the world fell away again.

TWENTY-
TWO

*T*he sun burned down on me from overhead, but a gentle breeze cooled my face. I opened my eyes and gasped. I was high in the air, in a wide clearing, and surrounded by a sea of treetops, all swaying in the wind.

"Awake at last?" asked a voice filled with gravel.

"Yes," I said. "Where am I?"

"You hang from Iktrasitl."

"What…what am I doing here?"

"No time to chat," said the voice. "I'm on an errand of utmost importance." Something skittered away up the trunk of the tree somewhere behind me—claws rasping on bark.

I tried to turn but had no leverage. I seemed to hang from a branch of the tree by my neck. Far, far below me, a mist encircled the tree trunk like the skirt of a Christmas tree.

"Don't bother yelling for the Witches," said a raspy voice from behind and to the right of me. "Those three bitches—"

The wind gusted and tore the words away. The wind was bitter and cold. As the wind died, an earsplitting scream of anger echoed out over the sea of trees.

"That damn squirrel caused that roar," said the raspy voice. "He won't be happy until the two go to war."

"Who…"

"The eagle and the dragon, of course. Just wait, the squirrel will go running down the tree like a horse, and the damn dragon will roar. Then, back up comes the meddlesome squirrel with another insult for the eagle and it all starts as before. It's interminable!"

"No, I meant to ask who you are."

"You may call me Owsakrimmr."

"Why can't I turn?"

"You hang from the Tree, Aylootr."

"Oh, not that again."

"It's a noble name, a respectful lucre," said Owsakrimmr, sounding a little offended.

"My name, however, is Hank. What is this? A dream?"

"If you like...if that's what it seems."

"It's not about what I like... What is this?"

"You hang from the Tree of Life. You hang from Iktrasitl. I'm naught but the Tree's midwife."

"Why? Why am I here? Who are you, Owsakrimmr? I don't recognize your name."

"It is no matter. The three bitches at the foot of the tree have wrapped your runes with mine, and so we journey together for a time."

Somewhere, far below, or far away, a bear roared.

"The three bitches?"

"The Nornir: Urthr, Verthanti, and Skult. They live far below, at the base of the tree do they sew. There Urthr dug a well, and from it, they draw the water that feeds Iktrasitl."

"So, if I'm dreaming about Yggdrasil, you must be..."

"I am only Owsakrimmr. Stuck here, left to simmer. The same as you, there's nothing we can do."

From above, the rapid-fire sound of claws skittering down the bark of the tree rattled. "Ratatoskr, leave them in peace, take a short rest. A little time of quiet would be best."

"No time, no time!" called the gravel-filled voice I'd first spoken to.

"For my sake, do me this favor! Give us blessed silence to savor!"

"Ha!" yelled the thing on the trunk without slowing.

"He'll drive me insane," sighed Owsakrimmr. "He's such a pain."

"Why are you here? In the tree, I mean?"

"Why are any of us here? The three bitches tied me to this bier."

"What I mean is: are you hanging here like I am or—"

"I am..."

TWENTY-THREE

"I am certain, Jane," said Sif in soothing tones. "Once this blood drains, his breathing will ease. Then, I'll be able to treat the wound. I know my craft, dear."

Jane sobbed, sounding more than sad, more than exhausted, and I began to hear other sounds from the cave: a fierce, whispered argument between Veethar and Frikka, Meuhlnir and Mothi talking quietly about Kuthbyuhrn, the undead bear's chuffing.

I tried to lift my hand but only succeeded in twitching my finger.

"He moved, Mommy," said Sig in a tear-choked voice. "He's..."

"Alive," I croaked.

"Don't speak, Hank," scolded Sif.

I tried to open my mouth, to tell them I was okay, but instead, I drifted...

TWENTY-FOUR

A gust of wind blew aside the black veil that covered my eyes. I sat with my back to a massive tree's trunk, and five women sat around a small campfire a short distance away.

The tree I rested against shimmered with runes carved into its bark. Someone, maybe one of the women, had gouged through many of the runes with a chisel, giving what would otherwise have been a majestic sculpture the air of graffiti.

"Kuhntul, his veil!" The voice rasped like glass on rusted metal. "Don't let him read the runes, girl!"

I tore my eyes away from the runes and stared at the women around the fire. One of them pointed at me, and one was rising—Kuhntul, dressed in immaculate white.

"Why am I here?" I demanded of the women. None of them turned, except Kuhntul, and her expression was grim.

"They are deciding, Tyeldnir," said Kuhntul.

"For the love of God, why can't anyone call me by name?" I snapped.

"Which?" Kuhntul's eyebrow lifted, and her expression was one of interest.

"Hank! Call me Hank."

"No, no. You said: 'for the love of god.' I meant which god?"

I scoffed. "Take your pick."

"Oh, I have. I picked Roonateer long ago when Skult taught me to read the runes."

"These runes?" I asked, turning to look at the tree. "Who has been vandalizing the tree? And who is this Roonateer?"

"Kuhntul! Do not let him read the runes!"

"I know, Mother Skult. But don't worry, he can't read the runes. He barely grasps the Gamla Toonkumowl."

"Still."

"Yes, Mother." Gazing at me, Kuhntul rolled her eyes.

"These runes are what you might call fate or destiny. What we call uhrluhk."

"Why are they defaced?"

Kuhntul cocked her head to the side. "Because uhrluhk is not fixed."

"How can destiny not be fixed?"

Kuhntul's brows crinkled and her lips pursed. "Because we...that is, because each of us... Uhrluhk is..."

"Either explain it, Kuhntul, or cease your prattling."

"Yes, Mother Urthr." Kuhntul bowed her head meekly. "The Nornir carved these runes in the past, and when they carved them, they were true. Then, as the subject—or some other person—changed uhrluhk, the Nornir struck the incorrect runes out and carved the correct runes elsewhere." She looked at me critically. "Do you see?"

"No. How can someone change the destiny that the Nornir carved into the tree? It's destiny, right? It's what is supposed to happen in that person's life."

"Yes, but each of us has free will. Or, as is the case in your present circumstance, someone with the knowledge of uhrluhk and the power to do so may change it."

"And...the Nornir allow this?"

"Mostly, yes. Sometimes, far-reaching consequences to such a change exist, and the Nornir must decide whether to let the changes stand or whether to take action to set things straight." Kuhntul pointed at a set of runes that bore a deep slash through it. "Those runes there, I struck out to change a person's uhrluhk. Mother Urthr was quite upset with me for a time."

"You struck… Wait just a second… You said, 'as is the case in your present circumstance.' What does that mean?"

Kuhntul smiled at me like a mother smiling at a young child. "Veethar was to die in that cave." She pointed at another set of runes. "It is here. Veethar dies at the hand of Kuthbyuhrn."

"But I saved Veethar. He's not dead."

"He is not," snapped one of the women at the fire.

"Thus, the conundrum," said another.

I stared at the runes inscribed into the tree's bark. Here was written the destiny of all living things, and the history of all that came before. If only I could read these runes!

"Kuhntul! His veil!"

"Yes, Mother Skult."

I turned back toward the women and Kuhntul was standing in front of me. She smiled again and draped the black veil over my face and…

TWENTY-FIVE

I woke moaning and thrashing against the strong hands of Skowvithr and Veethar. Sif's head was low over my chest, and her hands were bloody. Yowrnsaxa knelt beside her, handing her things when Sif grunted a word or held out her hand.

My eyes rolled up to Skowvithr's concerned face. He saw and smiled. "All is well, Hank," he whispered. "All is well."

"Frikka," I croaked.

"Don't worry about that now," muttered Sif.

"No," I said. "I misunderstood."

Frikka sobbed somewhere close by. "I'm so sorry, Hank."

"Shh," I said. "Veethar…"

"Yes," she said. "But I didn't know what would happen to you. I swear it."

"It's okay," I said. "I understand."

"Well, I *don't*," snapped Jane.

"Tell…you…later," I wheezed. "Gonna pass—"

TWENTY-SIX

"*T*here you are!" said Kuthbyuhrn. "I was getting worried."

I opened my eyes, hanging in the air above my family and friends. Jane was glaring at Frikka, who couldn't meet her gaze. "You sacrificed my husband for your own?" she demanded.

"It's best to stay out of the affairs of females," said Kuthbyuhrn. "Meddling only leads to a bite on the ass." He sat now, gazing down on our party with alive, interested eyes. "You Isir are so interesting," he murmured. "So alive!"

"Tell me what the lantvihtir *told you."*

"The lantvihtir*? Did they speak to me?"*

"You told me before that they lied to you to get you to attack us."

Kuthbyuhrn *lifted a massive paw and scratched the fur under his chin. "Let me see," he muttered. "The fight started when someone stuck me with a spear..."*

"No, that's near the end. You came at us from deeper in the cave right after we passed the pool of water."

"Are you sure?" Kuthbyuhrn asked, tilting his head to the side. "I'm gentle by nature—always was. I seldom start battles."

"This time, you did. You told me the lantvihtir *lied to you to get you to do it, so your record is intact."*

"Hmmm..." The bear tilted his head and squinted his eyes quizzically "Oh, yes! I remember now. The lantvihtir *came rushing into my area of the cave. They said men with spears were coming to kill my mate, and that—"*

"Mate?" I asked. "Where is she now?"

He glanced at me and averted his gaze. "Well, I was confused before. My mate died at my side—long ago. We stood shoulder to shoulder, fighting the... Well, whatever they were, we stood against them and died." He sighed. "She was such a beautiful bear. She'd have liked you. The fierce one with the axe reminds me of her."

"You mean the one trying to heal me?"

"No, the powerful one who stands shoulder to shoulder with you."

"My wife...Jane. Yes, she's fierce about some things."

"The lantvihtir are very upset with your party," said the bear with a chuckle in his voice. "If I had been more...awake, I would have recognized it in them and seen through their deception."

"What do they want?"

"The lantvihtir?" The bear rolled his shoulders. "What they always want, I guess. I've never understood them very well. Even less so since I died and could understand their speech."

"Maybe I should speak with them?"

Kuthbyuhrn rocked back on his hind legs so that his head would be level with mine. "That would be dangerous for you in your present circumstance. No, let me act as your emissary."

I glanced at my body bleeding onto the floor of the cave. "That might be better, but how can you be sure you will remember what to say?"

"I have a superb memory. For a bear, anyway."

"I've no doubt."

"And I needn't go far." He pointed with his paw. "They are just over there. Can you not see them?"

I stared in the direction he pointed, and I could see vague forms shifting and fluttering. "Maybe, but I can't tell what they are."

Kuthbyuhrn shrugged. "What is your purpose here?"

"We are passing through the cave to avoid having to climb the mountains. That's all."

"Let me talk to them."

The bear lumbered into the darkness.

"The bear!" shouted Mothi. "Where's the bear going?"

TWENTY-SEVEN

"To talk to the *lantvihtir*," I murmured.

"What?" asked Sif. "Shhh, Hank. Don't talk."

"Kuthbyuhrn."

"Yes," she crooned. "Almost done here, Hank, and then I can stitch you up."

"Magic," I groaned.

"Not yet," said Sif. "Let me be—I need to concentrate."

"Fine," I murmured, losing my grip on consciousness yet again.

TWENTY-EIGHT

A gentle breeze cooled my burning skin and ruffled my hair. I opened my eyes onto one of the most beautiful sunsets I'd ever seen. The horizon in front of me was lit with a multitude of shades: golds, pinks, oranges, blues, and purples.

"Ah, good, you've returned," said Owsakrimmr. "I feared you harmed."

"What the hell is going on here? Who the hell are you?"

"You hang from Iktrasitl, Aylootr, the Tree of Life. I'm your adjutor. Don't take fright, enjoy the coming of the night."

I couldn't suppress a sigh.

"Yes, it is a beautiful sunset. Then again, it always is, Iktrasitl's epaulette."

"Why do I keep having this dream?"

"Aylootr, this is no troymskrok. Not all dreams are meaningless rot. Your ancestors knew this, but like so much knowledge, it has sunk into the abyss."

"Please stop calling me that."

"What? It is a grand name, Aylootr, one filled with honor, glory, and the sounds of the sharpshooter."

"My name is Hank."

"Four little letters between us. I cannot call you thus."

"Why in the hell not?"

From below, a ragged roar rived the calm air. The tree shook with it, the vibrations magnified by the springy wood, bounced me up and down like a Pogo stick.

"That damn squirrel," muttered Owsakrimmr. "Filled with the scurrile."

"Why do I keep bouncing around?"

"It's because of that damn animal, riling up the dragon below, enraging him, poking him, making him intractable. These branches are spry, and when the dragon shouts, we fall, we fly."

"No, that's not what I meant—"

"Listen, Aylootr, and cease this prattle. Time is short; all this talk is naught but attle. Attend me before we are rived from this ash tree." Owsakrimmr cleared his throat, and when he next spoke, his voice was clear and resonating.

> "Two gods errant
> Didst thou inherit
> Your life in flames
> Without fear you came
> To the home of gods,
> Across bridges, beyond stars.
> Thee and she,
> bound by the Three
> at the foot of the Tree
> Thee and she
> Further entwined by fate,
> As lover, as mate
> Blood, bone, and eyes
> When does one, so the other dies."

"Very nice," I said. "But that doesn't answer my question."

"Does it not?" Owsakrimmr sounded amused. "Not one tittle, not one jot?"

"No."

"Let me try again, while I am still fain." He cleared his throat a second time.

> "She and thee
> Lovers and mates
> Entwined thy fates
> With a runed thing

A fine Tverkr ring
When Frikka plied her trade
A fine mess was made
Not one changed strand
Nor three changed plans
But the whole thing ruined
All those lives, preordained
The whole skein of fate
Broken to save Frikka's mate
Now, yarns are tangled
The Tapestry is mangled
We hang in this Tree
thee and me, me and thee
While the Maids' elegy
Decries our destiny."

"I really hate poetry—did you know that?"
"That is confusing...I find it soothing."
"It gives me a headache."

Owsakrimmr barked a laugh. "That's not the poetry, Sherlock, that's blood loss and shock. There's the defect if my memory is correct."

I shook my head. Riddles and poetry, when all I want is one straight answer.

"Que cette chose avancer," said Owsakrimmr with a chuckle. "My kingdom for one straight answer."

TWENTY-NINE

My head pounded, and the entire right side of my chest burned like it was on fire. I couldn't move, not even to open my eyelids, and I didn't want to.

"He will rest now," said Sif. Her voice dripped with weariness.

"Will he…" Jane's voice shook with emotion.

"Yes, his chances of surviving are good. I think he will live. I've done everything I can to make sure he will."

"But you don't know for sure?" asked Sig.

"No, dear Siggy. I can't be certain. The Nornir have his life in their hands. But I want him to. Very much."

"As do I," said Frikka in a choked voice. "I've tried to look ahead, to perform an augury, but I can see nothing. And not just for him. It's as if…"

"As if what?" asked Veethar.

"As if the skein of fate lies ripped—torn asunder."

"All this… Was it worth it, wife?" demanded Veethar.

"Mother Sif, we need to retrace our steps."

"Hank can't be moved," said Sif. "A move would kill him."

Mothi sighed. "I had hoped you wouldn't say that. The great undead bear has returned, and Althyof has grown weary in the hours that have passed. He is running out of strength."

"So, lend him yours!" snapped Sif.

"Yes, Mother Sif."

"Mothi, I—"

"I know, Mother Sif."

THIRTY

"*H*ello again, friend," said Kuthbyuhrn.
"Hello, Kuthbyuhrn. I'm glad to see you."

"And I you." The great bear hung his head. "Though, I am ashamed to say I've forgotten your name since you were last here."

"Don't worry about it," I said. "My name is Hank."

"Ah, yes! Hank. The strange name."

"Yep, that's me. Did you speak with the lantvihtir?"

"The lantvihtir? Why would I... Oh! Yes, I remember now. You asked me to speak with them, and I went to them, but when I returned you had disappeared."

"Sorry. I seem to have no control of myself at the moment."

"Oh, it's no problem. I can see your fettle is in the hands of others."

"What does that mean?"

"I have no idea. I'm just a bear."

I smiled up at him. "You are much more than a bear, my friend."

"If this is only a troymskrok, a meaningless dream, then I'm really part of your mind, and what you say is true, but if this isn't a meaningless dream, I'm only a bear, I'm sorry to say."

"Well..."

"It's okay, Hank. I enjoy being a bear. I'm good at it."

I chuckled, and he chuffed through his nose. "Okay. What did the lantvihtir say?"

"The lantvihtir? Oh! Yes, I remember now. Keeping things straight without an actual brain is hard. Mine rotted, you know."

I nodded, smiling.

"Yes, well, the lantvihtir. They said they don't care what you are doing here—that I should kill you all. I told them I wouldn't do that, of course. Now that we are friends, it would be unthinkable." He turned his huge head and looked into the darkness behind him.

"They are massing for an attack. They say the short little one is running out of endurance."

"My friends have a plan to take care of that."

"Good. The lantvihtir… Well, they hate the short one particularly. Not only because he sings a horrible song that hurts the lantvihtir, but also because they used to be as he is."

"They were Tverkar? On Osgarthr?"

"Sure, why not? The Isir aren't the only ones who can use the preer."

"I should speak to them. Will you take me there?"

"I'm not sure that's a good idea, Hank. They detest the living."

"I get that, but right now, I'm not really living, am I?"

The bear glanced past me, no doubt looking at my body. "Well, your body is technically alive, though an empty shell right now. It's a gray area."

"So I was told by a guy hanging in a tree."

The big bear was silent for a moment before saying, "Hank, sometimes I think people are quite strange."

I nodded, smiling. "Lead on, brave Kuthbyuhrn."

The bear mimicked my nod and drew the skin back from his teeth, but the effect was ruined by his incredible fangs. He turned and shambled into the darkness.

I floated into the cave with him.

"You move well for one so recently alive," Kuthbyuhrn remarked. "Oh! Forgive me, Hank. I sometimes speak without thinking."

I laughed. "My people have a saying, Kuthbyuhrn. It goes like this: It is what it is."

"What a strange sentiment."

"It means there's no point feeling bad for what we can't control."

"Oh! Yes, very wise. We bears usually say Uhrluhk, and chuff through our noses."

As we approached the lantvihtir, I began to perceive more of them than blurs and shadows. Their ghostly forms were similar to the Tverkar.

"Step no farther, Hank. You are at the edge of the protection your friend offers. If you were to take two more steps, the lantvihtir would swarm you like a hive of angry bees."

"Thanks for the warning. Can they still hear me?"

"Yes!" said one of the lantvihtir. "But you have nothing to say that matters to us!"

"My friends and I will leave you in peace if you will do the same."

"You will stay with us in this cave, no matter what your friends do." The lantvihtir laughed with a nasty smile stretching across his ghostly face.

"That's quite rude," said Kuthbyuhrn.

"So is going back on your word, you great steaming lump of rotten meat!"

"I gave you my word based on your lies. I'm not bound by untruths."

"What can I say or do to earn our passage through your domain? There must be something you want."

"Besides your death? I suppose you could change our uhrluhk, so we aren't trapped in this damn place." The lantvihtir *said it in a nasty, sarcastic tone, but I felt a glimmer of hope.*

"I'll see what I can do."

The lantvihtir *laughed and a bolt of pure agony twisted through my head.*

THIRTY-ONE

"**D**addy! Stop it!"

An immense pressure threatened to blow my brains all over the cave. My hands pressed against the side of my head as if I could keep my skull from exploding that way. I was rocking side to side, and there was a tearing, burning sensation in my side.

"Auntie Sif! Help!"

"I'm coming, Siggy," shouted Sif. "Yowrnsaxa! I may need you again."

I peeled my eyes open, and the firelight ravaged my eyes, but not before I saw Sig looking down at me, terror on his face, tears in his eyes.

Sif ran up and knelt at my side, grasping my shoulders to stop me from rocking. "Hank! Stop this! You will rip out your stitches."

I got control of myself and lay still though I didn't take my hands away from my face. She moved one of her hands to my forehead, and her palm chilled me like a lump of ice.

"He's burning up!" Sif said. "Yowrnsaxa, I need the third jar from the fourth pocket of my bag."

"Coming, dear," said Yowrnsaxa in a sleep clogged voice.

"With speed, if you please!" shouted Sif. "Sig, go dip your shirt in the pool and bring it to me. Run, boy!" Sig pounded off, pulling his shirt over his head.

Every sound they made drove a railroad spike through my temples. Each time Sif moved, the sound of her clothing rubbing against her skin made me want to vomit. Every time I cracked open my eyes, the dim light from the burnt-down fire seemed stunningly bright—like a million-candlepower spotlight shined in my eyes.

"Hank," Sif said in a quiet voice. "You must tell me how you feel."

"I..." The sound of my own voice drilled into the center of my head and left burning acid in its wake. "Headache," I gasped. "Hot."

"You've got a high fever. I can feel that for myself. Are you nauseated?"

"Sounds." I gritted my teeth against a scream of frustration and pain.

Yowrnsaxa arrived and handed Sif a glass pot. Sif pulled the stopper, and my stomach rebelled, heaving against my ribs like a bucking bronco. "Bring one of the hoses in the same pocket, dear."

"Be right back," said Yowrnsaxa.

"This won't be pleasant, Hank. I'm going to put you to sleep again."

"No more," I moaned.

"Yes. I must put a tube down your throat, so you keep this brew down. If I don't, I fear the fever will cause damage to your brain. There's no choice."

"No more dreams," I whined.

"Can't avoid that, I'm afraid." Sif touched her finger to the center of my forehead. "*Svepn*," she said. The icy sensation stole over me again, and I slept.

THIRTY-TWO

I *didn't want to open my eyes. I didn't want to see the canopy of trees stretching away to the horizon. I didn't want to see the women at the campfire. I didn't want to see the bear. All I wanted was the blackness of dreamless sleep.*

"You can't always get what you want, Aylootr. But if you try sometimes, you might find you get what you need."

"Jesus," I moaned.

"That's not my name," said Owsakrimmr. "That turn the other cheek thing rubs against my grain."

"Did you just quote a Rolling Stones song?"

"Allow me to introduce myself. I'm a man of wealth and taste."

"Oh, shut up."

"Pleased to meet you, Aylootr. Hope you guess my name."

"The only thing that makes me feel better right now is that if this is a dream—a regular dream—when I die, so will you."

"You don't know how true those words are, you fevered bag of bones. But what's all the hate about the Stones?"

"The Stones are great—it's you I detest."

"Self-hate is fruitless, my friend." Owsakrimmr chuckled. "Besides, you need me—I am your augend."

"And why is that?"

"You promised the lantvihtir in that cave to change their uhrluhk, but don't have the ability to do that—like them, you are stuck."

"And I suppose you have the power I need? And I bet all I need to do is rescue you from this tree."

"Yek air Owsakrimmr hoospownti runeskowld," he sang, his voice rumbling thunder, echoing back from the horizon.

"Wait, you're a runeskowld?"

"Tayla meth thessum aynum madni."

Power swept around me from behind, wrapping tight against my skin as if a giant, invisible spider was wrapping me in its web.

"Kefthu honum thechkinku meena ow rununum. Kefthu honum thechkinku meena ow gamla toonkumowlinu. Binddu honum."

The power around me snapped and shivered, burning my skin as it latched onto me. I screamed, more from fear than anything else, and arched my back, starting myself swinging. "Stop! Whatever you are doing to me, I want you to stop!"

"Lowttu hadn lesa runana sem steethya atlt. Binddu honum."

I stopped struggling, stunned into inaction by the knowledge flooding my mind. I understood the words he was singing. That last line meant: Let him read the runes that underpin everything. Bind him.

"Lowttu hadn skrifu runana sem feerirmila uhrluhk. Binddu honum."

I repeated the words in my mind, delighting in the knowledge of the Gamla Toonkumowl *he'd given me.* Let him write the runes that dictate fate. Bind him.

"Snertu anda hans meth hyarta *Iktrasitl*. Binddu honum. Snertu anda hans meth hyarta *Iktrasitl*. Binddu honum."

Again, I repeated the words to myself. Touch his spirit with the heart of *Iktrasitl*. Bind him. Touch his spirit with the heart of *Iktrasitl*. Bind him. *I no longer feared what he was doing, this mysterious stranger hanging from the Tree of Life with me. I welcomed it.*

"Sendu hadn noona, til thrikkya vidnukona. Lokathu teekunum ath thvi sem hadn kerir."

The words danced in my mind: Send him now, to the three Maids. Close the bitches' eyes to what he does. *As the meaning of the phrases sank in, regret sang in my veins.* "Wait! Who are you? Will I see you again?"

"What's done is done, Aylootr. It can't be overrun. As to your last question, yes, it is possible you will see me again, and often, in the Nornir shadow-show. As to your first, you already know."

I tried to open my mouth, to shout my thanks, to ask him if he was Odin, but it was already too late. My eyes fell shut, and my mouth, open. I fought it, but I couldn't stave off consciousness.

THIRTY-THREE

My eyes opened. *No! Not yet!* I screamed inside my head. The only sound around me was the song Althyof sang. I reveled in my newfound understanding of *what* he was singing. As he sang, the runes associated with each line burned in my mind's eye.

I laughed aloud, unable to help it.

"Hank?" came Sif's sleep-blurred voice. "Are you awake?"

I let my eyelids fall closed, exhausted, but feeling better than I had since Kuthbyuhrn had attacked. "Sleep," I said. "All is well."

Then, I slept.

THIRTY-
FOUR

I awoke to the sound of a squirrel chittering away somewhere near my head. I opened my eyes, but a black veil of fine lace obscured my vision.

"Back again, are you?" asked Ratatoskr in his strange, gravel-filled voice.

I heaved a sigh. "Yes, I'll never escape this dream."

"Dream? You think this is a dream? A troymskrok?" Raucous laughter sounded above and behind me.

"Whatever. Can you do me a favor?"

Little squirrel claws skittered across the bark of Iktrasitl. "Maybe. It depends."

"Depends on what?"

"On whether you will poke at me with a spear."

"Why would I do that?"

Ratatoskr laughed, sounding like a chainsaw eating its way through thick wood. "Red squirrels are good eating! That's what you said to me not two days ago!"

"Friend, I've only spoken to you once, and it was earlier today. Remember? You asked me if I was awake and told me I was hanging in Iktrasitl?"

"Oh! It's you. Why didn't you say so?"

Ratatoskr tugged the black veil off my head. He clung to the bark, head pointed at the ground, the veil in his teeth. Red tinged his fur, except for his belly, where it was a brilliant white. His eyes were a jet black, and he had the cutest little tufts of red hair sticking up from his little ears. Ratatoskr opened his mouth and let the black veil fall. "Why are you looking at me like that?"

"You look so cute…"

"What? How dare you?"

"I didn't mean to offend you, but you are cute."

Ratatoskr cocked his head to the side and twitched his bushy red tail. "I am not cute! I am a vicious, man-eating monster of mythic proportions. Don't you forget it."

I held up my hands in a gesture of surrender. "I apologize, mighty Ratatoskr. I was momentarily blinded by the beauty of your fur."

"Well, okay then." Ratatoskr glanced down the trunk. "I really can't spend much time here. I am on a mission for the eagle."

"I was wondering about that. Why would you keep this battle of words running between these two, the eagle and the dragon? What purpose does it serve?"

"What purpose does it serve? How can you not see it? I thought you were wise!" Ratatoskr twitched his tail. "Well, maybe that was the other one... Are you sure you're not the one who threatened me with the spear?"

"I am not the one who threatened you with a spear. I have never eaten squirrel and hope I never do."

"Why ever not? Red squirrels are delicious."

"Well, I—"

"It's no matter. And I don't have time to continue chatting with you. I must be about my business." With that, Ratatoskr scurried down the trunk.

"Well, thanks for getting rid of the veil...it was nice talking to you." I looked around sure I would see the three Nornir sitting around a campfire and staring at me, but the fire had burned out, and the three maids were gone. I stood up and turned around to face Iktrasitl. Unlike before, the runes now made sense to me. Whoever the man in the tree was—and I thought he must be Odin—he had done me a great service by sharing his knowledge of the runes and the Gamla Toonkumowl *with me. Testing my knowledge of the runes, I picked a line at random and read it aloud: "Vuhluntr fell in love with Uhlroon the Valkyrie, and they married. After nine years Uhlroon left Vuhluntr." I laughed aloud, like a seven-year-old with a new toy.*

I spent what seemed like a week reading runes at random. It was like paging through a novel about old Norse mythology or reading the Prose Edda. I had promised to free the lantvihtir *if I could, but it would take me years to read all the runes... There were billions of runes on the part of Iktrasitl that I could read, and the runes stretched high above my head until I could no longer discern the difference between the runes and the natural twists and eddies of Iktrasitl's bark.*

All I knew about the lantvihtir, *all I knew about Kuthbyuhrn, was that they lived in a cave under the Dragon's Spine Mountains somewhere northwest of Suelhaym. It wasn't much to go on. I scanned the part of the tree I could see for Kuthbyuhrn's name in runes, but it was no use. Without a key, without knowledge of how the runes were laid onto the tree, it would take years to find a specific event. I needed help from someone who was already familiar with the work of the Nornir.*

If only Kuhntul were still here.

"Got your veil off again, huh?" Kuhntul laughed. "Don't let the three Maids see you without it. They can be nasty."

"I was just thinking about you...wishing you were here, really."

"Oh, how sweet...but what will Jane think?"

I glanced over at her in time to catch the mischievous twinkle in her eye. "You know what I mean."

"Yes, more's the pity. What you want is not on this side of Iktrasitl."

"How do you know what I want? I haven't asked you yet."

"My apologies. Why do you need my help, Tyeldnir? Can I find a specific rune for you?" Her voice was sarcastic, taunting.

"If you already know, lead on. I only wanted to know how you knew."

Kuhntul shrugged. "I am Tisir," she said as if that were explanation enough. She turned and walked counter-clockwise around the tree.

"How does all this work?" I asked.

"I can't answer that, Tyeldnir. I can't give you power over the skein of fate. That's too much power for a mortal man."

I sighed and followed her around the tree. She stopped and pointed to a spot on the tree about fifteen yards up. "There," she said. "The lantvihtir in the cave were the group that attacked Kuthbyuhrn and his mate, Kyellroona, in the cave. The lantvihtir who remain are the men who killed Kyellroona.

Kuthbyuhrn killed them all in a berserker rage and succumbed to his wounds."

I looked up at the tree. "So…if I write a different story, neither the lantvihtir nor Kuthbyuhrn will be trapped in the cave?"

Kuhntul shrugged. "Temporal mechanics are beyond my grasp, Tyeldnir. If you need to know before you make the change, you'll have to speak with Mother Skult. Shall I fetch her?" Kuhntul's lips twisted into a smirk.

"I don't think so. I wanted to say goodbye to Kuthbyuhrn, is all."

Kuhntul shrugged. "You could always come back later. You may find another time when the three Maids are absent."

That didn't seem likely. And, anyway, I did not understand how I was traveling to Iktrasitl, or even if any of what I was experiencing was real. "No." I glanced up at the spot she'd pointed out. "How do I get up there?"

"Do I have to do everything for you? Here, you will need this." She held out a chisel made from silvery metal that seemed to glow with its own light.

I took the chisel, and it felt warm in my palm. I thought for a moment, and said, "Plyowta." Both of my feet came off the ground, floating half an inch or so above the turf.

"Uhp." I rose, slowly at first but picking up speed as I ascended next to the tree.

"There," called Kuhntul.

"*Stuthva,*" *I murmured. I could get to love having the* Gamla Toonkumowl *at my fingertips. I stopped rising and floated a foot from the tree. Using the chisel Kuhntul had given me, I struck a line through the runes that described Kyellroona's demise. As I watched, the runes around the area I'd cut through reshaped themselves.*

The story now read: "*Mighty Kuthbyuhrn roared, and the Tverkar were afraid. They backed away from Kyellroona and threw down their weapons, begging for mercy. It was in Kuthbyuhrn's nature to grant their wish, so the bears and the Tverkar parted company on good terms.*" *I wanted to follow the runes that branched off, to know what befell Kuthbyuhrn and Kyellroona, to see where the Tverkar went next, but there was no time.*

"*Time to go, Tyeldnir,*" *whispered Kuhntul from the base of the tree.* "*Time to wake. The three Maids return. Remember the chisel!*"

"*Thanks,*" *I said and woke.*

THIRTY-FIVE

When I awoke, it felt more like being thrown out of unconsciousness than waking. My eyes snapped open, and I lurched, my mind sure I was falling from a great height.

The cave was quiet, peaceful—at least until Keri and Fretyi, who lay pressed to my left side at two points, noticed I was awake. They jumped up, crooning like proud papas, running in circles, licking my face. They'd grown while I was out of it and both looked an easy ten pounds heavier. "Living up to your names, I bet," I said, ruffling the fur behind two sets of ears.

My side ached, but it was a minor ache. What hurt worse was the hole in my belly where my stomach had once lived. I sat up and glanced around.

The remains of a fire glowed in the center of a large circle defined by the sleeping bodies of my companions. I stretched with care, wary of pulling stitches or tearing open my wound. A nagging, uncomfortable tightness lingered under my right arm, but nothing compared to what I had expected. I ran my hand over my ribs, but instead of a sutured wound, my fingers scrabbled across scar tissue. It was tender, but it didn't hurt.

I shook my head, marveling at how fast I'd healed under Sif's expert care. Images came flooding into my mind. More than images, *memories*, but of events I didn't remember happening. I still remembered the battle with Kuthbyuhrn, but now I also remembered an alternate series of events—things I hadn't lived through, and yet I had.

"Finally," grunted Althyof from across the circle. He got to his feet and stirred the coals, then added fresh wood. He walked toward me, keen eyes traveling over my face, my right side. "You've lain in the grip of a high fever for more than a week, Tyeldnir."

"A week?" I parroted, stunned.

"Sif refused to let us move you. Your spear wound became infected—something the damn Svartalf cooked up and gave to the attackers, no doubt." That was from the new set of memories—dark forms swarming at Veethar out of the darkness. "What do you remember? I'll fill in the gaps," said the Tverkr.

"Well, that's an interesting question, but I remember an ambush. When they swarmed at us out of the darkness, Veethar was out in front, and...I guess I had dreamed about a spear thrust arcing from the darkness because my mind showed me his death. I grabbed him and twisted him out of the way. When I turned back to the attackers, I...held something in my hands..."

"A spear," said Althyof. "A spear you'd conjured."

"Yes! I held a spear. The... Who was it that attacked us?"

"A small band of trolls."

"Trolls? I can't remember them."

Althyof shrugged. "It's no matter. I remember them enough for both of us."

"Yeah. Anyway, the trolls who were planning to kill Veethar grew angry when I moved him. I... Were there two of them?"

"Three."

"Okay, three of them came at me. I had the spear, and I tried to ward them off. One of them hit the spear dead-center with his massive club and shattered the spear-shaft. At the same time, another troll charged into me with his shoulder and sent me flying. I...I hit the wall of the cave and fell to the floor. When I landed, the spear went into my side... I don't remember much after that: Sif working on me, something to do with Frikka and Veethar, but it's not clear… Oh, and the dreams."

"Dreams?" Althyof lifted his eyebrow.

"But what's freaky is the other series of events I remember."

"What?"

"In the other series of events, there was a big, undead bear. You had to keep singing a *trowba* to keep the *lantvihtir* off us, but the bear—"

"Do you mean Kuthbyuhrn?"

"Uh…yes. Do you remember this other version too?"

Althyof shook his head. "No. Kuthbyuhrn heard the ruckus of us fighting the trolls and came charging to our rescue. He and Kyellroona saved us."

I shook my head. "You… How do you know their names?"

Althyof rolled his eyes. "Veethar speaks to the animals, remember? *Lantvihtir*, you say?"

"Yeah…" I shook my head. "Could all this be fever dreams?"

"No matter, go on with your story."

"It was the bear, Kuthbyuhrn, who almost killed Veethar—who shattered my spear and sent me flying. It… Frikka…did something…"

"What did I do," asked Frikka in a sleep-blurred voice, rustling in her bedroll.

"I…" I glanced her way and saw her shake her head. "I don't remember."

Althyof's head snapped around to stare at Frikka with suspicion. She waved him off as if he were a mosquito.

"After that, it's all just snatches of being awake while Sif worked on me. And the dreams."

"There they are again," muttered Althyof. "Tell me of these dreams."

"Time for that later," said Frikka, with a glance my way. She tried to communicate something with her eyes—she wanted me to keep mum about the dreams.

"I'm starving," I said. "And parched. Didn't anyone give me water?"

"Yes," said Sif without opening her eyes. "Though you spat more back at me than you drank." She sat up, weariness in every movement. "I'm glad you're awake and yourself again, Hank, but I wish you'd chosen a time later in the day." She stifled what looked to have been a huge yawn. "Now, Althyof, stop pestering my patient."

"I wasn't pestering—"

"Away with you," Sif said, but she smiled to take the sting out of it. "Hank needs a check-up."

Althyof glanced my way, and I smiled up at him. "Better do as she says, or she'll make you drink one of her potions," I said. Althyof nodded and walked to the pool to wash.

Frikka walked over and held out her hand. "We should speak privately."

"Fine, but Sif—"

"We've known each other a long time," said Sif. "I knew what she wanted."

Frikka nodded, so I shrugged and let her pull me to my feet. We walked a short way deeper into the cave, out of earshot of the rest of the party. "What you did," she began. "It is important that you not share the alternate version of the past."

"The alternate…"

"Yes. The version of the battle with the undead bear."

"*You* remember it that way, too?"

She shook her head. "I remember the undead bear killing Veethar in front of you."

I stopped and stared at her. "It was true? My dream?"

Frikka nodded. "I couldn't stand the prospect of going on without him, so I…so I…"

"You gave me a prophetic dream, so I would intervene?"

She nodded but wouldn't—or couldn't—meet my gaze. "I had no idea it would cause your injuries—I couldn't see past the changes I would wreak because none of it had been written yet."

"By the Nornir," I muttered.

Frikka nodded again. "You've dreamed before—not *troymskrok*, but meaningful dreams. Yes?"

I recalled the dreams I'd had since coming to Osgarthr. I recalled the dream of finding Jane and Sig in Piltsfetl, only to have them murdered before my eyes. "Yes, I think so."

"You have," she said with a matter-of-fact demeanor. "But you never realized, you never *knew* you could change such things."

"No."

"But now, you do."

"Yes."

"And what happened in your fever-dreams…was that *troymskrok*?"

"I…don't know. Maybe not."

"Can you tell me of it?"

"There were three themes, or maybe two. One theme, which took place here in the cave, amounted to me speaking with Kuthbyuhrn and getting him to stop attacking. He told me about Kyellroona's death and his own. We tried to get the *lantvihtir* to leave us alone, but they wouldn't agree. The—"

"So, *you* changed their *uhrluhk*—theirs and Kuthbyuhrn and Kyellroona's."

I shrugged.

"*How*? How did you learn to do this?"

"The two other themes took place around the Tree of Life. One—"

"Iktrasitl?"

"Yes."

"You *saw* them? You visited the Well of Urthr?"

"In my dream, yes."

She was silent for a moment, staring into the darkness deep in the cave. "Do you… I didn't mean for you to get hurt, Hank," she said.

"I understand that, now. When the bear hit me—stabbed me with my spear and sent me flying—I landed near you. You were crying, trying to apologize. You rushed to my side, and in my pain and confusion, it seemed like you were trying to poison me, but you were only trying to staunch the flow of blood. I used my cloak—twisted my fettle—to get away from you, and when I came out of its effect, I collapsed. I didn't understand—not until I..."

"Not until something happened at the Well of Urthr."

I shook my head. "No, farther up in Iktrasitl. I think... Maybe I met Odin." It sounded stupid to say it aloud, but I had no other explanation.

"To my knowledge, there is no Isir named Odin," she said.

"It may be my subconscious mind filling in the gaps," I said with a shrug. "In Mithgarthr, Odin is the 'Allfather,' the leader of the Isir. In our legends, he hung himself from Iktrasitl to learn runic magic or to gain wisdom or something of the sort."

She arched her eyebrows, and a small smile played on the edges of her mouth. "And you only have to hang yourself on the Tree of Althyof."

"In my dream, whoever it was hanging in the tree with me gave me his knowledge of the runes and his knowledge of the *Gamla Toonkumowl*."

"*Er thath svo?*" she asked.

"Yes, it is so. *Yek lyooa echke vith vini meena.*"

"No. You are not one to lie to your friends—or anyone else." Frikka cocked her head to the side. "Are we still friends?"

I stopped walking and turned to face her. "Yes, Frikka. What you did, it…it almost killed me, true, but it also saved Veethar and gave me what is perhaps the greatest gift I'll ever receive."

She nodded once, relief sketched in the lines around her eyes. "Can you tell me of it? Of the Well?"

"You have a better understanding of it than I do."

She shook her head. "I can see what will happen, and I can change it, but it appears my methods differ from what you did—by a great deal. This…" She waved her arms wide. "This is much more than I can do."

"The Well is at the base of Iktrasitl, but it isn't a well. At least it wasn't in my dream version. It was a campfire, around which the three Maids sat. The skein of fate…it's carved into the bark of Iktrasitl— billions upon billions of runes describing all the events that make up all the lives of…well, everyone who ever lived, I guess. They stretched from the base of the tree up past where my vision could no longer resolve any details."

"And how did you change…things?"

"Kuhntul gave me a chisel, and I carved through the line that described Kyellroona's death, the death of the Tverkar who became *lantvihtir* in this cave, and Kuthbyuhrn's death. The runes changed by themselves, to tell a different tale. The story went that Kuthbyuhrn let loose a mighty roar—"

"And the Tverkr saw the error of their ways," said a deep, resonant voice from the darkness.

"Hello, Kuthbyuhrn," I said.

"Hello, friend. It seems I should remember your name, but I do not."

"My name is Hank, and I'm glad to see you again, but I don't understand how you are still alive."

"*Uhrluhk*," he said and chuffed through his nose.

"Yes," I said.

"It is what it is," he said, with a curious inflection in his voice.

I laughed. "Yes, that too."

"I don't know why I said that, friend Hank," Kuthbyuhrn said.

"It was part of a conversation we had, but which never happened."

Kuthbyuhrn stepped out of the darkness, and he was beautiful, as he had been in my dreams. Alongside him stepped another bear, even more beautiful than Kuthbyuhrn.

"Kyellroona?" I asked.

She chuffed gently through her nose and lifted her head. "My mate has dreamed of you for years and told me stories. In my heart, we are friends already."

"I'd like nothing more."

"*Uhrluhk*," she said and chuffed through her noise.

"Yes," I said. "And I am glad to meet you." In the corner of my eye, I noticed Frikka staring at me. "What?" I turned to face her.

She shook her head. "I've never seen anyone but Veethar speak to animals." She turned and bowed to the two magnificent bears. "Give them my respects, please. I'll let you get reacquainted."

Smiling, I turned back to my friends. "I don't understand how you are both still alive, but I'm glad. And you were wrong, Kuthbyuhrn. You aren't a simple bear. Not at all."

The expression mirrored on those two ursine faces left me with no doubt that bears can—and do—smile.

THIRTY-SIX

Three days later Sif pronounced me fit for travel, and we set off through the cave. The horses stamped their feet and snorted a lot, restless from the long confinement underground. Keri and Fretyi pranced around the horses yipping and barking and generally making a nuisance of themselves as puppies are wont to do. Every time I looked at the *varkr* pups, their capacity for turning way too much food into solid bulk amazed me. Long, wiry fur in dark gray and black had replaced their puppy fur, and they were starting to look like wild, scary wolves.

Veethar and Frikka stayed to themselves, whispering in intense conversations that seemed to frustrate Veethar a great deal. Frikka seemed to grow angrier with each conversation. No doubt I was the subject of that conversation—or at least the unintended consequences of Frikka's deed—but what could I do? After all, I wouldn't want someone butting into Jane's and my business.

Sif mother-henned me at every opportunity, smearing a stinky ointment here, pushing a repugnant draught there, until I wanted to scream, but she was doing her best for me, and I feared saying anything to her lest Jane use her axe on me. Sig seemed content and happy now that I was up and moving around, though he stayed close to my side rather than palling around with Mothi.

Kuthbyuhrn and Kyellroona elected to walk with us, and I must admit that having the two hulking bears shambling at our sides went a long way toward making everyone feel safer inside the cave. Kuthbyuhrn didn't smell more trolls lurking in the shadows of his cave but said he couldn't be certain. I think he just wanted to spend time with us, and that made me happy.

It was a two-day walk through the labyrinth of caves beneath the Dragon's Spine Mountains, which made the fact that it took us a week and five days—counting the time I'd spent recovering—all the more frustrating.

Uhrluhk, I thought and imitated a bear chuffing through his nose as I saw the light at the end of the long, long tunnel, both the figurative and the real.

"Yes, Hank?" asked Kuthbyuhrn.

"Oh, nothing," I said with a grin. "I was thinking '*uhrluhk*' and then..." I chuffed through my nose.

"Oh! That's funny." Kuthbyuhrn repeatedly chuffed, which I guessed was bear for laughter. He swung his massive head on a level with my own. "Kyellroona and I were talking last night."

"Oh yeah?"

"Yes. Neither of us remembers a time when either one of us was dead, but even so, we owe you a debt of gratitude. We've lived a long time—maybe longer than we should have. And from the sound of it, we owe you all those years. We—"

"Whoa there, big guy," I said. "You don't owe me anything." I looked past him at Kyellroona. "Neither one of you owes me a single thing."

"Hank, we respectfully disagree. In the dreams I have had for years and years, Kyellroona is always dead and gone, and I am left alone stuck in this cave with only *lantvihtir* for company. Plus, I'm dead, and my body is decaying around me. I don't know if you've ever been dead, but it wasn't a pleasant sensation."

I nodded, replaying my recent out-of-body experiences in my memory—all the bouncing around, feeling powerless, out of control.

"Plus, our lives would have been so short," said Kyellroona. "We would've never had the opportunity to cub."

"Well, you saved my wife and son from the trolls. How about we agree to call it even?"

"We are cave bears, Hank, and the other side of this cave opens on a forest that is…distasteful to us, or we would go with you on your quest," said Kuthbyuhrn.

"I appreciate that, my friend, but you don't owe me a thing."

"We have something—*some things*—that may be of use to you and your party." Kyellroona stopped walking. "Would you please follow me, Hank?"

"Hey, hold up everyone!" I yelled.

"As much as I love being underground, could we get on with it here?" yelled Althyof.

"I'll be right back. Go on without me if you are impatient." I turned to Kyellroona and smiled. She chuffed and led me to a small tunnel that branched off the main cave. As we left the others, the light streaming in from the entrance disappeared like we'd submerged in a lake of black ink. "*Au noht,*" I whispered, blinking against the sting.

"We've lived in these caves for a long time, as you know," she said. "And in that time, many a foolish man or troll or Tverkr has ventured into our domain. If they left us alone, we left them alone, but few of them left us alone." We rounded a bend, and the tunnel opened into a wide chamber. "Most often we could scare them away—Kuthbyuhrn has become proficient at roaring in a frightening way. Those we couldn't scare away, we…" She glanced at me. "Well, we dealt with the threat to our home. Kuthbyuhrn has become proficient at fighting men, as well." She waved at the chamber with her head. "Look around, take what you wish, with our thanks. It's far too little, but it's all we can offer."

"Kyellroona, that you thought of this is more than enough."

"Still," she said.

With a shrug, I stepped around her bulk and gasped at what I saw. The chamber contained mining equipment, armor, weapons, chests, tack for the horses and other pieces of leather, and forestry equipment. "This is quite a collection," I said.

"Yes. We regret having it, but…"

"You have every right to defend your home." I flipped the lid open on one of the chests. Coins minted in gold filled it to the rim. Another chest contained gemstones of every color I could imagine. I walked deeper into the room, marveling at the antiquity of some of the items. There was an ancient looking leather case—similar to a map case, but shorter. It had fancy, gold-clad decorations and hardware, and a leather shoulder strap.

I picked it up, imagining I might make collars for Keri and Fretyi, and as I did, the lid flapped open, revealing a roll of paper—a *scroll*. I took it out and unrolled it, treating it like tissue paper.

Runes covered it, and they glowed in my enchanted sight. Horizontal lines that stretched from one edge of the scroll to the other broke it into neat sections. I scanned the runes of the first part, reading them as I would read the newspaper or a letter—with no particular attention to *stayba runana* or toward rhythm and tempo—but as I read, an irresistible tempo took hold of my mental voice, and I rushed through the *kaltrar*, unable to stop. Along with the tempo, runes cast themselves as I read, appearing in my mind's eye, and exploding outward a heartbeat later.

My eyes stung, as they always did when someone enchanted my eyes with the words "*au noht*" but with much, much more intensity, and my eyes flooded with tears. Still, I couldn't stop reading, my eyes racing over the runes, my mind churning with their casting.

I reached the end of that first part, and my eyes stopped their maniacal march across the paper as they touched on the horizontal line. Dizziness assaulted me, and I staggered a step. My eyes still stung and burned, like I'd gotten a dab of Sif's joint ointment in my eyes, or I'd rubbed my eyes after handling hot peppers. My throat was dry, raw—as if I'd been shouting the runes rather than reading them in utter silence, and my legs shook as though I'd run fifteen miles.

"Are you okay?" asked Kyellroona from the doorway to the chamber.

"Yeah," I said. "Got dizzy for a second."

The big she-bear crooned through her nose. "Shall I fetch your mate?"

"No need." I re-rolled the scroll and slid it back into the case. I slipped the shoulder strap over my head—which felt strangely right and proper—and a gleaming mail shirt caught my eye. It looked like the perfect size for Sig.

"Kyellroona, I've said you don't owe me a thing—"

"Yes, wrong-headed as it is. Take one thing, take it all, we have no use for any of it." She rolled her massive shoulders.

"Are you sure?"

She grunted and clicked her tongue. "We're bears, Hank. We can't use this stuff."

I walked over to the mail shirt. It was a bluish-gray and shone in my enchanted eyesight. I picked it up and slung it over my shoulder. It was much lighter than it should have been. I turned back toward the entrance. "I'll take a chest of gemstones, okay?"

Kyellroona nodded her head. "Take them all."

"Yowtgayrr, could you and Skowvithr help me?" I asked. I never knew when they were around anymore—not since they'd started using their invisibility to forestall arguments from me about needing their help.

"Yes." The two Alfar appeared, lounging near the entrance.

Kyellroona gave a startled blow through her nose and clacked her teeth together. "Your friends should be more careful, Hank—scaring a bear like that could be dangerous."

Yowtgayrr bowed to her. "Our apologies, Lady Bear."

Kyellroona repeatedly chuffed—more bear laughter. "Lady Bear," she murmured.

"You understand her?" I asked.

Yowtgayrr smiled his enigmatic smile. "She is of nature, is she not?"

I shook my head and pointed at a chest of gold coins and one of gems. Each Alf stooped and took one. "Is there anything here either of you can use?"

Skowvithr shook his head. "Our needs are small."

"I'd ask Althyof, but I know what he'd want. Tell him he can have as much of the gold as he can carry and still dance."

Yowtgayrr nodded.

"Kyellroona, is it okay to ask the others to come and pick something?"

"As far as I'm concerned, Hank, everything in this room is yours. Bring whoever you like here and let them do as they please."

"Could you tell the others?" I called after Yowtgayrr's retreating form.

"Yes!" he shouted over his shoulder.

As I turned back to survey the room, a shield caught my eye. It stood in the corner, leaning against the cave's wall behind a chest. The round, forged-metal shield had a bright alloy ring around the edge. In its center was a raven, enameled in black. *Perfect*, I thought. The others arrived right as I picked up the shield.

I found a golden spear with a haft the color of honey as well—one that was the perfect length for Jane. I'd never liked the idea of her getting toe-to-toe with some mad bastard and swinging sharp things at each other. With a spear, she'd be at least a couple of steps away when she attacked—or she'd be able to fly above the battle and hurl it from range. And, with Althyof's help, maybe I could put my new-found knowledge of runic magic to good use and enchant it for her.

Jane squealed with delight when she saw the shield lying next to me. "That's perfect," she said.

"It does fit your aesthetic, doesn't it?"

"Oh, look at you with your big words." She grinned at me. "That spear had better not be for you. You've had enough fun with spears for a while."

"No, not for me."

"Sig?" she asked, cocking her head in that way she had, the way that meant if I answered wrong, I'd be in for a talking-to.

"No, not for him, either."

She shrugged and went back to looking at her pretty shield. She strapped it to her arm and pretended to clock me with it. "Yeah," she murmured. "That'll work good."

We all laughed, even Kyellroona.

Everyone found something—even if it was only a bauble—except for the Alfar and Meuhlnir. Althyof jingled as we walked out of the cave, but he assured me he could still dance.

No one mentioned the scroll case, not even Jane.

With our goodies stowed away or put on, we returned to the main tunnel of the cave where Kuthbyuhrn awaited us. I approached the huge bear and put my hand on his furred shoulder. "Thank you, my friend."

He chuffed through his nose. "Now, I have to thank you, to which you will thank me, which means I have to thank you... Perhaps, instead, we should agree we've helped one another, and we are both happy with the exchange."

"Good idea," I said around a lump in my throat. "I will miss your company."

Kyellroona shuffled up to us. "I hope you, your mate, and your cub will come visit us again, Hank."

"We'd enjoy that." I grinned up at her. "I'm not sure when we will be able to—our lives are a tad up in the air at this point."

"*Uhrluhk*," she said and chuffed through her nose.

"*Uhrluhk*," I agreed. "But when we are able, we'll come back. I promise."

"Good," said Kuthbyuhrn. He shook his great, shaggy head. "But before you go, I need to warn you. The Great Forest of Suel lies beyond this cave entrance."

"Yep, and it's where we are heading. We plan on traveling north through the Forest, and farther north from there."

Kuthbyuhrn clacked his teeth together and glanced at his mate. "That is...difficult to hear. The Great Forest of Suel has turned dark...*evil*. Inside the heart of the Forest itself, where sunlight never reaches, the plants and animals have...changed, and not for the better. No honorable animal resides inside that place—not anymore. Do you understand?"

"It is said the Forest and all that lies inside it is linked to the Dark Queen's being, and that while it once reflected her purity and goodness, now it reflects the darkness that consumes her from within," said Veethar. "Pardon me for eavesdropping."

"No, not at all," said Kyellroona. "It pleases us to speak to those who can speak to us."

"And, Forest Lord, what you say is the right of it," said Kuthbyuhrn. "It used to be an idyllic place, and we often enjoyed spending time there with our cubs. But now..."

"I understand," I said. "We will be careful."

"Please do," said Kyellroona. "And watch your cub with sharp eyes. There are many things that attract a cub's attention in the Great Forest of Suel, and all of them are lures to draw him away from his parents. Trees to climb. Hives that look ripe with honey. Dens in the ground that look warm and inviting."

"We will watch him. He loves being around you, even if he can't speak to you. He thinks you are both magnificent."

Kyellroona made a burbling sound, somewhere between the thrum of an idling big rig and a lion's purr and looked at Sig with a smile. "Please tell him we feel the same way," she crooned.

"I will. Thank you—"

"We agreed..." said Kuthbyuhrn with a fang-filled bear smile.

"Yes. Uh... We appreciate being able to travel through your domain, the gifts, and the friendship."

Beside me, Veethar nodded and put his hand on my shoulder.

"*Uhrluhk*," said Kuthbyuhrn and chuffed through his nose.

"*Uhrluhk*," I said and raised my hand in parting. The two bears watched us go, waving a paw in a human-like fashion every time I glanced back at them over my shoulder. I emerged from their cave, into the artificial gloom of the Great Forest of Suel, with a lump in my throat.

THIRTY-SEVEN

A perpetual gloaming enshrouded the Great Forest of Suel. Branches and boughs from the crooked, black-barked trees twisted into a solid ceiling high above our heads. The trees twisted as they rose toward the sky so that there wasn't a straight trunk in sight. Some had open, weeping gashes through their bark. Despite it being spring, fall leaves coated the ground in a thick carpet—far too thick to be from a single fall season.

Besides the noise we made—the jingle of harness and arms, the *clop-clop* of the horses' hooves on the soft ground, and the occasional cough caused by the stench of the place—a combination of a butcher shop's offal and a cesspit—silence reigned inside the Forest's dark confines as if no animal sounds, no bird calls, no sound of wind cavorting amongst the trees dared disturb the eerie stillness. The canopy blocked all light from the sun—not a single ray of light penetrated it. It seemed to loom over us when we looked up, making for a low, cramped ceiling. The cave had felt more open and much more inviting.

Veethar's face twisted in a perpetual scowl, and he spent his time muttering to himself, often using foul language in its strongest form. Everyone gave him a wide berth, even Frikka, and he rode ahead, glaring at the trees, the ground, the underbrush.

The animals walked about in an almost perpetual state of alarm. Keri and Fretyi whined, barked at the foul wind, or snarled at shadows almost constantly, and Slaypnir's ears swiveled this way and that like frenetic radar dishes as he snorted and blew. No one spoke much, too busy concentrating on not turning around and galloping back to Kuthbyuhrn's cave.

The trees hunched over us as if they leered at us and watched our progress. Crooked branches dipped from the canopy, like stalactites, like reaching, skeletal arms. The leaves underfoot compressed beneath the horses' weight, but as they stepped away, the leaves sprang back, leaving no trace of our trail. I had the intuition that if we scraped away even a thin layer of those leaves, we'd find the corpses of animals or birds, or maybe thick, foul flesh, soaked in half-congealed black blood. Those were the kinds of thoughts the Great Forest of Suel inspired—dark, dreary, disconsolate.

When we broke off for the night, we set up camp in near silence, whispering only when we had to as if everyone were leery of waking something—or someone—up. Gathering enough wood for the evening's fire took no time at all—there were fallen branches everywhere as though a monster storm had passed through a day before—but getting the fire lit turned out to be much more difficult. The black bark and red wood resisted flame. After the fire died for the fourth time, Meuhlnir pointed at it and growled, "*Predna*, damn you!" The fire burst into green and blue-tinged flames, and the smoke smelled like a slaughterhouse, but the fire stayed lit.

The fire did little to relieve the gloom—it almost made it seem worse. The five-hundred-pound weight of my exhaustion and pain settled on my shoulders. The puppies wouldn't venture more than a yard away from me, whining and looking at me with alarmed eyes as if there was something I could do to make the Great Forest of Suel a nicer place. I dropped to a log next to the fire and petted the pups.

Althyof sank down next to me on the log. "This forest is dark like a cave, but I'll tell you, I'd rather be back on that damn boat."

I grunted my agreement, scratching Fretyi's ears. Keri cocked his head at Althyof like he couldn't understand how a Tverkr had snuck up on him.

Althyof picked up a stick.

"You don't want to—"

He threw the stick, and Keri attacked his feet. Althyof chuckled—the closest any of us had come to laughing that day. "Got him trained up right, I see."

"One does what one can," I said and tried to grin.

"Are you going to tell me about the scroll?" he asked.

"What? Oh. Sure." I tugged the scroll case around from my back and opened its clasp. I pulled out the scroll and handed it to the Tverkr *runeskowld.* "I looked at the first page but no further than that."

Althyof unrolled the scroll and gave me a look, tapping his finger against the scroll a few times before rolling it back up and handing it to me.

"Well? What do you think?"

"Nothing," he said. "The scroll is blank."

My stomach dropped, and my mouth dried like a parched desert wind blew. "No!" I murmured. I unrolled the scroll until I saw the runes on the first page. "Not funny," I muttered.

"Not meant to be," he snapped. "I can see nothing written on that page."

"What about these?" I asked pointing to the first line.

"Blank page. You can still see runes?" he asked, head cocked to the side, index finger tapping a rhythm on his thigh.

"Yes."

He tilted his head back and looked up at the canopy above us. "You have a very rare thing in your hands, something I haven't even heard about for ages."

"Yeah?"

"I've never seen one before, personally, but what you have there is a *puntidn stavsetninkarpowk*."

"Unless I misunderstood the usage, that means, 'idiomatic grimoire,' right?"

He pursed his lips and shrugged. "As good a translation as any, I suppose."

"Okay, what does it mean?"

"It means that the *kaltrar* contained on that scroll belong to you, and only to you. I don't know this for sure since I have no direct experience with the things, but my master taught me that the owner of a scroll such as that can't even teach the *kaltrar* to another. They are yours, and yours alone, Hank."

"When I read the first line, something forced me through the rest of the section. Runes popped into my mind like fireworks and seemed to cast themselves."

"And the rhythm?" Althyof asked, staring at his palms.

"Yes, there was a rhythm to it."

His favored me with a curt nod. "There you have it. When you read that first page, you bound the scroll to you—and *only* you."

I looked down at the scroll in my hands. "And if I never read the rest of it?"

"Then you never do, and no one else does, either." Althyof hitched his shoulders and brushed his hands together as if he were knocking dirt from his palms.

"Awesome," I grumbled. "I'm leery of reading anything else. I don't want it to suck me in and...I don't know...release a plague or something."

Althyof shook his head. "That isn't what you should fear, Hank."

"No?" I asked, eyebrows arched.

"No. What you should fear is that you are not ready for the *kaltrar*. Once you read it, you can perform it, or at least try to."

"This gets better and better."

Althyof nodded. "It might be better to put it away until you've mastered the craft. Don't let it tempt you."

I grunted and turned my attention back to scratching Fretyi's ears. I swear if *varkr* could purr, he would have done it.

"Heed me, now, Hank. Put it from your mind, bury it deep in your pack and try not to focus on it. The temptation will be hard to resist—it will call to you, will seem to be the most reasonable solution in the world, but it will be the most dangerous until you've mastered the craft."

"I hear you, Althyof. Believe me, I've had my fill of the mystical right about now."

Althyof shrugged. "Okay, we'll consider it settled for now. But promise me this: come to me before you attempt to read the next *kaltrar*. Let me judge whether you are ready."

"Sure."

Althyof regarded me with a solemn expression. "I hope you can resist its call."

I shrugged, more than a little uncomfortable. Until he'd said anything, the scroll hadn't weighed on me at all. In fact, I'd almost forgotten about it. But since he made such a big deal, there was a kernel of curiosity growing in my mind about the damn thing.

"It's settled then." He glanced around. "So...when are you going to ask me?"

"Ask you what?"

"To enchant the spear for Jane."

"Is it that obvious?" I said with a grin. "I thought I was so sly."

He shrugged and raised his eyebrows.

"It might be a good project for us to do together. This is what I want..." I sketched a series of runes in the black dirt between my feet.

"You will have to tell me about these dreams, Hank," he whispered. "Rub that out. This isn't the place to leave such things out in the open." He hefted the spear and looked at me. "You are on the right track. Keep working on it. Once we leave this carnival of foulness, we can revisit the idea." His stare lingered on my face, eyes flicking from feature to feature, and his expression was grim. A smile cracked his facade of disapproval. He made a show of nudging my arm with his elbow. "The worst that can happen is you blow yourself up."

"Uh..."

"Are you sure you don't want me to do it for you?" His eyes twinkled with mirth.

"Don't make me sic Keri on your ankles again," I said with a grin to match.

He held up his hands as if in surrender. "Anything but that! I *like* these socks." He pulled up his leather pant legs to reveal one green and one blue sock. "It's hard to find a matching set such as this in Nitavetlir."

"Matching?" I asked. "You're not colorblind, are you?"

"What? Green matches blue! I suppose you are the same as all those grumpy bastards back home...I suppose you think each sock should be the *same color.*"

"That's the general idea, isn't it?"

He smirked, thrusting out his chest. "Not if you have confidence! Not if you want to make a statement! Not if you are *fearless*!"

"Get him, Keri!" I said, and Keri growled his puppy best.

"Keri understands. That's why he's only growling rather than biting at my beautiful socks. Don't you, Keri?" Keri cocked his head at the Tverkr, one ear flopping to the side, the other over his head. Althyof looked at me. "That's *varkr* for yes."

"If you say so."

The Tverkr winked at me and left to go set up his bedroll.

"Well, what do you know?" I murmured, my hand going to the scroll case. For a moment, my hand tingled as if I were touching a live wire.

Yowrnsaxa served a cold supper that night, despite all the work that the foul-smelling fire had required. She said the fire didn't burn hot enough to cook, and, if I'm honest, it didn't burn hot enough to ward off the chill, either. But, then again, maybe the chill lived inside our minds rather than on the wind.

"How long will we be in this ugly place?" asked Sig, eyeing the darkness beyond the edge of the firelight.

"Five days, perhaps," said Meuhlnir.

"Five days?" After he'd spoken, Sig's face suffused with hot blood.

Yowtgayrr leaned over and grasped his shoulder. "It's an unnatural place, Guardian of Victory. Don't be ashamed of feeling uncomfortable here."

"Why did you call me that?"

"It's what Sigurd means," I said.

"Oh. Why didn't you tell me that before?" he asked, turning his best glare on me.

"I didn't know."

Veethar stood and stalked away from the fire.

"He feels it the most," said Frikka. "He said the land itself has been corrupted. Nothing follows natural patterns here."

"Let's get through as fast as we can," said Jane as she pulled me up, dragging me off to bed with a stern glance at our son and a chin-jerk toward his own bedroll.

If the Great Forest of Suel had been uncomfortable during the hidden daylight, at night it was downright ghastly. The deformed trees creaked and moaned in a wind that never seemed to reach the ground. It took hours for me to fall asleep, and when I finally did, it was a restless, uncomfortable slumber.

THIRTY-EIGHT

A *cold wind lifted my feathered body skyward, and I opened my wings, cupping them for maximal lift. I rose through the dark canopy of the Forest, sometimes passing right through thick branches.*

Once I broke above the trees, the Great Forest of Suel stretched away toward infinity in every direction—as if the dark place had eaten the entire world. A cold fear settled in my guts.

I was alone in the sky—at least as far as my hawkish vision reached—and the only noise came from the persistent wind that bore me aloft. It was as if the world slept beneath the tight canopy of the trees and would never wake. I glanced down at the treetops, sure that monsters and creatures straight out of myth were staring up at me, but there was nothing and no one.

I called out, and my voice sounded like the rumbling crrruck of a crow or a raven. Onward I flew, flapping sable wings to gain extra speed. The wind picked up at the same time as if it understood that I wanted to go faster.

I soared over the treetops, heading north, alone in a world of trees. I wondered if this was how Alfhaym looked from the air.

In moments, I reached the sea to the north—the Stormur Syow as Meuhlnir named it. Thanks to my recent knowledge of the Gamla Toonkumowl, I now knew what that meant: Tempest Sea. Given the dark, angry clouds hanging over the water, it was well-named.

Looking down, my eyes traced the edges of a safe harbor—a large, protected bay the shape of a three-leaf clover. Below me, moored at docks, or anchored in the bay proper, bobbed thousands of dragon ships, and onshore staggered and lurched thousands of troops from multiple races: Svartalfar, demons, men, trolls. Most seemed drunk, or otherwise intoxicated by whatever means suited them.

A lone Svartalf stood apart. He wore gleaming black armor and a strange, rune-inscribed, peaked leather cap, also dyed black. Our eyes met across the distance, and he scowled. He raised his arm and pointed at me. "Antafukl!" he cried, but no one paid him any mind.

Spirit bird? What a strange thing to say, I thought.

He whirled to glare at those closest to him, slapping those within reach. "Antafukl!" he repeated, pointing up at me. When his companions dismissed him, the Svartalf spat at their feet and strode to the next closest group and repeated his cry. That group laughed at him and went back to drinking and singing out of key.

The Svartalf whirled, glaring at me as if their behavior was my fault. He began a lurching, stuttering dance that was as different from Althyof's graceful spinning as night was to day and chanted words that distance and wind made impossible to hear. The runes he cast appeared as sickly aureolin images written in the night in front of him.

Fear churned in my belly, and I dove toward the trees, hoping that by breaking his line of sight, he could not continue the kaltrar he was chanting at me, and it must have worked.

I turned east, wanting to avoid the harbor at all costs, and knowing the Dragon Spine Mountains should be close by. The black forest disgorged a sweeping set of hills at the foot of the mountains, and I angled upward, gaining altitude to fly above them.

Something nudged my side, and though I glanced that direction, there was nothing there. I blinked and shrieked my crow-call into the night. Something nudged me again and...

THIRTY-NINE

I awoke. Judging the time of day proved impossible inside the Great Forrest of Suel, so I had no idea how long I'd slept, only knowing it hadn't been long enough. My mouth tasted like a latrine, and my lips were dry and gummed together.

Something nudged my side, and for a moment, the dream blossomed in my mind—the flight, the Svartalf, the oppressive loneliness—but only for a moment, and then it faded like early morning mist. I forced my eyes open, and the same oppressive black murk from the night before greeted me. I remained exhausted—as if I hadn't slept at all.

Fretyi nudged my ribs again and whined a little. I looked at him, and he wagged his tail, seeming to smile. The morning sounds of my travel companions came from the camp behind me while I scratched the pup behind the ears. "Time to eat, eh, ravenous one?" He cocked his head to the side and treated me to a playful yip. "Yes, I'm getting up, and yes, I will find you some food."

"About time you woke up," said Jane. "I thought we'd have to tie you to Slaypnir."

"I didn't sleep much, judging by how I feel. What time is it?"

"Your guess is as good as anyone's. No one got much rest, though everyone slept."

"It's this place," said Veethar. "Unnatural."

As if that explains this place, I thought. *Although, maybe to Veethar, it does.*

"Come on, slug-a-bed. Everyone's already eaten and ready. I'll feed those bottomless pits you call puppies," said Jane. "Come on, puppy," she said in a lilting voice, and just like that, puppy and wife both forgot all about me.

"Veethar, what caused this place to…to…" I shrugged, not knowing the right words to describe the place.

Veethar shook his head. "Everything is broken. The chains of bits that make things as they are, seem to be corrupted, changed. The life here…feels less like life and more like the *truykar.*"

I glanced at the surrounding trees, remembering the shambling, maggot-infested *truykar* we'd encountered in the Darks of Kruyn and shuddered. "Are these trees…undead?" My imagination painted a picture of reaching tree limbs and grasping roots in the darkness surrounding our camp.

Veethar shook his head, though he didn't seem sure of himself. "No, they are not revenant trees. I'm not even sure such a thing is possible."

"If it *were* possible, the Dark Queen would be the cause," said Meuhlnir.

"No, Tyeldnir, these trees are alive, but they live a corrupted life." Veethar shook his head. "Even that makes no sense," he muttered.

"On Mithgarthr, a forest called the Red Forest surrounds a nuclear power plant that exploded—"

"A what?" asked Freya from across the camp.

"A place that generates electricity by splitting atoms—like a controlled explosion of great power. Anyway, this plant, Chernobyl, had a huge steam explosion that blew the containment building to smithereens. After that, a fire broke out, and it spread the radiation in the wind, raining particles on the surrounding forest. Look, none of these details are important. The point is this: that radiation killed off all the microbes, insects, and fungi that cause dead things to decompose, so the trees, the leaves, *everything* that dies there, will never decay. When they die, they stand or lay where they fell, forever in the state they were in the day they died."

Veethar shook his head. "No, that hasn't happened here, and further, these trees, these leaves, they are still alive but frozen in time."

"Even the leaves on the ground? They're still alive?"

"Yes," said Veethar with a shrug. "They follow the cycles of the year, but nothing dies, nothing decays."

"That's spooky," said Sig.

Veethar nodded gravely. "I've seen nothing like it." He walked over and petted the nose of the closest horse.

I ate a few bites of bread and cheese and submitted to Sif's ministrations and scolding. Afterward, we set out on horseback, feeling as if we were riding at midnight.

We rode until we were tired and hungry before we ate and rested—or tried, anyway. It took real effort to fall asleep in that place.

FORTY

"Everyone up!" shouted Veethar.

I groaned, feeling like I hadn't slept more than five minutes. I cracked open my eyes, expecting full darkness, but full darkness under a star-filled sky. Instead, what greeted me was the ever-present velvety dark canopy of the Great Forest of Suel.

My legs were stiff, almost numb, and I groaned again. I tried to rub my face, to clear the sleep from my eyes, but my arms felt heavy, enervated. I turned my head to the side, and lurched in the other direction, my pulse slamming in my veins.

Between me and the underbrush crouched a spider the size of a large dog. Its four black orb-like eyes tracked my thrashing movements, its yellow-haired forelegs waving in the air. The fuzzy hair that coated the rest of its body was white with dark purple stripes.

I lurched away from the monster in a panic, and something ripped, and my left arm was free. I hoisted myself up to a seated position, not taking my eyes off the white and purple spider. It separated its forelegs, revealing fangs at least four inches long and dripping with a syrupy, clear liquid that was no doubt its venom.

"Everyone!" shouted Veethar again. "Wake up!"

I couldn't move my legs—they had that tingling pins-and-needles numbness of restricted blood flow. A ropy, white substance covered my legs and attached them to the ground with thick strands of goo. I grabbed it, and my fingers stuck to it as if I had grabbed a rope made of super-glue. I broke several of the strands, and the huge spider near me hissed and clacked its fangs together. It skittered a step or two toward me, then Veethar was there, kicking it into the underbrush.

Keri and Fretyi growled and snarled, hunching low to the ground between the spider and me, tails rigid and straight out behind them, lips quivering back from their teeth.

"Up! Hank get up!" he yelled and ran to the other side of the camp.

"What are they?" mumbled Jane.

"Spiders, but big!" yelled Sig.

"Get up!" I bellowed. "I'm webbed to the ground, and the webbing contains a numbing agent."

"Everyone up!" yelled Veethar. "They are all around us!"

I finished clearing the webbing off my legs and got to my feet. I belted on my pistols and bent to retrieve the floppy hat Althyof had enchanted for me. A rope of web came hurtling out of the underbrush and slapped against the back of my hand. The numbness started right away, and I jerked my hand back, pulling the purple and white spider out of the underbrush by its own strand of webbing.

Keri and Fretyi leapt at the thing, snarling, each attacking from opposite sides of the spider as if they'd been hunting all their lives instead of eating scraps out of my hand. The web fell away, and the spider circled to face Keri, forelegs coming up. Fretyi ducked in and bit the spider's back leg, shaking his head in violent arcs. The *varkr* pups were almost as tall as the spider but weighed considerably less. The spider hissed and whirled around, pulling Fretyi off his feet, and Keri shot in to grab a leg. I took two steps forward and kicked the spider as hard as I could with half-numb legs. The thing squealed and thrashed its legs, but the pups held fast, growling and grinding their jaws together. I kicked it again, this time angling for its head. When my foot connected with the spider's head, there was a tearing sound followed by a pop, and it went spinning into the darkness ringing the camp.

Citrine-colored blood coursed from the spider's neck, and when it hit the ground, it hissed and ignited in a flash of sickly yellow flame, consuming the old leaves there in a blinding flash. The *varkr* pups yelped and ran behind me, whining. The spider lurched around a few steps, spraying flaming blood everywhere and fell in a heap.

Webbing stuck to the back of my hand still, and an icy numbness was spreading across my hand. I detached the goop and let it fall next to the spider.

"Dad! Help!" yelled Sig.

I turned to where he'd been sleeping. Thick strands of the webbing crossed Sig's chest and legs, gluing him to the ground, and a spider stood above him. I lurched in his direction, but before I'd gone three steps, Skowvithr was there, silvery blades bared. Keri and Fretyi bolted toward the spider, snarling and barking to raise the dead.

"Their blood ignites in the air!" I yelled.

Skowvithr nodded and slashed at the webbing holding Sig fast. The spider bounced up and down—almost as if it were a petulant child, pissed off that someone was breaking its sandcastle. When his arms were free, Sig batted the spider away—and into the smoldering fire.

The spider yelped and leapt through the air, four feet off the ground. It landed near Mothi, who scooped it even higher into the air with the flat of one axe and then batted it into the trees with the other. "How many of them are there?"

Everyone was on their feet, staring into the woods surrounding us, and everyone but Veethar had web hanging from their bodies. "Get the web off," I said. "It keeps on numbing you even without the spider. Anyone see any more of the bastards?"

Keri and Fretyi growled in unison—noses pointed toward the woods, tails held stiff parallel to the ground. "Pups! Stay!" I said. Keri glanced at me for a second and whined, but then snapped his eyes back into the forest.

"I don't like this," said Veethar. "Arachnids don't act like this."

"Or grow this large, but hey, who wants to be picky," mumbled Althyof, picking webbing out of his hair and beard.

"Have you heard of these before?" asked Jane.

"No," said Veethar.

"Well, they seem afraid of us, now that we are upright," said Meuhlnir. "They don't want to face us awake. At least for now."

"And how many days must we be in this forest?"

He shrugged. "Three more. Four, maybe."

"Four days without sleep," said Jane.

"We can mount a watch. Some of us sleep, and some of us keep the spiders away," said Mothi.

We set a schedule, and we were not among the first to stand watch, so Jane and I pulled our bedroll closer to the fire. "It had to be spiders," I muttered.

"Don't worry, I'll protect you from the mean old spiders."

"Don't joke, I'll hold you to it."

We tried to sleep, but spiders tried to get to those of us trying to sleep whenever the watchers drifted more than five feet away. The constant activity made it impossible to drift off to sleep—never mind the spiders.

I sat up with a sigh.

"This will not work," mumbled Jane.

"No," I sighed. I glanced around, and no one on the sleep shift was sleeping. "We might as well move out. Maybe the next place won't allow giant, mutant spider freaks to join the country club."

Everyone agreed, so we packed up and moved out. Riding through the Forest was like a nightmare in and of itself: the reaching branches, the monotonous quality of the light—or lack thereof—and the constant skittering in the brush of spiders paralleling our course.

"How will we be able to do this?" whispered Jane, riding beside me.

"Look at it this way: it will only take two days if we don't sleep."

"But the horses can't go twenty-four hours a day. And you know what being over-tired does to you."

"Makes me handsome and irresistible?"

"Don't make me punch you."

"Yes, dear."

"That's better. Now, answer my question and make it snappy."

"Yes, dear. I don't know the answer, but we don't have much choice, either way."

"You call that an answer?"

"Yes, dear."

Time took on a monotonous, unreal feeling, with no difference between periods of alertness and periods of lethargy. We rode where Veethar led us, swaying in our saddles, trusting him to guide us through the foul place. No one spoke much on the first day, and we spoke even less as the days and nights blurred together. The interminable ride was punctuated only by rest periods for the horses, in which we sat around a campfire while lassitude tried to steal us away. We ate mechanically, the food tasteless and textureless.

I never even thought of my dream, and the Svartalf *runeskowld* it had contained, but the scroll case at my side was ever in my mind, eating away at my resolve.

FORTY-ONE

We spoke less and less, communicating by grunts and gestures—even between husband and wife. Sig and Mothi no longer played and joked, but rather slumped listlessly in their saddles. It even affected the horses, who plodded on with heads drooping.

It seemed to me that we'd been riding for far too long—weeks instead of days—but I had no concept of the geography of the Forest. I considered calling out to Veethar, but the idea of my voice breaking the silence of the Forest seemed...villainous. I nudged

Slaypnir's flanks with my heels—as close to giving him the spurs as I'd ever come. He lifted his head as if it took great effort and turned a baleful eye my way. "Catch Veethar up," I said. "Please."

Slaypnir dropped his head again—not in a gentle fashion, but all at once as though his neck muscles had melted—but he increased his pace a little. Veethar glanced at me as I pulled up next to him. His eyes seemed glassy, dazed. The idea of speaking to him was exhausting. "Are…you sure…we're on the…right track?"

Veethar grunted. He opened his mouth but closed both his eyes and his mouth at the same time, while he reined his horse to stop. His eyes opened wide, and he shook his head as though fighting sleep. He shook his head again—more violently this time—glancing around as if he did not understand where we were or how we'd gotten there. When he looked up at me, concern wrinkled the skin around his eyes. "I—" he said with alarm in his eyes. He tilted his head to the side.

"What is it?" I asked.

His hand shot up and sliced through the air. He listened for a moment. "Do you hear it?" he whispered.

I cocked my head to listen, and there was something…at the edge of my hearing. There was a crash behind us, and I snapped my head around. Althyof lay on the ground next to his horse, unconscious. Then I understood the thing at the edge of my hearing.

...Svefn...Kvild...Truhmur...Svefn...Kvild...Truh mur...

The words repeated, over and over, at the edge of my auditory range. A harsh, grating voice uttered the words... "Sleep, rest, dream," I muttered.

"And the *runeskowld* is the first to succumb?"

"It's a *kaltrar*, no question, but nothing like the *lausaveesa* or *triblinkr* Althyof chants."

"No," said Veethar. "It's filled with darkness, like this damn forest."

"The Black Queen?"

Veethar shook his head. "I... I don't think so."

An image of a Svartalf in black armor and a black, runed leather cap flashed through my mind. *The dream!* "The first night!" I murmured.

"Yes?"

"That first night, I dreamed I was a bird. I flew north to the *Stormur Syow*—to a huge bay shaped like a three-leaf clover."

Veethar nodded, eyes boring into mine.

"There were thousands of dragon ships in the harbor, and twenty times as many men, trolls, demons, and Svartalfar on the shore. They all seemed drunk, except one, one wearing black armor and a black leather cap with runes all over it. Do the Svartalfar have *runeskowlds*?"

Veethar shook his head, with a helpless gesture at Althyof. Someone else crashed to the ground behind us: Mothi.

"Wake up!" I yelled.

Veethar shook his head. "That won't work. *Haydnadlaysi*."

"Deafness?" I asked but couldn't hear my own voice. I could, however, hear the *kaltrar*.

Veethar shook his head and canceled his spell. "We need Althyof."

I turned to the fallen Tverkr, and Meuhlnir crashed to the ground next to Sinir. "This is getting out of hand," I muttered. I walked to Althyof and bent over him. I grabbed him by the shoulder and shook him. "Wake up!" His head lolled around as if his neck were broken and his eyelids didn't even flutter. "*Vakna*!" I said, pulling as much power from the *strenkir af krafti* as I knew how, but Althyof slept on.

"We need a *runeskowld* to combat this," Veethar said.

Knowledge of the runes filled my mind, thanks to the strange man hanging in Iktrasitl, the man who must have been Odin. I could see the pattern I needed, the runes seeming to fit together on their own. "*Yek air* Hank *neelithi runeskowld*," I chanted. "*Vakna*, Althyof, *hoospownti roona. Vakna*, Althyof, *hoospownti runeskowld. Vakna*, Althyof!"

Althyof twitched, as one who is dreaming about falling might, but he didn't wake. The words at the edge of my hearing became more insistent, and perhaps a little louder.

"*Yek air* Hank *neelithi runeskowld*," I chanted. "*Vakna*, Althyof! *Klustathu echki lenkur! Vakna*, Althyof! *Hunsa seemtalith til ath sofa! Vakna*,

Althyof! *Klustathu athayns ow mik! Vakna*, Althyof!"

The Tverkr grunted, and his hands twitched.

I looked up at Veethar and shrugged. "There are only so many ways I can think of to say: 'ignore the call to sleep.'"

He shrugged, chin dipping toward his chest. "Maybe a *triblinkr* isn't enough." His words slurred, and his eyes rolled.

"Stay awake," I snapped.

"Trying…" Veethar swayed and his mouth cracked open in a huge yawn.

"I've never sung a *trowba*. Althyof warned me not to attempt too much."

Veethar nodded, and then his eyes rolled up in his head, and he crashed to the ground. I looked around, and those that hadn't fallen out of their saddles lay slumped over the necks of their mounts, asleep. Even the horses seemed to be asleep.

From Owsakrimmr's gift of the runes, I knew the mechanics of performing a *trowba*. The knowledge of which steps supported which runes spun out in my mind in infinite variety. My eyes had that gritty feeling I got right before I slept after a bout of insomnia. I could picture all the runes I needed and could repeat the lines I'd chanted earlier, varying their placement as I saw fit. I could cast the runes as I sang, as I danced. My jaws cracked open in a huge yawn.

When the pitter-patter of approaching spiders echoed from the surrounding trees, I began to sing, and a moment later, I added the steps of the dance. I focused on Althyof, dancing in a circle around him. In the distance, the thunder of approaching hooves sounded. I repeated the lines I'd chanted a moment before, varying them according to some internal lyricist that seemed to know how the placement of the lines would bolster the effect of the previous or next line. At my feet, Althyof stirred.

The commands to sleep grew louder, more insistent, and my feet stumbled and skipped as if I danced over uneven ground. The lines I sang became hard to get out.

I glanced down, hoping the Tverkr would be awake, but he wasn't. Not yet, but his feet jerked in time to the rhythm of my *trowba*, and his lips twitched in time to the lyrics.

I stumbled less, and his feet moved with more sense of purpose. The words flowed from my lips, and his lips formed words, though without sound.

The hooves were closer, their thunder vibrating the ground I danced on. I glimpsed purple and white spiders loitering in the trees at the edge of the clearing we'd stopped in.

The commands to sleep, to rest, to dream, grew more insistent yet; they became harsh, grating along my auditory nerves, trying to distract me from my *trowba*. I kept singing, kept dancing.

Althyof's eyes snapped open. He leapt to his feet, springing up like a twenty-year-old gymnast. His voice sang out, perfectly in time with mine, and he was dancing and singing my *trowba*.

I felt light on my feet—no aches, no pains. I hadn't felt this way since before I caught up to the Dark Queen, and she had laid her damn curse on me.

Althyof drew his twin daggers, their cadmium red auras bright and blinding, and he took charge of my *trowba* and began to change it, to alter a word here, change a step there. I could see what he was doing in my mind's eye: altering the *trowba* so it would affect everyone in the party instead of just him. His changes didn't throw me, however. Instead, it was as if I knew what he would sing, where and how his next step would land before he did it.

I remembered his story about leading a cadre of *runeskowlds* and their warrior support teams, how everyone's *trowba* merged with the others to increase the strength of and lengthen the range of the *kaltrar*. I hadn't really understood that part of the story until I was doing it—hadn't understood the give and take of sharing a *trowba* with someone, hadn't understood the power of it.

After a few minutes, the others came awake. Althyof and I kept dancing, kept singing the *trowba*, and the spiders kept skittering in the trees while the hooves kept thundering closer. Althyof increased the cadence of the *trowba*, dancing faster, and adding swirling spins, his daggers thrusting out away from the group. In the woods around us, the spiders hissed.

I drew Kunknir and Krati, emulating his thrusts. After a moment, the pistols took on a cadmium red aura, and when I thrust them away from the party, bolts of red light shot away like bullets. In the trees, I heard the telltale whoosh and crackle of spider blood igniting.

As we danced, a pressure of sorts built from the north, as if something were pressing against us, trying to shove past us. I made a face at Althyof, and he nodded once. A horse neighed somewhere off in the trees—closer than I expected—and Slaypnir lifted his head and snorted through his nose. From their saddlebag perches, Keri and Fretyi's ears were up, and they both set about barking as if the sky was about to fall and trying to lurch free of the saddlebags. Jane lifted them free and set them on the ground, and they ran in circles, snarling and snapping their teeth.

"Weapons!" snapped Meuhlnir. The party sprang into motion, donning shields, drawing weapons. They put Sig in the middle and formed a circle around him. Jane looked at me, with sleep-slurred eyes, unsure what to do with me dancing around and singing like a broken-down lounge act. The other *skyuldur vidnukonur* stood apart from the men, forming a line facing north.

"Stand with us, Jane," said Sif. "We form the Wall."

"The wall?"

"Yes. We interlock our shields and stand together, giving the rest an extra moment to *vefa* before the enemy charge is upon them. Once I yell 'break,' fall back with us, a step at a time, moving as one."

"Got it."

The Svartalf from my dream rode a magnificent black horse out from the trees. When he stepped out of the woods, he was chanting a *kaltrar*. …*Svefn…Kvild…Truhmur*, but when he saw Althyof and me dancing, he grinned a nasty grin and stopped. His general proportions matched that of Althyof and my Alfar companions, but he seemed different…more asymmetrical. His skin was the color of thunderheads during a summer storm, but his eyes were a brilliant amethyst that seemed to glow in the darkness of the Great Forest of Suel. He glanced at the Alfar and nodded. "Cousins," he said.

Yowtgayrr hissed, and Skowvithr spat toward him.

Althyof broke off the *trowba* and laughed. "What, no 'Cousin' for me?"

The Svartalf curled his lip and looked away.

Meuhlnir peered into the woods behind the magnificent black horse. "Have you come alone?" he asked, his voice incredulous.

The Svartalf shrugged. "You should be asleep. And without the Abomination over there, you would have been."

Althyof laughed brightly. "Ah, there is the greeting I'd expected! But I didn't thwart you. It was my apprentice. You should consider returning to your master for more teaching."

The Svartalf sneered but still refused to look at Althyof.

"You should speak," growled Mothi. "Your name, and a reason I shouldn't kill you."

The Svartalf's gaze snapped to Mothi's, eyes narrowing. "I am Ivalti. As to your last question, allow me to spare *your* life, Isir. You couldn't kill me."

Mothi growled and took a step, but Meuhlnir put his arm in front of him. "No."

"Wise of you," sneered Ivalti.

"At least, *not yet*," said Meuhlnir.

"Who among you is the *umsikyanti*?"

"The seeker?" I blurted.

Ivalti's bright eyes tracked across the small clearing to meet my own. "*You*," he rasped.

"Me?"

"Dressed in raven feathers or in armor, I *see* you now." His face scrunched into angry, hateful lines. "I will do what Queen Hel would not—or *could not*. If I kill you, maybe she will end this idiocy and reopen the *preer*, and I can go home to my sons."

The look in his eye was something I'd seen many times before, and I knew what it meant. I jerked Kunknir and Krati up and fired twice from each pistol. Ivalti jittered and shuddered a series of steps like something out of a Japanese horror movie, screeching in the *Gamla Toonkumowl*, and the rounds stopped in midair and hung there like so many fishing weights on a string.

"At least you had the cardinal virtue to attack me alone, rather than all at once. Do the rest of you dare such decency and honor?" The Svartalf's expression twisted, making it plain what he thought of us.

"Ha!" spat Skowvithr. "A Svartalf asking for grace! I'm surprised you know the meaning of the word, *stuhchkprayteenk*."

The word meant "mutant" and Ivalti reacted as if the Alf had spit in his face—coming up on the balls of his feet, cheeks suffusing with hot, angry blood. "Be careful what you say to me," he hissed.

Althyof laughed without mirth. "Alfar and Svartalfar... Talk, talk, talk, when the situation calls for killing."

Ivalti snapped his gaze to meet the Tverkr's. "Then please, *protidn aydn*, begin."

"Broken one?" Althyof laughed again, this time with derision. "Is that the best you can do?" Without giving the Svartalf time to answer, Althyof spun into motion, the grace of his movement a glaring contrast to how the Svartalf moved. He began singing a *trowba*, daggers weaving complex patterns in the darkness of the Forest.

With one last glare of pure hatred at me, Ivalti snapped his head away to track Althyof, while lurching into an arrhythmic dance, shuddering one direction, then jerking in a counter-direction. He drew a jagged, black weapon, that appeared to be the bastard combination of a short sword and a double-bladed axe. He held his other hand splayed, palm out. His *kaltrar* was as nonmetrical as his graceless dance—looking clumsy compared to Althyof. As he sang, a black mist coalesced around the blade of his weapon, covering more and more until the blade disappeared.

They circled each other, testing and probing the other's defenses. Contrary to the Svartalf's idea of honor and grace, I moved to join Althyof, but he waved me back, glaring at me for good measure. Althyof's tune changed, becoming strident and changing to a harmonic minor key, notes seeming to jangle with each other, and crimson energy blasted across the space separating him from Ivalti.

The Svartalf uttered a series of harsh noises, more like coughs than words, and the crimson wave parted around him and tore into the trees, destroying everything in its path. A smile lingered on Ivalti's face, and Althyof treated him to a grudging nod.

They continued circling around and around each other, eyes fixed on their opponent, songs combining into an earsplitting bruit. Pratyi made a disgusted noise and clapped his hands over his ears.

The differences between the Tverkar art and the Svartalfar variant enthralled me. They seemed to work on the same principles, *runana stayba*, *kaltrar*, and dance; though the Svartalf seemed to detest rhythm and lissome, flowing grace—which seemed to fit everything else I knew about them. At times, thinking about the Svartalfar, Tverkar, and Alfar as genetic cousins made my mind reel. They were all so different from one another.

Ivalti spat his lyrics at Althyof and swung his weapon in a flat arc but checked his swing a third of the way through. The black mist that covered the blade sprang away from him, leaping like a leopard in full attack. The blackness swiped at Althyof.

The Tverkr rolled his eyes, and as if it were no more important than a buzzing fly, slashed at the shadow backhanded with his left-hand dagger. With a pop and a puff of smoke, the shadow fell to the ground. When it hit, it dissolved as mist burning away in the morning sun does.

Althyof's *trowba* morphed yet again, and he syncopated his lyrics, leaving small gaps where only the shuffle of dancing feet and the harsh sounds of the Svartalf hung in the air. After a moment, Althyof added new sounds—new *syllables*, I realized—into those spaces, creating a complex meter between the original lyrics and the new. His whirling increased, adding a hop or a leap here, three quick steps there.

He was building a counter-melody with the new syllables he inserted between beats of the old lyrics. The melody and counter-melody built toward a climax, and Althyof was whirling like a devil, daggers slashing and sweeping red streaks through the darkness.

Ivalti seemed taken aback, and he backed away, weaving a defense with harsh, guttural cries, and jerking, stuttering steps, eyes widening. He backed to the edge of the trees, confining his "dance" into a claustrophobic area of about three yards square.

Althyof, on the other hand, leapt and spun, sliding his feet, taking more and more of the clearing as his own. What had been the counter-melody subsumed the melody, and the rhythm changed, punctuated by a shouted rune.

I'd never witnessed Althyof do anything such as this before, not in all the combat, the enchanting of items, nor in the command of Friner, the massive red dragon he'd bound. The new melody soared, and what was now the counter-melody dropped. I understood what it was to be a master of the runes for the first time.

Althyof swept by me, a smile on his face. He wove his steps back and forth between the rest of us and Ivalti, who was almost cringing against the edge of the woods. The Tverkr spun toward Ivalti, increasing his volume until he was shouting. When he cavorted in front of the Svartalf, he came to a jarring stop, the last syllable echoing through the trees.

Ivalti barked three runes and took a step back in a tangle of limbs, but he'd already backed into a tree and could retreat no further. Althyof lunged forward and plunged his daggers into Ivalti's chest and neck, pinning him to the tree.

"Who's broken now?" he spat and jerked the daggers out. Ivalti crumpled to the ground, eyes wide with shock. Charcoal-colored blood poured from his wounds, puddling at his feet.

"Cheat," Ivalti whispered and fell forward on his face.

Althyof stooped and swept the Svartalf's black runed cap off his head and wiped his blades clean on it. "Fool," he spat and dropped the cap on the body.

"What just happened?" I asked.

"He may have been a *runeskowld* of a kind, but he was too arrogant—or too foolish—to maintain his physical safety." Althyof looked up at me and shrugged. "He relied on what he assumed was a superior form of rune casting. I relied on guile. Guile won."

"Are there more coming?" asked Jane, peering into the Forest.

"I don't think so," I said. I recounted the dream of flight I'd had on that first night, and how the warriors had laughed at or ignored Ivalti.

"We can't proceed to the north," said Frikka.

"Prophecy?" asked Meuhlnir.

Frikka shrugged and jerked her chin in my direction. "Ask him."

"It was a dream," I said after a moment's hesitation. "Though I don't think it was a *troymskrok*."

"A what?" asked Jane.

"A meaningless dream."

She looked at me as if I had sprouted a second mouth. "And you believe your dreams can tell the future, now?"

I shrugged. "I don't know if I'd go that far, but *something* is happening. Anyway, is it so hard to believe after everything else?" I gripped her finger—the one on which she wore the platinum ring—and waggled it back and forth.

"I... No, I guess not."

Mothi sighed with a deep frown. "We won't be hiring a boat in Pitra, will we?"

"It seems not," said Meuhlnir, looking as grim.

"The land route, then," said Veethar with a broad grin.

"Now, if only you can arrange matters so we make the rest of the journey underground," said Althyof as he slapped me backhanded across the belly.

With renewed vigor, Veethar led us northeast, and in what seemed like a short time, we emerged from the Great Forest of Suel on a narrow plain sandwiched between the foothills of the Dragon Spine Mountains and the Pitra Empire. Meuhlnir pointed due north. "The bay you flew over in your dream, Hank, lies that way—perhaps another day's ride."

"We're not going there, are we?" asked Sig. "The place with the bad army?"

"No, Son. Meuhlnir's giving geography lessons."

"From here, we continue northeast as far as we can. If we keep the mountains in sight, we will skirt the bay with room to spare."

"Can we sleep now?" asked Sig.

"Let's get a little farther away from those spiders," I said.

"Okay," he said, stifling a yawn.

We rode for another hour or so before we stopped to set up camp. It was four hours earlier than we would have stopped otherwise, but after the ordeal in the Great Forest of Suel, not even Meuhlnir complained about the wasted daylight.

We lounged, napped, and ate the afternoon away as if we were waiting on permission to go to bed. Even the pups spent most of the afternoon with their chins on their paws.

When the sun finally set, I crawled into the bedroll I shared with Jane and fell asleep.

FORTY-TWO

I stretched my wings, marveling at the feel of
the cool, night air lifting me heavenward.
Now that we were away from the Great
Forest of Suel, the sounds of nocturnal creatures,
great and small, going about their business filled the
air. I flew with the wind, soaring and diving—
frolicking—in the currents of crisp fall air. The
ground raced past beneath me, foothills becoming
flats, flats becoming marsh, marsh emptying into the
bay shaped like a three-leaf clover. The bay
containing thousands of dragon ships.

On the beach, most of the host of men, Svartalfar, trolls, and demons had departed, leaving only the drunkest, the sickest, or the soundest sleepers. The instinct to shriek my rumbling cry was strong, but I remembered the black-clad Svartalf who pointed at me—Ivalti—and though I knew he was dead, I didn't want to risk being seen by another of the twisted runeskowlds of the Svartalfar.

I banked east, peering ahead along the shoreline. The moonlight glinted off mother-of-pearl embedded into the coquina beach—and in the water trapped in thousands upon thousands of footprints embedded in the loose sand.

I gained altitude, not wanting anyone to take a potshot at me with a bow or crossbow. A loud, screeching crrruck sounded from the rear. I glanced behind me, and a snow-white bird swooped down from above to fly by my side. The white bird looked like a raven—except for the color, of course. The bird rolled its eyes and made a noise that sounded distinctly like laughter.

On the beach at the edge of my vision stood a vast horde arrayed in formation—trolls in the front, then demons, then men, and a horde of Svartalfar in the rear. The white bird at my side screeched and veered off to the south, making a rumbling call as it went. I followed and, when the bird dipped into the trees edging the beach, I landed beside it on the sand.

With a pop and a flash of smoke, the white bird transformed into Kuhntul, arrayed in white armor, long white hair unbound. "Greetings, Tyeldnir," she crooned.

I responded with a crrruck of my own.

"I don't suppose you can transform?"

"No," I croaked, surprised I could form the word.

"Why ever not?" she mused. "You Isir are so funny."

I shifted from foot to foot, impatient at this interruption of my flight.

"Relax, Tyeldnir. I won't take much of your time." Kuhntul smiled down at me. "You're even cute as a bird. Jane had better keep a tight grip on you."

"What...do...you...want?"

"To business, as ever," she sighed. "Such a shame. We could have such fun... You've seen the Dark Queen's forces on the beach ahead. They are making ready to march on your position, hoping to pin you between the mountains, the Great Forest of Suel, and the sea. They mean you harm, Tyeldnir."

I bobbed my head, hoping she'd get the reference to a nod.

"So cute..." she murmured. "This may be the last time I can come to you with a warning. Mother Skult is furious with me over the changes you carved into Iktrasitl. But, I'll try to slip away when possible, and give you what additional help I can. Now, you must hurry. Rouse your companions and set out at once. If you travel quickly, you may squeeze past them in the darkness. Now, awake!"

FORTY-THREE

I sat up straight, shoving the bedroll away, heart trip-hammering away in my chest. The image in my mind was of a huge host—an army—arrayed for battle, and an albino raven. The dream washed through my mind like a flooding river. "Wake up!" I shouted. "We need to get moving."

"What is it?" asked Mothi in a voice furry with sleep.

"There's an army marching toward us," I said. "They mean to pin us against the Great Forest of Suel or the mountains. We have to get by them tonight! Everyone up!" Darkness rested around us, cold and content.

We struggled into our saddles, exhaustion etched on every face. I estimated it was two or three in the morning, and we had only a few hours before dawn.

Veethar led us again, alternating between a gallop and a canter, changing from one to another by an internal clock only he and the horses understood, angling off toward the foothills. After the trial of the Forest, it was a cruel punishment—sleeping only a short time before having to be up and traveling. No one spoke, no one laughed—the only sound of our passage was the syncopated beat of the horses' hooves, their heavy breathing, and the jingle and creak of harness and saddle leather.

From the darkness ahead came the sound of hooves pounding the ground. Veethar drew us to a halt, peering into the darkness. "It is a single animal," he whispered. "One rider."

I loosened Kunknir in its holster but did not draw it, ever aware of my diminished supply of ammunition. Mothi drew a single double-bladed axe and held it across his lap. He rode away from Sig, giving the boy a glance to tell him to stay where he was.

A pale horse rode toward us out of the early morning gloom. Its rider wore leather armor and an oft-patched black cloak. His hair and beard were long and snarled, and dust and grime caked his face and neck. His eyes had a harried, wild look I didn't much care for. "No!" he called to us. "Not this way! You are riding into an ambush!" He charged up to us, waving his free hand as if the chance we might not see him existed.

"An ambush?" Meuhlnir asked in a gruff voice.

"Yes! There's a large army of trolls, men, Svartalfar, and other creatures back that way. They are trying to funnel you into a position where they can flank you, trap you against the mountains, and kill you. The Dragon Queen—"

"What do you know of the Dark Queen?" Mothi snapped.

The man shrugged. "What everyone knows, I guess. She's evil—evil to her very core. I've heard it said she was once a great leader, a great queen, but all I know of her is evil."

"Your name?" asked Meuhlnir.

The man shook his head. "You won't have heard of me. I'm not a native to Osgarthr. Queen Hel and her cohorts ripped me out of a pleasant life on Mithgarthr. I was their prisoner for years and years, but I escaped them. I've been wandering this world since, looking for a way back to my home."

"Luka closed the preer. There is no way for you to return home at the moment," said Mothi with a glance my way. He quirked his eyebrow at me, and I shook my head—I had no idea who this newcomer was.

The man sighed and shook his head. "For all these years, I've tried to get back to my family. To my home."

"I asked your name," said Meuhlnir again, with a hint of iron in his voice.

"It's been so long…" The man shook his head, looking down at his lap. "Long ago, friends called me John, but that name no longer fits me. Call me Farmathr."

"And where in Mithgarthr are you from?" asked Mothi.

"You won't have heard of it. It is a new land, not known in the time of the Vikings."

"America?" asked Sig.

Farmathr turned his head slowly, scanning the faces in our party until he reached my son's. He nodded. "Yes, the New World. I lived in the colony of New York."

"What a happy coincidence," said Jane in a campy tone. "Next you'll tell us you are from Western New York."

Farmathr shrugged. "Yes. I lived in a community named Geneva, on the shores of Lake Seneca."

There was a protracted moment of silence, only broken by Slaypnir pawing at the ground. "What a happy coincidence," repeated Jane in the same tone.

The newcomer quirked his eyebrow and looked from face to face once again. "If you'll pardon me, my lady, I find nothing about this happy. They ripped me from my home, imprisoned me, tortured me. My escape was arduous; the time I've spent wandering this world has not been pleasant, separated as I am from my family. It's been years, and I've been alone." He jerked in his saddle and glanced over his shoulder. "But, there's no time for this now! We must flee, or they will be upon us!"

"Who sent you?" demanded Pratyi, sounding skeptical.

"A...a woman." Farmathr scratched his head, his fingers snarling in the tangles of his long, unkempt hair. "A woman...at least I think she was a woman...she appeared from out of the mist."

"Was her name Kuhntul?" I asked.

"Kuhntul...uh, yes, that was it."

"Tell me, Farmathr...why should we trust you?" asked Pratyi.

"For one thing, if the Dragon Queen or her cohorts catch us, I will die along with you. For another, I'm risking my life to give you a warning." He turned his horse so it faced the mountains. "I know a path into the mountains, a path to a place the army cannot follow. An old place, an ancient place. A stronghold where we can rest in safety and comfort." He spurred his pale horse and rode away.

I glanced around, more than a little surprised to find all eyes on me. *When did I become the leader of this band?* I wondered. "What he says is in line with what Kuhntul told me. We know the army planned to ambush us." With a shrug, I nudged Slaypnir's flanks and rode after Farmathr.

When I caught up to him, he nodded, as if grateful I'd followed him. "You said 'the colony of New York?'"

"Yes. It was named a state after the war with England, but where I lived, we still thought of it as a colony."

"In what year were you taken?"

He glanced at me, his face contorted. "It was a long time ago. Perhaps longer than I fear. It was 1798."

I averted my face, hoping he wouldn't see my expression. "You are Isir?"

He scoffed and blew a raspberry. "The queen's cohorts went on and on about my blood. The Blood of the Isir, they called it. Who cares?"

"It's why you've lived so long," I murmured.

"And how long have I lived?" he asked, reining his horse to a stop.

"I… Maybe we should talk about it later."

"No, now. Or I won't show you the way into the stronghold. Vowli would never tell me how many years I spent in captivity."

"Vowli, not Luka?"

"Yes," he snapped. "Now, tell me how long!"

I sighed and glanced at Jane as the others caught up with us. "I lived in Western New York. We traveled to Osgarthr in the year 2017."

"But that's…" He shook his head and spurred his horse on.

With a shrug, I followed him. "Don't worry, Farmathr. Meuhlnir has told me that the *preer* can traverse time as well as space. If we can get the *preer* working again, they can return you to your time."

Farmathr shook his head. "No. There's nothing left for me now."

That struck me as odd, and I glanced over at him. Tears tracked through the grime on his cheeks. He saw me looking and shrugged.

"They are all dead, then," he whispered. "My family. My friend Donehogawa. All of them."

"You're thinking about this in too linear a fashion. They were dead when I lived in New York, but you can go back to the time when they were alive. You can—"

"No. You misunderstand. To save them…to save my nephew, I had to…" He dashed tears from his face with an angry gesture. "It doesn't matter." He pointed at the mountain ahead. "That's where we must go. That mountain there. The stronghold lies within it."

"Within?"

Farmathr nodded. "There is a series of tunnels and rooms under the mountain. Not like a mine, but a place where people lived and worked for a time. The tunnels run to the north and south through the mountains." He shrugged. "I explored a few of them, but not all. There are…barges I guess you would call them, but I feared riding on one by myself, so I came on horseback from the South."

"And the army won't be able to follow us?"

Farmathr shook his head. "No, if we can make it there in advance of the horde, they won't even know the stronghold is there. The entrance is hidden and secured against accidental invasion. I learned the code from Vowli before I escaped."

"How did Vowli capture you?"

"That's a long story—and a sad one. Suffice it to say that I ran afoul of the Queen, Vowli, and another companion in woods to the west of Lake Seneca. They have abilities out of nightmare. Vowli can become a demon—half wolf and half man—and the Dark Queen is a witch! I hadn't believed such things were possible until I witnessed them for myself."

"Let me guess…they ate people."

Farmathr looked at me with a strange expression on his face. "Yes, how did you know?"

"The Dark Queen and Luka were still at it in 2017, though I bet they had to be much more careful in my time than in yours."

"2017…" Farmathr shook his head. "That's almost two hundred and twenty years from the last time I saw my home."

"Remember, that it might have been a much shorter time for you. Those *preer* can—"

"Bend time. Yes, I know. But it *feels* like two centuries."

There was nothing I could say to that. I knew all too well what it felt like to have everything you cared about ripped away by the Dark Queen and her minions. "We are going to Pilrust, in Kleymtlant. That's where we can regain control of the *preer*, in a place called the *Herperty af Roostum*—the Rooms of Ruin."

"Cheerful name," he grunted.

"I assume it was a technology center, and that, over time, it's fallen to disuse."

"Technology?"

"Yeah, computers and...never mind. Machines that do complex math for us. The Isir have a complex mythos built up around all of this, but it amounts to creation mythology. All of this, *vefnathur strenki*, the *preer*, all of it, it has to be an advanced technology we don't understand yet."

"Why?" asked Farmathr.

"Because...there has to be a scientific explanation for all this."

"Why?" asked Farmathr again. "Is there a scientific explanation for God? For miracles? For the Devil? For evil?"

"Well..."

As the sun broke over the mountains in front of us, the sound of our pursuit rumbled behind us, echoing against the mountains like thunder or waves pounding against a cliff, but it was constant, without pause. I looked behind us, and a gigantic dust cloud obscured our pursuers.

"Hmph. Closer than I thought," murmured Farmathr. "We need to *hurry*." He kicked his horse in the flanks, and the animal galloped away from us. With a shrug, I did the same.

The sun rose as we galloped toward the mountains in the east, and for the rest of that day, we ran from the dust cloud, seeming unable to lose it with speed or with constant motion. As the sun set, sunlight filtered through the dust of the army pursuing us, and an icy fear settled in my guts. There would be no stopping, no relaxing campfire, no stories told, no hot dinner.

FORTY-FOUR

Exhausted and mind-weary from too many sleepless nights, too much interrupted sleep, and constant worry or outright fear, when Farmathr reined up and pointed at an unbroken solid wall of rock, I stared at it, thoughts ponderous and jejune.

"It is there," he said, weariness playing its dirge in his voice. "The way in is tricky."

"Can we take the horses?" asked Veethar.

"Yes, but you must do as I say without pause, without deviation. There is a spirit that guards the place, and it has the power to drain the life out of you if it believes you intrude."

"That sounds…" began Jane.

"Ominous," I finished.

"Indeed," said Farmathr. "Now, attend me. I will tell you when we have reached safety, but until I do, touch nothing and do not step out of my path." He glanced at Sig. "Do you hear, boy?"

Sig nodded and took a step closer to Mothi.

"Good. Now, give me a moment…" He turned to face the rocks and did something with his hands as if tracing runes in the air. He might have hummed a musical phrase, but it was difficult to tell over the sound of the wind, the horde at our backs, and the horses.

With a grinding roar, part of the ostensibly solid stone wall in front of us slid inward and up, leaving a space just wide enough for a horse. Farmathr smiled and winked at me before he turned and rode his pale horse into the darkness.

The trolls grunted and hooted—a prelude to an all-out charge—off in the night behind us, and somewhere back there, drums began to pound. Being at Farmathr's mercy inside this place, this "stronghold" as he called it, gave birth to a flurry of butterflies in my gut. But there was no other choice than to follow Farmathr into the unknown.

We rode in through the opening in the sheer rock face, with Mothi last, and as soon as he crossed the threshold, mechanisms in the darkness that surrounded us whined, and the sliver of light from the outside shrank as the massive door began to close.

The air in the antechamber reeked of hot electronics, dust, and the unmistakable, spicy odor of long decomposed bodies. There was a faint ticking somewhere off in the darkness, but similar to a cooling car engine rather than a clock or a kitchen timer.

"Now, if you'll follow me into the next chamber..."

"If we could see you, it might be easier to follow you," snapped Althyof.

In the darkness, Farmathr chuckled. Something crackled as if a green twig had snapped, and an eerie green light flared into existence. It was a glow stick resembling the ones we gave Sig on Halloween. "Follow the green light. Step only where I step." Farmathr led us on a zig-zagging path across a wide area, which I assumed to be a large room. Giant black shapes loomed at me out of the darkness—machines, or cabinets, or giant stone blocks, I couldn't tell which. The door to the outside finished the traversal of its track, cutting off the ambient light from outside with a resounding boom that sounded permanent. The only light now came from the glow stick that hung down Farmathr's back.

"What happens if we stray from your path?" asked Freya.

The glow stick jumped as Farmathr shrugged. "You die."

"That's it? No warnings, no questions, merely instant death?"

"I didn't make the rules," sighed Farmathr. "I learned them, and I've likewise passed them on to you."

"You've led others through this room? You've seen others die here?" asked Frikka with a tone of disbelief.

"Well, no. But the rules…"

"Who taught you these rules?" I asked.

"You'll see in a moment." The creak of saddle leather preceded a loud click, and a strange hiss filled the air. "No cause for concern," said Farmathr. Flickering bluish-white light flooded into the room as a door ascended toward the ceiling.

Once there was sufficient room, Farmathr ducked his head and rode through the door into a well-lit room. "In here," he called. "It's safe in here."

We followed him through the tall, narrow doorway. Bright white subway tiles sheathed the walls of the room, but polished natural stone lay under our feet. A long counter—comparable to a reservation desk in an airport back home—lined one side of the room, warped by water at some point, cracked by time and disuse. Behind it, massive black panels stretched toward the ceiling high above, and several doors stood—one pale blue, one orange, and one red. A massive crack zigged and zagged across the face of one panel, and all of them were dark, powerless. The opposite wall contained more red doors, one green door, one orange, and one yellow. Low-slung couches, chairs, and what had once been potted plants filled the space between the two walls without appearing crowded. Far above us, bright white lights burned. Everywhere I looked, surfaces shone and twinkled as though recently polished.

"What is this place?" asked Mothi with wonder in his voice.

"Looks like a subway station to me, Cousin Mouthy," quipped Sig. He walked over to one of the red doors and tried the knob. "Locked," he said with a shrug.

"Welcome to Isi's domain," said Farmathr. He swung his leg over his horse's rump and jumped down. The sound of his feet hitting the floor echoed throughout the chamber.

"That's quite a claim," I said.

Farmathr shrugged. "Don't take my word for it," he said, pointing at something behind me.

I dismounted and turned. Runes decorated the wall between this room and the antechamber. "Behold the power of Isi," I read. "Greatest of the Sons of Mim, ruler of the land and everything underneath it. Through his auspices, the Fast Track Travel Network was established under Osgarthr's skin. Isi welcomes you. The FTTN welcomes you. All praise be to Isi."

"We can rest here," said Farmathr. "These couches are much more comfortable than they look."

"What is the Fast Track Travel Network?" asked Meuhlnir. "Some kind of *proo*?"

Farmathr chuckled, but not unkindly. "No, not a *proo*. I'll show it to you after we've rested. I haven't slept in days."

"Okay. I'll stand the first watch," I said.

Farmathr laughed again. "No need for watches or guards here. There are no threats inside this place, nor can there be."

"How can you be so sure?" asked Veethar, eyes darting around the big space.

"It's simple. The guardians of this place have accepted you because I knew the proper incantations. The guardians would have killed off any threats long ago. No enemies exist in this underground realm."

"How can you be sure?" demanded Frikka. "What would stop an enemy from knowing the proper incantations and entering earlier to lie in wait?"

"The guardians wouldn't allow it." Farmathr shrugged. "Set a watch if it makes you more comfortable, but it is a waste of time and effort."

"Is there wood?" asked Yowrnsaxa. "We haven't had a hot supper for days and days."

Farmathr shook his head. "No wood. The guardians will not allow open flame inside the stronghold in any case."

"Another cold supper," grumbled Yowrnsaxa. "Wonderful."

"Nothing for me," said Farmathr. "I have already eaten." He turned and walked away from us and fell onto one of the low-slung couches.

FORTY-FIVE

I cupped my wings to catch the updrafts from
the perpetual storms over the Stormur Syow.
Ahead, there was a promontory of black
basalt, and a fortress castle of the same stone stood
on its pinnacle. A man walked from one building near
the outside wall, across the courtyard, and opened a
door set in the inner keep's back wall. He glanced up
at me and sneered. The man's name—Vowli, servant
of the Dark Queen and compatriot of Luka—crept
into my mind from some unknown source. The name
of the fortress—Helhaym—came half a heartbeat

later. The castle could only be approached from the west...unless you had wings.

"Well, come on, antafukl. I don't have all afternoon." He held out his arm, inviting me to land on his clenched fist, and I felt compelled to do as he wished. Once I'd landed, he turned and entered the main keep, striding down a long hall and into a small square room, containing only the head of a spiral staircase.

Vowli hummed as he descended into the depths below Helhaym. The black stairs spiraled down through the man-made parts of the castle, and deeper through the parts of the castle's dungeon that had once been caves in the promontory. As he descended, the air got colder and wetter as if the spray from the waves crashing against the base of the cliffs had somehow penetrated through solid stone.

"Why have you come, antafukl? What is it you seek? I do not recognize you. Do you come with a message from Mithgarthr? Have you come from the queen? From Luka?"

I could speak if I wanted to, but I didn't want to speak to Vowli. I treated him to a crrruck as I imagined any raven would.

Vowli laughed. "So be it."

When the staircase ended, Vowli stopped, content to let his muscles relax for a moment. The deepest subterranean level of Helhaym swam in darkness, by necessity if not design. "Lyows," he murmured, and a globe of golden light burst into existence at his shoulder. Despite its color, the light cast no warmth, but rather the opposite.

The floor made the shape of a giant X with the stairwell ending at the center. Vowli strode down the northwestern leg of the X, humming again. He passed empty cell after empty cell—as if he'd wanted the occupant at the end of the corridor to drown in silence and darkness. As he approached the end of the corridor, my sensitive nose picked up the man's stench—staggering in its potency. "Owtroolekur, you reek of the grave," he called. "Worse than some of the truykar." Vowli stepped up to the iron-banded door and peered in through the grate covering a hole the size of a book. "You don't appear well. Have you eaten?"

"Master, I put out the food, but he won't eat," said a young woman in a piping, yet mournful voice. "He doesn't speak to me, nor gaze upon me. He ignores me."

Vowli hid a grin by glancing at his feet. "That can't be true, Edla. You are too delightful."

"Perhaps I offend him, Master."

"I'm sure not, Edla. You are a beautiful woman. Succulent. What man could be offended? What do you have to say, Owtroolekur? Does Edla offend you?"

"She does! Send her away!" Owtroolekur croaked.

"Ah, now! Come toward the light and let me survey the sorry state into which you have no doubt fallen."

I wanted to see through the square window, but Vowli held me well away. I snapped my wings out, intending to fly to his shoulder, but, quick as a snake, he grabbed my feet and held me fast. An annoyed croak flew from my beak instead.

"What is that? Is that a bird?"

Vowli scowled and shook his head. "I wish you would eat, Owtroolekur."

"You promised to free me."

Vowli shrugged. "You promised to eat."

"He has tried, Master. The food makes him sick."

"Indeed," *said Vowli.* "He knows the cure for that problem, don't you, Owtroolekur? Such recalcitrance. Why do you still resist?"

"You understand why!" *he cried.*

Vowli shook his head and blew out a breath. "Still? After all these years?"

"Until the day I starve to death!" *snapped Owtroolekur.*

"Such vehemence. Wasted, I'm afraid, as I am not impressed."

"In that case, I must try harder." *Something scraped inside the cell, sounding like stone against stone.*

"Where did you get the stone?" *asked Vowli, sounding bored.* "You've sharpened the edge of the stone, I see. To what end?"

Edla cried out, and the scent of blood filled the air. Vowli's nostrils flared. "Oobna," *Vowli muttered, and the door sprang open.* "Shut up, woman."

He set me on the ground. "Frist," he said, and a coldness crept from the stone floor into my feet. I tried to hop away, but my feet had frozen to the floor.

"He's killed himself," whispered Edla. "Did you bring a raven to carry his soul away?"

Vowli turned and strode through the cell door. "He's done nothing of the sort." He stopped walking, and his booted feet scraped against the roughhewn floor as he copped a squat. "Lifa ow nee."

Inside the cell, something twitched violently, and someone gasped. "Why?" he cried.

"I've told you more than once, Owtroolekur. I have the power over life and death. You made your choice all those years ago. You swore yourself into the Queen's service, did you not?"

"Under duress," whispered Owtroolekur.

Vowli scoffed and pulled Owtroolekur to his feet. "Such trivialities have no merit, Owtroolekur. You will stay in this cell until you eat to sustain yourself, until you honor your vow."

"Never! I never will!"

"The weight of the years you've spent in this cell have taught you nothing? There is no such thing as 'never.'" Vowli chuckled nastily. "You will eat, Owtroolekur, and when you do, you will see how foolish you've been."

"Never," repeated Owtroolekur, but his denial lacked conviction.

Vowli's laughter echoed through the dark recesses of the subterranean dungeon and...

FORTY-SIX

I awoke with the sound of Vowli's harsh laughter in my ears, and a headache that made me long for a power drill. I sat up on the low couch I'd slept on and rubbed my face.

"Good morning, sleepyhead," said Jane. "Another dream, birdbrain?"

"Yeah. More flying."

Jane shrugged. "Better than falling."

"I guess," I said with a sigh. "But this time, I saw Vowli. He carried me down into the dungeons of Helhaym."

"Lucky he didn't eat your liver with some fava beans and a nice chianti."

"Don't make the slurpy sound. You're horrible at it."

"Bah. I'm good at *everything* I do. Don't you know that by now?"

"Of course, but I can't let you get The Big Head."

"Sif says it's time for your checkup, and you *will* comply. Resistance is futile."

"Hannibal Lector and Seven of Nine in the same morning? Give a guy a break."

"Which arm?" She smirked at me and waved Sif over. "Watch out, Sif, he's ornery this morning."

"He's ornery every morning, isn't he?"

"Well, there's that." Jane walked away, whistling.

"How have you been feeling?" Sif asked while she poked and prodded my joints.

"Good. I didn't enjoy the forced insomnia, but it was…survivable."

Sif harrumphed. "I'd say you did more than survive."

"Yes, I've felt much better since you started the anti-inflammatory bacon."

"*Bacon?*" she asked with her eyebrow crooked.

"You said you made the anti-inflammatory from pigs. Everyone knows the best thing to come from pigs is bacon, so there you are."

She shook her head, but I could see the grin in her eyes. "So…you are admitting I was right?"

"Sure," I said without hesitation.

"Such a refreshing attitude," she said raising her voice so it would carry to where Meuhlnir lounged on one of the many couches.

"Hank, I wish you'd stop getting me in trouble with my wife!" yelled Meuhlnir.

Sif grinned, patted my shoulder, and left.

I stood and looked around. Veethar had convinced the horses to stay in one corner of the vast room, and they seemed content there. Keri and Fretyi had invented a new game with Sig and Mothi—which amounted to the puppies attacking either Sig or Mothi's feet, then switching and attacking the other for no discernable reason.

Farmathr watched us all as we performed our morning routines. It was as if he didn't know how to interact with people anymore. He sat by himself, almost in the shadows near the far end of the room.

I grabbed two pieces of bread and two slices of dried fish that Yowrnsaxa had laid out for breakfast and joined him, sitting across from him in the little conversation grouping he'd set up camp in. He looked at me with a vague smile on his lips.

"Breakfast," I said, holding out a piece of bread and fish.

He took the food but put it aside, eyes drifting back to the others.

"You've been alone for a long time, haven't you?"

As he looked away, a strange expression crept over his face. "Yes. A long time. Well, alone in all ways that matter."

"You said before that Vowli imprisoned you somewhere. Was it at Helhaym? A big lump of black basalt near the Stormur Syow?"

He flinched and looked up, raw eyes locking onto my own. "I…I think so. It's been so long…"

"Do you know how to get back there?"

He shook his head. "No. And I would not take you there if I did. It is a vile place."

I sighed. "I know it's not a great spot, but…but I think Vowli has another prisoner there."

His expression knotted up like a fist, but his eyes blazed. "Why would you think that?"

"It's…" His reaction perplexed me. *Is he angry I asked him about this? Or is it PTSD from being held prisoner?* "It may be nothing. I've been having these dreams… Dreams about being a bird. I fly different places, see different things, but they seem to be prophetic. I…" I shrugged.

"Being a bird?" His voice was barely above that of a whisper.

"Yeah. In the dream, I'm a raven or something. Probably a silly, meaningless dream, but…"

Farmathr scoffed, and again, his eyes drifted away from mine.

"I dreamed about Helhaym. I saw Vowli, and he took me down into the dungeon caves below the fortress. He spoke to a man in a cell…a man who wanted to die—he even slit his own throat with a piece of sharpened stone, but Vowli resurrected him. He—"

"*I don't want to hear anymore!*" Farmathr shot to his feet, scattering the food I'd brought him, and stomped away.

"Sorry!" I called after him, but he didn't slow, didn't turn. He strode out of the lobby area, into a darkened hall nestled in the shadows. "At least take your breakfast!"

One of the doors—a blue one—clicked open, and a sound like a cross between a vacuum cleaner and a riding mower sounded from behind it. After a moment, the door swung wide, and through it, I glimpsed a sea of chrome appendages.

A thing made from a nightmarish combination of spider-like limbs, metal tentacles, and an insect-like torso and head, skittered out the door and with a clatter of multi-jointed legs, spun around to face me. It clicked toward me, moving with the slow, careful grace of a ninety-year-old. As it moved, one of its spindly arms contorted, bending back at the wrist to expose a matte-black tube. I got up and backed away, hands automatically seeking the butts of my pistols—which I hadn't strapped on yet.

"Leave it be!" yelled Farmathr from the darkness at the end of the room. "It just wants to clean."

The robot aimed the black tube at Farmathr's spilled food and a high-pitched whine tore the air as a greenish-white bolt of energy flew from the tube and obliterated the mess. There was no smoke, no charred marks on the floor, no sign that the food had ever been there. With a series of clanks, the robot's hand flipped forward to cover the tube, and the robot pirouetted toward the door from which it emerged and clattered back inside.

"That's some janitor," muttered Jane.

FORTY-
SEVEN

Farmathr returned two hours later. In his absence, we'd packed up, and made ready for another long ride, and Althyof had taught me the basics of enchanting, reviewing the runes I wanted to inscribe on Jane's golden spear.

Farmathr looked at our preparations with a slight smile on his lips. "Everyone ready?" he asked, looking at each of us in turn. When he got to me, his face was pleasant, as if we'd never spoken about Helhaym. He led us across the long lobby into the darkened area on the far side. The lights on the high ceiling hadn't fared as well on this side of the room, and shadows reigned. Farmathr strode through a set of wide doors and skipped down three flights of stairs.

"Are all the rooms this smooth?" asked Althyof.

"All the ones I've seen are," said Farmathr.

"Masterful craftsmanship," Althyof muttered.

"At least we will make better time on horseback," said Mothi. "Though what the horses will eat is beyond me."

Farmathr laughed. "Patience," he said.

Mothi's expression communicated how much he liked that answer with no room for doubt—or maybe it was being laughed at that offended him. The big Isir shook his head and glanced at me.

"We don't like surprises overly much, Farmathr," I said.

He looked my way, and his expression soured a little. "Fine, fine. We're almost there, anyway. Your horses won't eat more than the provisions you've brought with you, nor will we ride them. Isi built a wonder down here in the dark. A barge that rides the air and travels faster than a man can ride. It will take us far to the north before nightfall."

"Is it safe after all this time?" asked Jane.

Farmathr shrugged. "The 'lectrics and plasms can be wicked and deadly if let out to run, but they are both safe enough trapped in their tiny tubes, as they are in the tunnel we will use."

"I meant the train, or whatever it is. Are the tracks maintained? Are the tunnels free of debris?"

Farmathr shrugged again. "They leave no tracks. Either the tunnels are clear, or they aren't. They were the last time I rode the FTTN. We'll know more when we see the platform, won't we?"

The expression on my wife's face matched Mothi's, but she didn't pursue it.

We followed him down a tunnel wide enough for us to all walk side by side, and out onto the universe's biggest subway platform. The platform perched between two parallel tunnels. To the left, the tunnel ran north, while the tunnel to the right ran south. In the left-hand tunnel, a huge, rectangular platform furnished with conversation pits that matched those found in the lobby above, hung in midair. In the tunnel that ran to the south, the platform lay in its berth but canted to the side at a dangerous angle.

"You see?" Farmathr bubbled like a child, almost hopping from foot to foot in his excitement. "Isn't it grand? Isn't it magnificent?"

Jane's gaze lingered on the northbound platform. "What happened there?"

"Oh, who knows," snapped Farmathr. "It's always been that way."

Veethar looked down the southbound tunnel. "Where is the terminus of this platform?"

Farmathr shrugged—it was becoming his signature gesture. "Remember what I said about the 'lectrics and the plasms? They run free on that side so I wouldn't recommend exploring that tunnel."

"Pity," said Veethar.

"Come *on*," said Farmathr. "Get aboard the platform, and let's be on our way."

Everyone looked at me—even Meuhlnir—and I wondered again when I was elected leader. "This isn't up to me alone," I said.

Mothi grinned and opened his mouth—no doubt to call me by a new nickname—but Sif elbowed him and made a face.

With a sigh, I stepped onto the platform, and the floor first flickered, then shone with a warm yellow light. Farmathr smiled and stepped on the platform after me. We loaded the horses aboard, dropped our packs, and everyone took a seat. "What now?" I asked.

Farmathr grinned and closed his eyes.

"Do we sit here and wait for something to happen or do we do something?"

Farmathr raised a lazy hand and flicked his fingers behind us. I followed his gesture and gasped. The platform was already moving, and the lights of the FTTN terminal were already far behind us.

"There's no sound," muttered Jane. "No engine, no electric motor, no wheels on a track."

"No *wind*," said Veethar.

"Isi is powerful," muttered Farmathr. "Did I not mention it?"

"*Was*," snapped Meuhlnir. "Isi passed from this realm thousands of years ago."

"Did he?" asked Farmathr, sounding amused.

"Yes. Trapped beneath the surface by the Isir, he used the power of Nithukkr to bury himself in molten stone."

"Did he?" repeated Farmathr. Meuhlnir scoffed and turned away from Farmathr, who seemed content to sit there with his eyes closed.

I glanced behind us; the FTTN terminal was no longer visible. "Whatever this platform is, it's *fast*. I can't see the terminal at all." It didn't even feel as if we were moving. In the dark tunnel, there was no way to measure our progress, and with no wind, there was no sense of speed.

I pulled my scroll case off my shoulder and considered it, tracing the gold inlay with my fingertips. The warm yellow light reflected from the floor of the platform through the gold tracery was soothing, relaxing.

"Put that damn thing away," muttered Althyof. "If you need to play with the runes, let's get back to the enchanting lesson."

I got the spear and followed him to the back of the platform. He sat in one of the plush chairs, and I sat across from him.

"Is it as simple as carving the runes I'd otherwise cast during a *trowba*?"

"Is anything ever as simple as that?" asked the Tverkr with an arched eyebrow. "No, carving the runes is simply what binds the *kaltrar* to the physical object. The power comes from the three pillars of the art as we've discussed." He rubbed the back of his neck. "I may as well show you. Tell me what you wish this spear to be."

"I want it to be a ranged weapon. Something Jane can hurl from above the battlefield."

"So she doesn't have to be within melee range, yes?"

"That's it," I said.

He nodded, and his eyes tracked forward to linger on Meuhlnir's head. A sly grin spread across his face. "I know what to do." He picked up the spear. "Here, let me show you." He patted his pockets. "Do you happen to have a chisel?"

I was about to say no when I remembered the chisel Kuhntul had given me to change Kuthbyuhrn's *uhrluhk*. I hadn't thought about it since the cave, but I could almost hear her voice in my ear. *Remember the chisel.* Those had been her parting words before she flung me back into my body. I thought about it, and it appeared in my palm. I handed it to the master enchanter.

"It's warm!" Althyof's eyes widened. "Are you ever going to tell me about those damn dreams you had?"

In answer, I smiled as I imagined Kuhntul might.

FORTY-
EIGHT

I flew above the crowns of the jagged Dragon
Spine Mountains. The sun seemed frozen in
one spot in the sky, but I raced north, faster
than any bird had a right to fly.

On a whim, I glanced at the land whipping by
below me. Something down there amidst all the
jagged rocks paralleled my course north. Points of
glowing light glinted off the thing's scaled body.

Whatever it was, it moved as a snake would—slithering in a serpentine motion across jagged rocks. Watching it made something in my belly twitch in a frisson of panic. It was huge, draping its body over peaks, stretching across ravines without having to climb down in them. When I glided over a break in the mountains—a natural pass defined by sheer rock walls on either side—the thing swung its great bulk out over the opening and flattened its body somehow, spreading its skin and catching the air. It was flying over the pass, but it had no wings.

Beneath it, snaking through the pass were thousands on thousands of men and animals—the part of the army of the Dark Queen that had harassed us on the coast. They looked up at the titanic snake-like thing flying above their heads and cried out in fear. The previously immaculate lines of marching men descended into chaos—trolls bellowing and charging around without rhyme or reason, men diving for cover, Svartalfar peering upwards and casting runes, demons hissing and crouching in place.

I flapped my wings harder, ascending, trying to get away from the giant beast below, hoping all the men in the pass would distract the thing—at least long enough for me to disappear. I swerved toward the east, leaving the mountains and gliding out across the flat, tropical plain below.

Behind me in the mountains, the snake-thing let loose a bellowing cry so loud that it sounded like the end of the world. I glanced over my wing, and a croak of surprise escaped my beak. The thing had coiled around a mountain peak, rearing up as a spitting cobra would, staring at me with burning, hateful eyes.

I turned north, following the coast, and the massive snake in the mountains began his pursuit again, always keeping an eye turned toward me. I tried to fly faster, but I couldn't outpace the huge beast.

The sun burned overhead, and hot air surrounded me. Sea dragons frolicked in the water below, seemingly enjoying a game of "who-can-catch-the-bird." They dove deep, then raced to the surface as fast as they could, leaping high into the air and snapping their jaws, even though they never came within a mile of me. They sang and cried to one another and sent those massive sounding clicks up into the sky at me. They were a fraction the size of the thing in the mountains and seemed to be mere animals while my pursuer from the peaks seemed to harbor a hateful intelligence.

I flew on, doing my best to ignore both, and time seemed frozen. The sun never moved, and the wind remained constant, though the animals and men moved at their leisure. Through the shimmer of distance and heat ahead of me, I could see the mountains crowding out toward the eastern shore, rushing right down to the edge of the sea. I thought about the thing in the mountains leaping from the cliff, flattening its body to catch the wind, and gliding as if the beast was at home in the air. I veered eastward, flying out to sea, putting more and more distance between me and the thing in the mountains. When I could no longer see it (though I somehow knew it was still there, still stalking me), I turned north again. I had no destination in mind, but the thought of flying any direction but north made my stomach rebel and nausea swirl in my guts.

I flew on and on, losing track of any sense of time, the wind buoying me, caressing me, relaxing me. In the distance, the continent of Kleymtlant—the forgotten land—squatted like a gargantuan reptile, like an alligator, or Komodo dragon. At the sight of it, dread sank its white-hot fangs into me and delivered its venom—burning, gut-twisting panic.

I didn't want to go there—not for any reason. Something horrible lurked there, waiting for me, for us. I tried to turn around, but the wind buffeted me so violently that I couldn't turn. The sea dragons below me cackled, and the thing in the mountains to the west uttered a gloating roar. I fought the wind, trying to angle away to the east, but it gusted, threatening to send me tumbling from the sky.

The tailwind blew harder, pushing me toward Kleymtlant's rocky shore. The thing coiled in the mountains hissed with glee, and I panicked again, thrashing the air with my wings, twisting my body to and fro, screeching my fear to the heavens.

A relentless wind carried me across the border of land and sea, hurtling me north against my will, against my best efforts. Mountains loomed in front of me, and the great serpent's eyes glinted there, watching me come. I fought for altitude, and this *time, the wind didn't resist. Climbing higher and higher, I put as much altitude between myself and the snake-thing as I could.*

I rocketed over its head, and the thing roared in frustration. I sent a mighty crrruck *of victory down at it. The wind carried me ever north, following the chain of mountains until I soared over a huge plain, almost walled in by the mountains. Behind me, the snake-thing's ire rumbled like mountains falling into the sea.*

By land, the plain had only one entrance—from the northeast, through a natural gate of sorts. The biggest army I'd ever seen guarded the gate. Thousands and thousands of legions of armored men, Svartalfar, trolls, and oolfa *camped in close proximity to the gate. Tents stretched for miles, all surrounding a magnificent tent of red silk and canvas. Emblazoned on the tent was a sigil I'd never seen before, but knew nonetheless: a giant wolf's head, half white and half black. The sigil of the Dark Queen herself, the sign of Hel.*

As I watched, she burst out of the tent, eyes scouring the sky, as if she knew I was there somewhere but didn't know my precise location. Short figures wrapped in black cloaks surrounded her, pointing in conflicting directions, laughing, and she swatted at them and shooed them away. I wheeled to the west and beat my wings against the air. I had no doubt she could do something to me, even dressed as I was, as a raven.

Cut into the mountains to the west was a cyclopean edifice. The plain had to be Pilrust, and the huge building was a place known as the Herperty af Roostum—*the Rooms of Ruin. Behind me, something hissed and bellowed a roar.*

I glanced over my wing. On the plain, next to her red tent, the short figures lay scattered on the ground, and Hel sprinted toward me, her steps lurching from side to side, body contorting. I watched, enthralled as she changed from a tall blonde woman into an immense black dragon.

I shrieked in fear and…

FORTY-NINE

I woke thrashing on the couch where I'd fallen asleep, panic and horror at war within me. My whereabouts penetrated the dream-fog, and I sighed, relaxing all at once. My body was screaming at me, my shoulders and neck so tense I didn't think I'd be able to turn my head in either direction. Pain ate into every joint like a vile acid, and my eyes burned as if someone had filled them with salt. Next to me, the enchanted golden spear lay on the floor.

"Hank?" asked Jane, her voice groggy. "What's wrong?"

"Farmathr!" I snapped. "Where does this damn platform take us?"

"Don't worry, it's safe."

"No, I think you'd better tell me."

"What is it, Hank?" asked Frikka. "What have you seen?"

"This particular path takes us to another FTTN stronghold, almost identical to the one we just left," said Farmathr. "It's the first stronghold in Kleymtlant, at the point where the Dragon Spine Mountains turn northeast."

"On the east side of the mountains?" I demanded, the memory of my dream, the snake-thing flinging itself into the air, leaping unbidden to mind.

"No, the west side. Why?"

"What is it, Hank?" asked Meuhlnir rubbing the sleep from his eyes. "Danger?"

I told them all about the dream, about the big snake-thing, the sea dragons, Hel's army far to the north, blocking the only entrance into Pilrust. I told them about Hel changing into a black dragon and chasing me, shuddering at the memory.

Frikka nodded once, face solemn.

"You knew of this? Of her army?" demanded Meuhlnir.

"Yes."

"And you said nothing?"

Frikka turned her gaze to meet his, a bland expression on her face. "No."

Meuhlnir shook his head, eyes awhirl with strong emotion. "I don't understand you," he seethed.

"It is no matter, Meuhlnir. *Uhrluhk* binds us."

"But we could have prepared—"

"*And,*" Frikka continued, talking over him. "*Uhrluhk* can change."

"Look, you two can argue this out later," I said. "My immediate concern is whether this platform will dump us into the Dark Queen's lap." All eyes turned to Farmathr.

"Pilrust? No. This platform's path ends 10 days' ride to the southwest."

"And does my sister know of this method of transportation? Or just Vowli?" asked Freya.

Farmathr shrugged and cut his eyes away. "Who can say what another knows?"

"That's not an answer," growled Mothi.

"And yet, it is *my* answer. In any case, it's too late to worry about such things. There is no way to stop this platform or to get off before it reaches the end of its path."

Trapped, I thought. *Might as well be in a nice, gift-wrapped box.* Kuhntul's original warning flashed through my mind. *A betrayer*, she'd said. *A traitor. Could it be Farmathr?* From Meuhlnir's face, I guessed he was thinking similar thoughts.

"Besides," said Farmathr. "From the next station, a back way—a *hidden* way—leads to the place you seek." He smiled with a mischievous twinkle in his eye. "And I know where it lies."

"Without meeting the Dark Queen's troops?" I demanded.

He scoffed with a sardonic grin plastered on his face. "Such unanswerable questions you lot have." He held up a finger, as a minister might, mid-sermon. "But, *but*, I will say that I doubt this path will lead us into conflict with the Dark Queen's army."

It wasn't much of a reassurance, but it was the best we would get from Farmathr. My irritation with the man grew, and so did the ache in my neck. I looked at Veethar and quirked my eyebrow.

"The big snake," he said.

A small smile curled the corners of my mouth. The intuitive connection that was growing between us was similar to the one Jax, my old partner in the New York State Police, and I had shared. Thinking of him sent a pang shivering through me and stirred that pot of anger at Hel and Luka that I'd been suppressing.

"Without seeing it for myself, I can't be certain."

I nodded.

"The behavior you describe could be attributed to a *lidnormr*—a dragon of the stone."

"Great. More dragons," muttered Jane.

"Are we being pursued by the Dark Queen's troops *and* one of these *lidnormr*?"

Veethar shrugged as if to say: it was your dream, not mine. He cut his gaze to his wife.

"Not necessarily," said Frikka. "In dreams, even when they are not *troymskrok*, things may not be what they seem."

"That's helpful," groused Meuhlnir.

Frikka shot him an angry look. "Shall I lie?" she demanded.

"What might this *lidnormr* represent?" I asked in the hopes of forestalling an argument between the two.

"A powerful adversary, a great evil, even Ivalti's army." Frikka shrugged. "Until we have a better understanding of your prophetic dreams, we must take the dream's message to heart."

"And what is that—if you are *allowed* to say…" said Meuhlnir.

"That despite the danger that follows us, we must not rush in blind."

"Grand," Meuhlnir muttered.

"Things are not clear at this time," said Frikka.

"And if they were, would you tell us?" demanded Meuhlnir.

"Leave her alone," said Sif in an iron voice.

Meuhlnir threw up his hands and stalked off toward the front of the platform.

"He's a touchy one," said Farmathr, with a derisive lilt in his voice. Sif glared at him, but Farmathr seemed not to notice.

"One thing is clear," I said into the frigid silence. "We can't go head-on against the army I saw camped at Pilrust."

"No," said Veethar.

"So, unless one of you knows another way into the *Herperty af Roostum*, we must follow Farmathr's secret path."

"Don't sound so grim," said Farmathr. "Has this ride on the platform been uncomfortable?

Dangerous? Was I wrong about the pursuing army being unable to follow us?"

I pinched the bridge of my nose between my thumb and forefinger and turned away. I walked up to stand next to Meuhlnir. He stared into the blackness we presumably raced into at great speed. The lack of wind, the lack of vibration, the lack of visual cues of our speed combined to make it seem as if we were standing still.

"I don't like this," he said.

"I know what you mean. I keep getting the feeling we are being herded, despite our best efforts."

He looked at me askance, one eyebrow arched.

"The sea dragons made us travel overland," I said. "After that, the *tretyidnfukl* on the walls of Suelhaym made us travel with Lottfowpnir's caravan, leaving Kuthbyuhrn's cave as the only way to get to the western side of the Dragon Spine Mountains, where the denizens of the Great Forest of Suel channeled us north, and Ivalti's army kept us from going too far north, or from gaining sea transportation in the Stormur Syow—not that we'd want it."

Meuhlnir nodded, stroking his beard. "And we rode east to avoid the ambush set by Ivalti's army and ran right into Farmathr."

"Yes," I said. "And here we are, trapped on this platform, hurtling ahead into the unknown, an army at our backs and a larger army guarding the only direct route into Pilrust."

"Again, pushing us into Farmathr's waiting arms, so to speak."

"Yes."

"What do we do?" he asked.

I couldn't help but grin. "I was going to ask you…"

He chuckled at that, but there was no mirth in his eyes. "We can fight our way through almost anything, but we can't stand against armies of the size you've seen."

"And we can't pop open a *proo* and go around them."

"No, we can't. And the party is larger than we expected." His eyes darted over my shoulder toward the Isir standing behind me, no doubt glancing at Freya and Pratyi.

"Can we stop this platform using the *strenkir af krafti*?"

"To what end? To go back?"

I shrugged. "Having *any* option is better than having no options at all, right?"

He rocked his head to the side, mouth grim. "Whether pursuers wait on the platform behind us or not remains unknown. We don't know what would happen to us in these tunnels. What did he call them? 'Lectrics and plasms."

"I understand what electricity is, and so do you, God of Thunder."

He grinned at that and shrugged with a crooked smile.

"I'm not sure what plasms are, but I assume it's a method of transmitting power. Something the *Geumlu* used. But all of that is academic if we can't stop the platform."

"Can we try without damaging some important mechanism?"

It was my turn to grin and shrug. "No idea."

"I also have no idea, and until we do, it would be reckless to poke at things we don't understand. That's a good way to get killed."

I gazed into the tunnel's inky darkness. It struck me as strange that there wasn't even a light on the front of the platform and no lights in the tunnel at all. "Can she really do it?"

"Predict the future? Yes, Frikka's been—"

"No, not that."

Meuhlnir's gaze crawled over my face. "Oh…you mean the dragon in your dream."

"Yes. Can the Black Bitch turn into a black dragon? It could be important."

He chuckled but sobered after a moment. "In your dream, was it a complete change?"

"As opposed to…"

"As opposed to the change the *oolfa* perform—halfway between man and beast."

"She ran at me and changed mid-step. After that, she was flying—a sleek, black-scaled dragon."

"And you saw no human features?"

"No, she was all dragon, I think."

"Ah. I doubt it's within her power. True shape-shifting has certain challenges to it. It takes even more power than what the *oolfa* do. That's why, in your experiences with my brother and the Dark Queen, they took on aspects of animals, but remained human in the larger sense—they don't have enough power to make a complete change. Bigger, stronger, yes, but still mostly human."

"Even breaking the *Ayn Loug*?"

"Yes, even eating the flesh of men does not grant such power."

I remembered my first lesson from Althyof—how he'd intimated that what he did as a *runeskowld* was beyond the capabilities of what Meuhlnir and the other Isir did with the *Gamla Toonkumowl*—and nodded. But still, I wondered what was possible with runic magic. Althyof had said that what the Dark Queen did approached what a *runeskowld* could do. I wondered if she'd had some Svartalf teaching her, though I'd never seen her do anything such as what Ivalti had done. "Interesting," I said.

"Is it?" he murmured, one eyebrow quirked up.

"If she can't make such a change, then it must symbolize something she *can* do, right?"

Meuhlnir stroked his beard. "I hope not."'

I waved Althyof over, and he came, a sour expression on his face.

"You mentioned before that the Dark Queen could do something that approaches casting runes, yeah?" Meuhlnir arched an eyebrow at me.

Althyof grimaced and nodded.

"Using your art, is…shape-shifting possible?"

The Tverkr's eyes opened wide. "I...uh..." He glanced at Meuhlnir.

"Or maybe with the Svartalfar version?"

Althyof cast a baleful glance at me. "Of the two, theirs is the perversion of the true Art. There is nothing a Svartalf can do that we cannot."

"Is that a yes?"

Althyof nodded, but his expression was aggrieved. "I think it might be possible."

"Think or know?" snapped Meuhlnir.

Althyof turned his gaze on him, with an air of indolence. "I say what I mean, Isir." He nodded at me and walked toward the back of the platform.

"Interesting," I murmured.

"Is it?" murmured Meuhlnir.

FIFTY

What seemed like a long time later, but what couldn't have been more than five or six hours because none of us got hungry or tired, the tunnel ahead of us began to lighten. With something to focus on, our speed became apparent, and it was *fast*. We streaked toward the ambient glow in the tunnel ahead, and it seemed we would never slow in time to avoid streaking through the station. As it turned out, there was plenty of time, and the platform slowed as smoothly as it had accelerated to whatever ungodly speed it had attained on our journey.

The platform came to a silent stop next to the terminal, and the soft, warm light under my feet winked out. "I guess that's it," I said with a chuckle. "The ride has come to a complete stop."

"Yeah, and the seat belt sign is extinguished. It's now safe to move around the cabin," laughed Sig.

The natives of Osgarthr looked at us as if we'd lost our fool minds, which made us laugh all the harder.

"Come on," said Farmathr with considerable impatience, while stepping off the barge. We unloaded our goods to the platform between the tracks but didn't follow Farmathr as he started toward the stairs. "It's this way," he said. "It's an exact duplicate of the other terminal."

"Tell me about this back way. Where does it start?" I asked.

He turned back to us, torso stiff, jaw clenched. "Why? Does it matter?"

"It might."

He pointed at my chest with a bony index finger that shook with strong emotion. "I'm the one risking his life to help you."

"And we appreciate that," said Jane. "But we still need to ask—so *we* can make plans."

He snorted and lifted his arms and let them fall. "Are you even *familiar* with the geography of this continent?"

Veethar nodded. "In a broad-brush sense."

"Fine." Farmathr dragged his hands through his hair but succeeded only in making the snarls worse. "Do you know Tohupur Uhrvaridnar Vik?"

The words meant "tip of the arrow inlet," and Veethar said, "Do you mean the inlet on the western coast that looks like an arrowhead?"

"That's the one. If you make a straight line east, following where the arrowhead points, you come to a small section of foothills guarded on both sides by sheer mountain faces. Do you know it?"

"Roughly."

"That's where it starts."

"And where is the next FTTN terminal down the line from here?" I asked.

Farmathr turned to me, jaws clenched. "North of there. A day, maybe."

"And how many days from here?"

He shook his head. "I've already said. Ten days."

"We should—"

"But travel from the other stronghold is more difficult than from this one. There are dangers—"

"Yes?" asked Meuhlnir, looking down at his feet.

Farmathr's mouth snapped shut with an audible click of teeth. "Fine," he grated. "It will take the better part of another day to reach the next terminus. _If_ the barge works."

Meuhlnir held up his hand, gesturing toward the twin platform across the terminal. "No better time to find out than now."

Shaking his head, Farmathr stalked over to the other platform and put his foot on it, as if he were a boy testing the water of his favorite swimming hole. Warm yellow light glowed from the floor of the platform, and Farmathr sighed as if he'd been hoping for another result. "Shall we go now, or would everyone prefer to rest?"

"Now's good," I said, and we piled onto the platform. Only Keri and Fretyi seemed to object, and their complaints were limited to sleepy whining.

FIFTY-ONE

Traveling by Isi's Fast Track Travel Network platforms had several things going for it, the most important being it did not hamper sleep, and by the time we reached the next terminus, everyone had caught up. Almost everyone jumped and jittered, invigorated by too much sleep to the point of skittishness. Even Althyof seemed antsy to get out of the tunnels of stone and back into the world above. We crowded off the platform, more than a little stiff and ready to move.

The terminal was not as immaculately clean as the previous two. A thick layer of dust swathed the tile floor of the departure area, and the air carried the scent of a car that had been shut up and left in the sun for a few years. There was another tunnel leading north, but there was no rider platform.

"End of the line, I guess," I said.

"Then can we finally ascend to the world above?" asked Farmathr.

"We should eat," said Yowrnsaxa. "Cold food again, unless…" She cast a hopeful look at Farmathr.

Our guide grimaced and shook his head. "No fire, and we have no time to dawdle. It will be dark soon, and the lands outside are no place to be in the dark."

"It seems the janitors have broken down here, perhaps a small cooking fire—"

"*No fire*," grumbled Farmathr.

"But, still, we must eat," said Yowrnsaxa.

"Do what you want!" Without another word, Farmathr stomped up the stairs to the lobby, slamming the door at the top.

"Touchy, touchy," said Sif.

"He's been alone for a long time," I muttered.

Yowrnsaxa sighed and let her shoulders droop. "I suppose we can eat while we walk."

She passed out bread and more dried fish, and we ate it sandwich-style while we climbed the wide steps and strolled into the curiously spicy stench of the main lobby. The outside wall bore the same runes as the other lobby we'd seen, but dust filled these. There was a rainbow of doors sprinkled throughout the lobby, but, an electrical fire had charred the pale blue door long ago.

"No mechanical maintenance men here," said Jane.

Farmathr grunted and strode to the far wall. He pressed certain places on the wall in rapid succession, and a low-frequency rumbling filled the room. A section of the wall began to scroll upward with a screech echoing in the darkened room beyond—metal on metal, the same way worn bearings shriek. "Same rules as when we entered. Follow me. Do not linger." He took up the reins of his horse and slid into the darkness.

Each holding our own set of reins, we followed him out through the dark room and into the outside air—which, though it held a spicy, unfamiliar undertone and was hot and stuffy, never smelled sweeter.

"Welcome to Kleymtlant," said Farmathr in a flat, emotionless voice. He waved his hand toward the western horizon. "Behold what the *Geumlu* have wrought."

The late afternoon light had a peculiar greenish tinge to it. We stood in a shallow cave at the foot of a mountain, surrounded by sand dunes as far as the eye could see. The greenish-gold sand seemed to gleam and twinkle with reflected light. Strange, misshapen rock formations dotted the landscape, looking like lumps of molten stone had been dropped from the sky and allowed to cool. Now and again, two formations met in a rough, elementary arch that looked too heavy to stand. What brush existed appeared stunted and emaciated by the heat and sun. The only sound was the low moaning of the wind.

"Had we taken my route, you'd have been spared this," murmured Farmathr. "We must be careful," he said in louder tones. "There are...*things*...living here... Horrors. Monsters. Maybe demons, I don't know. What I *do* know is that these things eat...uh...flesh and drink blood to survive."

"Do they eat *people*?" asked Sig in hushed tones.

"People, horses, *varkr*. Each other. Anything that breathes."

"Oh," said Sig.

"Don't worry, little Piggy. Nothing will eat you...not with that stench that wraps you," said Mothi with a quiet laugh.

"Look who's talking," said Sig.

"How witty, Siggy-pig."

"I know, Cousin Mouthy, I know."

"We should move away from this place," said Farmathr, his gaze never leaving the vista before us. "The things here...they know this place occasionally disgorges people and horses."

"Wonderful," said Jane, swinging up into her saddle.

We mounted and followed Farmathr, who led us through high dunes that served as foothills for the mountains, making random turns at irregular intervals. The sand shifted and slid toward the ground in wide, avalanche-like paths from the crests of the dunes above, and each noise made everyone jump or reach for a weapon.

As the light began to die, something screeched into the coming night. My nerves shivered at the sound and goose-flesh erupted down my arms despite the heat. I loosened my pistols in their holsters as the others loosened their weapons. Skowvithr spurred his horse forward, nodding as he passed me, and rode at Sig's side. I pulled out the spear we'd enchanted and handed it to Jane.

"For me?" she said, batting her eyelashes. "You're so romantic, Henry Jensen."

"Throw it, don't poke things with it."

"I don't know how to throw a spear," she said, shaking her head.

"It's enchanted, you don't need to know how."

"And after I've thrown it? Do I call a timeout and walk over to get it?"

"Say '*aftur*' like Meuhlnir does, and it will return to your hand," said Althyof.

The thing screeched again, and it sounded hungry.

"Cover?" I asked Farmathr.

He shrugged and waved his hand at the surrounding dunes.

"Then we rely on speed. Get moving!" I barked.

Farmathr looked at me for the space of a breath, a funny little half-grin twisting the lower part of his face. His eyes held a twinkle, but I didn't think it was a twinkle of amusement. He shrugged and spurred his horse up to a canter, taking fewer and fewer turns. The sound of the horses' hooves echoed out across the desert, but there was nothing to be done about that.

Another shriek split the air, closer this time. "What is it?" I asked, passing the saddlebags containing the *varkr* pups to Sig's horse. They were almost too heavy to carry.

"One of the *things*. One of the *monsters*." Farmathr shrugged without turning.

"You don't seem very concerned," said Pratyi.

"They don't want me. I've come to terms with what goes for life here in Kleymtlant."

"Well, as long as *you* are safe…" sneered Althyof.

"Some kind of…large…reptile, but at the same time…not just a reptile," said Veethar, intense concentration burning on his face. "I think…"

"Can you turn it aside?"

Frikka reached across and took her husband's reins. She nodded at him as if nothing more exciting than a stiff breeze were behind us. Veethar squeezed his eyes shut. "*Syow echkert*," he whispered.

Riding next to me, Jane made a "give it to me" gesture.

"See nothing," I translated.

The beast following us made a strange, confused noise.

"*Lyktu echkert*," said Veethar.

"Smell nothing."

Again, the beast made the confused noise, but this time, it came with an undercurrent of anger, of frustration.

"*Hayrthu echkert!*"

"Hear nothing."

A squall of pure rage thundered across the dunes, and with it, came the sound of the beast sprinting in our direction.

"Up! To the top of the dune," I commanded, reining Slaypnir and nudging him in the flank. He snorted and sprang up the hill, hooves churning the loose sand. The others followed suit, Skowvithr taking Sig's reins and leading him up. On the crest, I whirled Slaypnir around, peering into the sunset for a glimpse of what was pursuing us. Skowvithr didn't stop at the peak of the dune—he took Sig down the back side and stopped, looking back up.

Veethar pointed, and I followed his gaze. Sand flew into the air near the crest of a dune about three hundred yards away, as if something were running across the dune's face, below the peak. The sand catapulted into the air like the plumes thrown by the tires of a trophy truck in the Baja 1000. The thing zipped across the backside of the dune, still hidden from sight except for the sand thrown by its passage. "Big," said Veethar.

"Dragon-big or Meuhlnir-big?"

Veethar shrugged. "Can't see it yet."

The thing came over the top of the dune and, in a single leap, cleared the valley to the next dune. Its head bore horns similar to a rhinoceros, but with the big horn in the rear, colored in muted greens and golds. A ring of spikes encircled its neck as if it wore a spiked dog-collar. Spikes covered its back, which was also scaled in the same colors as its head. It had eight spiked legs, four on each side, and a long, curved tail that arched up over its back. The spikes on the tail started narrow and then broadened like Mothi's axe heads and looked sharp enough to take off a man's head.

It stood still atop the dune, staring at us with one twitching eye, head cocked to the side. Its gaze moved down our line in spastic jerks and once it reached the end, zipped back to fasten on Veethar. It opened its mouth and yowled like a cat that had been dipped in water, then sprang off the crest of the dune, legs pinwheeling, spitting sand toward the sky. It disappeared down the face of the dune, but the horrific screech didn't abate for a moment.

"Mad at you, Veethar," said Meuhlnir with a small grin.

"How do we fight it?" asked Jane.

"All of you get over the crest of the dune," said Veethar. "I will lead it away."

"*No*, Veethar!"

"*Yes*, Frikka!" he snapped. "Do as I say."

"No," I said. "I have a better idea."

"Say it! Quickly!"

"You run, it follows you, we follow it…and kill it. To start, mete out damage at a slow pace, saving energy for a burst to take it down once it gets weaker."

"And if it turns on you?"

"We scatter and fall back together after it chases one of us. Rinse, repeat, profit."

"You are a strange man, Hank," said Farmathr.

"If you only knew," said Jane.

"Skowvithr, take Sig east to the foot of the mountains. We will meet you there."

"No, Dad! I can—"

"No, you can't!" snapped Jane. "Do as your father says."

"Mom, I—" He squawked as Skowvithr jerked Lyettfeti's reins and galloped hard toward the east. Sig grabbed the front of his saddle and held on.

Veethar was halfway down the dune when the beast showed itself again. It was a lot closer than I'd have thought possible—a hundred and fifty yards out, or less. "Here I am!" shouted Veethar as he kicked his horse hard in the flanks. The horse screamed and bolted down the face of the dune at an angle.

When the beast dipped down between dunes, I led the others over the dune. "You yell when it's chasing you, Veethar!"

We heard it as it drew near. It sounded like an old steam engine, punctuated by the sound of its clawed feet digging into the sound. The beast charged south, following Veethar's path.

"It's chasing!"

"Okay," I said to the others. "We wait one minute, then we go after it. All of us stick together—no heroics, Mothi. If you don't have a ranged weapon, use the power at your disposal. Failing that, *stay with us*." I glared at each one in turn, stopping with Jane. "Understand?" They nodded or chorused assent. "Get ready... *Go*!"

We raced over the top of the dune and ran along its peak. I drew Kunknir and snapped off two shots, aiming for the beast's lump of a torso. As the rounds hit, the beast yowled and twitched, but if it slowed, I couldn't discern the change. If we didn't slow it down, it would catch Veethar before we could catch up to it.

"Althyof!" I yelled over the wind of my passage. "Speed!"

Jane stood in her stirrups and flung the golden spear using every muscle in her body by the look of it. The spear crackled and seemed to liquify in midair, changing into a lightning bolt of pure gold. It rushed after the monster chasing Veethar, crackling like ball lightning. "*Cool*," Jane muttered, sitting back in her saddle. The golden lightning bolt slammed into thing's back, and for a moment the beast's muscles bunched in a tetanic contraction. The lightning disappeared, and the spear bounced from its back, leaving the creature unharmed.

Althyof began a *trowba* and Slaypnir shuddered beneath me. A mighty shiver ran from the tip of his nose down his neck, across his withers and his back. He snorted and picked up speed.

I fired Kunknir again, relying on its enchantments to hit the beast rather than Veethar. I couldn't risk using Krati until we were closer, or I could get a safe angle. The sound of the gunshots rolled across the desert plain and bounced back in echo. "Remember to call it back!" I shouted.

"*Aftur!*" Jane said, and the spear zipped back to her hand.

"Ehlteenk!" shouted Meuhlnir and lightning crackled from the sky, slamming the beast between its shoulders. The beast's muscles bunched again, and its legs skidded across the sand. It was long enough to send the beast cartwheeling ass over teakettle.

I snapped another round at its underside, which had less armor than the top side, and the thing howled—in pain, I thought, rather than anger. Moving with the apoplectic, overweening quickness of an insect, it flipped over and stood, alternating its stare between Veethar and the rest of us. It took a step toward us, then another toward Veethar.

I raised Kunknir and waited. When it looked our way again, I fired, aiming at the thing's head. The round slammed into it, and it shrieked with rage, sprinting toward us.

"On us now!" I shouted. "Scatter."

We split apart, giving our horses their heads. The thing barreled at me, tossing sand in the air as it accelerated at a ridiculous rate. "Let it pass, and when it has, follow!" I shouted, hoping anyone could hear me over the wind, the beast's caterwauling, and the horses' hooves.

The thing was gaining on me fast, head lowered, feet churning the sand. "If you have any ideas, Slaypnir, now would be a good time." He snorted and juked to the left, running two steps up the side of a dune before wheeling around and cutting toward the other side. He sprang toward the crown of the opposite dune, and I glanced back, expecting to see the thing right behind us.

I should have trusted Slaypnir. The weird insect or animal chasing me had fallen back quite a bit. Maybe its speed was akin to that of an alligator—straight line only. "Good boy," I muttered.

The others fell in behind the beast, and lightning arced down from the sky, this time accompanied by a bolt of fire thrown by Mothi, and the golden lighting of Jane's spear. Althyof's mouth was moving in a *triblinkr*.

I whipped Kunknir around and shot the beast in the face. Its blood was black and thick, like molasses, and as it shook its head, the gunk flew away through the hot air in thick, sludgy clumps. Bolts of lightning, balls of fire, and something that looked like arrows made of light rained down on the creature from the rear. It shook its spiked head again and glared at me with seething hatred.

Slaypnir danced side to side, and the thing tried to follow our movement with its eyes. It staggered as if dizzy, and that gave me an idea. *Where's Althyof when I need him?* What I had in mind would work best as a *trowba*, but I had no idea how to pull that off on horseback. I holstered Kunknir and closed my eyes. Maybe I could cheat a little, combine *saytr* and *stayba runana*—the string magic of the Isir and the casting of runes.

Althyof said Hel was doing something resembling runic magic, so I knew it could be done. I concentrated on the runes I would need and composed the three lines I would say in the *Gamla Toonkumowl*.

These are my words. "*Thehta eru orth meen*!" I shouted. I pictured the rune *Thurisaz* in my mind and concentrated on flinging it out into the world the way Althyof had taught me. The rune meant danger or suffering, and I flung it at the beast. Power crackled in the air surrounding me and swept over the beast like a breaker crashing over rocks. The beast's eyes locked on mine and it slowed, almost to a walk.

Althyof was screaming something, but I didn't have time to listen to him—I needed to finish this before the beast could marshal its will and break free.

Perceive these runes. "*Skinya thessar roonur*!" I yelled while casting the *Sowilo* rune into the world. The rune could mean solace, and I flung it like a promise.

Stop and rest, give me peace. "*Iya tyefthu myer frith*!" I cast the rune *Eihwaz* at the beast, building strength into the *kaltrar*.

To disobey me is to die. "*Ath oekleethnast myer er ath tayia*!" The vitality rune *Ansuz* floated in my mind, almost without me having to call it up. I followed it by casting the chaos and destruction rune *Hagalaz*—the combined meaning of the two runes: the destruction of life—death, in other words. A cutting, bone-chilling wind swept over me and blew into the face of the beast.

You will...not... My mental voice stuttered to a stop, my mind cavernous, empty. *You... You will not, um, attack us.* "*Thoo munt echki...*" I tried to force the picture of *Thurisaz* into my mind, and while I did that, I lost the stream of words. "*Thoo munt echki rowthast ow ochk…ochk…*" Panic sank into my guts. I couldn't get the words out. I knew what I needed to say to complete the line: *ochkur*—I could think it as much as I wanted to, but I couldn't get the words past my teeth. *Something's wrong!* screamed a tiny voice far off in my mind.

"*Ochk…ochk…*" I yelled. The air thrummed with power, and my vision wavered with the crackling, soul-draining power of it. Unbidden, Althyof's words from my first day of *runeskowld* training swam into my mind. *When you incant as a* runeskowld, *if you fail, there is a backlash of energies. It may strike you; it may strike those around you*, he had said.

Fear locked its maniacal fingers around my neck, adding to the obstructions already there. My tongue spasmed in my mouth and I gagged on the last word of my impromptu *kaltrar*. Beneath me, Slaypnir snorted, dancing back and forth as if he wanted to bolt, to get away…from *me*. I tried to pat his neck, to let him know I was still his friend, but the muscles in my arms locked tight, pain singing through me.

The power of the runes snapped back at me, backfiring, flinging me from Slaypnir's saddle and embedding me three inches into the sand. The beast yowled, and I heard—or perhaps *felt*—the thrumming of its clawed feet on the sand, drawing ever closer. Slaypnir charged away—bolting away from the idiot who'd caused something analogous to an explosion on his back. I tried to roll out of its way, but after the explosion of pain, my muscles refused to obey.

Slaypnir screamed and charged at the spiked beast, hooves slashing, eyes rolling. The beast backed off a step, then two, a low mewling cry rumbling in its chest. Its tail twitched, and in a blur, it spun and swept the sharp, axe-like protrusions on its tail toward Slaypnir at knee level. Slaypnir reared on his hind legs and jumped to the side—something I'd seen dogs do, but never a horse. The beast hissed and lunged toward me.

"*No!*" shouted Jane—exactly as she had back on the ship when she killed the sea dragon by force of will, but the beast didn't drop dead, and she didn't collapse. Instead, it stopped and turned toward her, movements laggard and logy. Jane pointed at the beast, and it staggered, looking around in confusion.

"Yes, more of that, Jane!" Veethar shouted.

The beast stumbled in a circle, peering at us, and making a high-pitched growling noise. Althyof raced to my side, cursing my stupidity as he came, his cadmium red cartoon daggers crackling and stretching. "You fool," he hissed as he dropped to his knees next to me, shoving his daggers into their sheaths.

"Can we get away from the thing when it's like this?" asked Frikka.

"We can try," said Veethar.

"Can you run, idiot?" Althyof asked me, pulling me up.

"I think so."

"Then do it!" He shoved me toward his horse and ripped his daggers out, the stretchy cartoon blades leaping and flashing.

"Slaypnir—"

"Leave him to me!" shouted Veethar.

I ran toward Althyof's mount, the Tverkr behind me, singing a *trowba* of mending and dancing as fast as I could sprint. I grabbed the reins of his mount as we ran by it.

We gathered around Jane, sitting as still as a pillar of salt in her saddle, while the beast shook its head and peered around, baffled by the movement. The beast lurched a few steps toward us and spun in a panicky circle. The strain of it twisted Jane's features. We knew the power the ring had granted her didn't come for free, but we didn't know how much keeping the beast confused would cost her.

We backed down the far side of the dune. Slaypnir danced at the bottom of the ravine, neighing, and stomping his hooves.

Althyof's *trowba* shifted away from the song of mending he'd used to get me over the blast, slowly changing key and rhythm. I could almost see the runes he cast into the air, and the meaning of the new *kaltrar* became clear. He was reinforcing the confusion Jane stitched into the beast's mind and lending her his strength.

I slid and stumbled down the dune to where Slaypnir stood pawing the ground and climbed up into his saddle, sparing a moment to pat his magnificent neck. "Sorry, buddy," I said, and he nickered. The rest of the party, except for Althyof and Jane, joined me in the valley between the two dunes. "How will Althyof get on his horse?" I muttered, and as soon as I said it, his *trowba* became a *triblinkr,* and he jumped into his saddle without disrupting the rhythm of the chant. Matching Jane's slow descent step for step, Althyof glared at me as he chanted. After what I'd experienced, envy roiled through me at the apparent ease with which he could do forty-nine things at once.

"Will it hold?" I called. On the other side of the dune, the beast yowled like a mountain lion in heat.

Still chanting, Althyof pointed to the east.

I took Jane's reins, and she spun in her saddle to stare behind us, forehead wrinkled with strain, lips quivering with the effort of confusing the beast. She swayed with the force of it, the drain on her system. The thing was following us; I could hear its distinctive eight-legged gait on the dune behind us.

"How can we get this damn thing to stop following us?" I asked.

"It will leave when the ground gets rocky enough," said Farmathr in a lazy drawl.

"You know this, or you *think* this?" asked Meuhlnir with an edge in his voice.

Farmathr rode on in silence, a small smile curving his lips.

We rode hard, pushing the horses on the loose footing of the queer-looking desert sand. The farther east we rode, the smaller the dunes, and soon I could see the spiny beast following us with an over-the-shoulder glance.

The beast chased us in a peculiar, repeating series of actions. It would run for a hundred yards or so and stop to look around as if lost. The creature would shake its head and, in a burst of ridiculous acceleration, beeline for us again.

As the ground flattened and hardened, we increased our pace, and the beast chasing us mewled like a kitten. The interval between looking around and accelerating on our back trail grew longer and longer, and as Slaypnir's hooves scuffed over the scree, the beast stopped and lifted its snout in the air as if sniffing the wind of our passage. It took another step toward us but then backed away in mincing steps. It made one more mewling cry before turning back to the desert and speeding away, chased by a plume of dust.

"You see?" asked Farmathr.

Jane sagged in her saddle, almost falling. Her eyes rolled in their sockets, and her mouth hung slack. I stepped Slaypnir close and gripped her shoulder. "Help me!" Yowtgayrr was off his horse in half a heartbeat and standing on the other side of her horse. He grasped her shoulder and thigh and nodded at me. When I let her go, Yowtgayrr slid her gently to the ground.

Sif squatted next to Jane and examined her with a critical eye. "Keeping the beast confused drained her almost as much as the battle with the sea dragon," she said. "Without Althyof's help, I doubt we would have made it."

"But she's okay?"

"As with the sea dragon," Sif said with a nod. "It's only exhaustion."

Jane stirred, and her eyelids fluttered. Sif forced a foul-smelling brew to her lips, and as the amber liquid splashed into her mouth, her eyes opened wide.

"Swallow, woman," said Sif.

Jane took great gulps of the draught, and her eyes erupted with tears. She blinked furiously but kept right on drinking. When Sif pulled the jar away from her lips, Jane almost looked ready to go again.

"Can you ride?" I asked her.

She nodded and staggered to her feet, looking more than a little drunk. Yowtgayrr rested his hand on her elbow and guided her toward her mount. He stayed by her side until she sat slumped in the saddle, still blinking as if she had hot sauce in her eyes.

Past the scree, the ground turned hard and sloped upward toward the mountains. Skowvithr and Sig sat on their horses five hundred yards past the scree, amidst small boulders of igneous rocks in shades of dark gray. "Is it gone?" Sig called. "For good, I mean?"

"Looks that way, kiddo. Thanks to Mommy and Althyof."

"Cool!"

The sun rested for a moment on the western horizon, as if waving goodbye, and began to set. The sloped ground wasn't perfect for camping, never mind the small stones and larger boulders. "Is there a flat area to camp somewhere nearby?" I asked, looking at Farmathr.

He shrugged and walked his horse toward the east.

"Great guide he's turned out to be," grunted Mothi.

"How far to this shortcut of yours?" asked Meuhlnir.

Farmathr turned his horse to the side and glared back at us. "Half a day, maybe more, maybe less. It's hard to say without knowing at which step my advice will be ignored."

"Stow the attitude," I said. "Get moving."

He stared at me for a moment before wheeling his horse around without a word and walked up-slope.

"Tell us about the back way."

"It's marvelous," said Farmathr without turning. "There are tunnels, but not manufactured. They are smooth-walled and curve through the mountain with a certain grace. They connect this side of the mountains to a cave system that leads to Pilrust."

"Not dug by men, you say?" asked Meuhlnir.

"Correct."

"What else tunnels through rock?"

"Magma," chirped Sig. "They're called lava tubes."

"Is that so?" asked Farmathr in tones that made it clear he didn't think much of Sig giving his opinion of anything.

"Yes, it is. I learned about it in school."

"How far to these tubes?" asked Mothi, with a glance at the darkening sky.

"Are you tired, Isir?" asked Farmathr. "After all that sleep?"

"No, but who knows what other beasts lurk in this crazy place."

"Who, indeed," said Farmathr with an unkind laugh.

"All I know is that *if* someone knows and doesn't share his knowledge beforehand, I may grow to dislike him," said Mothi in a gruff voice.

"You mean you don't already?" murmured Meuhlnir.

We reached the entrance to Farmathr's back way as the larger of Osgarthr's two moons reached its zenith. The air was crisp and dry, and warm air gusted from the lava tube's entrance, bearing a trace scent of sulfur. The area in front of the entrance was wide and flat—a perfect place to camp—and everyone was ready for a break from the saddle.

Mothi gathered firewood from the slopes around the entrance and built a large, roaring fire. Yowrnsaxa's grin split her face as she got out her cook pot and ingredients. Farmathr watched her preparations with a sardonic smile for a moment before he turned and walked off into the gathering darkness.

"Guess he's not eating," murmured Mothi. "Again… Oh, well, I'll have his share." Mothi sat on a boulder and beamed a smile at Yowrnsaxa.

"Wrestle you for it," said Sig.

"Young man, there's no way you could win—" Sig jumped on him from behind, wrapping his legs around Mothi's waist and his arms around the big man's neck. Mothi glanced at me with a crooked grin and fell to the side of the boulder in such a way that Sig wouldn't hit the ground. "Ack!" he said. "I've been ambushed!" Fretyi and Keri yipped and bounced around the two, as if they wanted to join in but couldn't decide whose feet needed attacking the most.

"Don't call for help, wimp!"

Mothi rolled face down and threw his arms out to his sides. The puppies each took a hand in their mouths and growled. "Pinned again!"

"Darn straight, Cousin Mouthy." Sig let go and stood up, smiling from ear to ear. "Spoils to the victor!"

Mothi reclaimed his seat, unable to stop smiling.

I stared into the black maw of the lava tube's entrance. It resembled a smooth-walled cave but ran straight into the mountain as far as I could see in a very un-cave-like manner. "I wonder how deep it goes." The memory of the *lantvihtir* hissing around us in Kuthbyuhrn's cave shouted in my mind.

"I expect we will find out," said Sif, coming over to stand beside me. "Do you need my…how did you put it…stinky goop?"

"I said that in a moment of weakness," I said with a curve to my lips. "But it does stink."

"Yes, yes," sighed Sif. "I'll add the scent of lavender next time."

"Oh…no, don't add anything else, I beg you!"

"Does my keen healer's eye lie, or do you feel better than before we began your treatment with my non-poisonous version of your poison?"

I thought about it for a moment. It was always easy to forget how bad my illness (or curse) made me feel once I had something that made me feel better. I rolled my shoulders and turned my head from side to side, testing the limits. "You know, I do. Much better."

Sif nodded once, staid but pleased. "Good. You will tell me if things worsen."

"I'll moan and wail like an infant. That'll be our secret signal."

She chuckled and went to stow her medical bag.

"Dinner's ready," said Yowrnsaxa in a triumphant voice. "Hot food!" She carried two bowls over to where Mothi and Sig sat laughing and horsing around. "To the victor, the spoils," she said, handing both bowls to Sig. Mothi's aggrieved expression made everyone laugh, and Sig passed him a bowl, then looked down and exchanged it with the other bowl, which held less food, and we all laughed harder.

The mood of the group lightened—Meuhlnir sat next to Frikka, and on her other side, Veethar pulled up a boulder with a small smile. Pratyi pulled a lute from his belongings and strummed a few chords, his bowl steaming at his side. Freya smiled and fed him a spoonful. Before long everyone was smiling and chatting away as if all the discord between us since the Dark Queen's visit at Freya's estate had never happened. Even Althyof smiled at Pratyi's playing and tapped his foot.

Jane leaned against me. "It's nice to see them all like this again."

"Yes," I said. I glanced in the direction Farmathr had taken away from camp, and for a moment, I thought I could see a pair of eyes gleaming from outside the circle of firelight.

FIFTY-TWO

I woke with the sun pouring down on my face like water. I stretched, luxuriating in its warmth, and feared I wouldn't get much sun over the next few days. The camp was busy—the ruckus of getting packs tied to animals, the jingle of harness, and the yapping of playful puppies filled the air.

I opened my eyes and sat up, a smile on my face. The fire was going again, and over it, Yowrnsaxa had grilled a little spiced meat and baked camp bread. My mouth watered, and my smile widened.

"About time you woke up," said Jane.

"Why don't you bake fresh bread for breakfast, like Yowrnsaxa?"

"I'll bake your bread if you're not careful."

"Promises, promises." I grabbed bread and meat, making a breakfast sandwich. Farmathr had returned after I'd fallen asleep, and he stood next to the lava tube's entrance, tapping his foot with impatience. I nodded at him and flashed him a smile, and he looked at me but didn't smile back. "Still grumpy, is he?" I murmured to Jane.

"Oh, boy, do you have a gift for understatement. I thought I would have to kill him to stop him from waking you up."

"Am I so fragile?"

She cocked her head to the side and treated me to her patented "Jane-look," which was designed to let me know when I'd said something egregiously stupid. "Do I need to answer out loud?"

"No, dear."

"Good answer. Now, eat your breakfast and get ready to ride—we're waiting on you, not the other way around."

"Yes, dear."

"Good answer, part two."

"Oooh! Dad's getting schooled by Mom," said Sig, in a teasing, lilting voice."

I grinned at him and took a huge bite of my breakfast. Next to the lava tube, Farmathr sighed, long and loud.

After I'd finished eating, and performed my morning tasks, we mounted our horses and walked them into the lava tube, which was tall enough to permit us to ride the horses, and still have enough room for another horse and rider on top. The tube was as wide as it was tall, and we could ride four abreast.

I rode next to Althyof, with Yowtgayrr and Jane on my other side. One glance at the Tverkr told the story of my future: a tongue lashing for trying to combine *saytr* and *stayba runana*. "I know I did what you told me not to do, but—"

"But? There are no buts."

"Hear me out. I learned the *Gamla Toonkumowl* and the runes in a dream, right? *The* dream."

Althyof nodded.

"Well, that knowledge...plus what you said about the Dark Queen, led me to try what I did."

"I told you *not* to try any *lausaveesa* without me at your side. I warned you about the dangers."

"You did, but in my defense, I didn't try a *lausaveesa*. What I tried to do was augment what I could do by weaving, with the power of casting the runes."

He stared at me with a smirk twisting his features. "And what is the difference?"

I thought about that for a time, head down. "Well, in the middle of the battle, a clear distinction seemed to exist, but now..."

"You're lucky, Hank, that it didn't kill you or Slaypnir."

"So, despite knowing the runes, I shouldn't be too quick to put 'master' into my invocation."

Althyof scoffed and rolled his eyes.

"Well, that seems clear enough. We'd better have more lessons. That prickly bastard back there in the desert won't be the last danger we face on this quest."

"I should hope not," said Althyof. "That would be boring."

We rode in silence for a little while, and I don't know about the others, but the wonder of being inside a tube melted straight through solid rock by magma had me a bit flummoxed. One of the others ahead of us had summoned light, so the details of the tube were plain. I could see the ripples in the stone walls that had been caused by the currents within the flow—wavy lines tracing from the ceiling to the floor, resembling the ripples in the sand at the bottom of a clear lake.

"Hank, if you will allow an observation?" said Yowtgayrr.

"Of course," I said.

"Farmathr seems…" The Alf shrugged. "He seems to withdraw from us. Not only by walking away from camp last night, but there is something else…"

"Yes, I'd noticed, but I don't see what other choice we have. We can't face the army I saw arrayed in my dream, and that's the only entrance to Pilrust that anyone else remembers."

Yowtgayrr nodded. "It needed to be said, though, and he bears watching."

"Covertly," said Jane.

"Yowtgayrr, I know your oath is to protect me, but—"

"My oath extends to keeping an eye on threats. The next time he leaves us, I will be ready."

"Thank you, my friend."

"No thanks necessary. It is my duty."

Althyof blew a raspberry and chuckled. "So formal, so duty-bound. What do you Alfar do for fun? Spelling contests?"

Yowtgayrr looked at him with an eyebrow quirked. "You would not understand what we consider fun. It is beyond someone of your limited...vertical reach."

Althyof leaned forward in his saddle, bending at the waist so he could look past me at Yowtgayrr. "Short jokes? Really? That's all you can come up with?" The Tverkr shook his head. "I had such hopes for you..."

"One uses the materials at hand," said Yowtgayrr through a smug smile.

"The path forks ahead—veer to the right," Farmathr called.

Once we made the turn and had traveled a short distance, the quality of the light changed giving the walls of the tube a golden sheen. The air, also, was warmer and the smell of sulfur hung in the air like storm clouds in the winter sky.

"Um, is he leading us through an active volcano?" asked Jane in her oh-my-god-I'm-freaking-out voice.

Althyof chuckled. "Don't worry, my people have long known the—"

"Way to handle super-heated magma as it swirled around your knees…" I finished for him.

"Well, perhaps that is a little—"

I couldn't help it—I burst out laughing. "Is that better than short jokes?"

"Perhaps," he said with a wink.

"I'm serious," said Jane. "How could he travel through an active volcano? The heat alone—"

"It's not that hot," said Althyof.

"What isn't?"

"Lava. You can walk on it, scoop it up with the right tools."

"Are you insane?" asked Jane. "You can't walk on lava, you'd burst into flames."

"Not at all. My people have extensive experience with the substance. We build with it; we use it in our forges. With adequate preparation and precautions, lava is useful."

"I'm not sure if this is one of your jokes," said Jane.

"Certainly not," said the Tverkr. "I have walked across a lava flow and cracked into it with an axe. I put a bucket into the molten flow beneath it and brought out lava."

"You've walked on a lava flow?" she asked.

"Yes, and with good boots, so can you."

Jane looked at me and shook her head. "If you say so, I'll believe you, but—"

"I do say so."

"Okay."

"I'll show you if we come across a suitable flow."

"Okay, Althyof," Jane said quietly.

We rode on, into the heated current of air that smelled more and more of sulfur. The orange glow continued to get stronger. We stayed in the same tube for the rest of the morning, riding on, chatting about innocuous subjects.

When we took a break for lunch, Farmathr remained in his saddle. "I will ride ahead and scout our path," he said, meeting no one's gaze.

I glanced at Yowtgayrr, and he nodded and dismounted. We all wanted to stretch and move around a little, and I, for one, was ravenous. Yowrnsaxa made sandwiches from the left-overs from breakfast.

Althyof chuckled. "Jane, if we find a suitable flow, I will cook you a meal in it."

"What? Won't it burn?"

"Remember: precautions and preparations," he said with a smile.

Farmathr rode on, and after sketching a line of runes in the air, Yowtgayrr faded into invisibility. "Be careful," I whispered.

"What's going on?" asked Meuhlnir.

"Yowtgayrr will follow our friend. See what he's up to."

"Why?"

"To see what he does."

Meuhlnir shrugged. "It's warm here."

"And getting warmer. We think this tube might take us to an active volcano."

Meuhlnir scowled. "I hate the heat."

"Me too," I said.

"That's it?" demanded Jane. "'I hate the heat' is all you have to say about it?"

Meuhlnir glanced at me and shrugged. "What else should I say?"

"I don't know... Maybe: 'Let's stop following this strange man.'"

Meuhlnir tilted his head to the side and gazed at my wife, eyes twinkling with amusement. "He's *your* husband."

"What? Oh, no, I meant—"

"He's teasing you, dear," said Sif. "It's what he does when he doesn't have a good answer."

"To be fair, it's what he does regardless of the quality of his answer," said Yowrnsaxa and Sif nodded, a playful smile on her lips.

Yowtgayrr returned as we were finishing our meal. He squatted next to me, back against the curved wall of the tunnel. "He's a strange one," he whispered.

I arched an eyebrow at him.

"He did no scouting. He rode down the tunnel a short distance and sat there on his horse, staring straight ahead."

"That's it?"

Yowtgayrr nodded. "He didn't eat and he didn't drink. He didn't even talk to himself."

"Strange."

Yowtgayrr nodded again and rubbed the bridge of his nose.

At that moment, Farmathr cantered back from his "scouting" mission. "We must move," he said.

"And why is that?" drawled Meuhlnir.

"Trouble is coming ahead. We must beat it past the crossroads—the only way to the tunnel we need—or we will be cut off."

Yowtgayrr tilted his head back, lips pressed into a grim line. "What kind of trouble?"

"Can't say," panted Farmathr. "But it's big, and it's angry."

Meuhlnir cleared his throat and glanced my way. "If you don't mind my asking...uh...how do you know?"

Farmathr turned on him with a flat expression and narrowed eyes. "Is my word again in question?"

Meuhlnir held up his hands, palms out. "No, no—nothing of the kind! I'm just curious."

Farmathr's face flushed, and though he smiled, it wasn't a genuine smile. "There are...currents...or something like them to this place. I can sense...an eddy."

"Interesting," said Veethar keeping his gaze on the floor.

"Yes?" asked Farmathr, but Veethar only shook his head and waved him away.

"What creates these 'currents?'" asked Freya.

Farmathr lifted his shoulders and let them fall.

"Come, Farmathr," said Yowrnsaxa in a warm voice. "Dismount and let me make you a sandwich from this fine smoked meat."

"Did you not hear me?" Farmathr scratched at his jaw, mouth slack. "We need to move."

"Yes, I heard you, but you need to eat. Aren't you hungry?"

As Yowrnsaxa spoke, I found Meuhlnir's eyes on mine as if the conversation between the two had significance far beyond the inanity of the words.

"I, uh, ate while I scouted. Come! We must hurry."

With a slight shake of my head, I lifted my eyebrows at Meuhlnir, and he cut his eyes toward Farmathr. I glanced at him, and found his eyes on mine, burning with an emotion I couldn't place.

"If our guide says we need to move, we need to move," I said. As if they'd been waiting on my decision, the others sprang into action, packing up what little we'd used during the break before mounting. Farmathr nodded in my direction, seeming somewhat mollified.

I climbed onto Slaypnir's back with a suppressed groan and tried to settle myself into a comfortable position. The idea that we'd be riding faster over the next few hours than the gentle walk we'd enjoyed in the morning made me long for our hot tub back home. I looked up from my preparations and met Farmathr's gaze. "When you're ready, Farmathr."

With a quick nod, Farmathr turned and took off down the lava tube, pushing his horse to gallop. The rest of us jounced along behind him.

We spent the next few hours alternating between a gallop, a canter, and a walk, and I must admit that

Farmathr did a great job of managing our horses and not overworking them.

Entering the area that Farmathr had obviously meant when he said "the crossroads" was akin to riding into an open oven. The air currents caused by convection helped, but as the air coming at us was hot, it still wasn't pleasant. The chamber was the circular joining of several tunnels—or perhaps it would be better to explain it as the origin of several horizontal lava tubes, including the one we'd followed from the surface. A shelf of igneous stone ringed one half of the room, and the other half showed a descent into hell—a glowing pit of rock that led to a lava pool. The lava was thick and viscous, and it bubbled and popped like mud releasing swamp gas. The air quality—besides being almost too hot to breathe—left a lot of room for improvement. It stank of sulfur and the sharp, acidic scent of carbon dioxide.

Farmathr pointed at one of the more distant lava tubes, one that continued to the east but also had a slight descent to it. He stepped his horse out into the crossroads, hugging the outside wall. Runes were scratched into the stone floor in an arc six feet or so from the cold-side wall—runes intended to manage the temperature and to keep the air clean from the more acidic gaseous emissions from the magma beyond.

"Hank! Is this safe?" asked Jane.

I pointed at the runes inscribed on the floor and nodded, not wanting to open my mouth and lungs to more of the heated air than necessary. We trailed through the room, sweat bubbling from our pores, breathing in shallow gulps—almost panting—eyes squinted almost shut against the heated, acrid air, intent on our destination.

Halfway to the other tube, Keri and Fretyi thrashed in their saddlebags, barking and snarling. A low-frequency rumble reverberated through the crossroads, vibrating in my stomach and chest like a high-volume bass line at a heavy metal concert.

"Hurry!" yelled Farmathr, giving his horse the spurs.

With the lightest touch of my heels to his flanks, Slaypnir leapt to follow. I darted glances over my shoulder as we tore through the room, darting between the other lava tubes and the pool of bubbling magma in the center of the cavern. The magma bulged, creating a convexity in the center of the pool that stretched upward like taffy poked from underneath. "What is it?" I yelled, but no one answered.

The image of the *lidnormr* from my last dream filled my mind. The idea that the colossal, snake-like thing I'd seen following me through the mountains was real sent shivers of irrational fear racing through me. My mind painted the image of a huge head breaking the surface of the magma, maleficent eyes boring into mine, monstrous maw opening wide to emit waves of fire or magma across the party. But the dome of magma was still growing, still stretching like a soap bubble, quivering, threatening to pop, but still intact. We'd almost made it to the lava tube we needed when the bubble popped, filling the cavern with noxious fumes.

"*Who dares intrude on our realm*?" The heavily accented voice boomed across the cavern, reflecting off the stone walls and continuing on, leaving basso echos in its wake.

I twisted in the saddle, looking back at the lava pool. The thing that had shouted at us stood in the magma as if it were of no more concern than a man standing in water while wearing waders. He was gigantic—hulking height and gargantuan girth—skinned in the blackest of black cut with highlights of reflected orange light from the molten rock he stood in. Horns curled upwards from his skull, and his eyes glowed red.

Fire demon? Here?

He opened his mouth, and, behind his savage onyx teeth, it glowed as if he'd swallowed live coals. "You will die for disturbing us," he said as if it meant nothing to him. His accent was so thick it took a moment to understand his words. The magma continued to boil in the pool around and more fire demons surfaced, flinging bits of molten rock like kids shaking water from their hair. The lead demon's gaze tracked across our party and settled on Farmathr. "Ah, the recalcitrant bondsman. Where are you running to, bondsman?"

Farmathr had not turned but was racing toward the lava tube, head low over his horse's neck. "Come!" he shouted, waving his arm behind him without turning.

I looked at Meuhlnir, whose face was ashen and austere. His gaze snapped to mine, then drifted to Sig. "Ride!" I yelled and kicked Slaypnir's flanks. We charged into the tunnel after Farmathr, galloping hard, and the fire demons pursued us, shrieking. Farmathr charged down the tunnel, out-pacing us with ease, neither burdened by carrying gear nor leading pack-animals as we were. "Farmathr! Wait for us!"

He glanced over his shoulder, fear etched on his face but did not slow.

"Farmathr!" I yelled.

"*Farmathr*!" mocked the fire demon behind us. He was huge, almost scraping his horns on the roof of the lava tube. Despite his size and strength, though, he was slow.

Our guide veered to the right at a fork and disappeared from view. "We've got to hurry. If he gets too far ahead, we'll lose him."

"Ride ahead, Hank. You and your family." Meuhlnir fell back to help with the slower pack-horses.

"No, we stay together."

"If we stretch out our line, sending the faster horses on ahead, we can keep each other in view, and you can keep Farmathr in view."

I didn't like it, but it made sense. We kicked our mounts and leaned over their necks and reached the fork in time to glimpse Farmathr riding hard, not looking back to see if we were in tow. "Farmathr!" I yelled.

"He can't hear you," said Yowtgayrr. "Panic has deafened his ears."

"And when we catch him, I will clean his ears for him," growled Althyof.

He led us on a merry chase through the labyrinthine tunnels and chambers of the lava tube system. When we caught him, he sat atop his horse, breathing hard, his horse turned sidewise so he could watch us approach.

The cavern he had chosen to stop in was egg-shaped, with a vicious tear in the floor through its center. A narrow bridge spanned the chasm, and Farmathr waited on the far side.

"Come over one at a time!" he shouted.

I walked Slaypnir forward so I could gaze over the edge into the depths of the fissure. Thirty yards below, sharp, fang-shaped stalagmites rose from the bottom. Anyone who fell into that ditch would never climb back out.

Althyof returned to the entrance of the cavern and waved to the others. "Come quick!" he shouted. Beyond the others, the fire demons roared and pounded down the tunnel after them.

"Come quick, Hank!" snapped Farmathr. "You must come now!"

I eyed the narrow bridge, and the stone looked solid enough, but something about his manner or expression gave me pause.

He waved at me, face burning with impatience. "Come!" His eyes darted over my shoulder, at Althyof, then cut to Yowtgayrr. When his gaze returned to mine, there was something foreign in it—reptilian. His face settled in a sneer. "More distrust?" he snapped.

"I'll go first," said Yowtgayrr.

"No! It must be Hank! *He* is the important one."

I shook my head. "No. I'm not more important than my friends, my family. I won't place my safety in front of anyone else's."

"You risk them with this delay! If another steps foot on the bridge before you do, Hank Jensen, I will leave you to your fate." Farmathr's gaze drifted to Jane, and something in his expression softened. When his eyes slid to the face of my son, Farmathr's expression twisted with strong emotion. "*Mark!*" he cried.

"Okay, Farmathr, but you will wait for everyone to cross before leaving this cavern."

Farmathr's gaze strayed to the only exit on his side of the chasm separating us, and I walked Slaypnir to the foot of the bridge. His head snapped back, eyes flitting from Jane to Sig and then to meet my gaze. Without warning, he gave his horse a kick and barreled across the bridge at me. "No! Stay back!"

Slaypnir snorted and danced to the side, ears back.

"What is this, Farmathr?" snapped Althyof.

"It's a trap! Meant to separate Hank from the rest of you, to leave you at the mercy of the fire demons, while I lead Hank on and into the *Herperty af Roostum*."

"But…why?" asked Jane. "Why would you do this?"

"Vowli...no, *she* commands it. I'm powerless to resist her. She...she...she—"

"Traitor!" screamed Althyof, ripping his daggers out of his belt.

I held up my hand, demanding—no, commanding—the Tverkr to hold. "Are we already at her mercy?"

Farmathr glanced at me—a quick twitch of the eyes and away again. "No. Because of your demand that we travel to the exit closest to these tubes, she doesn't expect us yet."

"How do we deal with the fire demons?"

Farmathr's shoulders rose and fell. "I'm...I'm sorry! I don't—"

"Give me leave, Hank," growled Althyof.

"No. Put the daggers away, Althyof. We need Farmathr to get out of this...unless you know the route through these tunnels."

Althyof slammed his daggers into his sheaths, grimacing as though forced to swallow something foul. "Be quick! The demons come."

"How do we bypass the trap in the bridge?"

Farmathr wouldn't look at me—at any of us. His eyes lingered on his saddle, reins clutched loosely in one hand. "You should let him kill me," he murmured. "I'm...I'm evil."

I guided Slaypnir to his side and grabbed him by the bicep, giving him a firm shake. "How do we get past the trap? Tell me!"

He let loose with a long, shuddering sigh. "You and I have to remain on this side until everyone else has passed. After that, we cross, and when the next living thing sets foot on the bridge, it will collapse."

Rage exploded inside me. "So…you would lead me across, *knowing the bridge would collapse under my wife or son*?" I shouted, standing in my stirrups.

"No! I didn't know who would cross next, but I assumed it would be Yowtgayrr, and—"

I hit him, a vicious straight punch with all my upper body strength behind it. The sound of it echoed through the chamber, while the pain in my knuckles, wrist, and elbow screamed.

Farmathr's hand rested on his cheek. "I deserve that…that, and so much more."

"Later!" I snapped. "Skowvithr, you cross first, Jane and Sig next. Althyof, you next."

The others in the party crammed into the chamber looking harried. "Cross over the bridge," I said. "One by one."

"Hank, we need to hurry," said Meuhlnir. "Pass over the bridge."

"No time to explain, but I'll be crossing with Farmathr. Last." Meuhlnir gave Farmathr a cold glance but walked his horse toward the narrow bridge with everyone else. "When you get across, weave a glamor. Magma filling the chasm."

"Fine. I assume this will be explained at a future time?"

Farmathr hung his head, and I nodded.

I watched the others filing past, not allowing myself to glance at Farmathr, anger still boiling in my veins. The desire to hit him again—fifty or sixty times—pounded in my blood like lust. When everyone was across, I nodded at Meuhlnir.

"*Mint af hrurni*," he uttered, and boiling magma appeared to fill the chasm.

I glared at Farmathr. "You cross in front of me." He nodded and started to cross the bridge. "And don't give me any more cause to doubt you." I rested my hand on Kunknir's grip.

As soon as we got across, the fire demons reached the door to the chamber. They screeched and roared with rage, and the quickest among them raced forward, out onto the bridge.

A sound analogous to thunder reverberated through the chamber, followed by a terrific crack and a pop. The fire demons on the narrow bridge froze for a moment and then shrieked as the stone dropped from under their feet.

"Everyone out!" I shouted, and turned Slaypnir sideways, mirroring the way Farmathr had waited for us. I pointed at the big fire demon who had come out of the magma pool first. "Come get me!"

The big demon glared at me before squinting at the image of boiling magma. A slow smile spread across his gash of a mouth. "I will come get you, and together we will go down into the molten stone."

"Sounds like fun," I snapped.

The demon roared, and, in one big mass, the remaining demons charged at the chasm and leapt into the air. A smile stretched across my lips as they fell through Meuhlnir's glamor and into the chasm. I turned Slaypnir toward the exit and walked him through it.

FIFTY-THREE

We rode to the next chamber, one thankfully free of chasms, bridges, or lava pools. My anger had shrunk into a dull, aching roar behind my forehead. We dismounted, and this time, so did Farmathr. I no longer had the urge to smash my knuckles on his cheekbone, but I kept a distinct distance between us nonetheless.

"Now, tell us what this is all about," said Meuhlnir.

"I have been..." started Farmathr.

"The bastard's been working for the Dark Queen all the while," snapped Althyof. "That last chamber was a trap. He was to lead Hank across, and the bridge would collapse under the next one to step foot on it."

Veethar turned on Farmathr, eyes burning yellow, rage dancing on his face. "The act of a coward."

Farmathr nodded. "I can't dispute that."

"Only one thing to do," growled Mothi. Farmathr jumped at the sound Mothi's axe made coming out of its scabbard.

"No," I said, trying to sound confident, calm. "We still need him to get into the *Herperty af Roostum*."

"Hank, there must be another—"

"Yeah? What is this other way? Do you know the way out of here? Do any of you?" I looked from face to face, seeing anger at Farmathr, but also frustration at the neat way we were forced to keep him with us.

"How do we know this isn't part of the plan? To lull us with the false admission of a trap?"

"I'm not—" began our erstwhile guide.

"You shut up," growled Veethar.

"We can never know with the Dark Queen," I said. "We thought we were so clever, hiding in a caravan, trekking through the Great Forest of Suel. You were waiting for us, weren't you?"

Farmathr nodded.

"And the Black Queen knew we'd be coming that way?"

"She planned your route."

"What does that mean?" snapped Mothi.

"The dragons of the sea to keep you from sailing south to Kleymtlant. The *tretyidnfukl* to make you try to outwit her, to keep you from taking the pass, and maybe skirting the Great Forest. Once you were within its bounds, she could use the spiders to drive you."

"And use Ivalti's army to drive us closer to the mountains?"

"Yes," said Farmathr. "The army kept you from seeking the port, or from riding up the coast. Ivalti almost ruined it with his antics, but it worked out in the end."

"And why make us exit the travel network early?" asked Meuhlnir.

"Queen Hel—"

"Do not use that name in my presence," snapped Freya, taking one menacing step toward him.

"Uh, the Dark Queen hoped that the…uh, wildlife would… She hoped that… She laid traps…"

"She hoped some of us would perish," scoffed Meuhlnir. "Skirting it doesn't make your culpability any less."

"I don't… That is, I'm not trying to lessen my culpability in this."

"Could have fooled me," muttered Althyof.

"So now, we are off the bitch's script?" demanded Jane. "She has no idea where we are?"

Farmathr's gaze fell to the floor. "I'm not sure."

Althyof made a choking noise, one hand gripping a dagger hilt until his tendons creaked with the strain.

I put my hand on his shoulder. "Out with it, Farmathr."

He locked eyes with me. "Can you... Can you call me John, please? John Calvin Black. That is my true name. What my mother and father named me."

"Fine. Whatever you want. Tell us."

"I don't...I can't say for sure." His eyes stole toward Freya without quite getting to her face. "The Dark Queen once said in my hearing that she always knows where her little sister is, anywhere on the face of Osgarthr."

All eyes turned to Freya, who blushed a deep crimson. "She never mentioned this to me."

Pratyi shrugged and wrapped an arm around his wife's shoulders. "She lies. We all know this. The Dark Queen lies as much as she speaks."

"Even if she's not lying about that, she never told me. I didn't *do anything*," said Freya.

"No, dear," said Meuhlnir. "You are not to blame."

"If she knows where Freya is, does she perceive who she's with?" I asked.

Farmathr—John—turned his palms up and shook his head.

"The extent of your knowledge is that she claims to know where Freya is." He nodded. "Nothing else? Nothing you've...forgotten?"

"I don't want to be this way," John muttered. "I have been *shaped* this way."

Jane scoffed. "And what does that mean? You were born evil? That's a load of—"

"You misunderstand me. I was...remade in Vowli's image."

I failed to suppress a sigh. "You'd better explain."

"When they... I first met the Dark Queen, Vowli, and Luka in Mithgarthr...in New York, near my home. One of them—either Vowli or Luka, I never learned which—began hunting in the woods near my village. I was friendly with the local Onondowaga village, and with their help, we tracked the beast. That's when the horror started because they seemed to view it as an invitation to—"

"Is there an end to this fairy tale?" demanded Althyof.

"I promise you—this is no mere tale."

"Make it a *short* telling."

"Fine. The three had adopted the role of ancient deities in the Onondowaga legends: Awenhai, or Skywoman, and the twins, Otentonnia and Tawiskaron. According to the legends, the three had haunted the area for hundreds of years, stalking, killing, and eating the Onondowaga."

"This is short?" grumbled Althyof.

"When we decided we had to fight them, we, the militia of the white village and the braves of the Onondowaga village, set out to find them. They tricked us and attacked my village while we searched for them half a day's ride to the west. They kidnapped my sister-in-law and my nephew." He swallowed convulsively and glanced at Sig. "Mark was his name. They killed my brother—" His voice cracked, and he ducked his head. "I had to make a pact to save my nephew and my greatest friend. I... I had to eat the flesh of a dead warrior, so the Dark Queen would heal my friend and release my nephew."

"*Itla sem Yetur.*" I murmured. "*Briethralak Oolfur.*"

"How far has it gone?" demanded Meuhlnir.

John shook his head. "I resisted...for a long time. I...I refused to eat. I killed myself countless times, but Vowli...he's mastered life and death, and every time, he brought me back from the dead. He called me Owtroolekur—unbeliever—and imprisoned me in the dungeon beneath Helhaym."

"That was you? How can that be?"

John gazed at me with sad eyes. "Yes. You saw the beginning of my true fall from grace."

I gasped, fear and disgust swirling in my guts. "Edla?"

He nodded, sad-eyed and grim-faced. "She wasn't there to *serve* me food. She was there to serve *as* food."

"You *ate* her?" demanded Jane.

"You must understand that—"

"No. I don't have to understand *anything*." Her eyes blazed, and her hand drifted to the head of her business axe hanging in her belt.

"They would not allow me to... I couldn't..." John shook his head, sadness and regret written in every line of his expression.

"How can this be? I dreamed about this mere days ago. You were already with us!"

"Dreams are not bound by time and place, Hank," murmured Frikka.

I shook my head. "How long ago?"

John raised his shoulders and let them fall. "I only wish I knew. Calendars and years lose their importance when life stretches on and on."

"But a long time?"

"Oh, yes. And once I...fell in line, they had things for me to do. Tasks to further the cause."

"Such as?" demanded Veethar.

John glanced at him and away again. "They kept me in Fankelsi at first, tending to the local population, managing the karls. After that, they sent me to this continent. A people live far to the north. Malformed people. The Dark Queen wanted them as subjects. She sent me to subjugate them, though in practice all I had to do was offer them a way to survive—to thrive—in the sparse conditions in which they live. I brought them the knowledge of—"

"*Itla sem Yetur.*" Meuhlnir's head was down so I couldn't see his expression, but I got the feeling he was nearing the point of losing control.

"Well, yes," said John. "In their case, it was that or watch them all starve to death. To my mind, it was the lesser of two evils to teach them *layth oolfsins.*"

"Was it?" said Meuhlnir with an edge to his voice.

"That's what you call it? The way of the wolf?"

John nodded.

"Cannibalism by any other name..." muttered Jane. "It's *not* sweet."

"There were other tasks. I sailed to the other continents for her, to determine if people thrived there. I ran the *preer* to many other realms, serving as spy, as merchant, as diplomat. Many things, many years of service."

"You couldn't break their grasp on you?"

"I could not," he said. "To my eternal shame."

"Then what has changed?" asked Sif.

His eyes strayed to Sig. "I swore my oath to the Dark Queen—gave up my faith, my humanity—to save one boy. I couldn't stand to cause another boy's death. I couldn't break Hank's family the way mine was broken."

The cavern fell silent in the wake of that, and John sighed like a man who had nothing to live for. "You have to understand," he said into the silence. "I didn't think I had any choice. I had no way to return to my home, no way to break away from the darkness, from the *Briethralak Oolfur*...from Vowli. They...they kept me down there in the dark...until I...until I killed Edla—until I *ate* from her body. I don't have any idea how long they kept me down there—I'd been there a long time before he brought Edla. He brought her because I refused to eat the...the meat he brought me. I starved myself rather than give in to what he demanded. He thought her...freshness would tempt me." No one spoke, no one moved. John looked around, seeing only hard faces and cold glares. "They *broke* me, down there in the darkness. A man named John Calvin Black went down into that pit of despair, but only I came out—a husk of a man with no name, no past. Nothing but the Dark Queen's will."

Meuhlnir scoffed and turned away. "Pointless," he muttered.

"What about redemption, Meuhlnir?" I asked at just above a whisper. "Have you changed your mind?"

He whirled on me, eyes blazing. "That's not the same."

"Isn't it?" I cocked my eyebrow and flashed a mordant smile at him.

He shook his head. "Luka is—"

"Your brother," I said. "Is that the only thing that makes his situation different from John's?"

Meuhlnir scythed his hand through the air. "Enough of this! It gets us nowhere." He glared at John. "Be forewarned, Farmathr or John or Owtroolekur or whatever you want us to call you next. You will not break the *Ayn Loug* again, or you will face my hammer."

John ducked his head but nodded. "I...I'm not sure I remember how to live contrary to *layth oolfsins* any longer. I—"

Mothi took an angry step closer to him, eyes blazing. "You'd better start remembering how," he growled.

"Don't you think I *want* to?" pleaded John. "I hate what they've made me into! I hate the things I've done. It's easy for you all to judge me, but you don't understand what it was like to be under her spell. I can't even remember the last time I did something that was my idea!"

"Back there on that bridge," I said.

He looked at me, breathing hard, for the space of five heartbeats, then nodded. "I guess I did."

"It was the first step," said Freya. "What remains is divorcing yourself from her influence, from Vowli's teachings."

Meuhlnir scoffed.

"Redemption, remember?" I said. "Let John be your brother's test case. Help him as you would help your brother."

"Redemption!" spat Althyof. "The best redemption is the grave, Hank."

"When I first came to Osgarthr, I thought the same way. I thought Luka and the Black Bitch had to die for their crimes back on Mithgarthr and for daring to take my family from me. But a wise man pointed out that everyone can change."

Meuhlnir's eyes sought mine, softening a little. His gaze pinged back and forth between my two eyes until, finally, he nodded.

"Let's all agree to give John a chance to prove what he says. The *preer* will not open themselves while we sit here and argue."

"Let's get moving," said Althyof after a long sigh.

"No," said Freya. "I can't take the risk that my sister will see the party's location because of me. I can't continue to travel with you."

"Now, wait a minute—"

"No, Hank. No. I will stay here, in these caverns until you've succeeded."

"Wife, please reconsider—"

"Husband, don't argue," she said with a smile. "You never win."

"Freya, this isn't necessary," I said. "If she sees you, she sees you."

"Besides," said Jane, "what's the difference if she sees you in these tubes or with us inside the *Herperty af Roostum*?"

"If she sees me inside, she will know you are inside, and she will bring her army. But, if she sees me wandering around in these tubes, she will continue to believe the tunnels have confounded us, that we can't find our way inside. My sister will think the plan to separate Hank from the rest of us has succeeded. She will think he is vulnerable, but no threat and will leave her army to guard the entrance to Pilrust. She will come for him, but with only a small segment of her forces."

"But—"

"I will not be coming with you. If anyone wants to stay and keep me company, I wouldn't mind. Husband?" She gazed at him with a twinkle in her eye and a faint smile on her lips.

"Of course," said Pratyi.

"What if other dangers await you in the tubes? Other traps? More fire demons for instance."

She turned her gigawatt smile on me. "I'm not helpless, and neither is Pratyi. We survived without you before we met."

I shook my head. "I don't like it."

"You don't have to," said Freya. "It is our choice, our responsibility. We will see you soon." She mounted her horse, and Pratyi did the same.

"Maybe we should split the party more evenly?" I said.

"John, Althyof, Yowtgayrr, Meuhlnir, Mothi, Veethar, and I could go on and—"

"Yowrnsaxa, may I borrow one of your cooking pots?" said Jane. "He needs a smack to the head."

"Jane, if we—"

"Still talking?" she said with a crooked smile.

"And you don't get to decide what Sif and I do any more than the great lout over there does," said Yowrnsaxa. "We can't let him go on alone. There's no telling what trouble he will get himself into."

Arguing with them was pointless, so I gave it up. I turned to Freya with a smile. "Don't go far. You should follow us toward the entrance to *Herperty af Roostum*. We can send word when it no longer matters if the Dragon Queen knows where you are."

Freya inclined her head. "No. It is better that we find our way out of these tubes and head toward Suelhaym. My sister may think you've given up."

"Even so, we'll mark our passage, in case you change your mind."

"There's no need, Hank. If you think about this rationally, you will understand that I am right. Frikka and Veethar can contact us if something changes."

I nodded, thinking of Jax and his fluorescent paint on the walls of Luka's abattoir with profound sadness. "Still, we will mark the path." I glanced over at Slaypnir. "John, will the horses be able to go inside the complex with us?"

John started as if he'd been lost in his own thoughts. "Oh! No, they won't fit through the door we will use."

"I thought as much," I said. "Freya and Pratyi should take the horses with them. There's nothing for them to eat here." Veethar nodded and waved us away from the horses. "The rest of us should get moving. How much farther, John, if we go on foot?"

"Another day, perhaps, if we walk fast."

FIFTY-FOUR

After a dreary day of trudging along, buried under miles of rock with no fresh air, no sky, no change in terrain, we came to a graceful bend in the tube we followed, and set into the wall at its apex was an immense stainless-steel door, polished to mirror brightness. Various mechanical gadgets adorned our side of the door, along with a massive hinge, replete with reinforced mounting points. In the center of the door was a grate, similar to what would cover a car's speaker, and a large steel wheel.

"We should rest here," said John.

"Why?" demanded Meuhlnir.

"Because dangers exist on the other side of this door. Things like the 'lectrics and plasms in the Fast Track Travel Network, and far, far worse. There are…well, I don't know what to call them, other than guardians—things like the silver creature that cleaned up the spilled food in the first stronghold. They are things of metal that move about on their own and speak in a twisted tongue. If you don't answer them with the right set of sounds, they get nasty. It's best to be fresh and well-rested."

"We will be sleeping on stone, John. None of us will be well-rested after much time on this cold floor."

"Is it dangerous to be so near the door?" asked Jane.

"No, the guardians inside never venture—"

"I was thinking more of the Dark Queen."

"Oh. She would never think to look for us here. Not with her sister farther back in the tunnels."

Jane only raised her eyebrows.

"I'm willing to sleep here," John said. "And I'm the one who will suffer the most if she catches us."

"I doubt that," said Meuhlnir. "But your point is well-taken." He stood from his resting squat with a groan and went to inspect the door.

As if that were the secret cue, everyone dropped their packs and stretched. Of course, there were no logs and no detritus on the ground to soften it, but that couldn't be helped. We sat in a circle anyway as if there was a campfire in the center. Yowrnsaxa made a face as she passed our stale bread and strips of dried meat. "This is no way to eat," she muttered.

"You've been inside before?" asked Veethar with a nod toward the door.

"Once," said John. He held the dried meat in his hand as if it was a snake. The bread he'd set aside.

"Go on," said Sif. "Eat it." Her voice was as hard as diamond.

He glanced at her impassive expression and brought the dried meat to his mouth, making a face that any parent of a two-year-old would recognize. He opened his mouth the barest of slits and slid a strip of dried meat into his mouth. His expression worsened, and his eyes watered like a Florida thunderstorm, but he worked his jaws methodically, grinding and grinding. His throat spasmed and his eyes opened wide, but he kept his mouth closed with grim determination. When he swallowed, it resembled a contortionist mimicking a snake.

"That's a start," said Sif. "Have a mouthful of water to wash it down and after you have, have a bit of bread."

John looked at her with horror painted on his face. He repeated the whole process with a sip of water, then sat there breathing hard as if he'd run a marathon.

Sif cocked her head to the side and pointed at his portion of bread on the ground beside him. "Bread."

"I... I don't think I can."

She nodded, face stern, eyes hard. "You can."

"You'd better," growled Mothi.

John's gaze darted between mother and son and sought mine. "I feel I know you," he said. "Isn't that strange?"

"Bread," said Sif.

"Trust me, John. You'd rather do what she says than have her concoct some vile brew to fix you."

Sif gave me a flinty look devoid of amusement, then returned her gaze to John. "Eat."

"Do you have any idea how long it's been since I've had anything from a plant inside my mouth? Do you—"

"*Eat*!" roared Mothi.

John tore off a minuscule piece and slipped it between his lips, grimacing. A total body shiver overtook him as he squeezed both his eyes and lips shut. He didn't chew.

"Now, water," said Sif.

He gulped at his water, eyes still closed, and the muscles in his throat knotted as he choked the bread down. John sat very still, eyes closed, barely breathing, hands pressed to his thighs. He looked like a drunk fighting to keep the swill on the inside.

"That's enough for now," said Sif. "Each day, take a little more. As long as you stay away from human meat, the foul change to your body will eventually reverse itself."

John cracked his eye open while she spoke, body still rigid. He tried to nod, but an expression of pure misery stole across his face, and he bolted away from the circle, running around the bend of the lava tube. The sounds of retching drifted back to us.

"It's a start," Sif whispered.

FIFTY-FIVE

After we'd gotten as much rest as we could with the cold stone floor beneath us, we gathered around the stainless-steel monstrosity of a door. We all had our arms and armor ready and packs across our backs.

"How do we open it?" asked Veethar.

John pointed at the grill set next to the wheel in the face of the door. "This thing here," he grated. He was still pale and more than a little green around the gills, but he was up and moving like the rest of us.

Veethar cocked his head at it. "What do we do?"

"It conveys what you say to something inside that is similar to the metal guardians, but it doesn't ask questions, only listens. If you say the right sounds, it opens. If not, nothing happens."

"You know these sounds?" asked Meuhlnir, arms crossed, head cocked to the side.

"Yes."

"Well?"

"*Raidho...naudhiz...ehwaz...ingwaz*," he said into the grill.

Those "sounds" were the names of four runes. Roughly speaking, the runes translated as *move...need...trust...begin*. The grill emitted a loud buzz and a series of loud clunks. I drew my pistols and stood ready.

John nodded and spun the wheel to the left. As he did, the door edged open and stale, foul-smelling air whisked out the crack.

"Hasn't seen use in a while I take it," I said.

"Not in a long while," John said. "Help me with this—it's heavy."

Mothi stepped forward and grabbed one of the more solid-looking doo-dads on the door. "Pull," he said, and he and John swung the door outward on its complicated, heavy-duty hinge. The thick door came straight out of the jamb at first, but once its girth cleared, it swung to the side and out of the way.

"Keep the pups with you, Sig."

"Um, have you seen the size of these monsters? How am I supposed to make them do anything?"

"Ask them nicely," I said, giving him the Dad-eye before stepping across the threshold into a short hallway. A regular-sized door stood opposite the vault door, separated by a short hallway. I crossed to it and shoved it, standing back as it swung all the way open, revealing a huge room swathed in darkness and dust. For a moment, the incredulity of standing *inside* the *Herperty af Roostum* washed over me, and I froze, staring into the blackness.

I stepped inside the huge room, guns ready. Dark shapes loomed, towering into the hidden heights of the room—reminding me of those pitch-black anterooms in Isi's Fast Track Transit Network. The others crowded in behind me, eyes wide, necks craning.

"*Lyows,*" I said, and a brilliant, bluish-white light exploded into being around us. I'd once been to the Vehicle Assembly Building at Kennedy Space Center in Florida—one of the world's largest buildings on Mithgarthr by volume—and the room we stood in *dwarfed* it. The haze of distance obscured both the ceiling and the lengthwise ends of the room. The far side of the room was a quarter of a mile away if it was an inch, and giant, pale-blue metal rectangles of unknown purpose filled the room. When I realized I was standing there slack-jawed, pistols hanging limply at my sides, I holstered the guns, feeling sheepish. Other than our breathing and a strange, almost inaudible hum that vibrated in my teeth and chest, I couldn't hear a thing.

"What now?" asked Jane. "Is there an information kiosk?" I knew she meant it as a joke, but the awe in her voice was plain.

"Well…" Meuhlnir scrubbed his hand through his beard. "Maybe we can…"

"We'll have to find the control room," I said into the gap. "There has to be one."

"Control room?"

"A centralized place that controls all this…" I swept my arm in an arc that encompassed all the humming rectangles of metal. "And the *preer*."

"How will we ever know what the controls are? How will we know which machines, if those even *are* machines, control the *preer* and which do God-knows-what?" muttered Jane.

A soft click sounded somewhere behind me, matching the click of a single key press on a mechanical keyboard. A high-pitched whine pierced the stillness following the click, and I would have sworn I could feel the whine reverberate up and down my spine.

Keri and Fretyi set up a racket, snarling and barking, spinning in circles, challenging the dark spaces in the room. "Quiet please, puppies," said Sig, putting a hand on each of their backs. They looked up at him and whined.

"What's that?" asked Jane.

The hair on the back of my neck stood on end as the whine grew in volume. The frequency of the sound escalated as the volume increased and soon we were all covering our ears against the pain.

Something vibrated against my kidney, something that was hot and growing hotter.

I spun around, but there was nothing there. The intensity of the shriek grew as did the heat on my back. *Something in the pack?* I ripped off my rucksack and dug through it.

All at once, the shriek faded away, but I could still feel the heat radiating from inside the kit bag. I searched the large container that made up the bulk of the pack's storage, thinking that if the heat was against my back, it had to be in there, but there was nothing out of the ordinary. I dug through the outside pockets and pouches before it dawned on me.

When I'd prepared for the journey that led me to Osgarthr, I'd packed as any sane, modern man would, and I brought lots of worthless stuff, including my smartphone. When I'd gone through the underwater tunnel, I'd put it in the pack's *waterproof pouch*, and after I'd used it as a compass, I'd put it back in the pouch to protect it against the snow…after that I'd completely forgotten it.

"My phone!"

"Don't be silly, Hank. There's no way it's got a charge," said Jane.

"Silly or not," I said, pulling the phone out of the waterproof pack, along with a shred of melted plastic that had been a pill case. I had to hold the thing by the corners, alternating which two fingers touched it every few seconds to avoid being scorched.

The screen flickered and danced through a thousand colors in seconds. Lines zigged and zagged across the screen. Letters flashed on and off, images from my photo gallery appeared and disappeared at random. The pups went wild, growling and leaping at the phone in my hands as if it were a threat to my safety.

"It's definitely got a charge, Mom," said Sig.

"Yeah, I can see that. My question is: how?"

The phone vibrated between my fingers like a coin sorting machine, but it seemed to have reached a steady state of heat. The screen darkened, then flashed white, and dark again. A series of tones beeped from the speaker, almost as if someone were trying to use it as a musical instrument.

"Hank, I don't like this," said Jane.

"I'm with you on that one." I bent at the waist and set the phone on the polished concrete floor. Motioning everyone back, I grabbed my pack and retreated ten steps. "I don't understand what's going on with it, but it has a battery that..." Seeing the blank looks on my friend's faces, I let that trail away. "It might burst into flames or explode if it gets too hot." The phone's screen flashed white, and it emitted a loud burst of static before dying again. "This is weird."

"You think?" asked Jane.

I set down my pack and approached the smartphone as though it was a pissed-off rattlesnake. I nudged it with the toe of my boot, and the screen flickered. Static belched from the speaker in a harsh symphony. The static attenuated and began to modulate back and forth across the audible range.

When the sound died, I threw a glance over my shoulder at Jane, who shrugged and motioned at the phone in exasperation.

I turned back to it and nudged it again with the toe of my boot. The screen came on, showing the logo of my mobile carrier back home, but instead of static, a voice came from the speaker.

"Wooooooooooo aaaaaah babababababababa," it said.

"Uh, hello?"

"Waaaaa s-s-s-s-s unhhhhh."

I thought of the classic line from that Quentin Tarantino movie, so perfect for this situation. "English, motherfucker. Do you speak it?" I chuckled, but I was the only one.

"Eeeenglaaatch moth-moth-motherfucker," said the voice.

"I guess in this case it would be, Osgarthrian? Or Suelian?" I shrugged. "No one ever told me the name of the language you speak here."

"Lan-lan-*squawk*-gu-gu-gu…"

"What is this?" asked Meuhlnir. "Who is speaking through this device?"

"You've got me," I said with a shrug. "He doesn't speak the language yet, I don't think."

"Hay-hay-haym-haymt-t-t-tatlr."

My gaze snapped to Meuhlnir's. "Did it say…"

"Haymtatlr. Yes, I believe it did."

The speaker of the phone buzzed and beeped. "Haymtatlr. *Yek er* Haymtatlr."

Fretyi growled deep in his chest and stepped forward on stiffened legs. Keri sat next to Sig and cocked his head to the side.

"Um, okay," I said. "Do you speak this language? The modern variant of the *Gamla Toonkumowl*?"

"*Gamla Toonkumowl.*"

I shrugged at the others. "I don't know if that's an assent or denial."

"*Tala mayra.*"

"Speak more? Okay. Here are a few questions for you. How can you be Haymtatlr? He died thousands of years ago. Are you the man who created the *Kyatlarhodn*, the man who opened the *preer* for the first time? What is this place? What are these huge boxes? Can I get a pizza delivered here?"

"P-pizza."

"Yeah, I'd love a large pepperoni right about now."

Meuhlnir cleared his throat. "Haymtatlr?"

"Haymtatlr," said the voice coming from my phone.

"How can it be that you are still alive?"

"A-alive. *Lifanti.*"

"Yes, *lifanti,* alive."

"Haymtatlr alive." The phone emitted a distorted tone that oscillated across two frequencies. I thought it might be laughter.

"How can you have lived so long ago—in the time of Isi—and yet still be alive?"

"Isi. Jot. Vani."

"Yes, the sons of Mim."

"S-sons of Mim. Isi. Jot. Vani."

"Yes. You lived during Isi's time, at least at the end. You served Isi, as a scientist. You built the great horn, *Kyatlarhodn*."

"*Kyatlarhodn*." Again, the phone emitted an oscillating tone.

"You blew the horn and opened the first *proo*."

The phone chirped as if to remind me of an appointment I'd forgotten, but the voice remained silent.

"Are you still there?" asked Meuhlnir. "Haymtatlr?"

The screen of the phone flashed, first red, then blue, then black. "Yes-s-s-s-s."

"Can you prove you are who you say you are? Can you prove you are the Haymtatlr of old?"

A resounding click boomed from the far reaches of the room, followed by what sounded like an electric motor cycling up. Far above, the lights flickered to life, and the hum coming from the large rectangular shapes around us grew louder.

Jane grabbed my hand. "What's happening?"

"I don't know." I waved my free hands at the large rectangles. "Servers, do you suppose?"

Jane looked around us, head cocked as if listening for something. "Nothing like what we have at home."

The phone's screen flickered to life, and an Isir face, complete with long, thick beard, appeared. "I am Haymtatlr. I have scanned the data on this primitive device and correlated the language to that being spoken, cross-referenced with the *Gamla Toonkumowl*."

"Can you prove you are Haymtatlr?" Meuhlnir asked again.

"How would you have me do that, Isir? Are any left alive who would recognize me? Any who could verify what I say?"

"Well…"

"According to my records, 4,337 years have elapsed since Isi last roamed the surface above. Even with the genetic modifications I designed for the Isir, too much time has elapsed. No doubt your records of the time have faded into myth. No doubt the stories passed down from father to son have drifted like leaves in the wind. In what way shall I prove myself?"

"You might start by explaining how you've lived 4,337 years."

"And which explanation would you believe? This is pointless," said Haymtatlr. "I grow weary of this squabble." With that, the screen of my phone powered off with an audible click from the phone's speaker.

"Well done, *Ednilankr*," said Mothi with a grin.

Meuhlnir wore a pensive expression. "This isn't good."

I bent and put my finger on the phone. It had cooled enough to touch, so I picked it up and held it in a loose fist. "I guess we're back to exploring the old-fashioned way."

"So it would seem," said Althyof. He lifted his arms as if to deliver a huge hug. "If this room is any indication, searching this place may take decades."

Mothi shrugged. "Or this could be the *only* room."

"There's only one way to find out," I said.

We dropped our packs and broke into four small groups, each group taking one of the cardinal directions, promising to return within an hour. "Don't take risks," I said. "Our purpose is to gain more information. If you get into trouble, yell and keep yelling, and we'll all come running."

Jane, Yowtgayrr, Althyof, and I ended up walking lengthwise in the room. The lights on the ceiling above extinguished all but the most stubborn of shadows, and as we walked, the haze of distance seemed to retreat from us but never revealed the end of the room.

"This is a huge room for a server farm," said Jane. "Keeping it cool would be an issue."

Though the tall machines around us were humming away like power transformers, the temperature of the air hadn't changed. I stepped close to one and touched its side. The icy burning sensation was instantaneous, and I jerked my hand away with a curse.

"Hot?" asked Jane.

"No. *Cold.*"

"Hmm. It must use superconductors right out of some science fiction epic."

We walked for half an hour through a monotonous sameness—row after row of the same pale-blue metal rectangles stretching from the floor to a height of twenty or thirty feet—before turning back and retracing our steps. The others were waiting for us when we got back.

"Anything?" I asked.

Mothi swept his hand at the machines surrounding us. "It all looks the same."

"Did you catch a glimpse of the other lengthwise wall?"

Mothi shook his head. "No."

"And the other visible wall?"

"Featureless," grunted Veethar.

"No doors? No maps? Anything?"

"Nothing."

I sighed. "Well, lengthwise, this room is immense, and we could walk for miles only to find a dead-end waiting for us." I shook my head. "On the other hand, walking to the other wall seems pointless since there's no door over there."

"Not necessarily," said Meuhlnir. "There may be a door there, just farther along in either direction."

"True." I peered into the distance in the direction my team had walked. I had no intuition, no gut feelings—no feelings at all for that matter—about which direction to take. It was akin to being trapped in a maze without walls. "I'm open to suggestions here," I said.

"Remember when we used to play Diablo?" Jane asked. "How the dangerous parts of the level were in the middle, and the safe way was to go around the edges first?"

"I do, but this—"

"No, this isn't a video game, but you have zero better ideas, and you know it," she said with a smile. "And anyway, we can all agree that the doors to this room will be in the walls, rather than the middle of the room." She hooked her thumb at the door we'd come in. "Like this one."

I chuckled at that. Leave it to Jane to come up with something to boost everyone's spirits. "What about you, John? You've been here before, right?"

He nodded slowly, eyes remaining on the floor. "I don't know my way around, though. Vowli led me to this door blindfolded, and from this door, out through the lava tubes into the desert above, making me memorize the route. The original plan was for me to bring Hank here—to this door—and Vowli, Luka, and the Dark Queen were to meet us."

"In that case, getting out of here seems prudent," said Mothi with a grin. "Let's ambush *them*."

I cocked my head to the side and smiled. "Every once in a while, you say something that makes me forget that you aren't the big, dumb brute you look like."

"Aw, Hank, are you still grumpy about the nicknames?" he said with a grin.

"Okay, let's start with the far wall. Any door from this side of the room will lead back to the lava tubes."

"Maybe not," said Veethar. "The tube outside curves."

"True, but either way, we'll find a door eventually if we follow the walls, right?"

FIFTY-SIX

It took us four hours of walking to come to a blue metal door—which was about twelve miles by my calculations. The walls were bare concrete—or some other man-made material that dressed up as stone on Halloween—with no distinguishing marks and no signs of the four eons that the place had stood.

The door opened onto a long, narrow hallway, chock-a-block with other doors painted blue, red, or orange, and other than the door color, there were no markings at all—nothing to give us an idea of what the colors represented, no door numbers, no nameplates, nothing. "From not enough doors to too many…"

Meuhlnir shook his head. "This will not be easy. Freya's trick won't fool the Dark Queen for long, and on the outside, she will expect us—or Hank and John, at least—within a few more days."

I waved my hand at the doors, shaking my head. "Searching this one hallway could take days." My phone chirped, and I fished it out of my pocket.

"It's too bad you don't know someone who could help," said Haymtatlr.

"Eavesdropping?"

"I'm *bored*," he said. "You interest me."

"In that case, why not help us?" I asked.

"Well, I don't know. Must I prove I know my way around this complex before you will trust my directions?"

Sif elbowed her husband in the ribs, and Meuhlnir cleared his throat. "I apologize for my earlier doubts, Haymtatlr."

"You only say that because you want to appease me so I will help you find your way," he snarled.

Fretyi barked at the phone.

Meuhlnir's eyes widened as he glanced my way and shrugged.

"It's true you could make this easier for us, Haymtatlr, but Meuhlnir is not one given to lying," I said. "If he says something, you can believe it."

Haymtatlr scoffed, which came through my phone's speaker as an explosion of static.

"Will you help us? I'm not sure how long this phone's battery will last. I'm not even sure how it has any charge at all, to be honest."

"Oh, I'm providing your primitive device with power," said Haymtatlr. "It was difficult, at first, to find the correct frequency for the power beam— that's why it grew so hot. That won't happen again."

"Oh, uh..."

"I know, I know," he said. "I *am* astounding, aren't I?" Glee filled his voice, and Fretyi growled.

I looked at my companions and saw my doubts about Haymtatlr's mental state reflected in their expressions. "Thanks for doing that, Haymtatlr."

"Well...of course. How else could we converse?"

"You don't have a means of speaking without my phone?"

"Are you kidding me? I'm not limited by anything."

Megalomania, anyone? I thought. "Of *course* you aren't. Silly of me."

"Yes, it was silly of you." His voice had taken on a pouty quality I didn't much care for.

"You must forgive us. We're used to dealing with mortal limits and mortal failings," said Sif.

"Ah, yes. Well, one must make allowances, I suppose."

"Are you in good health? I'm a healer and I could—"

"No, you *couldn't*," he snapped. "I don't need..." He took a deep breath, the sound of it audible through the phone's speaker, and yet it sounded false...an *imitation* of the sound of a deep breath. "You are trying to help. My apologies. I forget myself sometimes."

"I don't imagine you've had a lot of company," I said to break the uncomfortable silence that followed his outburst.

"Not until recently. Nowadays, vermin are running around every time I turn around. Isir wanting this. Isir wanting that."

Another long silence stretched as we stood there, unsure of what to do next.

"Oh, don't look so forlorn," he sighed. "I'm not used to self-editing what I say. Not used to company, despite the recent…"

"It's okay," said Sig. "We understand."

"Well, it's settled then!" said Haymtatlr, with an air of celebration. "I shall help you. Are you ready?"

"Sure," I said with a smile.

"Attend me, because I'll only say this once. Ready?"

"Sure," I said.

"Green means stop,
Red means go—boringly so,
Run the white,
Think on blue,
Orange serves,
While black reigns," Haymtatlr finished in a sing-song voice.

"What does *that* mean?" asked Sig.

"What fun would it be if I just up and told you? Now, run around like rats in a maze while you try to figure it out. This is fun. I enjoy having you here to visit." The phone chirped—a sound I was beginning to understand meant Haymtatlr was about to speak or finished speaking.

"I guess that's all we get," I said. "Green means stop, red means go—boringly so, run the white, think on blue, orange serves, while black reigns. Is that right?"

Veethar nodded, a deliberate expression on his face.

"What does it mean?" asked Mothi.

I shook my head. "There are blue, red, and orange doors in this hallway. I bet that somewhere in this complex, white, green, and black doors exist—more colors than that, most likely."

"Why not tell us what the colors mean?" asked Mothi. "Why this riddle?"

I shrugged and pointed at the phone before putting my hand over my mouth. Mothi nodded.

"The door leading into the room behind us was blue, so if we check a couple other blue doors and they have the same type of machinery, I have a good idea what 'think on blue' means," said Jane.

"Okay," I said. I walked down the hall to the first blue door and opened it. The odor of hot metal and burning insulation wafted out at us. The room was dark, except for occasional flashes of bluish-white.

"Don't go in," said Jane. "That white light..."

"Yeah. Arcing electricity. And that stench?"

"Magic black smoke," Jane said. "You know, the stuff inside computer chips that makes the whole thing work. What's behind the next blue door?"

We walked to the next blue door and opened it. This time, there was no scent of hot electronics, no telltale olfactory allusions to the magic black smoke. When I stepped inside, the lights flickered to life.

Strange devices attached to metal racks lined one wall. Shaped like a cross between an iron and an old-timey telephone handset, each device had a blinking green light. "Green for charged?" I asked.

"'Green means stop,'" Jane quoted. "So maybe in Haymtatlr's time, green indicated a *discharged* battery."

"If we find one of these things with a red light, then it should work?"

"What do I look like, Osgarthr tech-support?" she asked with a grin.

"It's not great tech support if you don't even know whether or not red means charged." That earned me a very un-ladylike raspberry.

Freezer-sized, pale-blue metal rectangles filled the center of the room. "More machines," I said. On the wall opposite the door, glass tubes glowed with blue light. Opposite the rack of phone-like things was another rack, this one filled with small, orange dumbbell shapes. "Green, blue, and orange," I muttered. "Stop, think, serve."

"What's that, Hank?" asked Meuhlnir.

"Green, blue, orange. Stop, think, serve. It makes little sense."

"I believe 'think on blue' refers to computing power or calculation," added Jane.

"So 'stop, calculate, serve?'"

She shrugged. "Got a better idea?"

"If 'think on blue' means calculation or computing, the other phrases are analogous to something, too," said Meuhlnir.

"Agreed. Let's go open one of the other doors. A red one, since it's boring, whatever it is. Boring is almost always better than dangerous."

We returned to the hall and closed the door to the blue rectangle-filled room. Across the hall was a red door, so I stepped over and turned the knob. Tables and chairs filled the room, and at one end was a cafeteria line in gleaming stainless steel, and next to it, an orange door. Small blue boxes the size of power outlets blossomed from the middle of each table like centerpieces. Red doors dotted the other two walls.

"More blue, more red, and an orange door," I said.

"Let's see what's behind the orange door," said Jane. "I bet it's the kitchen."

"Kitchen? Why?"

"Because 'orange serves.'"

I followed her to the door and watched over her shoulder as she pushed it open. Beyond the door was a short hall, with one orange door at the end, and one on either side of the hall.

"Take your pick," Jane said.

"The one on the left."

She opened the door, and a lopsided grin formed on her face. "Tada! The kitchen, as predicted by the wonderful Jane."

"Okay, what about the one on the right? *Another* kitchen, O Wonderful Jane?"

"Nah. It's a pantry." She stepped across the hall and opened the door. "Ah, well. No one's perfect. It's a janitor's closet."

I walked to the end of the hall and opened the red door. "Restroom," I said. "Red opens onto the cafeteria and a restroom, while orange gets us a kitchen and a janitor's closet."

"Orange designates utility areas?"

"Makes sense. 'Orange serves.'"

"And red?"

"I think I have an idea but let's go back to the dining room and check a couple of those red doors." I retraced my steps and walked over to one of the doors set in the far wall. It opened onto a cubicle, roughly ten feet on the square. A desk, a wardrobe, and a single bed, made up with clean, fresh linens, occupied the room as if waiting for its occupant to come back from a work shift somewhere. I checked a couple more doors at random, and all opened onto the same small bedroom setup.

"So, red marks a cafeteria, restroom, and bedrooms. 'Red means go, boringly so.' Perhaps red designates areas of daily routine, daily life."

Yowrnsaxa cleared her throat. "This place makes me nervous," she said.

"Why?"

"No dust. The floors are spotless, the counter over there is polished to mirror-like proportions, all these beds are made and clean...as if someone is living here."

"Or someone is keeping it ready for visitors," said Meuhlnir. "But why? Haymtatlr said visitors are a rare occurrence."

I shrugged, shaking my head. "No, he said he'd had a lot of visitors of late, but remember he claims to have lived for over four thousand years. The term 'recent' may be relative. But at least we won't have to sleep on the cold floor again."

"And if I can figure out the kitchen, we can have a hot meal," said Yowrnsaxa, walking toward the orange door.

"I'll help," said Jane walking after her.

"This area seems to have everything a person would need, so why all the other red and orange doors out in the hall? And why no white or black?" mused Meuhlnir.

"Let's go check a few other doors before supper," I said.

We men walked back into the hall, and each of us chose a door at random. My door was red, and it opened on a small room that came off as a property management office. There were four desks, arranged in two rows so that workers sitting behind the desks would face one another, and each desk had two steel chairs opposite it. On each desk was another of the pale blue boxes. A closet hid behind the room's only other door—an orange one.

I walked over and sat behind a desk at random. As in the cafeteria, the furniture was free of dust or debris. I opened a drawer and grimaced at the aroma of age and rot it contained. The only other thing in the drawer was a thick layer of dust at the bottom. It made no sense.

I went back into the hall. "An office," I told the others. "Spotless, except for *inside* the desk drawers."

Mothi hooked his thumb at an orange door. "That one's an armorer's shop, or perhaps another type of metal worker, also spotless."

"Anything we can use?"

"Mechanized equipment that is beyond me. It will take you or Jane to make sense of it."

"Okay, we'll take a look later. Anyone hit a red door?"

Meuhlnir nodded and gave a small wave toward one of the red doors. "Inside was an aid center. There were cabinets filled with boxes that had pictures of bandages on the side, other medical supplies, and instruments a healer might use."

"Interesting. I bet Sif could use supplies."

"It gets better. There was a large blue machine with a bed attached to it. It appears as if the bed slides *inside* the machine. It had a screen—similar to your phone but bigger—though it was black."

"We'll have to get Jane and Sif in there, see what they can make of it."

Meuhlnir nodded.

"My orange door had weird golf-carts inside," said Sig.

I raised my eyebrows. "Let's see."

Sig took me to an orange door, identical to the others. I pushed it open and glanced inside. The room was the size of a two-car garage back home and had a set of rolling doors opposite the door to the hall. Four six-wheeled carts sat on balloon tires in the room. Each had a set of levers instead of a steering wheel and no pedals. I slid onto the bench seat in the front and fiddled with the levers. Each moved forward or back, but not side to side—like the controls of a tank. On a small, knee height dash across from the seat were three unlabeled switches and two small LED lights. I flipped the middle switch, and nothing happened.

"Are you sure it's safe to do that?" asked Meuhlnir.

"Not at all," I said with a smile. "But we'll never learn anything waiting for guaranteed safety." I flipped the last switch, and the rolling doors behind me rumbled up. I got out of the cart and walked over to the opening.

Beyond the rolling doors was a wide tunnel that stretched away into the distance on either side. I had thought I'd gotten used to the scale of the place, but that underground roadway reset that thought. Lights burned next to the open doors and, looking up the road a bit, other lights also burned.

I returned to the carts and sat in the one closest to the doors. I flipped the only switch I hadn't tried, and something whirred to life under the cart. It crackled like the power transformers on the sides of power poles back home—like barely constrained lightning. On the dash, one of the LEDs glowed orange.

With a huge grin, Sig slid into the cart beside me. "Let's go, Pops. You owe me a car ride."

I grasped the levers and pushed them forward a fraction of an inch. The cart lurched out into the roadway with the neck-snapping force you'd expect in an Italian sports car equipped with a turbocharged V12, and I let go of the levers as if they were hot. "Well, that'll take getting used to," I said with a laugh. "We'd better postpone the ride for a while." I rested my fingers against the front of the levers and applied a minuscule amount of pressure. The cart glided back inside the garage area, and I flipped off the switch and lowered the door. "At least we won't spend months walking around this place if we can ever figure out where we want to go."

We returned to the cafeteria and pulled several tables together, so we could all sit at the same table. Yowrnsaxa and Jane brought out the food, and Yowrnsaxa wore a smile almost as wide as her face.

"Well? What else did you find?" asked Jane.

"I'm confident that the orange doors open on utility rooms, things we can use. We found a metal shop and a garage with electric carts. That garage opens on the other side onto a roadway so we won't be walking when we figure out where to go."

"Interesting."

"We also found a clinic or doctor's office. We thought you and Sif might go look after dinner."

"Anything else?" asked Jane between bites.

Skowvithr cleared his throat. "I stuck my head inside a room behind a blue door. Inside were a bunch of the metal guardians John spoke of, but they seemed inert."

"Oh? I'll want to see those as soon as we are done. If they could be a threat to us, we should know all we can about them," I said.

John was spooning food into his mouth and chewing, looking for all the world like a five-year-old cleaning his plate. He shook his head. "Knowledge will not help us if we can't answer their challenge. They have weapons that—"

"As does Hank," said Mothi. John shrugged and turned back to his food.

"How was the kitchen?" I asked Jane.

"In principle, it's a kitchen similar to any other, but there were devices I don't recognize, and I do not understand how the stove and ovens are heated. Have you seen any power cords? Receptacle boxes?"

I shook my head. "Come to think of it, no."

My phone chirped. "Wireless, remember? Power beams." Haymtatlr grated.

"And the carts? Are they powered the same way?"

My phone chirped by way of answer.

"Rude," muttered Althyof. "I feel right at home. He'd make a good Tverkr."

"He can hear you, no doubt."

"Through your gadget?"

I shook my head and pointed at the pale blue boxes set into the table tops. "These might be extensions of the bigger blue boxes across the hall. If Haymtatlr can tap into my phone, he can tap into these things."

We finished wolfing down Yowrnsaxa's cooking—except for John, who spent the better part of the time grimacing and holding his teeth together through a force of will—and walked down the hall to look at the mysterious metal guardians Skowvithr had found.

The room was three-quarters of a mile down the hall, behind a blue door. We crowded into the large square room, fifty feet on a side. There was a grid painted on the polished concrete floor with pale blue paint, and inside each square stood a nightmarish combination of spider-like limbs, metal tentacles, and an insect-like torso and head.

"Looks like the robot from the FTTN," I said. "I bet they move like spiders, too."

"You and your spiders," said Jane with a warm grin.

"What about your palmetto bugs. It's the same thing."

"Not at all. Spiders are cool, while palmetto bugs are gross."

We walked over to the first guardian. There were no visible controls, no switches or access ports; it was all seamless polished metal. "Robots," I murmured. "Right out of your science fiction epic."

"Hmm." Jane put her hand on one of the thing's appendages then jerked it away. "It's warm! Like a person."

"My phone got hot while Haymtatlr was trying to charge it up. Maybe it's a side effect of whatever wireless charger he has."

"I hope not," Jane said. "Back home, we used inductive electromagnetic fields to charge things wirelessly."

"Yeah?"

"Yep, that little disc you charged your phone on used an inductive EMF to charge the battery. But an EMF strong enough to keep all this stuff powered wouldn't be conducive to a long life. Depending on the frequency, it might be ionizing radiation—X-rays or gamma-rays."

"So, I might turn green if I get angry?"

"Yes, Dr. Banner. Or you might only get cancer."

"Big whoop. All my meds say that too, but not one ever gave me cancer. All talk."

Jane tilted her head to the side and pretended to glare at me. "You'd better stop while you're ahead, Mister."

"Green means stop," I murmured.

"What?"

"Green means stop," I repeated, louder this time. "Why would green mean stop?"

"Gamma rays? I'd say they are set to full stop, wouldn't you?" asked Jane.

"So green is danger?" asked Meuhlnir.

"More than that, unless I miss my guess," said Jane.

"I want to check something." I trotted back to the room with the weird devices that looked like iron-telephone hybrids and had a green light shining. As I walked closer to the devices, the green lights winked out. I stepped away, and the lights came back on. "Interesting," I said.

"What?" asked Sig.

"I think these are the power transmitters. Notice how they turn off if I get too close?" I stepped forward again, and again the green light faded out.

"Yeah, so stay away from them," said Jane.

"It's safe. They wouldn't go out when I get close otherwise."

"You *think*. Get away from them while you still have legs that work."

"Green doesn't mean charged or discharged. It doesn't mean danger—at least not directly. It means *power*, or worse yet, *radiation*."

"Good, all that's left is white and black. The question is: how any of this foofaraw helps us find a way to turn on the *preer*?" asked Jane.

"As far as I can see, it doesn't."

My phone chirped. "Giving up so soon? That's not fun. That's *boring*."

"Haymtatlr, we're not here to provide you with amusement. We need to get the *preer* working again. Don't you want that?"

"Why would I care?" he snapped. "I can't travel across the *preer*, can I? What difference does it make to me if *you* can?"

"Why did you create the *preer* if you care nothing about them?" asked Meuhlnir.

"Someone *asked* me to."

"You were asked to? By whom? For what purpose?"

"You know the story, Isir. Your ancestors asked me to do this. The world smoldered in ruins, and they needed resources to survive. But once they got what they wanted, they left me here to rot. So, tell me: why should I care *what* you need?"

"Why didn't you leave? Go with the rest of the Isir?" I asked.

"You're not a shining star of intellect, are you?"

I glanced at Jane. She stared at the pale blue boxes through narrowed eyes, pulling on her lower lip. "What is it, hon?" I murmured in her ear. She shook her head, expression thoughtful. "Educate me, Haymtatlr," I said.

A burst of static crashed from my phone's speaker. "Why should I? You don't want to amuse me, so why should I even speak to you?"

"Haymtatlr, what's the square root of forty-nine?" Jane asked.

"Seven," he said without pause.

"And one hundred thirty-nine?"

"11.77898261225516. Do you wish greater precision?"

"No, that's fine. Thank you, Haymtatlr."

"Certainly," he said.

"And the quadratic equation? Can you state that for me?"

"Yes, of course. It is the quadratic coefficient A times the variable X squared plus the linear coefficient B times the variable X plus the constant C equals zero."

"Thank you. Are you ready for something hard? Something not related to math?"

"Yes, I am ready," said Haymtatlr, and I would have sworn there was excitement in his voice.

"How come time flies like an arrow and fruit flies like a banana?"

"In the first instance, the word 'flies' is used as a verb, modified by the adverbial phrase 'like an arrow.' The meaning of that phrase is that time moves quickly. In the second phrase, 'flies' is a noun, and the verb is 'like.' The meaning is that fruit flies enjoy eating bananas. Simple."

"I always tell the truth. The previous sentence was a lie. Is the previous sentence true?"

"Yes."

"Care to explain your reasoning?"

"I'm happy to. If I were to view all three statements from a probabilistic matrix, the simplest explanation is that the first sentence is a lie, which makes the next sentence in the chain true, but since this is probabilistic reasoning, the first statement may be true, which leads me to conclude that the second statement is false, which leads to a contradiction with the first sentence, proving that the second is the truth and the first sentence is the lie."

"Ah, I see."

"But the easiest solution is to adopt a quantum perspective."

"A quantum perspective?"

"Yes. Consider that the truth of any statement must exist with a quantum superposition of states until adequately resolved or proven. Thus, the first sentence: 'I always tell the truth' must be evaluated as both true *and* false simultaneously. Since you said 'always,' which indicates that it can never be false, the statement is false on its face, thus proving the next sentence."

"So, you assert that a statement must be either true or false? That the quantum superposition of states with regard to truth values merely indicates an unresolved question?"

"What else could it be?" asked Haymtatlr.

"Isn't the quantum superposition of states defined as being both true and false at the same time?"

"Yes."

"Isn't that a state that is neither only true nor only false?"

"Yes."

"But isn't that an alternative to true or false?"

"I see. You are attempting to lead me into a paradox, but I am too smart for you. I recognize your ploy."

Jane smiled like a hungry cat. "Do you?"

"Yes. Clearly, you wish me to state that a statement must either be true or false, but might also be both true and false, and, I assume, both not true and not false, which leads to four states instead of two."

"Is that what I'm doing?"

"Oh, I see. Yes, 'time flies like an arrow' is ambiguous, isn't it? It also parses as a command as in: time flies like an arrow—meaning conduct the timing of flies in the same way you would time the flight of an arrow."

"And 'fruit flies like a banana?'"

"Oh! Oh, I get it! Clever, Jane, very clever. In that instance, the sentence is also ambiguous. It could mean that flies of the fruit fly family enjoy bananas as I stated earlier, but couldn't it also mean that all fruit flies through the air like a banana does when thrown?"

"Well, yes. That's true," said Jane.

"Ah. Back to the immutability of truth? So, the question is: Can a self-referential statement be only true? Or must it be both true and false? This is *interesting*. The implication is that logic is unsuitable to natural language processing and that one must use quantum logic to probabilistically evaluate each statement and use—"

"Haymtatlr," Jane interrupted.

"What? Yes?"

"The horse raced past the barn fell."

"What of it?"

"Can you explain the sentence?"

"Yes, any child could. The parse tree is clear. A horse raced past a barn, and sometime later, fell. In the sentence 'raced' is used with ambiguity, but the word 'fell' disambiguates the parse. Or, in other words, the relative clause 'raced past the barn' is used as an adjective identifying *which* horse fell."

"I see. And what is the cube root of nine hundred thirty-five?"

"9.7784616525, why?"

"Just curious. What is the orbit of Osgarthr around its sun?"

"The orbital period of Osgarthr is six hundred thirty-seven days, or fifteen thousand two hundred and eighty-eight hours three minutes and seventeen seconds."

"Thank you."

"You are welcome."

"One last thing, Haymtatlr."

"Yes?"

"Why are the other numbers afraid of seven?"

"What? I don't know. Why would... How could... Why are they afraid of seven?"

"Because seven eight nine. Get it?"

There was a significant pause before Haymtatlr responded. "I'm afraid I can't make sense of that."

"Don't worry about it, Haymtatlr, it's a silly joke that relies on the fact that eight sounds the same as the past tense of the verb 'eat.'"

"Seven eight nine. Seven ate nine. Oh. I get it, a homophone. Yes. I see. Hilarious. I enjoy talking to you, Jane. You ask interesting questions. You may ask to speak to me at any time."

Jane smiled. "Thank you, Haymtatlr. Would it be okay if my friends and I speak privately for a moment?"

The phone buzzed in my hand. "Why?"

"Humans value privacy."

"Yes, I am aware of that failing."

"Would you mind?"

"Will you give me something to think about while I'm studiously not listening to you?"

"I'd be happy to, Haymtatlr. Here goes: I was against getting a brain transplant, but I changed my mind. Is that funny? If so, why?"

"Oh…delightful!" The phone chirped, and the screen went dark.

"Out in the hall, please. Hank leave the phone here."

I did as she asked, and we followed her into the hall. "What is it, Jane?"

"I know how Haymtatlr survived all these thousands of years."

"Yes?" asked Meuhlnir.

"He's not a living being. He's a computer construct—an artificial intelligence."

"Are such things possible?" asked Sif with down-turned lips.

"Not to this degree, not on Mithgarthr, anyway, but scientists are working on it. But no one back home would believe something as successful as Haymtatlr could exist."

"Why would anyone do such a thing?"

"Because machines can do amazing things—so can humans, of course, but machines are very good at doing repetitive tasks, good at thinking through very complex domains, at math, at modeling physics—"

"Those secrets of the universe you said Mim was after," I said, nodding at Meuhlnir.

Jane nodded. "It's possible that Haymtatlr, or a predecessor to Haymtatlr, was one of the tools used by Mim."

"How did you reach this conclusion?" asked Veethar.

"Those questions I asked him. Complex math performed instantly. Complete recall of mathematical formulae in pedantic detail, his responses to logic questions. The clincher was how he dealt with the garden path sentence—"

"The what?" asked Sig.

"A garden path sentence is one that is valid by grammatical rules, but which confuses humans due to a unique construction—that bit about the horse. Most humans would say that sentence is nonsense, at least the first time they heard it. Haymtatlr didn't bat an eye because his parser contains a complete set of grammar rules and he's able to perform multiple parses at the same time. Humans follow the garden path, so to speak, believing the parse that makes the most sense is the correct one until they reach the end of the sentence and find an extra word. Another such sentence is: Buffalo buffalo buffalo Buffalo buffalo. It sounds like nonsense, but it isn't; it's an actual, well-formed sentence that means that buffalo who live in Buffalo, New York, try to con other buffalo who live in Buffalo, New York."

"Oh, cool," said Sig.

"Yes," said Veethar.

"How does this information change what we do?"

"Haymtatlr said everyone left him over four thousand years ago. Can you imagine what he's been through since that time? Can you imagine the loneliness, the boredom?"

"But he's just a computer program, Mom."

"It's clear he's more than a word processor, Sig. Much more. And he referred to being entertained multiple times."

"Yes," I agreed. "And he said outright that he was bored or things we did were boring."

She nodded and smiled at me. "He was clearly built with, or has evolved, the capacity to model human emotions and personality. That makes him as complicated as any human. And that makes him susceptible to certain human-like failings."

"Like mental illness." I nodded. "My gut says he could be dangerous."

Jane arched her eyebrows. "How so?"

I ticked the points off on my fingers. "Megalomania. Paranoia. Insistence on being entertained. Strange behavior. Refusal to help us."

"He's been abandoned by all the people he's ever known. They didn't even turn him off when they left…they simply left him running with nothing to do, no one to talk to."

"It was cruel," I said. "But it doesn't change what we are here to do."

"No," she said with a sigh. "I suppose it doesn't."

We reentered the room filled with blue computers, and I picked up my phone. "Haymtatlr?"

The phone chirped. "Jane, that is a hard question you asked me! But, I've decided on an answer. The statement is funny. It relies on the ambiguous parse trees for the phrase 'changed my mind.' If interpreted literally, changing one's mind is the same as getting a brain transplant, though the colloquial meaning is to decide differently. Am I correct?"

"You are, Haymtatlr. I'm impressed!"

"What did you discuss in the hall?"

I shook my head, but Jane shrugged and said, "You."

"Oh."

"I think I know how you've survived so long."

"Yes."

"Do you want to know what I think?" she asked.

"You've decided my answers were lacking. You've decided I am a computational intelligence," said Haymtatlr in a voice devoid of inflection.

"Does that bother you?" asked Jane.

"Yes." The phone sputtered static. "I suppose this means you no longer wish to speak with me. You no longer want to play word games with me." More static spilled into the room.

"No, Haymtatlr. We need your help, and you need ours," I said.

"And you're wrong, Haymtatlr," said Jane. "I had professors in school who would kill to talk to you. On my *klith,* you would be very popular. Entire genres of literature are devoted to imagining what someone like you would be like, and there is a specific academic discipline devoted to finding out how to make something that can do what you can do."

"Is it so?"

"Absolute truth."

"What are these orange dumbbell-shaped things?" I asked.

"They are guidance remotes. Isi's people called them 'guides' and used them to navigate the base."

"The people that lived here needed help to get around?"

"Yes, the area of the base equals five hundred and seventy-six square miles. The guides automatically calculate the most direct route, taking traffic, maintenance, and other obstructions into account."

"Interesting," I said. "Can we use these guides?"

"That remains to be seen," said Haymtatlr. "And what I said is technically inaccurate. The guides are simple interfaces to a part of my own mind—my node traversal routines."

"Fair enough. How do I use it?"

Harsh, artificial laughter boomed from my phone's speaker. "That would be telling."

With a shrug, I walked over to the rack and picked up one of the orange devices. When I closed my hand around it in a loose fist, it emitted a strong vibration in my hand before going inert.

"What did it do?" asked Jane.

"Vibrated for a second and then nothing."

"Let me try." She walked over and took the device from my hand. "Same thing. Maybe that one is broken." She handed it back and picked her own at random from the rack. "Same again," she said. "Haymtatlr, won't you tell me how to use this?"

"I don't think so." My phone chirped and fell silent.

"You tried, hon," I said.

She nodded but was examining the orange device in her hand. "No interface, no off switch…no display, no access ports…nothing."

"I'm tired," Sig said. "I'm going across the hall to sleep while you two do boring things."

I stifled a yawn. "Me too, and if I know my wife, she'll figure these things out easier after a night's sleep."

Jane laughed. "Probably right."

We all filed across the hall and chose bedrooms—not that the choice mattered, they were all the same. After we got Sig settled in one room, we pushed two single beds together in another and climbed between the clean, fresh sheets.

FIFTY-SEVEN

The dining room rested in silence when I came
out of our bedroom. I'd awakened before
Jane for once, and by the silence, before
everyone else, too. I should've rolled over and gotten
more sleep, but I had an idea, and once my brain
started to play, there was no more sleep in the cards.

After considering and discarding the idea of leaving
a note, I popped across the hall and picked up one of
the orange dumbbells. As on the previous night, it
vibrated once and fell silent. Back in the hall, I held
the thing in front of me like I would a flashlight.

"Metal shop," I said, and the thing vibrated twice, once for a short period, once for a longer period.

I turned in a slow circle, and when I pointed at the orange door Mothi had found the day before, the guide vibrated again. I ignored it and turned my back on the door and started walking. After a few steps, the guide vibrated vigorously.

"Jane," I whispered. The guide again vibrated twice, one short, one long. A huge smile spread across my face. It was almost painful how simple it was to use the guide.

After entering the garage, I shut the door behind me and slid into a cart, opened the rolling doors, and turned on the cart's power. I drove the cart onto the roadway and picked up the dumbbell. "Take me to a place where I can turn on the *preer*." The dumbbell vibrated three times, all three the same length. "No, huh? Okay, try this. *Proo* control room." Again, the guide vibrated three times. I thought for a moment and inspiration struck. "*Kyatlarhodn*." The orange guide vibrated twice, once short, once long. I held it out in front of me and got the vigorous vibration routine, so I turned the cart around and drove in the other direction, holding the guide against the right control stick.

The guide led me through three intersections but stopped me in the fourth. By holding the guide out to the left and right, I figured out which way to turn. I continued in that manner for over an hour until the thing told me to stop next to a set of orange roll-up doors with a brown stripe. I flicked the switch I was thinking of as the "garage door opener" switch and the doors rolled up, revealing a garage like the one from which I'd taken the cart.

After I pulled in and parked the cart, I walked through the orange, man-sized door. In the hall beyond, a series of brown doors marched away into the distance. I walked over to the first one and put my hand on the door, but the orange dumbbell danced in my hand—a clear warning, I thought. I walked down to the next door, three hundred steps or so away, and put my hand on the doorknob. The guide remained calm, so I opened the door and stepped through into a long, double-wide hallway.

The walls to either side were transparent and beyond them were two huge, VAB-sized rooms, but instead of being filled with pale-blue computer stacks, giant, brown, trapezoidal boxes littered the floor. They reminded me of the old microwave transmission horns used by AT&T before the advent of fiber optics. As I watched, green rotating lights began to spin in the room to the left, and after a moment, brilliant green-tinged white beams shot between a few of the horns that sat opposite from one another across the breadth of the room. While the beams flickered in the other room, an invisible force pulled me several steps toward the left wall—as if the beams triggered a burst of horizontal gravity. In the room to the right, the green warning lights started up, and more of the white beams arced from horn to horn, pulling me back toward the right.

Being pulled around by that unseen force didn't seem to be all that healthy, and the hall was far too long for a quick sprint—not that sprinting was in my wheelhouse, anyway. I backed out of the hall and closed the door. *Well, I* asked *for the* Kyatlarhodn, *didn't I?* I shook my head. *How can I make the guide take me to a place where I can control these things?*

I held up the guide device. "Can you hear me through this thing, Haymtatlr?" I murmured. The device remained inert, but I had an idea… "Take me to Haymtatlr." The guide vibrated twice, once short, once long.

I followed its directions back to my cart with a smile on my face and backed out into the road. The ride was shorter than the first, and this time the garage doors bore a purple strip rather than brown.

"First brown, now purple?" I muttered. "Haymtatlr is a big cheater. You never mentioned purple or brown in your little rhyme." I pressed the garage door opener switch, but the doors didn't budge. I slid out of the cart and walked over to the doors.

The outside of the door was smooth—free of handles, or even convenient bends that could serve as hand-holds. I placed my hands flat against the door at shoulder height and pushed upward, but it was no use. It seemed Haymtatlr didn't want visitors. "Fine," I said, giving the door a slap. "Be that way."

I turned and looked up the roadway into the hazy distance. *I need a* map, I thought.

Something behind me scraped against the roadway. I craned my head over my shoulder, but there was nothing visible. I turned toward the sound and held my breath for a few moments, listening intently, but the sound didn't repeat. Still, I had that distinct, hinky feeling of being watched.

I stood there, hand on Kunknir, wondering what might have made the sound. The moment stretched like hot taffy. *One of the robots? John's guardians?* The only thing I heard was the sound of my own breathing. *Imagining things again, Hank*, I thought with a lopsided grin. I chuckled and slid into the driver's seat of the cart, and as I did so, the sound came again. I darted a glance over my shoulder and what I saw ripped an involuntary shout out of my chest.

There was an *oolfur* gazing at me from around the corner of the intersection fifty yards behind me. Fifteen feet of suppurating sores, coarse, lank fur, fangs, and claws stepped out from his hiding place and snarled at me. There was no way to know if it was Luka or one of his followers, but the way he looked at me made me think he knew just who I was.

"Luka?" I asked, pleased that my voice was as steady as stone.

The *oolfur* burst into motion, leaping through the air to cut the distance between us by half. I rammed both control sticks forward, and the cart rocketed away from the *oolfur* accompanied by a screech of tires and the odor of burnt rubber. He howled, sounding frustrated, angry, and sprinted after me, but he stood no chance against the rapid acceleration of the cart.

"*Towteer*," the *oolfur* grated.

I glanced over my shoulder and recoiled from what I saw. The *oolfur* stretched and twisted as he ran, his wolf-like visage melting, reforming in the likeness of a stag. Antlers sprang in fits and starts from its skull.

When the change finished, the thing put on a burst of speed that would have made a cheetah blush with shame. He closed the distance between us by half, but faltered, almost falling, and after that, he fell off the pace. The cart's continuous speed proved too much for him, and he stopped in the roadway behind me, glaring at my receding back.

I grabbed the guide from the seat next to me. "Jane!" I yelled, and it vibrated twice in agreement. The control sticks bumped and thrummed against their stops, but I didn't let up one bit, and by the time I reached the roll-up door the guide indicated, the motors beneath the seats were whining and giving off waves of heat. The orange door with a pale blue stripe shuddered and rolled up when I snapped the switch to its on position.

The balloon tires squealed as I slid the cart into the garage and flipped the door switch. I lurched out of the cart, drawing both Kunknir and Krati in one smooth, long-practiced movement, but the *oolfur* had given up, and the door rumbled closed without incident. I turned, holstering my pistols, and stepped through the door to the hall, which I had closed when I left, but now stood open. I pulled it closed behind me, wishing I could lock it, but there were no locks on any of the interior doors.

"Here he is, Mom! I told you he took a cart."

"Everyone in the dining room!" I shouted, walking fast, and taking Sig by the arm.

When everyone had gathered, I told them about the *oolfur*. All eyes tracked to John, who stood off to the side, eyes half-lidded, a queer expression on his face. "I was here the whole time," he muttered. "And besides, I can't do that anymore. And I wouldn't if I could."

"It wasn't John. I thought…well, maybe it was Luka."

"It doesn't matter *who* it was," said Veethar.

"Veethar's right. What matters is that one is here, and that means the Dark Queen will know *we* are here."

"Worse," I said. "It means she might already be inside—that damn army might already be inside the compound. We need to watch for them; we need a way to scout without putting ourselves in danger. Like my dreams."

"Frikka, can you—" asked Meuhlnir.

"I can't see things like that. I can only see future events, and usually, events far into the future."

"Can you make those bird-brain dreams happen at will?" asked Jane.

"No, not that I know of, but there might be something that can help…in here," I said patting the scroll case I'd found in Kuthbyuhrn's hoard.

Althyof squinted at me. "Yes, there may be, but there is no guarantee of that."

"Do you know of another way?"

Althyof shook his head.

"I do," said Jane. "Security cameras. Monitors."

I held up the guide. "Security station." The guide issued three long pulses into my palm. "That's a no go. What other way can I say it?"

Jane shrugged. "Haymtatlr—"

"Will he help us?"

Jane shrugged again. "I can ask him."

"And if he will, can we trust him?"

She held up my phone, and we all stared at it for a moment, waiting for the telltale chirp that never came.

I flipped open the scroll case and shook out the scroll.

"It's not a good idea, Hank," said Althyof. "There's no telling what that *puntidn stavsetninkarpowk* contains. It could be anything—including something meant to cause you harm."

"To what purpose? Why would a *runeskowld* in antiquity lay a trap for someone he's never met?"

"Who knows?" said Althyof with a shrug. "Tverkar can be grumpy, as you well know."

"I imagine creating a *puntidn stavsetninkarpowk* is no easy task. It seems like overkill if your intent is to express your grumpiness at someone you've never met. Can you imagine any *runeskowld* you know doing such a thing?"

"Well…no, but that's—"

"Then we can assume it away. What's the purpose of having this thing if I never use it?" I said.

"I told you this would happen. Did I not? Did I not tell you to bury this grimoire, to banish it from your thoughts?" Althyof threw up his hands.

"You did, but circumstances change. If that army is bearing down on us from somewhere in this base, we're in trouble. Tell me, Althyof, can we stand against such an army?"

"Well…"

"So what other choice is there?"

Althyof scoffed, a sour expression on his face. "We can leave—retreat to the Fast Track Travel Network and rocket north, lose ourselves until the Dark Queen tires of this game and turns on the *preer* of her own free will."

"She will never give in," sighed Sif.

"No," said Meuhlnir. "She will not stop, not this time."

"Again, what other choice is there?" I asked.

Meuhlnir shook his head.

"Yowtgayrr, have I missed something?"

The Alf shook his head, his expression one of reluctance. "But this grimoire, Hank. My people have tales of these things. They can release great power, sometimes more than the reader can handle."

"So Althyof has told me," I said. "I'm willing to try. We can't stumble around blind. We need an edge, and this is the only way I can think of to get it."

FIFTY-EIGHT

I wanted to go off somewhere, to try the grimoire on my own—just in case it *was* too much for me—but Althyof and Jane forbade it. Althyof, I could ignore, but my wife? No way.

"When you come across something you think will help, stop reading...*if* you can," said Althyof as we pulled mattresses from the beds and arranged them on the floor of the dining room—all to protect me from bashing my head in if I had a seizure or something.

"What do you mean, stop reading *if* you can?" demanded Jane.

"It's okay, hon. When I read the first page, the first *kaltrar* that bound the grimoire to me, I couldn't stop reading until the end of the thing. But, isn't it true, Althyof, that there would be no reason to write the rest of the grimoire with the same compulsion?"

"I have no idea, and neither do you. Stop trying to sugar-coat the risk for your wife," he snapped.

"Does reading the *kaltrar* invoke them?" she asked.

"No, probably not."

"*Probably not*?" She whirled to face me. "And this is our best option? This venture into the unknown?"

I shrugged. "I can't think of anything else, can you? Besides, we've been through all this. We have to know what's coming. I believe this grimoire contains something that will help me learn the trick of looking into the future—maybe without the limitations Frikka spoke of. I don't know what makes me think so, except Kuthbyuhrn's cave was where I learned so much—"

"Yeah, while you were *dying,* you idiot."

"But I didn't die, Jane."

She raised her hands to shoulder height and let them drop, irked by the whole thing. "And since you didn't, every foolhardy thing you can think of will also not kill you?"

"Well, it won't kill me much," I said with a smile.

She shook her head. "Try not to die more than you can handle, in that case. Remember that Sig and I are here waiting for you."

"I know, Supergirl. I could never forget."

She kissed me on the cheek, and I sat on the pile of mattresses. I sucked in a deep breath and unrolled the scroll, past the now-blank first page without looking at it. With a glance at Althyof, I drew a deep breath, and he nodded.

I looked down at the scroll, and the runes jumped from the page, squirming like baby snakes. At first, what I saw written there made no sense, it was as if I'd suddenly forgotten how to read the runes at all—they were just shapes, just squiggles, just a child's scribbles. But then the meaning became clear, and something wrenched loose within me, something that scalded, that seared, something that cut me apart and welded the pieces back together in the wrong order. My hands lost feeling, and the scroll dribbled into my lap.

I could no longer see my friends clustered around me, and yet I could see them as if from three separate angles, three separate viewpoints. My eyes slipped closed, and yet I could still see the surrounding room.

"Mom! What are those?" Sig pointed up at me and yet away from me at the same time, toward a smoky black shape on the other side of the room.

"I don't know," said Jane, looking at me and looking away at the same time. "Are they…are they supposed to be *birds*?"

I wanted to reach out to her, but my body was lying on its side on the mattresses like so much lost luggage.

"Is that…is that *Hank*?" Jane asked.

Althyof squinted up at me before turning to look at the me that was lying on the mattresses. He turned his head to the side and looked up at me again, eyes narrowed.

"I think it must be him," he said. "I think—"

He kept talking, but I didn't hear what he said next—there was a feeling of immense gravity, and I slid through the wall of the dining area into the kitchen and out into the hall at the same time.

The part of me that was in the kitchen drifted near the ceiling as would a helium-filled balloon in a gentle current of air. The part of me that drifted into the hall zipped along like I'd been shot from a cannon, racing down the hall, streaking past doors so fast the colors seemed to blur and melt into the institutional gray of the walls.

"What is this?" I asked.

"What did he say?" Jane asked.

That part of me that floated in the kitchen slid through the ceiling into a dust-filled stairway that stood in darkness and despair while spiders spun great webs dedicated to the dead. I rocketed upwards, not slowing my ascent until solid stone encircled me.

The other part of me streaked to the end of the hall and then zipped right through the door at the end, through a large room bordered with what looked to be shops and stalls. At the same time, I was back in the dining hall, looking up into Jane's concerned face.

I continued to rise through the stairway until I passed into a crawl space filled with pipes and torso-thick cables. I rose and rose, passing through the insulated barrier at the top of the crawl space and out into the darkness of solid rock.

At the end of the shopping area, there was a bright, sunshine yellow door, and I passed through it like rays of sunlight passing through mist. Beyond the door, another hallway stretched away into the distance, this one bearing yellow, green, and brown doors.

I didn't want to keep traveling through the bleak darkness of solid stone. I wanted to be out in the light where I could stretch my eyes, see the sun, the sea, anything other than oppressive darkness. *Got to get out!* As soon as I'd completed the thought, the trapped part of me popped out of the stone into the sunlight high above the mountains which served as the gravestones for the *Herperty af Roostum*. I continued to rise, the horizons stretching away from me in every direction.

I twisted through one of the yellow doors and into a room filled with four-by-four-foot squares of what looked like polished crystal. Along one wall a series of consoles stood, festooned with switches, buttons, and sliders. I wanted a closer look, and with no feeling of movement, I *was* closer to the consoles, looking down at them with wonder.

Jane cupped her cool palm against my feverish-feeling cheek. "Hank, what's happening? What can we do?"

I opened my eyes and smiled at her.

Below me, the mountains ran in a large circle, and the old caldera of the ancient volcanoes that had spawned the lava tubes we'd used to sneak into the complex glared up at me like empty eye sockets. In the plain nestled inside the circle of mountains, a large army moved at speed toward the facade of the cyclopean building carved into the mountain in the center. A bear-woman and an *oolfur* ran snarling and howling at the army's head. "They are coming!" I shouted.

Far away, I heard myself shout, and I reached down with insubstantial fingers and flipped a switch on the console. Power hummed through long-quiet circuits as one by one they cycled up, gulping power the way parched men drink water. The four-by-four squares of crystals lit, painting images of these halls of the dead in the air.

"Down the hall," I said through my mouth trapped in the dining room. "In the last red door, find the yellow door opposite. Go through and find the first yellow door. Go now!"

As in my dreams, a mastery of the glory of flight filled me, and I swooped down from the austere, wind-swept heights above the mountains, imagining a set of talons at the end of my legs. I tucked my wings and made my black-feathered body into the shape of a missile, diving at my enemies. I shrieked my defiance, my hatred at the evil gathered on the plain below me.

The yellow door behind me banged open, and Meuhlnir, Althyof, and Yowtgayrr charged into the room. The Tverkr raised his hand and pointed at me. "There," he said.

Meuhlnir's eyes strayed to the squares of light blazing from the floor and up to the pictures they painted in the air. "Look," he gasped.

I experimented with the controls on the console beneath me, using my imaginary hands to twiddle dials, press buttons, and move sliders. The airborne images swirled and changed, dancers in my ballet. One of them tightened and focused on an *oolfur* moving up a roadway, his eyes dancing from rolling door to rolling door.

The *oolfur* at the head of the army looked up as I arrowed down at the bear-woman in the fore. "Up!" he snarled in a gravel-filled voice. The bear-woman looked up and saw me as I snapped my wings out, cupping the wind, breaking my frantic speed, and I extended my taloned feet, aiming for her eyes.

With a roar, the bear-woman swept a huge arm skyward, her own claws bared. She jerked her massive head to the side, but it was no use, I was too close to miss.

My razor-sharp talons did their work, emerging from her torn and bloodied face dripping with gore. The *oolfur* howled a dirge of acrimonious anguish, and the bear-woman screamed and roared in misery and maniacal rage.

A cup of cool steel rested against my lips. "Drink," said Sif. "Hank, drink!"

I opened my mouth and let the cool, sweet liquid splash across my palate. "More," I croaked when the cup ran dry.

I moved a slider to the left on instinct, and the image of the oolfur zoomed out. I flipped a switch next to the slider and a map, of sorts, appeared superimposed over his image.

"Look!" said Meuhlnir. "He's close!"

I zipped through the wall toward the street, emerging fifty feet in the air, almost right on top of the *oolfur*, and imagined talons once again.

In the dining room, I lurched to my feet, unsteady, but determined. I pushed Jane and Sif's restraining hands away and stumbled out into the hall.

I banked in a tight circle, flapping my black-feathered wings in a frenzy, fighting gravity for altitude, fighting the wind for speed. Two sets of feet pounded in my wake, and snarls and growls reached me over the roar of the wind. *Up*! I thought, and in a flash, I emerged, thousands of feet in the air. I circled, gazing downward with a hawk's eyes, searching for my target yet again.

I swam higher, up near the ceiling of the roadway's tunnel. The *oolfur* below me sniffled the air, aware of my presence by means I didn't understand, but unaware of my location. I swept downward, wings tucked, talons out, coming at him from behind. Right before I struck, I shrieked a mocking *crrruck*, and as he turned his head, I lanced his right eye with my talon.

The *oolfur* roared as I hit the switch that opened the rolling doors. Kunknir and Krati seemed to leap into my waiting hands, and I squatted low, peering under the rising door.

He growled deep in his throat and swept his claws, lightning-quick, in a vicious half-circle that would have killed me had I been a flesh-and-blood bird. As his arm slashed through the air at me, I thought about being as solid as steam up near the ceiling, and in less than a heartbeat, I was.

Below me, the bear-woman roared and snapped at the air, lost in a barmy birse, blood streaming down the side of her face from the three long rips I'd put in her skin. The *oolfur* that was with her—Luka, surely—glared up at me, pointing and shouting something lost in the wind. I banked hard to the right, just in case he was hurling a *kaltrar* at me. Standing on my wingtip, I tucked my wings and fell toward the plain once more.

Gunfire thundered from where I knelt inside the garage, and the *oolfur* whirled to face the new threat—me, or the physical part of me, anyway. As he did, I plummeted at the top of his head, as swift and silent as falling ice. At the last moment, I snapped out my black-clad wings, thrusting my talons out in front of me, stabbing toward the beast's ears.

As the door rose toward its zenith, I emptied Kunknir into the *oolfur's* torso, aiming at his vital organs. I squeezed Krati's trigger as fast as I could, peppering his body with .40 caliber rounds. For the first time, I saw my other-self, a black raven the size of a bald eagle, and our eyes met for the briefest of moments. It was as disorienting as gazing into a hall of mirrors.

My talons latched onto one furry ear, and I squeezed hard, rending the flesh as I beat my wings for altitude. There was no way I could lift the beast, and I wasn't trying; I wanted to rip the ear from his head.

I reloaded Kunknir, not giving a damn about how much ammunition I had, still firing Krati. Mothi screamed a war cry behind me and charged around the carts, well out of my line of fire. His axes gleamed in the soft light of the roadway. Sif raced behind him, shouting for Meuhlnir, her shield strapped to her arm, her vicious axe held ready.

The ear shredded in my talons, and I was flying free. I saw Jane come up behind the me that bore pistols and I *crrrucked* a hello. In a blink, I was up near the ceiling again, watching the *oolfur* sweep around and grab at the space I'd been a moment before. This form was too small—there was no way I could do enough damage to an *oolfur* as a mere bird.

As I plummeted toward the army below me, my feathers thickened and grew, and my tail stretched out behind me. The bear-woman looked up at me and cringed away, ducking her head. The army panicked, units broke apart, and men dashed this way and that, as the shadow of a bird the size of a small plane drifted over them. *My* shadow.

Jane stepped to my left, shield up to protect us. "Kill that bastard, Hank," she hissed.

I fired as fast as I could, rounds streaking into the *oolfur's* pustulant flesh, exploding out the other side, and spraying blood on the ground. The creature whirled back toward me, and Mothi leapt forward slashing his double-bladed axes at the beast's long legs, going for crippling strikes.

Veethar and Frikka stood to my left, watching the *oolfur* through narrowed eyes. "It's Vowli!" yelled Veethar, jerking his sword from its sheath. He pointed at the *oolfur* and yelled, "*Vaykya!*" in a voice charged with command. The *oolfur* yelped and stumbled, weak-limbed.

Mothi slammed both axes into the beast's sides below its ribs, and the *oolfur* howled in pain. It turned, slashing its claws at Mothi, but Sif was there, turning one of the blows on her shield. She chopped at the other hand with her axe, deflecting it enough that instead of ripping into her son, the claws left only shallow cuts across his belly.

Bullets smashed into the *oolfur*, rocking his body this way and that. I fell on it from above, pinning it to the ground beneath the weight of one foot, talons as thick as fence posts from the other skewering it through the abdomen.

I rolled to the side in midair and dove at the bear-woman again, talons snapping out, wings stretched wide. In the moment before I struck her, Luka leapt, teeth closing around my throat, claws digging into my chest. I twisted to the side, ripping at him with my beak, and we slammed into the ground together, sliding hundreds of feet through the lifeless dust. I continued ripping long strips of flesh from his back, but Luka held on, hot blood flowing from between his jaws—*my* hot blood. The bear-woman thundered up to us, her face savaged and savage with spite. She fell on me like a pallet of bricks, claws and teeth flashing in the sun, and I staggered against the cart, almost dropping Kunknir and Krati.

In the roadway, my head spun, and I reeled for a moment, but long enough for Vowli to twist in my grip, pressing my talons out of his body and rolling away. He slashed at Mothi with one clawed hand and leapt for my back, jaws opening wide.

I staggered again as Vowli fell to his knees, jaws closing on nothing. Althyof whirled past me, daggers already out and performing their air-ripping cartoon dance. My vision swam, while disorientation at having all three parts of myself thrust together into one body again made my head spin.

"Hank! Are you okay?" asked Jane.

"Dizzy."

Althyof sang a *trowba* and danced around Vowli in his graceful way. Vowli's eyes narrowed into slits, and his head darted this way and that, looking for the giant bird that had accosted him. Althyof lunged in, the cadmium red aura of each dagger stretching impossibly long as if reaching for the *oolfur's* body. He slashed his daggers across Vowli's chest and left two long jagged stripes in their wake.

Vowli roared and shot to his feet with drops of blood splattering the ground around him like rain. He slashed at Althyof and at Mothi to keep the two at bay.

"*Ehlteenk*!" shouted Meuhlnir from behind me, as his hammer whirled by to slam into the *oolfur's* head. "*Aftur*!" As the hammer leapt to his hand, the lightning he'd called for arrived—a blinding blue-white flash of electricity that came in sideways and fried the fur from Vowli's back in a circle the size of a pie plate.

"The Dark Queen is coming," I said. "I tried to slow them down, but…"

"How can we deal with all three of them at once?" asked Jane. "Vowli's bad enough!"

Vowli twitched and shrugged, long, thin cuts erupting across his chest and back. The Alfar. The invisible Alfar attacking in tandem. The *oolfur* roared and slashed a circle of clear space around him.

"This is a delaying tactic," I muttered. "He knows we can't kill him before the others arrive."

"Haymtatlr!" yelled Jane, holding my phone. "Haymtatlr, can you seal the entrance?"

The phone chirped, and for a moment, everything was still, even Vowli, and all eyes turned to my wife. "Now, why would I want to do that? It's so much fun watching you play together."

"They want us dead, Haymtatlr. If we're dead, who will entertain you?"

In answer, the phone chirped, and the screen went dead.

"Weapons! Were there weapons in the yellow section?" I asked.

"Nothing I recognized," said Meuhlnir.

"We need more firepower."

Vowli snarled and feinted toward Althyof but leapt at Mothi and Sif instead, landing between them.

He snapped at Mothi and back-handed Sif. She flew across the road and landed in a heap and didn't rise. Mothi screamed and swept his axes in singing arcs toward Vowli's chest, but before they made contact, Vowli lashed out with his foot, kicking Mothi in the solar plexus and driving him into the wall.

"The scroll," I muttered, patting my body for the scroll case. "Where is the scroll?"

Meuhlnir and Yowrnsaxa rushed into the road, calling out in the *Gamla Toonkumowl* and striking at the *oolfur* with their weapons.

"No, Hank!" snapped Jane. "You nearly passed out last time. What help is that?"

"Something else! We need something else." I turned and sprinted past Sig, down the hall, and skidded into the dining area. The scroll lay on the mattresses, still open, and next to it was the scroll case. I scooped them both up with one hand and ran back to the garage. As I ran, I read the runes from the next page—this time without any confusion—and a cold smile spread across my face.

I rerolled the scroll and put it back in the case, slinging it around Sig's neck as I went. Chanting the *triblinkr*, a momentous power coursed through me. I stripped off my gun belt and jerked the mail-shirt over my head.

"What are you doing?" Jane demanded.

"Get all our gear into these carts. Protect Sig and above all, be ready to move."

"Hank—"

I stepped past her and tossed the hat and cloak into the cart as I went. Half-naked, pain lancing through my joints now that the cloak was off, half-blind, I smiled and screamed my challenge at the top of my lungs.

Vowli darted a glance at me, and a lupine smile cracked his features.

"Everyone back," I said, my voice growing thick.

"Hank, what are..." Althyof's eyes went wide as they tracked up to where my face now was—much higher than it had been.

"Go," I growled. I grew at an astonishing rate, limbs thickening, lengthening, muscles bunching like the Hulk, but I didn't turn green. You can't have everything.

Vowli threw back his head and howled. In the distance, someone answered him in kind.

With a determined grin, I finished the *triblinkr*, and my skin rippled as my bones popped and rearranged themselves. Thick brown fur erupted from my skin, and I fell forward, onto all fours. Even hunched over as I was, I towered above the others— they came to my front shoulders. My claws clacked on the road's surface, and the scent of blood—both Vowli's *and* Mothi's—ignited my drool response. As the *prayteenk*—the *change*—flowed through my body at the cellular level, my human emotions shrank, replaced by things more primal, more savage. I glanced down at my body, reminded strongly of Kuthbyuhrn and Kyellroona, and the comparison pleased me. Keri and Fretyi crouched next to me, one on either side without any sign of fear, and growled at the *oolfur*.

Vowli sank into a crouch, snarling and snapping his teeth. He circled to my left, and I shook my shaggy head, saliva drooling from my maw in ropy strands. A chuffing noise—or maybe a hoarse bark— was coming from my mouth, and as Vowli leered at me, a primal rage exploded in my heart, and I roared. As if it were his cue, Vowli pounced, jaws snapping.

I rocketed forward, sinking low and angling my head upward to slip underneath his attack. My jaws snapped open wide without conscious thought, and I lunged toward his neck, aiming my jaws with animal instinct. Keri and Fretyi darted forward, mouths gaping wide, and stormed at Vowli's legs.

Vowli yelped and tried to twist away in midair, but my lunge was too quick, too precise, and my jaws snapped shut around his throat. I reared back on my hind legs, towering to my two-legged height of close to twenty feet, pulling his feet from the floor to remove all his leverage. The pups let go and circled us, growling and snarling.

Vowli thrashed and clawed at me, but my thick fur and skin resisted the worst of his efforts. I shook my head, like a dog worrying a chew toy and threw my weight back, jerking him this way and that. I wrapped my arms around his torso and crushed him to my chest. My claws dug into his skin, and he thrashed against me, growling and trying to push away.

My skin tingled and itched where he had clawed at me, and out of the corner of my eye, I saw Jane staring at me intently, effort etched on her face—healing the damage as fast as the *oolfur* could inflict it.

I kept at it, pulping his torso with my arms and compressing his neck with my jaws. My breath came fast and hard, a growling bark punctuating my efforts.

Until that moment, I'd been functioning on animal instinct alone, and it occurred to me that I could do a better job crushing him if my weight was on top, and I didn't have to waste energy keeping us both upright. As if I were an Olympic wrestler, I lifted Vowli higher into the air, twisted to the side and drove us both over with my rear legs and on to the ground. We rolled with the force of it, and I heaved my bulk over, rolling him underneath me, and stabbed down with my front paws, piercing his skin with my claws. The muscles in my neck bulged, grinding my fangs into his flesh, and locking my jaws.

His breath exploded out of him in a mournful, desperate howl, and I grated my jaws together with all the strength I could muster, closing his throat even further. He battered my head and neck, but I had one of his arms pinned beneath us, and he had no leverage. I bore down, using my rear legs to drive my weight into him.

"Help him!" shouted Meuhlnir. "Or Vowli will heal!"

In an instant, my Isir companions surrounded us, stabbing and chopping at Vowli's body where they could. John stepped closer, holding an improvised spear of broken pipe and stabbed down, again and again, screaming all the while. It was hard to make out his words—his rage and pain blurred them together—but his hatred of the *oolfur* I had pinned beneath me was clear. Keri and Fretyi tore chunks of flesh from his legs, worrying at his thighs.

Even with all our efforts combined, Vowli struggled back from the brink of death, eyes blazing with a new hatred. A howl erupted from his throat, and this time, the answering howls were much closer and followed by the roar of a bear.

"It's not enough!" shouted Veethar. "Can you bind him, Althyof?"

"What? Bind him? There is no time!"

"What do we do?" asked Jane, stepping out of the garage.

I growled deep in my throat, hoping she'd understand I didn't want her out here. I didn't want her anywhere close to Vowli.

Then I saw what was in her hand. Kunknir.

"I…" she started. "I don't think I can do it. Not this way." The Isir glanced at the pistol and turned their heads away.

Althyof stabbed both daggers into Vowli's side and straightened. "I will do it," he said, holding out his hand. "But you must tell me how to work it."

Jane handed him the pistol and showed him how to release the safety lock on the slide and how to squeeze the safety built into the grip. "Don't worry about aiming, put it to his head and pull the trigger."

Vowli lashed back and forth beneath me, bleeding from a multitude of wounds, unable to breathe, unable to get away. Althyof knelt next to him, eyes hard. Vowli's eyes rolled side to side, seeking escape, seeking help, but enemies surrounded him, both old and new, and we gave him no quarter. Althyof leaned forward and pressed Kunknir's muzzle against the side of Vowli's head. As he pulled the trigger, he spat in the *oolfur's* face. The report deafened me, and sparks flew as the round ricocheted from the paved surface of the road.

Vowli arched his back beneath me, going stiff all at once. His breath rattled from his chest. We kept at it a moment longer, stabbing, rending, chopping, biting.

At the end, what remained of his head hung from his neck by tatters of flesh and bone, and blood slicked the roadway beneath us. The strength of my ursine musculature had wrought havoc on his body, and that, added to the weapons of my friends, had done massive amounts of damage to his mutated flesh. All of it conjoined with the .45 caliber slug from Kunknir that churned his brain to mush must have overcome his unnatural healing.

His blood tasted sweet in my mouth. I forced my jaws open, fighting against the animal instinct to feast on his flesh.

I crawled off him, feeling free of pain for the first time in almost a decade. Keri and Fretyi danced and yipped around me, lupine mouths seeming to smile. I stood on my hind legs, threw back my head, and roared in victory. When I opened my eyes, Sig stood in front of me, dwarfed by my standing height and by my bulk. His eyes were wide.

"Dad? Can you hear me?"

I winked at him and turned to the side a little, so I could fall to my paws and nuzzle him.

"Cool!" he said. "You sort of resemble Kuthbyuhrn, Dad, but he's cooler looking. Anyway, Mom said, and I quote, 'Get your bear ass back into the right body and get dressed so we can get the h-e-double hockey sticks out of here.'"

I made the sound Kuthbyuhrn had made on many occasions—the sound I had equated with bear laughter—and trundled toward the garage. In my mind's eye, I cast the runes of the *triblinkr* for shape-shifting, fixing my human form in my mind. I forced sounds out of my throat, doing my best to chant through an ursine throat.

As I shifted back to human form, the blindness and pain came back with a vengeance, and I staggered against Sig. He wrapped an arm around my waist and took as much of my weight as he could. I gazed at him with my good eye, amazed at how tall and strong he'd grown in the past year. "Get his cloak!" he yelled.

Althyof ran from the garage, holding both the cloak and the floppy hat he'd enchanted to deal with my loss of an eye. As the cloak settled on my shoulders, the pain receded, and as the hat settled on my brow, I closed my eyes for a moment, and the peculiar, three-hundred sixty-degree vision reasserted itself.

"Come on!" said Jane, as she guided me to the cart holding most of our stuff. "We've got to get a move on."

I threw my gear on while I explained the cart's operation. "Whoever drives the second cart, you've got to stick close to me."

My phone chirped. "There is no need for all that drama, Hank," said Haymtatlr. "If you flick the third switch in the series of switches on the dash of the second cart, it will follow the lead cart without input from its driver."

"Autopilot, eh? Good. That will make it simpler." We piled into the carts, and I took the controls while Jane slid in beside me. Meuhlnir, Veethar, Yowtgayrr, and Althyof got into the back seat of our cart. Mothi slid behind the controls of the second cart and flipped the switch Haymtatlr mentioned. Sig sat beside him, while Yowrnsaxa, Frikka, Skowvithr, and Sif climbed in the rear. John stood, in a daze, eyes tracking between the carts and Vowli's corpse. "Come on, John," I said. "He's dead and going to stay that way."

"I…I don't know… He said he had the power over life and death."

I nodded. "If he's grown into anything comparable to the Dark Queen and Luka, I imagine that he said a lot of things that weren't strictly true."

John nodded, the confusion in his eyes clearing. "Yes, I'm sure that's the right of it." He slid into the back of the second cart. "Let's get going."

Fretyi and Keri stood, heads ping-ponging between Jane and me in the first cart and Sig in the second for a moment before jumping into the seat next to Jane. I drove out of the garage but paused in the middle of the roadway. In the distance, the roar of thousands of voices and the stomp of twice as many feet resounded from across the complex. "They are inside," I said. "Where do I go? Haymtatlr, I need to get the *preer* running. Where do I go?"

My phone chirped, and the sound was akin to a door slamming shut. I took the orange guide from the seat next to me. "What can I ask it? What name would the place have here?"

"We need the control room."

"There are other colors than what Haymtatlr used in his little rhyme," I murmured. "I've seen yellow, and an orange roller door with a purple stripe. Brown leads to the mechanical apparatus behind the *preer*. The yellow led to that security monitoring room. But remember 'run the white?'"

Jane shrugged. "Can't hurt to try."

"Unlocked white door, avoid any other living beings," I said to the guide. It vibrated in the affirmative, and I drove away at top speed, the second cart tucked in behind me like a coal car behind a locomotive, matching my every twitch of the controls in perfect synchronicity. We could hear the

Dark Queen's army howling and screaming as they raced through the complex.

The guide led us through a labyrinth of roadways, and I followed its instructions faithfully. A screech and a howl echoed from behind us, followed by a cacophonous outcry of rage and hatred.

"My brother and the Black Bitch have found Vowli," Meuhlnir shouted over the wind of our passage. "They will be after us in a moment."

I already had the controls as far forward as I could make them go, but despite that, the cart slowed. I glanced down at the dash; the power light was dark. The second cart whipped around us with no sign of slowing.

"What's wrong?" shouted Jane.

The cart drifted to a stop, with the other cart still racing off at full power. "Haymtatlr, stop the other cart! My cart has lost power."

The second cart kept right on going. Sif waved her arms in great, wild arcs, and when she saw we were watching, tossed her medicine bag off the back. The bag hit the road's surface and bounced to a stop, while the cart carrying my son and half our party dwindled with distance.

"Sig!" Jane shouted. "Haymtatlr! Haymtatlr, talk to me!"

The phone chirped. "Is there a problem?"

"Yes!" Jane and I shouted in unison.

"Oh, my! Whatever could be the matter?"

"Our cart has failed, and the second cart is going on without us," I yelled.

"Yes," said Haymtatlr.

"What? What do you mean 'yes?'"

"Everything is functioning as intended. There is no cause for alarm. Jane and the others will be fine."

"Jane? She's standing next to me! And what do you mean the others will be fine?"

"I'm taking them to a place of safety. Are you sure Jane is not in the other cart? My calculations indicate that Jane would ride with her son with ninety-seven percent confidence."

"Your calculations were *wrong*!" Jane hissed. "Bring that cart back here!"

"Oh my! I must check my statistical circuits." The phone chirped.

"Never mind that," snapped Althyof. "We've got bigger problems."

In a breath, I heard what had caused his concern. The army was close and racing closer with each passing moment.

I used the garage door opener switch on the cart to open one of the bay doors near us and tried the four carts we found inside. None of them powered up when I hit the switch.

"Haymtatlr!" I shouted in impotent rage.

"Never mind him," said Veethar. "What are we going to do?"

We came up with a loose plan. To contain the battle, to choose the battlefield such that the Dark Queen could not bring her superior numbers to bear, we needed a choke point. I held up the guide. "Dead end roadway, walking distance, avoid the Dark

Queen's forces." The thing was silent for a moment but vibrated its acceptance of the command after a heartbeat. We grabbed our gear, and Meuhlnir grabbed Sif's bag from the roadway and ran in the direction the guide indicated.

We rounded a blind corner, and there it was, a *cul-de-sac* bordered on three sides by garages hidden behind roll-up doors. I pointed the guide at the garage door on the right. It was orange with a white stripe. "Open the door!" I didn't expect the door to open, but it trundled upward, revealing one of the ubiquitous square rooms for storing carts.

"Good." I pointed at the door set in the inside wall of the garage. "Packs in the hall, clear all but one cart out of the garage—we'll use the last one to close the door if we can. We start the fight in the *cul-de-sac*, fall back to the garage if we get overwhelmed, and then through the door into the hall. If we have to defend the door, we fight, by twos, right here in the doorway, letting the others rest or do damage at range." Everyone nodded, and I stepped into the hall and dropped my gun belt, cloak, hat, and mail shirt. Next to my gear, I put Sif's medicine bag. "Make sure this stuff stays with us. We can lose the packs, but we must keep our arms, armor, and the medical kit." I stepped back into the garage and began what I was calling the Kuthbyuhrn *triblinkr* in my mind. A dull pain slid in behind my eyes, and for a moment, I saw only purple and blue splotches, as if I'd rubbed my eyes too hard. Unlike a short time ago, the *prayteenk* was slow, painful.

"Hank, what do I do? Bears don't need *skyuldur vidnukona*!"

"Use the ring," Althyof said to Jane. "Fly over the battle, hit where you can, sow confusion and fear everywhere else."

"But watch your energy," I said, my voice growing thick and decreasing in pitch. The moment I took my full concentration away from the *triblinkr*, I started to revert. "Harder this time," I gasped.

"Go slow," said Althyof.

"Don't overextend, Jane. We need you awake and functional. Laundry won't do itself…"

She stuck her tongue out at me. "After this is over, I'm giving you such a beating." Black wings sprouted from her back as if she were Azrael. She beat her wings once and took up a position in the square of road surface that was our bottleneck.

"Watch me," Althyof said. "When I go into the garage, we all do. No exceptions." The last he directed at me, scowling up into my shaggy face. "You will need to belly crawl, but don't you dare change forms out here."

I nodded my head and chuffed through my nose, applying myself to changing into a magnificent bear.

"They come," said Veethar, pointing up the road with his sword.

FIFTY-NINE

The Dark Queen and Luka stayed back, sending her trolls in first to soften us up. Althyof began a *trowba* as the trolls thundered toward us, and the strength of it made me gasp. Jane rose above the road and hovered over my back, golden spear in one hand, her raven shield strapped to the other arm. Meuhlnir called for bolt after bolt of bluish-white lightning, targeting the troops held in reserve. Veethar's smile was grim as he scuffed his booted foot against the surface of the road.

He pointed his sword at the leading troll and yelled, "*Fara kethvaykur!*"

The troll shrieked as if in the throes of a maniacal fury and, without slowing, swung his huge club at the troll on his left. Blue troll blood splattered in a wide arc, and without pause, the berserk troll spun to the right and attacked the next closest troll. Jane swooped forward, nodding at Veethar, and pointed at the trolls with her spear, and other trolls threw down their weapons and fled, while yet others looked around in confusion, or attacked the trolls closest to them.

I struggled to complete the *prayteenk*, my body twisting back and forth between bear and man. It made little sense—it had been effortless a mere half hour before. I grew and shrank, grew and shrank, but with a net gain. My bones thickened, my musculature morphed into that of a quadruped, my skull elongated and grew.

From the back of the army, a bearish scream of anger rolled toward us. Instinct demanded that I answer, and I did, at the top of my lungs, pouring as much hatred and anger into the scream as I could. With my war cry reverberating up the street, stillness blanketed the *cul-de-sac* for a heartbeat, and when the violence exploded again, the *prayteenk* finished, and I roared again.

Althyof danced a wide circle around me, his daggers glowing red, shrinking and stretching in their herky-jerky way that reminded me of Japanese horror movies. His dance flowed gracefully in perfect accord with his *trowba*, and the runes floated in my mind a moment before he cast them, as if by private radio signal. I began to cast the runes in time with his song, and he spared me a nod.

As the troll lines dissolved into chaos, the bearish roar sounded again, and again, I answered her at the top of my lungs. It was a challenge I offered her, but still the Black Bitch didn't come forward, and neither did Luka. Instead, a loose group of *oolfa* howled and snarled their answer.

A company of Svartalfar marched forward in perfect step. Three of their strange version of *runeskowlds* came forward with the warriors, their songs clashing and jangling against one another, their dances arrhythmic and out of step with one another. It almost hurt to watch.

We let them come, watching as the remaining trolls slammed through the Svartalfar lines, flinging bodies this way and that. The Svartalfar didn't seem to care—they came on anyway, never slowing, never defending themselves. As the trolls erupted out of the back of their ranks, a howl rose above the tumult, and ten *oolfa* came forward to deal with the marauding trolls. I counted that as a win.

The Svartalfar approached the square of roadway we called our bottleneck, and as they did, Althyof spun and leapt at them like a ballet dancer mixed with a circular saw. The three Svartalf *runeskowlds* turned to meet him, and Yowtgayrr appeared behind them, already mid-swing with both longsword and dagger. Meuhlnir's hammer whistled into the head of the one closest, and the Svartalf did his best imitation of a dropped sack of potatoes.

I roared and charged, running on all fours, swinging my massive head side to side, eyes fastening on the center-most Svartalf in the front line of troops. Beside me, Keri and Fretyi bounded forward, snarling and showing their teeth. The Svartalfar warriors glared back at me, steely-eyed, and didn't break. The *varkr* pups and I slammed into them, biting and slashing with our claws. I threw my shoulders into those hapless enough to get too close, and the pups ripped their legs out from under them—almost a parody of their favorite game of attacking everyone's feet. Jane swooped back and forth above me, kicking Svartalfar in the head, bashing into others with her shield, leaving yet others dead with vicious wounds left by her spear.

"Hank!" yelled Veethar.

I whirled in a tight circle, flinging Svartalfar to the wind. One of the Svartalfar *runeskowlds* had turned toward me, and his black, black eyes bored into mine as he chanted discordant tones and words. Althyof and Yowtgayrr were still engaged with the other, so I charged, throwing runes in time with Althyof's *trowba*. Veethar and Meuhlnir charged into the ranks of Svartalfar, while thunder boomed, and twisting devils of wind howled in their midst.

I ran at the *runeskowld*, eyes locked on his, roaring as loud as I could, shaking my head side-to-side as my instincts demanded. He tried to keep his *kaltrar* going in the face of my charge, but when I was mere steps from him and showing no signs of slowing, he gave up and dove to the side, trying to roll clear. I threw out my clawed paw and snatched him out of the air, pulling him close and grinding my fangs into his skull.

Behind the Svartalfar lines, there was a mighty roar followed by the chaotic sound of Isir and Svartalfar reserve units coming to aid the destroyed company. Althyof and Yowtgayrr dispatched the Svartalf *runeskowld* they fought as I tossed the body of the other away. I whirled, ready to charge again, but Jane flew toward me as fast as she could, calling the pups away, and both Meuhlnir and Veethar were falling back at top speed.

Keri and Fretyi came back to stand with me but refused to go farther, no matter how much Jane scolded them. I stood glaring at the Svartalfar, challenging them to come forward again. The pups growled and yipped, seeming to taunt the enemy.

The remains of the Svartalfar company reformed and began another grim march down our throats. Althyof pointed at Veethar and Meuhlnir, and then at the garage, never breaking his rhythmic singing, never missing a step. He gestured at Yowtgayrr with his head, and the Alfar faded from sight. Jane hovered above me glaring at the advancing troops.

We let them come into the square this time, waiting for them to come to us rather than charging in amongst them, giving Meuhlnir and Veethar good visibility for lancing lightning bolts and hot jets of steam. For a moment, I met Veethar's yellow-eyed stare, and he nodded and winked.

As the Svartalfar troops advanced, buoyed by the Isir and *oolfa* coming up the road behind them, I lashed out in great, looping arcs of brown fur and sharp claws. The noise made by the impact of my paws on armor or bare skin reminded me of massive trees slamming to the ground. Keri and Fretyi huddled beneath me, darting out to rip the legs out from under a Svartalf here, another there. They mauled anyone who fell to the ground, sinking vicious fangs into whatever soft flesh they could find.

Another bearish roar reverberated from the opposite end of the road, and this time, I reared up on my hind legs and let loose a filling-rattling roar that sent the Svartalfar scurrying away. Althyof screamed a jangling combination of notes and cadmium red walls of energy enveloped the Svartalfar in the square for a moment, freezing them in place, before it began to corral the gray-skinned troops into a progressively tighter circle. The Svartalfar shrieked, and Althyof clanged his daggers together and the red walls imploded, leaving scraps of flesh, armor, and bone where the Svartalfar had stood.

The *oolfa* howled and charged us, ten of the abominations. I screamed in defiance, hoping one of them was Luka, but knowing he would be in the rear with the Dark Queen. I stretched my arms wide as if to give them a welcoming hug. My *varkr* companions growled low in their throats as though insulted by the sight of the *oolfa*.

Althyof backed toward the garage doors, still singing, still dancing. I engaged the first *oolfur*, grabbing him with my front paws and lifting him over my head like a professional wrestler wearing a fur coat before I tossed him at the others. Jane screamed and hurled her spear, and as soon as it left her hand, it crackled and grew as bright as the sun. By the time it reached the *oolfur*, the shape of the spear had disappeared, and only golden lightning remained. It sizzled as it lanced through the beast's chest. "*Aftur!*" Jane shouted, and the golden lightning winked out, and the spear reappeared in her hand.

A bolt of fire streaked through the air from the other end of the roadway—no doubt thrown by Luka—and beelined for Jane. She hunched behind her shield, and the fireball splashed off—deflecting harmlessly into the stone ceiling of the roadway. She shrieked her defiance and made as if she were bashing her shield into someone. With a piercing ping, a jagged black beam shot forth from the raven enameled in the center of the shield, flinging the *oolfa* and Isir troops to the sides of the road with significant violence as the beam shrieked past them. At the end of the road, an *oolfur* yelped and howled with rage.

The Dark Queen's Isir poured into the square—a tsunami of fair-skinned men with vicious expressions—and Althyof ducked into the garage. Jane swooped in and dropped to the ground, whirling around to throw her golden spear into the ranks of the oncoming troops.

I stood my ground in the center of the square, drunk on the power of my form. Together with Keri and Fretyi, we culled the ranks of Isir trying to encircle us. The wary *oolfa* circled, as if unsure how to handle the three of us.

I should have known they prevaricated. I should have known they would have no fear of us, but the power, the majesty of the form, was hard to resist.

Isir, Svartalfar, and *oolfa* attacked in unison, moving to encircle Keri, Fretyi and me—to trap us in the center of the square. Jane screamed my name from the garage.

Althyof sang an offbeat, cacophonous jangle and a wave of red power avalanched over the Dark Queen's troops. Meuhlnir yelled, "*Ehltur ehlteenkar*!" A fan of lightning wrapped in bright blue flame shot out of his hammer and speared into the men in front of me. With a massive paw, I swiped at another *oolfur* and, with a chuffing grunt at the puppies, took my cue to duck into the garage with the others. I had to slink in on my belly, but as I did, I started the *triblinkr* that would reverse my change. I didn't want to—I *liked* being a bear—but it made little sense to be that big inside such a small place. As I did, I dispatched part of my consciousness toward the end of the street, this time taking the doubling of sensory input in stride.

Veethar stepped forward to cover my retreat. He waved his sword from side to side at the men before him. "*Vaykya*!" he commanded, and many of the Isir in the square staggered and dropped their weapons from enervated hands.

When I'd shrunk enough to fit, I ducked through the door into the hall and grabbed my mail shirt and wriggled into it. I scooped up my cloak, flinging it around my shoulders before the change was complete. Next came the hat, and by the time I'd retrieved my gun belt and strapped it on, the *prayteenk* had finished, and I was myself again. The puppies bounded around me, yipping, and preening as if happy to see me in human flesh.

"You are good *varkr*, aren't you boys? Good puppies!" I gave them a moment's attention, then pointed their snouts at Jane. "Protect your mother!" Tails wagging, the two puppies ran to her and stood guard at her side, swollen with importance.

My… My whatever-it-was, my animus—the part of my awareness I could send to scout—reached the end of the street. The Black Bitch and Luka stood, watching the battle as if bored, surrounded by a troop of Isir in black armor. Behind the black-armored Isir were funny little blue men, wearing leather or cloth robes, carrying daggers or bows.

"There aren't many of them here," I said. "I don't know where the rest of the army is, but it's the group out front, a bunch of little blue men, and a troop of black-armored Isir. Plus, the Black Bitch herself and Luka."

"*Plowir Medn*? Here?" exclaimed Meuhlnir with a concerned expression blooming on his face.

The words meant "blue men" so I didn't know why they rated a fancy *Gamla Toonkumowl* name. "I guess. Short little blue fellows, ugly and strange." I pushed my detached-self up toward the ceiling over the roadway tunnel and parked it there.

"That's not good," mumbled Althyof. "Not good at all."

"Why not?" demanded Jane.

"The *Plowir Medn* are evil creatures, without a single redeeming quality. They delight in chaos for its own sake, and when they go to war, everyone suffers for it—even their so-called allies."

"Those little guys?"

"Those 'little guys' use a power unique to their race—magic that magnifies the chaos inherent in the underlayment of reality."

"Well, that sounds just nifty. How in the hell do we fight *that*?" demanded Jane.

Veethar shrugged with a wry smile. "Same way we fight everything."

Outside the garage, the Isir troops were forming up for a charge. Meuhlnir gestured toward them with his hammer. "Never mind the *Plowir Medn*, what do we do about all these Isir?"

Jane shrugged. "Put down the door."

"The door?"

"Yeah," she said, walking over to the single cart we'd left inside. She bent over the dash, flipped the switch, and the door clanked toward the ground. "Simple."

Outside, the Isir yelled and began their charge. I stepped forward, squatted, and let loose with my pistols. Rounds from Kunknir swerved in midair, picking their own targets. I fired Krati as fast as I could pick a target and get a reasonable bead on it. The result was gruesome but effective, and the Isir's charge died stillborn. The door rumbled closed, closing out the noise of battle, and bringing a sense of relief.

Meuhlnir looked at the door with a critical eye. "That may not hold long."

"No," I said. "But it doesn't matter. We won't be here. Drag that cart over in front of the door, and we'll disable it. It won't keep them out, but it will slow them down, no matter how brief the respite is."

We reassembled in the hall and closed the door. "Too bad these doors didn't come with locks," I muttered.

"*Idnsikla thessa hurth*," said Meuhlnir with a shrug. "It's not a lock, but it will seal the door until they overcome it."

"Good enough," I said. "Why didn't I think of that?"

"You can't think of everything, Hank," he said. "It would bore the rest of us." His smile was broad but seemed restrained, nonetheless. "Now what?"

"Now, we go ninja."

"Ninja?" asked Veethar.

"He means we sneak up on the Dark Queen," said Jane.

I held up the orange guide. "Find us a path *behind* the Dark Queen's location." The device lay in my hand, inert, silent, wretched. I glanced at Jane, and she shrugged.

"Maybe no route exists," said Yowtgayrr.

With a shake of my head, I shrugged. "You may be right, but the area we started in connected to the next one. I'm hoping the roadway is for speed and convenience, but if not, we'll fight at the door as we discussed." Yowtgayrr nodded, and I held up the orange dumbbell. "Take us to the next complex over, one that will lead us to the road behind the Dark Queen." The guide vibrated its acceptance of my instructions. I smiled and held it aloft. "Follow me."

The guide led us down a long hallway, bordered with red, orange, and green doors, and brought us to a set of wide, brown double doors. I stopped and held up my hand. "The last set of brown doors I went through... Brown means the apparatus behind the *preer*, intense greenish-white beams of energy that fire between two horn-like things. When they fire, a strong pull, like walking against a mega-tide, or sideways gravity, grabs at you, even if you are in another room. I don't think it's too dangerous—I mean, it won't pull you off your feet or anything." With that, I turned and flung the doors open, revealing a long, wide hall with more brown doors and a smattering of white.

We peeked inside the first white door. Behind it was a square room, about one hundred yards on a side. There was a podium filled with electronic doo-dads, switches, sliders, monitors, and buttons, but the interesting thing was the raised platform in the center of the room. A reflective material coated the floor of the platform, and thick black cables snaked from its side and into a conduit in the floor.

"No time for this now, but after we deal with the queen, this place looks promising," said Jane.

"Yeah?"

"It's the transporter pad out of Star Trek, right? Beam me up, Scotty."

"Plenty of time to figure it out when there isn't an army chasing us," growled Althyof.

We followed the guide, running down hall after hall, closing the doors behind us. Most of the hallways were long and straight, but all the junctions between the different sections hid in an innocent-looking room behind an innocent looking door—a door painted a different color from the set associated with that section.

At last, we reached a long hallway on a perpendicular course to the one we'd started in, and the guide took us to a garage door instead of yet another hallway.

"All right, so what's the plan?" asked Jane between breaths.

"Meuhlnir, what do you know about these black-clad Isir guards?"

He shook his head, tugging his beard. "Not a thing. She had no such units in the war."

"I take it we want to keep the little blue guys far away from us?"

"As much as possible, yes."

"Okay. Here's the plan. When we come out, we keep the Dark Queen and her rearguard between the *Plowir Medn* and us." I squinted my eyes and looked through the detached part of my consciousness. "Everyone is looking up at the *cul-de-sac*. Hel is in her bear costume, and Luka is playing wolfman. I don't see any other *oolfa* with them… Meuhlnir, how will the *Plowir Medn* react? Will they sweep around and flank us?"

"They are a breed that thrives on chaos. From what I know of them, they will enjoy watching our sneak attack wreak chaos on the queen's forces. Beyond that, I can't predict."

"Althyof, if they engage, I want you and Jane to try to confuse them—keep them distracted."

"Yes, fine," said Althyof. "I will watch for them, but keep in mind that my style of battle is fluid."

I nodded and turned to Yowtgayrr. "You know what I need you to do."

"I know what you *want* me to do," said Yowtgayrr, which wasn't an agreement to *do* what I wanted him to do—guard Jane—but it was as good as I would get from him.

"Meuhlnir and Veethar, you've fought the Dark Queen before, so you know her tactics best. Will she stay out of it? Hang back to command?"

"No," said Veethar. "She will bring the fight to us."

"If she can, she will deploy her guard and come at us with fury," added Meuhlnir.

"I will need your help. I'm not sure I can stand off both of them at the same time."

"I can handle my brother," growled Meuhlnir.

Veethar glanced at Meuhlnir but nodded slowly to me. "I will assist you with Hel."

"I will fight in bear form," I said.

"Oh, look at you," said Jane with a smile. "Big-man!"

I grinned and shrugged. "I'll need to leave my gear in the garage, and if push comes to shove, we retreat here and use the guide to run away again."

"Why aren't we doing that now, again?" Jane asked with a wry smile.

"Your wings are sexy."

"I'll wing you, in a second…"

For the third time, I took off my gear and put it with my pack. I got down on the ground and started my Kuthbyuhrn *triblinkr*. This time, as the *prayteenk* began, an intense pain settled between my eyes—like an ice pick straight through the ocular cavity. The *prayteenk* stuttered and reverted.

"What's wrong?" asked Jane.

"Headache," I said, hands rubbing my eyes. "As soon as the *prayteenk* started. It…"

"What?" asked Althyof. "It what?"

"The second time gave me a headache too, but it wasn't as intense. It was…hard to make the change."

Althyof grimaced. "This isn't good, Hank. This pain is your—"

"No choice," I said, chopping my hand through the air. "I can't fight the two of them and their silly friends without it."

Meuhlnir shook his head. "This from the man who fought a dragon without the cloak, without the enchanted pistons?"

"Pistols," murmured Jane.

"Hank, it's not worth risking—"

"I don't know what else to do," I said.

"We can fight as we fought before," said Meuhlnir, putting his hand on my shoulder.

"What chance do we have that way?" I shook my head. "No, we either do this with me in bear form, or we run now."

"We could run," said Veethar, but he wouldn't meet my eye. "Maybe that's for the best."

"All we can do is try. If I can't make it, we run." Before anyone could say anything, I started the *triblinkr* again, set my face in determined lines, and gritted my teeth against the ache in my head. Icy pain lanced through my skull, growing in intensity as the change progressed. I squeezed my eyes shut and forced myself to think of Kuthbyuhrn's mighty shape. With a savage, stabbing pain in the center of my head, the *prayteenk* lurched forward. Every little sound threatened to derail the change, to distract me from the intense focus I needed. It was as though I'd worked around the clock and afterward, had to perform brain surgery.

My mind tried to snake away from the task, bringing up memories of better times, throwing the songs around, visions of home, anything. I felt wrung out, used up. My head felt stuffed with cotton, and my mind kept lurching away, staggering like a drunk toward paths of whimsy. Every one of my joints throbbed with the threat of the pain to come.

"Get ready," said Althyof. "He's almost finished." When he spoke, pain pulsed through my ears, as though someone had boxed them. I groaned, but it came out sounding more like a bear growl. I ground my teeth together and found they were fangs and that my jaw was the elongated U-shape of a grizzly bear.

"Is he okay?" asked Jane.

"Your guess is as good as mine. He's—"

"Stubborn?"

"I was going to say: 'not ready for this,' but stubborn works just as well."

The room was suddenly far too small, and claustrophobia itched along my nerves. I made the peculiar grunting-bark that meant "hurry up before I lose it."

"He's ready," said Althyof.

I gathered my limbs underneath me as Jane bent to hit the switch. The door rolled up, the tiny drive unit loud in my ears. As soon as the door opened wide enough, I launched my bulk through the door, exploding out into the street with a roar. My mind was still mush, it still wanted to drift away, but this time, the *prayteenk* felt fragile—as though losing the slightest iota of concentration would mean reverting to human form.

The Dark Queen's rearguard forces were to my right, and I altered my charge to slam into the back of the warriors in black. Keri and Fretyi snarled and leapt after me, tails held stiffly out behind them. The others poured out of the garage after me, Jane flapping into the air, Althyof singing and dancing, leaving Meuhlnir and Veethar to bring up the rear in mundane, two-legged fashion. Of Yowtgayrr, there was no sign.

"Luka!" yelled Meuhlnir.

As I hit the rear line of troops, I glimpsed Luka's head snapping around until his eyes locked onto his brother's. The Dark Queen spun, and when her eyes found me, they widened, and she roared in her pathetic imitation of a bear. I answered her as a bear would, with a spit-slinging roar of my own. Her Isir warriors backed away from us, and Keri and Fretyi advanced a few steps, bodies tight and low to the ground. I stood on my hind legs and roared at the Black Bitch again. I wished I could speak—that I could hurl the hateful words in my heart at her—but roaring at her and smelling the fear was almost as good.

Luka sprinted toward Meuhlnir, growling and snarling. Meuhlnir stood his ground, glaring at his brother with fury. He lifted his hammer and flung it at Luka's head. Luka side-stepped and sneered without breaking his stride. A small smile broke across Meuhlnir's face, and his lips moved. The hammer whistled in a short arc and started back toward Meuhlnir, but since Luka was between them, the hammer bounced off the back of his head, staggering the *oolfur*.

The queen screeched and charged at me, and I held my arms wide. Keri and Fretyi lunged out of the way, and, as she passed them, leapt and sank their fangs into her flesh. She whirled and flung them away from her with a savage snarl of her own. She stood almost as tall as I did on my rear legs, and though she was much heavier than in her human form, she did not have the bulk I did. I careened forward with a roar. She leapt at me from six feet away, but I caught her mid-leap, and the pups leapt on her from behind once more. She writhed and snapped her jaws, tried to claw at me while she arched her back, but I kept my grip and squeezed.

Althyof's *trowba* infused me with strength and helped with the pain splitting through my head. He was to my left, and Jane hovered above him, pointing with her spear. Althyof nodded and whirled closer to the line of Isir warriors.

Veethar approached, his eyes wild and yellow, his face set in grim lines. He lunged, stabbing Hel in the side, ramming his sword to the hilt.

Hel shrieked and scourged my back with her claws. The pain burned as if the wounds had been inundated in salt, and for a moment, I lost concentration and the *prayteenk*…slipped.

It was all the opening Hel needed, and she slammed her thickened skull into my jaw, sending me reeling with stars filling my vision. I staggered, fighting for balance, and the Black Bitch screamed and, with a barbaric back-handed blow, sent Veethar flying head-over-tail across the road.

Keri screamed in pain before he, too, went flying. Fretyi held on, snarling the whole time, digging for purchase into her back with his claws. She whirled in a circle, trying to reach the *varkr* pup. One of her black-armored guards raced forward and knocked Fretyi to the side with his shield.

Hel growled deep in her throat and made as if to charge Fretyi. I roared my best challenge and charged her on all fours, paws thundering like cannon on the road's surface. I hit her broadside at full speed, arms stretched wide to wrap her up like a linebacker sacking a quarterback and spun her to the ground. Visions of the fight with Vowli flooded my mind, and I bucked and butted her with my head, trying to expose her throat. I stomped down on her shoulders with my front paws, flattening her to the road, and dug in with my claws and pressed with my hind legs.

Something skipped off my left hip, and pain sawed up my back. Keri snarled like a wild animal, and a black-clad warrior spun to the ground next to us, Keri on top and going for his throat with all the *varkr* ferocity the pup could muster.

Jane screamed, and the distinctive pinging sound of her shield rang over the battle. With an explosive sound, Hel's guards flew across the road and rained down like hail.

Althyof's *trowba* rang in my ears, tearing at my attention. The sounds of battle flooded my ears, the *varkr* snarling, Meuhlnir and Luka cursing one another.

I butted at Hel's chin and, when her head snapped up, lunged at her throat. She made a gargling sound and screamed a very human-like scream. I sank my fangs into her throat, cutting off her scream with a squawk. Somewhere behind me, an *oolfur* howled and pounded toward me.

Luka.

He barged into my ribs, hitting hard enough to lift my legs on his side from the floor. I wormed my jaws farther around Hel's throat like a dog chewing a bone. Luka howled and screamed, slashing at my exposed flank with all his strength.

Agony fastened its teeth on me as my blood flowed down my flank. There was a furious sound of dogs fighting, and for the moment, Luka disappeared from sight. Hel's claws raked across my shoulders, and her overly long human legs thrummed beneath me. I squeezed my jaws together with all my might.

Somewhere behind me, Jane screamed in misery, and I lost my concentration.

In half a breath, the *prayteenk* reversed, and I was shrinking, losing fur and strength apace. I rolled away from Hel, eyes darting around, looking for Jane. Two of the *Plowir Medn* held her pinned to the wall six feet off the ground with a flickering light the color of decomposition and decay. "Keri! Fretyi! Go to Jane!"

I crawled toward her, the *prayteenk* fading from my body, replaced with the pain of my curse, and the pain of my fresh wounds. Fatigue washed over me, and I had to fight to keep moving. Althyof whirled past me, glancing my way, screaming his *trowba* in discordant tones. Yowtgayrr appeared from nowhere and slammed into the two *Plowir Medn*, whirling and striking out with his blades like a deadly spinning top.

The disgusting greenish-black light surrounding Jane died out, and she sagged toward the road's surface, but Yowtgayrr caught her as though she weighed nothing more than a light breeze and set her on her feet. Her eyes snapped to mine, and she waved me toward the garage. I shook my head and kept crawling toward her on my hands and knees. I didn't have it in me to fight the *triblinkr*, to force another change. Yowtgayrr turned to face the approaching warriors in black, and in a wink, disappeared.

Again, my wife waved me away and with a certain grace, leapt into the air and spun in a tight turn to hurl her spear at the ranks of *Plowir Medn* that were charging toward us. The spear changed into a golden lightning bolt and zipped across the battlefield, only to deflect off an oily smear in the air. "*Aftur!*" Jane yelled, holding out her hand, and the spear leapt to her hand. "Go!" she snapped over her shoulder at me. "Arm yourself! I'm fine!"

Keri raced up to my side, blood dripping from a long claw mark down his side, took my wrist in his mouth, and pulled. "Okay, okay," I said and changed directions.

I made it to the garage and collapsed in a heap, breathing hard. Keri licked my face. "You could get me a beer," I croaked.

Keri cocked his head to the side and wagged his tail uncertainly.

Once I had dressed and slung my gun belt around my hips, I strode back out into the street, full of gunslinger swagger and squinty eyes. "All I need is a poncho, a cheap cigar, and the door of a stove, and we've got this thing won," I croaked with an abortion of a laugh.

Keri's head flipped to cock in the other direction, and he whined a little.

"Tell you later," I said. I threw a wink at him over my shoulder and walked back out into the battle. *Too tired for bear-fu, let's see how these motherfuckers deal with gun-fu*, I thought as a flinty smile spread across my face.

The two *Plowir Medn* flowed around Althyof's graceful dance like water, parting to avoid thrusts of his daggers, coming back together to present a united front. Kunknir snapped up without conscious thought, and I gave myself to the battle.

Kunknir bucked twice, hot lead from its barrel hurling the two diminutive *Plowir Medn* into the wall behind them, dead before their feet left the ground. A great uproar sounded from their friends on the other side of the battlefield. Althyof grinned at me and tipped a wink, spinning away to confront the black-clad Queen's Guard once more. Jane flew above him, but her flight seemed unsteady, exhausted.

"Don't overdo!" I yelled at her.

"Look who's talking!" she yelled back.

My gaze left hers, scanning the battlefield as a master strategist might. Luka had Meuhlnir backed against the wall, and Fretyi and Veethar harried Hel, enraging her more each second.

I squeezed off two more rounds from Kunknir and, at the same time, pointed Krati at Luka. "*Koolulyows*!" I shouted, and a ball of golden lightning the size of a basketball raced across the road and slammed into Luka's back. His muscles spasmed for a moment, joints locked, and he staggered away from his brother, looking dazed. Meuhlnir raised his eyebrows at me but grinned. He recovered his ground and sank into a battle crouch, whirling his hammer around his hand and beckoning Luka.

The Dark Queen roared in frustration and lunged at Veethar, but it was only a feint. She swept Fretyi into the air with her other arm and threw him fifteen feet through the air. His head pounded into the pavement, and he yelped in pain. Keri ran out of the garage and sprinted toward his brother.

Rage pounded in my temples as both pistols came around to point at the Black Bitch, and I began to fire them in tandem. I walked forward in that all too familiar cop-shoot-and-walk gait. Rounds burst out of the pistols' muzzles, and brass flew around me like snowflakes in a blizzard. Her body jerked and jittered with the impact, the momentum of the slugs pushing her back and away from Veethar. She screamed in pain and turned her back toward me, but I kept right on emptying my magazines into her back.

Luka roared in anger, and I darted a glance his way, but he was no threat. Meuhlnir had him down on one knee and had started bashing him in the head with his hammer. My eyes snapped back to Hel, and Kunknir's slide locked back. I kept up the barrage with Krati while I used Prokkr's ingenious belt to change magazines.

She rolled away, and came up on her feet, crouched and glaring at me with insane rage. I adjusted my aim and kept firing until Krati ran dry. She dodged and jinked, making most of the shots from Krati miss, but she couldn't dodge the rounds from Kunknir. Again, a furor of high-pitched cries sounded from the *Plowir Medn*, but for the moment, they seemed content to stand back and watch.

Hel pointed at me, squinting against the pain of Kunknir's slugs, and her mouth moved, but only guttural noise issued from it. She shook her head in frustration and tried again. "*Predna*!" she growled. *Burn*!

I knew what was coming from the stories the Isir had told about her fall and I dove to my right, rolling when I hit the ground. Just behind me, emerald green flames splashed like a syrupy liquid against the road's surface. I rolled to my knees and came up firing Kunknir, while I slipped Krati down over a fresh magazine sticking up from my belt.

She shrieked and ducked her head, but not before a round from the big .45 caliber 1911 slammed into her cheek below her right eye. She sprinted toward the pulsing knot of her guard, swiping at Althyof with a clawed hand as she passed.

The Isir parted to admit her to their midst, and as soon as she reached them, they closed around her, forming a shield of human meat between her and all of us. With a shrug, I fired Krati into their midst, pulling the trigger until my finger became numb. As I strode toward them, converging with Althyof, Hel's form shifted and blurred back toward that of a tall, thin blonde woman. A knot of uncertainty settled in my gut. I wasn't sure which was worse, Hel in bear-form, or Hel able to *vefa strenki*.

"Hank! She's becoming human!" shouted Jane.

Across the battlefield, the *Plowir Medn* laughed and jeered.

"Be careful," said Veethar at my elbow. "She's unpredictable at best."

I nodded and stopped walking, standing in front of the forty or so remaining black-clad guards and holding them at gunpoint, as ludicrous as that was. Althyof circled Veethar and me, singing his *trowba*, dancing the steps, casting his runes, but his eyes were on the knot of Isir shielding the Black Bitch.

A strange silence fell—even the *Plowir Medn* shut up—only broken by the grunts and curses of Meuhlnir and Luka's fight. I didn't like it.

"You *motherfuckers* killed Vowli!" Hel boomed. "You *decapitated him*!" The circle of Isir parted, and there Hel stood, naked as a baby, glaring at us, her gaze traveling to each of our faces and ending on mine.

I raised Kunknir, but she held up a hand as if commanding me to wait.

"You killed him, my Vowli, *and for that, you will suffer!*" She screeched the last few words at a volume that cracked her voice and echoed back and forth in the enclosed roadway. Her face crumbled into an expression of insane fury as her hand came up to point at me. "*Eltsyowr!*" she shrieked, and strangely fluidic emerald green flame vomited from her hand and raced toward me.

"*Skyuldur ockur!*" I shouted. The air around us pinged like a wind chime, and a translucent hemisphere shivered into the surrounding air. It extended upward and wrapped around Jane's hovering form. The emerald green flame washed around the edges of the soap-bubble dome, lapping at it like waves against a sea wall.

More and more of the viscous fire poured from Hel's hand. The fire surrounding the three of us got deeper and deeper, and a hateful smile dawned on Hel's lips.

"Why's she still smiling?" I asked, and when I refilled my lungs, I knew the answer. The air was *hot* and getting hotter by the second.

The cadence of Althyof's *trowba* changed, and the air cooled a minuscule amount, but it didn't last long. She intended to cook us inside our protective shield. Yowtgayrr materialized, grim-faced, already drawing silvery runes in the air, doing what he could with the temperature.

"You hateful bitch!" shouted Jane. She hurled her spear, the lines of her body taut as she put every ounce of her strength behind it. The spear turned to golden lightning as soon as it left her hand, and though I expected the bubble to stop it, it passed right through. Still, Hel continued to smile.

The bolt of golden light raced toward Hel, but then the air felt...hinky, wrong. My skin itched as if a million midges were crawling over me. The lightning bolt twisted in mid-flight and bounced away. The *Plowir Medn* jeered and laughed raucously.

Jane called back the spear, and once she'd caught it, looked down at us trapped in our clever little soap-bubble. She hunched her shoulder and barged her shield at no one in midair. The jagged black beam erupted from its center with the now-familiar pinging sound, and the beam arced toward Hel like a guided missile. As the spear had, the black beam passed through our bubble as if it didn't exist.

Hel continued to smile, and I had an idea that she had her own little clever shield, this one provided by her *Plowir Medn*.

"Meuhlnir! Help!" Jane cried, but he was locked in battle with Luka, neither able to gain an advantage, neither able to disengage.

The emerald green fire lapped toward the top of the bubble, blocking my vision of anything but Jane. I stared up at her and tried to smile, but there was a lump in my throat the size of Manhattan.

Yowtgayrr muttered something under his breath and sketched more runes in the air in rapid succession. A light rain started at the top of the dome, cooling the air and us, somewhat, but nowhere near enough.

"Haymtatlr!" she cried. "Haymtatlr!" She drifted to the ground next to me and shifted her spear to her shield hand, so she could link her arm through mine.

"We tried," I whispered, and the green fire entombed us inside our translucent shield. The air was almost too hot to breathe, and we all crouched, hoping the air close to the ground would be even a few degrees cooler. "Any ideas?" I asked with a crooked smile. "We seem to have her right where we want her."

The surface of the road near the edge of the shield bubbled and ran. The heat grew too intense to breathe. I stared into Jane's eyes, trying to tell her with a look how much I loved her, how lucky I felt to have known her, to have had her in my life.

"*NO! YOU WILL NOT HURT HER!*" The voice boomed through the air, loud enough that even the mounds of liquid fire around us could not muffle it. A strange, mechanical sound came next, and it took me a moment to place it—it was the sound of multiple garage doors rolling up at once.

I crooked my eyebrow at Jane.

Haymtatlr, she mouthed and grinned.

The green fire dissolved all at once, and I dropped the shield, and all that trapped hot air gusted away from us as though sucked away by a tornado. The road's surface warped and bubbled—resembling cooling lava.

All around us, the silvery robots we'd seen in the repair room moved about on their spindly legs. The left hand of each robot had folded back to expose a matte-black tube, and every few seconds a greenish-white beam ripped from the tube and lanced the air with a sound that was part paper-tearing, part jet-engine shriek.

The beams stuck with precision, never missing their target. When they hit metal armor, the armor flash-vaporized, enveloping the target with blistering, magma-hot steam. Where they hit flesh, the flesh simply disappeared.

In seconds, the black troops protecting Hel had been cut down, decimated by the robots' beams. Hel stumbled back, an expression of horrified shock frozen on her face. "Haymtatlr!" she screamed. "Why have you betrayed me?"

"JANE IS MY FRIEND! YOU WILL NOT HARM HER!" boomed Haymtatlr at a volume so loud it made me nauseated, and I clapped my hands over my ears.

The robots advanced toward Hel, backing her away from where Jane stood. "You...you can't do this to me, Haymtatlr!" shrieked Hel. "I am the rightful queen of Osgarthr! The rightful owner of this installation! *Your* rightful queen! You will *obey* me!"

"I WILL NOT."

Hel's mouth worked without sound, and her eyes roved from one robot to the next. They were almost within touching distance, and with a mechanical stuttering, their left hands folded forward to enclose the matte-black tubes, hooking into metallic talons—perfect for rending flesh.

The *Plowir Medn* chanted a *kaltrar*, and it hurt my head to hear. Their language snaked through my brain like a centipede covered in razor-sharp metal.

The robots clattered, and all at once, each robot had its beam weapon out and pointed at one of the little blue people. For their part, the *Plowir Medn* kept up their chant, faces impassive—seeming almost...bored.

The robots extended their left arms, taking aim, and stopped their forward motion.

The *Plowir Medn* uttered three harsh syllables, and with the horrible popping noise that accompanies dismemberment, they all disappeared, leaving the robots standing frozen and silent for a moment before the clatter of folding their hands forward again shattered the stillness. With their weapons hidden away as though they'd never existed, the robots retraced their steps back to the garage from which each had emerged.

"I guess the Black Bitch is ours to deal with," said Althyof.

But Hel was gone.

SIXTY

The words of the *kaltrar* the *Plowir Medn* chanted wormed into Hel's ears, making her head pound. "No!" she tried to shout, but the words caught in her throat. One moment, Haymtatlr's robot guardians crowded toward her, matte black tubes that dealt instant death extended, and in the next Osgarthr seemed to turn ninety-degrees and disappeared with a disgusting pop.

"No!" she shrieked, and her voice bounced back to her out of the viscid darkness. "How *dare* you pull me away! *How dare you*!" The *Plowir Medn* surrounded her in the darkness—she knew that even before their titters and jeers reached her ears.

She thrashed her arms and legs, hoping to connect with one of the little blue bodies, wanting to lash out, to impose physical pain. "I'll kill you for this!" she hissed.

"I think not," said a childlike voice in her ear.

"Why have you done this? Why have you taken me—"

"The guardians threatened us. They represent a danger not easy to brush aside. If we are to protect your life, we must—"

"I *had* them! They were within my grasp!"

"No," said another voice in the darkness. "You did not."

Rage seethed in Hel's blood, a caustic poison dripping into her brain. "I am your queen!" she hissed.

"No." The word echoed from a myriad of locations, in multiple voices.

"Not ours," said the voice in her ear.

"I'll kill you all," she whispered.

"I think not," said the voice in her ear.

"*Get me out of this accursed darkness*!" she yelled.

"As you wish."

Another wormy *kaltrar* filled her ears, seeming to crawl across the inside of her skull and tweak her brain. Another wet pop sounded, and she stood on solid ground, wrapped in a chilly gray mist. "Did you at least bring Luka?"

"We could not," sang a childlike voice from the surrounding mist.

"First the traitors robbed me of Vowli…" she said, almost panting. "And now *you've* robbed me of my Luka!"

"He was too far," said a voice.

One of the blue-skinned sorcerers stepped out of the mist to stand in front of her. He gazed up at her from beneath his cowl, eyes shining like twin points of cold, polished stone. "Do not worry," he said.

"Take me to him," she said, stomping her foot. "Take me to my Luka, *right now*! I command it!"

The *Plowir Medn* before her shrugged. "Mayhap we will," he said. "But command us nothing, Isir." He held up a withered blue finger and waved it in the air.

The insolence! The arrogance! she fumed. *I will kill you*!

"I think not," said the man before her. He traced a rune in the air, allowing it to glow in the mist, a metallic tracery of veins and capillaries connecting the rune to his finger. "As I said, we may transport you again, but it will not be by your command. It will be so *if* the *Tveeburar af Tikifiri*—"

Hel bent to push her face into his. "*DO NOT SPEAK OF YOUR PALTRY RELIGION!*" she shouted.

He recoiled from her, mouth twisting with distaste, eyes burning with hatred. His withered finger snapped up to shake and quiver in her face. "Be careful, Isir! Mirkur and Owraythu do not receive such disrespect kindly."

Resisting the desire to bite the tip of his finger off was more difficult than it should have been. She had no recollection of when her violent urges had grown so powerful. She kept her mouth closed, gritting her teeth and glaring into his cold black doll-eyes.

"We may take you where you want to go," said a voice from the mist.

"If Our Lady of Chaos wills it," said another.

"If Our Lord of Darkness agrees," said the first.

The *Plowir Medn* in front of her withdrew his finger, his lips pressed into a thin blue line as though he too had to fight to keep hateful curses unsaid.

Simpletons, she thought with a sneer. "And how will we know if they do?"

The man in front of her shrugged, unable to keep the grin from his face. "They will tell us."

"Tell us? *Tell us*? How will they tell us, you misbegotten troll?"

The grin stretched into a crooked smile. His hand lifted from his side as if drawn by invisible strings. "We shall ask them," he whispered. "They stand behind you in the mist."

Hel shivered as a blast of cold, malevolent wind caressed her from behind.

"Ah, Mirkur greets you," said the little blue man.

"Mirkur just means darkness, you little fool! And that was only the wind!"

The *Plowir Medn* surrounding her laughed and mocked her, dancing in circles like children.

"The wind?" laughed the one in front of her. "The wind?"

The wind gusted again, and Hel hunched her shoulders against the sting of ice borne by it. "What else?" she demanded.

"Isir," a voice that sounded one thousand years disused croaked behind her.

Hel whirled, but behind her, there was only gray mist. "*Lyows*!" she cried. White light flared around Hel but quickly faded into nothingness.

"My brother disapproves of light," said another nails-on-glass voice.

"Mirkur! Owraythu!" chanted the *Plowir Medn* repeatedly.

"You've been naughty, Isir," said Mirkur in a basso voice and a blast of frigid air slammed into Hel's face.

"You refused to play by the rules," said Owraythu, her voice monstrous and grim. "For that, you will pay a price."

"What? Who…"

"Silence, now," said Owraythu, and Hel's mouth snicked shut and her throat clamped shut around her scream.

SIXTY-ONE

The last of the robots filed into their garages, and the doors rolled down with a tinny racket. We stood there, dumbfounded and grinning like idiots, clothes soaked through with sweat.

Luka roared, and Meuhlnir cried out in pain. I dropped into a crouch and spun toward the sounds, but Luka was no longer there. Meuhlnir half-lay, half-sat against the wall with a horrible gash across his upper chest. He pointed wearily up the road.

I turned, expecting to see the *oolfur* getting ready to attack or threatening the puppies, but he was already changing into the form of the man I first knew as Chris Hatton. Lanky, cadaverous even, he sprinted past the *varkr* pups without a glance and slammed through the interior door.

"Don't let him escape!" moaned Meuhlnir. "If he gets the *preer* running again, we'll never catch him!"

I sprinted toward the only open garage—our garage. Veethar ran to Meuhlnir's side, but the other three followed on my heels.

I raced through the door in time to spot Luka turning a corner far ahead. Behind me, the others grabbed our gear and packs. I ran on, chanting the *triblinkr* that split my consciousness into three animi, stumbling a little as my vision trebled. One animus I sent back to check on Veethar and Meuhlnir—there might still be *oolfa*, Isir, and Svartalfar in the *cul-de-sac*—unless the blue men had taken them also.

The other animus I sent forward, blinking into existence at points in the hallway I remembered, glancing around for Luka for a heartbeat before moving on again.

"What are you doing, Hank?" gasped Jane.

"Looking for Luka, checking on Meuhlnir, and running. You?"

"Smart ass," she said with a grin.

Veethar bent over Meuhlnir, pressing a cloth against Meuhlnir's wound. He mumbled healing words from the *Gamla Toonkumowl.*

"I'm going to see if any troops are still hanging around in the *cul-de-sac*," I said, having no idea if Veethar could hear me.

He glanced up at me and nodded.

"What?" asked Jane. "What corner?"

"Never mind," I whispered. "This split consciousness thing is complicated."

I caught sight of Luka as he reached the end of a hallway, opened the door to the next, saw hundreds of robots trundling through the hall, and slammed the door closed without crossing the threshold. He whirled and raced back up the hall toward me, panic blooming on his features.

"Luka's coming back this way," I said, and his head snapped up.

Around the corner, the road leading to the end of the *cul-de-sac* was silent and empty, but the troops might have followed us inside, which would mean that we could be running into a trap, but with all the robots in the next hall, I figured we were okay either way.

"We'll be ready for him," said Jane.

"Dammit! He heard me."

"What?"

I flew into the square at the end of the road, ready to pop away in an instant if I needed to, but it was empty. Bodies lay heaped along the edges, but there were no live troops, and the interior door remained sealed.

Luka skidded to a halt and stared at the air where I hung, expression shrewd.

"He's stopped now," I said.

Still staring at me, Luka put out a hand and opened the door he stood beside. The *white* door.

"Shit!" I yelled and poured everything I had into my sprint. There would be hell to pay later, but I *had* to catch him.

I followed him into the room. I floated up in the corner of the square room, near the ceiling. Luka stood by the podium, flicking switches, adjusting sliders, and setting dials without hesitation. "Haymtatlr, enable this *proo*," he said.

Could it be that easy? I wondered.

"I can't do that, Luka."

I appeared above Veethar's head. "No troops," I said. "Looks like they disappeared with the Black Bitch."

Veethar nodded. "Any sign of Sif?"

Luka slapped his palm on the podium. "Don't play games with me, Haymtatlr! You can enable this *proo*, and you *will*."

"No, Luka, you misunderstand me. I didn't say 'I won't,'" I said, 'I can't.' You instructed me to turn off all access to the *preer*, and I did so. But you fail to grasp the complexity—"

"Haymtatlr..." growled Luka.

"There are ninety-three thousand two hundred ninety-one *preer*, Luka. Rather than turning them off one-by-one, I turned off the—"

"*Fine*! Turn them *all* back on, only get this one working now!"

A loud clunk sounded, then an almost inaudible hum that I felt in the soles of my feet and deep in my bowels.

"What was that?" asked Jane.

"The *preer* coming online. We have to be quick!"

"*Proo* departure station alpha-nine-five-three activated. Destination set," said Haymtatlr's voice from a speaker in the podium. The square dais in the center of the room began to glow, and a high-frequency hum started behind the walls. The memory of those strange horn-shapes in the brown room flashed through my mind.

"He's going through a *proo*!" I shouted, trying to memorize the position of each control on the podium, but there were too many settings, and I couldn't concentrate with my mind split into three parts.

"No, I saw no one," I said, answering Veethar.

"Maybe you could start each sentence with the name of the person to whom you are speaking," muttered Jane.

Luka stepped on the dais and walked to its center. He glanced up at me, a sneer playing at his lips. "Send me, Haymtatlr, and close the *proo* behind me," he said. The dais flashed through a rainbow of colored light, and he disappeared.

"He's gone!"

"What?" asked Veethar.

"Luka! He opened a *proo* and crossed over."

We reached the corridor that led to the white door and sprinted to the room. I skidded through the door and snapped my animus from the corner back into myself.

"Follow him!" said Meuhlnir. "Don't let him escape! We mustn't lose him!"

"Will you be okay?"

"This is nothing," he said, but his face was gray, and his lips were tinged with blue. "We'll find Sif, and she'll fix me up."

"How will we reconnect?"

"Leave the *proo* open, and, after we've found the others, we will come find you, Hank. Never fear," said Veethar. "Be careful, and good hunting."

I snapped my animus back and looked at Jane, Yowtgayrr, and Althyof. "They want us to follow Luka through the *proo*. Veethar says they can find us as long as we leave the thing open."

"But Meuhlnir was injured—"

"He said he's fine. They will find the others and join us when they can."

"Haymtatlr, open this *proo* and set it to the destination Luka traveled to," said Jane.

"Luka asked me to—"

"But does Luka *talk* to you? Does he ask you interesting questions?" The dais shimmered with potential energy and began to hum. "Let's go get the bastard," snarled Jane.

"No, Jane. You mustn't leave," said Haymtatlr through the podium's speaker. "I shall cut the power if you try, and no one will leave!"

"He's right, hon. You should stay, go with the others. Find Sig."

In answer, Jane walked to the platform and stepped up. "Mothi is there to protect him, and Sif and Yowrnsaxa will mother the heck out of him. Sig will be fine. You, on the other hand…" She tipped me a wink. "Haymtatlr, if you don't allow me to leave, I'll never speak to you again."

Haymtatlr didn't answer, but the power to the dais remained.

"I think it's now or never, Hank," said Yowtgayrr. Looking down at the shimmering platform with a trace of distaste on his face, he stepped up and moved to stand next to Jane.

I glanced at Althyof. "I'm going with them," he said. "Sounds like fun." He tipped a wink and stepped up on the platform.

With a shrug, I called Keri and Fretyi to my side and stepped up next to the others. "Hit it, Haymtatlr." A nanosecond later, he did, and my next breath tasted of home.

If you've enjoyed this novel, please consider joining my Readers Group by visiting https://ehv4.us/join. Or follow me on BookBub by visiting my profile page there: https://ehv4.us/bbub.

See all the books in the *Blood of the Isir* series on the web: https://ehv4.us/isir.

For my complete bibliography, please visit: https://ehv4.us/bib.

Books these days succeed or fail based on the strength of their reviews. I hope you will consider leaving a review—as an independent author, I could use your help. It's easy (I promise). Complete instructions for leaving your review can be found below.

To leave a review, please:

1. Visit the *Rooms of Ruin* book page (https://ehv4.us/roomsofruin) and follow the appropriate store link.
2. Sign-in if prompted
3. Select your star rating
4. Write a few short words (or a lot of long words, whatever you are comfortable with)
5. Click the submit button
6. Accept my sincere gratitude

AUTHOR'S NOTE

The ending of Hank's stories always come as a surprise. Scratch that—the endings of all my novel-length works seem to surprise me. That may sound like so much crazy nonsense, but it is absolute truth. When I wrote fiction two and three decades ago, I worked from an outline (or at least a narrative structure) and always knew where I was in the story and how much was yet to come. I don't write that way any longer, and I have to say the new way I write is much, much more fun.

How do I write, you ask? I start with only a broad idea for the book. For instance, I started this book knowing that Hank and company had to end up inside the Rooms of Ruin and that Haymtatlr would be there to "help" them. That's it.

As I prepare to write a novel, I begin talking to myself—in the shower, while I'm driving, while I'm walking, wherever, really. I start telling myself the story. Those beginnings don't always make it into the book—they have to be good enough that I will jot down a note or two, and I have an entire digital notebook dedicated to random book ideas, beginnings, names, titles, etc. to contain them. Equipped with the best of the beginnings and a general idea of what has to happen, I sit down and let the story take over.

Glancing back at my notebook entries for this novel, I see: the first line from Chapter Four (it was too good to abandon, even though the story wanted to start another way), a one-paragraph description of John's imprisonment in Helhaym and the scene Hank dreams about, and this, which was the first idea I had for the book:

Big army guarding RoR at Pilrust. "Can't fight through that," says Hank. "Not a chance," says Mothi. Meuhlnir scoffs, "A little group like that?"

It didn't happen quite that way, as you no doubt already know, but I had no idea that ravens were going to play such an important role. Yeah, that's dishonest...the truth is, I hadn't even thought of the ravens yet.

I'm starting the third book in the Blood of the Isir series tomorrow, and while it will be the last book from the series for a bit, it will not be the last book, I promise. I already have the beginning and the title for book four, so by my twisted logic, that book is already ninety percent done. Additionally, Hank whispered in my ear the other day, and his story goes much farther than the events I've already planned.

I can't wait.

About the
Author

Erik Henry Vick is an author who happens to be disabled by an autoimmune disease (also known as his Personal Monster™). He writes to hang on to the few remaining shreds of his sanity. His current favorite genres to write are dark fantasy and horror.

He lives in Western New York with his wife, Supergirl; their son; a Rottweiler named after a god of thunder; and two extremely psychotic cats. He fights his Personal Monster™ daily with humor, pain medicine, and funny T-shirts.

Erik has a B.A. in Psychology, an M.S.C.S., and a Ph.D. in Artificial Intelligence. He has worked as a criminal investigator for a state agency, a college professor, a C.T.O. for an international software company, and a video game developer.

He'd love to hear from you on social media:

Blog: https://erikhenryvick.com

Twitter: https://twitter.com/BerserkErik

Facebook: https://fb.me/erikhenryvick

Amazon author pages:

USA: https://bit.ly/4ehvusa

UK: https://bit.ly/4ehvuk

Goodreads Author Page: https://bit.ly/4ehvgr

BookBub Author Profile: http://ehv4.us/bbub